Victoria Corby wa   e
travelled and work   before
returning to London to work in advertising and PR. She
now lives in south-west France with her husband and
three daughters. Her novels *Something Stupid* and *Seven-Week Itch* are also available from Headline.

Up to No Good

Victoria Corby

HEADLINE

First published in 2001
by HEADLINE BOOK PUBLISHING

First published in paperback in 2001
by HEADLINE BOOK PUBLISHING

10 9 8 7 6 5 4 3 2 1

ISBN 0 7472 6513 5

Typeset by
Letterpart Limited, Reigate, Surrey

Printed and bound in Great Britain by
Clays Ltd, St Ives plc

HEADLINE BOOK PUBLISHING
A division of Hodder Headline
338 Euston Road
London NW1 3BH

www.headline.co.uk
www.hodderheadline.com

For Plum

I'd like to give particular thanks to Theo Wayte for answering lots of small queries, and Maître and Madame Cavalie and the Langon Gendarmerie for taking the time to explain some of the details of French police procedure, and to Dinah Wiener for thinking up the title.

CHAPTER 1

Several pairs of eyes bored into me accusingly and gave me the entirely intended impression that if I didn't agree to do what was demanded *immediately*, I could hold myself responsible for ruining everybody's holiday.

I squirmed under the searchlike glares of disapprobation. In true Gestapo style, someone – Maggie probably – had saved me the chair on the terrace that faced directly into the sun, so I had to squint as I tried to focus on the three others on the opposite side of the wrought-iron table.

As far as I know there is absolutely no psychic ability in my family; no seventh daughters of seventh daughters, no one born with a caul over their head, not even a tea-leaf reader. Great Uncle Henry is reputed to have had a prophetic dream about the horse he'd put his shirt on trailing in last in the Derby – but that was hardly surprising since Great Uncle H's ability to pick a sure-fire loser was so marked that his regular bookie used to take him out for a slap-up lunch once a year. However, some distant relative somewhere must have been a dab hand at crystal-ball gazing, for I'd known, just known, that when Oscar suggested that what I really needed after being so ill was to join him and a group of his friends for two weeks' recuperation in a cottage in France, *it wasn't a good idea.*

I'm not sure why. A pretty cottage with its own pool in the middle of peaceful vineyards, excellent wine from the château, wonderful food, sunshine – what more could I ask for? Even the English couple who owned the château and cottage were friendly and charming, Oscar reported, quite different from the normal sort of proprietor who seemed to think they breathed a more rarefied air than their tenants. What's more, I could remember him enthusing about the cottage when he'd stayed here for a few days with Maggie a couple of years ago, so I knew he wasn't just indulging in hyperbole. It wasn't even that expensive. Not that I minded paying, since my only other option for a bit of R & R was with my parents in Chatham, where I'd have to fend off my mother's anxious enquiries about whether I was warm enough, would I like this rug over my knees and how about a nice hot drink?

Yet still I'd dithered. Partly because I wasn't certain about going away with four near-strangers, though Oscar blithely assured me that I'd get on like a house on fire with everyone. Even at the time I'd had a feeling this statement was based less on conviction than the need to fill the gap left by the last-minute cancellation of Maggie's sister and her toy boy. (He'd broken his ankle rollerblading, and though he'd said he didn't mind in the least being left behind, Maggie's sister had apparently felt it unwise to leave six foot two of tanned nineteen year old on his own in case some other female offered to come in and tend his plaster.) Somehow Oscar swept away all my doubts, persuading me that my forebodings were merely a previously unknown side-effect of taking too many antibiotics, even dismissing my protest that I'd have to leave early for my grandparents' diamond wedding anniversary by pointing out that I could go back by train to England with only one easy change. Surely even I could manage that? So here I was, having nearly two weeks' intensive convalescence in France.

I barely knew Maggie, though since we were mutual friends of Oscar's we'd stop to exchange a few words if we met at parties on the PR or advertising circuit. Shooting stars like Maggie couldn't afford to spend much time on copywriters much lower down in the firmament when there were so many other, more valuable contacts to be made. She was reputed to be very clever, very good at her job. Indeed, she'd won an important award at a PR aren't-we-all-clever do – and, according to my Art Director, had also come top of the straw poll conducted amongst the males present of who they'd most like to see doing a major presentation wearing only suspenders, seamed stockings and high heels. Maggie was strikingly good-looking, small and curvy with large toffee-coloured eyes and lots of tumbling dark hair, and while other women were increasingly trying to be one of the boys she made no bones about playing up her femininity to the hilt. Her dresses were floaty yet still managed to show off an excellent figure, her heels were high, and she never appeared in public without expertly applied makeup. Like other people reputedly annihilated by Maggie, it seemed I'd made the fundamental mistake of assuming that anyone who bore such a close resemblance to a kitten, all big eyes and soft gestures, must be as fluffy and cuddly as one too. Right now Maggie was being about as fluffy and cuddly as her Prime-Ministerial namesake. And as set on getting her own way.

She leaned forward earnestly. 'I can't see what you're making all this fuss about, Nella.' Fuss? *I* wasn't making a fuss. How could I, since every time I opened my mouth to speak, someone else cut across me and drowned me out? 'Anyone would think that Oscar had Disgusting Personal Habits, or something.'

I glanced over to where Oscar lay sprawled on a sun-lounger, studiously not taking part in the conversation. Amused by the sudden attentive tilt of his head, I was tempted to retort, 'You should see the way he cuts his toenails . . .!' I haven't actually, so I said, 'I'm sure Oscar's personal habits are all that's fragrant and civilised,' though I refrained from adding, 'as far as any man's ever are.'

'You must have shared a room on holiday before, so what's the big deal?' she demanded impatiently. Well, primarily that I wouldn't have come at all if a condition had been sharing with Oscar. I'm very fond of him, he's one of my best friends, of either sex. We'd just spent the last two days driving through France without having a single row over map reading, whether we had classical, jazz or soul playing on the stereo, or if this was really the best place to stop for a picnic of pâté, baguette and *vin plastique*. Nor a single cross word over my driving, which in itself deserved a gold medal for tolerance and a mention in *The Guinness Book of Records*. But it still

4

didn't mean that I wanted to share wardrobe space with him. Boarding school is supposed to teach you how to rub along with others and accept their foibles. Mm, maybe. All being in a dormitory with seven others taught me was that there's only one decent reason for sharing your sleeping accommodation – and that's if he's about six foot two and makes you weak-kneed with lust.

'You do *know* Oscar's gay, don't you?' Maggie asked, as if this was something that in six years of knowing him might have completely escaped my notice.

No wonder I'd had doubts about coming. I'd even mentioned it to Oscar, but as he always does when anything gets in the way of what he wants, he'd brushed it aside, saying I was imagining things. I wasn't. Maggie didn't like me. Well, that was all right – the feeling was mutual.

Goaded, I raised my eyebrows and stared back at her. 'Actually, Maggie, Oscar's not *completely* gay,' I said, matching her superior tone.

Unfortunately, as withering material, it didn't work. Maggie merely looked at me, probably amazed I was daring to answer back, then her eyes swivelled round to settle speculatively on my travelling companion. 'I can't see that occasionally taking a girl out really counts,' she proclaimed loftily, as her eyes came back to rest on me. '*You'll* be quite safe, don't worry.'

I don't know who had the most reason to be offended. Oscar for the aspersions on the strength of his sexuality, even if it had to be admitted that the exquisite young man in pale primrose cotton trousers, still remarkably uncreased after six hours' driving, who was playing idly with his earring didn't look like most people's idea of rampant heterosexuality. Or me for the implication that even if by some strange chance Oscar was concealing a supercharged vein of testosterone, my virtue would still be as safe as if I was immured in a convent.

In fairness to Maggie I couldn't really blame her for being pretty dubious about my prowess as a man magnet. Consumption might have done wonders for the looks of La Dame aux Camellias; pneumonia had done absolutely nothing for mine – even if, much to my delight, I could see my hipbones for the first time since I was ten. Given a week or so's rest and a bit of a tan I might begin to look halfway decent again. Might. A complete makeover and a new wardrobe were probably needed too – and a Wonderbra. Sudden weight loss has unexpected disadvantages.

'Perhaps Oscar wouldn't be safe from *me*,' I retorted crossly. Oscar sat up looking pleased, a bit *too* pleased in my opinion, and I found my wavering resolve begin to harden. After all, the whole point of being here was to get myself back on my feet again after a bout of illness that had nearly landed me in hospital, and my convalescence was hardly going to be aided by being constantly on my guard about my roommate having ideas of *that* sort. Worry that I might show off my bits as I got in and out of bed – inevitable given the length of the T-shirt I wear to sleep in – wouldn't help my stress levels either. And what if it was really hot and I wanted to sleep in the nude? I certainly wasn't going to do that when sharing a room with Oscar, whether he was in one of his gay phases or not.

I decided to make one last-ditch attempt to stand my

ground before I was steamrollered into giving up my bedroom for this Jed whom I'd never even met, and who wasn't even supposed to be staying here in the first place.

'Um . . .' I floundered. Everyone looked at me expectantly with 'What now?' expressions on their faces, while I sent a meaningful stare at my proposed roommate. I was absolutely certain Oscar viewed the prospect of our bunking up together with as little enthusiasm as I did. He widened his yes and smiled at me blandly. In other words, over to you, Nella. Typical! I thought crossly. Oscar was an expert at ducking out of unpleasantness.

I sought frantically for a cast-iron, copper-bottomed, rock solid reason why we shouldn't share, which no sane person could possibly refute and which wouldn't result in everybody making a dash for the door when I entered the room. 'I talk in my sleep,' I said at last. 'All the time.' This didn't seem to be making much of an impression on my audience. 'It used to drive George mad,' I added, putting on a tragic face. 'He couldn't stand the noise.'

'*Really*?' asked Oscar with deep interest. 'He never told me that.' Not surprising, since it wasn't true, but I wondered uneasily what George and Oscar *did* talk about when they met up for a drink in the City after work. Oscar claimed it was about things like England's chances in the next Test, but that topic wouldn't last halfway down the first bottle of Beck's. 'Is that one of the reasons why you two broke up?'

I nodded, although 'nocturnal noise' was one of the few faults George didn't choose to ascribe to me when explaining at length why he'd decided I was no longer fit to be his particular bit of arm candy – not that he, of course, would have lowered himself to use such an expression. My faults had included my chronic untidiness, my completely unreasonable refusal to handwash his silk boxer shorts, and my inability to make a bread and butter pudding as good as his nanny's.

I beamed at the others. 'It just wouldn't be fair on Oscar. I'd keep the poor thing awake.'

Maggie didn't look as if she thought this was a serious consideration. Sally, her best friend and sidekick, a slim girl with light brown hair tied back in a pony tail, leaned forward saying, 'Wouldn't the answer be earplugs?'

'No, it would not!' Oscar said indignantly, at long last spurred into action. 'Besides, why should Nella share with me? She's been ill, she needs her rest.'

Hear, hear, I thought, glad that at last someone had seen fit to mention this point. It was obvious from Oscar's expression that his heels were now dug in immovably. Even Maggie realised she was flogging a very dead horse, for she cast us both a scorching look – I could see who was being awarded the lion's share of the blame – and muttered something deeply reproachful about what on earth was she going to say to Janey now.

Delicately brushing off some insect that had landed on his arm, Oscar said, 'What's Janey got to mind about? We're doing her the favour. And there's still the sofa bed. I can't think why you didn't suggest this Jed slept on that in the first place.'

Maggie hesitated. If she said she didn't want to have the sitting room cluttered up by a strange man sleeping on the sofa bed I really would give into temptation and clonk her. I waited expectantly. To my slight disappointment she said,

'It doesn't look very comfortable.'

I didn't see how anyone could assess the comfort of a sofa bed while it was still folded up, but felt it wouldn't be wise to point this out. 'If it's that uncomfortable, why can't Jed go in the twin room with Oscar?' I suggested.

I got a look which implied that I'd just come bottom in the class IQ test. 'I don't think Jed would like that at all,' Maggie said, with a pointed glance towards Oscar.

'Actually, *I* wouldn't like it either,' said Oscar firmly. 'I'm very fussy about who I sleep with. Frankly, Maggie, I don't see why we've been landed with someone none of us knows in the first place.' Neither did I, but I'd been too busy fighting my corner to ask this question. The news that I was now sharing a room with Oscar to make way for this Jed had been sprung on me almost before I'd had time to swing my legs out of the car. 'At the very least you might have asked the rest of us before you promised Janey we'd have this bloke to stay,' he added.

Charlie, Sally's other half, who had been sitting back in his chair, eyes fixed on the horizon as if he wanted to stay right out of this, nodded in agreement. Sally sent him a furious look which he didn't appear to notice.

'Well, I felt we had to help Janey out . . .' Maggie cast a glance for support at her boyfriend Phil, a slim wiry man with, according to gossip, a severe case of wandering hands. He was too busy lighting a cigarette to see it. 'She's been terribly good to us. We got a special rate on the cottage after all.'

'Only because you went direct to her to book it and she didn't have to pay her letting agents a commission,' interrupted Oscar.

'Maybe,' she admitted, conceding the point, 'but it is much nicer than anything else we could have got for the price.' OK, we had to give her that. From what little I'd seen of the cottage so far, it was as charming as Oscar had claimed. The Provençal tiles in the loo were certainly very pretty.

'When she gave us the key yesterday evening she was virtually tearing her hair out because she can't fit everyone in at the château.'

'She's so pushed for space in that enormous great pile she's driven to bludging for bedrooms off her tenants in the cottage?' asked Oscar sceptically.

'Absolutely,' Maggie said earnestly. 'It's not really that big.' No? OK, it was small compared with Longleat or Blenheim perhaps, but in my opinion any house which has ten windows in a row on the top floor counts as big. 'The rooms are large but there aren't that many of them,' she went on, 'and Tom's daughter and her boyfriend are there, one guest room is being decorated, and yesterday the electrician who was fixing something in the attic put his foot through the ceiling of the other guest room, so of course it can't be used until the repair's done. And she's got Jed arriving today for a week's stay, with no room for him.'

'She could have put him off for a while, couldn't she?' Oscar said.

'No, that wouldn't have been fair. He's coming down here on business, and he's already fixed his appointments so she couldn't cancel him.' Maggie looked at us both to ensure that we properly appreciated the chain of disasters that had struck the hapless Janey. 'She was going to send

him to someone in the village who does bed and breakfast, but they're full up, then when she realised that we
can sleep eight here and there are only six of us, I thought
that it really wouldn't bother us much to help her out and
put him up for a few days.'

No, it wouldn't have bothered *her* much, would it,
since she hadn't been planning to have her own sleeping
arrangements disturbed. Oscar was now eyeing her with
the sort of steely expression that I suspected was
mirrored on my own face.

Maggie looked as if she might start squirming, but then
Sally chipped in with, 'Otherwise she'd have had to put
Jed in the room with the rotten ceiling and it might have
fallen on him at any moment.'

Oscar looked singularly unmoved by this dire prospect.
Maggie went on quickly, 'Janey says he's charming and it
isn't as if he'll put us to any trouble over meals and things
as he'll be eating up at the château. So really we'll hardly
notice he's here at all. And it'll probably only be for a few
days until the ceiling is fixed.' She looked hopefully at
Oscar and me and we stared back silently. She sighed
meaningfully, the major part of the sigh being reserved for
me. 'If you really insist, he'll have to go on the sofa bed
then,' she said in the disapproving tone usually saved for
those who say they positively dislike puppies.

Another silence indicated that indeed we did insist.
She sighed again. 'Janey's asked us to come up for a
drink to meet him this evening,' she said, as if she had
just announced we were about to be entertained by a
duchess at the very least. So was this the reason why
Maggie had been so keen to offer house room to this

11

Jed? I wondered. So she could have a chance to experience a little of *la vie au château*? In Tuscany last year I stayed in a cottage converted from an old stable block, and the owners of the main house, though absolutely polite, had done little more than show us where the light switches were. Perfectly understandable; if they started fraternising with their tenants they'd find the whole summer was spent entertaining people they hardly knew. But we were hardly going to be run-of-the-mill tenants if we were putting up one of Janey's friends, were we?

'We're due up at the château at six-thirty, so as we're already running behind,' Maggie said with an irritable glance at me, 'we'd better be ready to leave in a few minutes.'

It was obvious that the invitation included all of us, and equally obvious that like the voluntary church services at school, we were all expected to attend. I slumped back in my chair, tempted to see what the reaction would be if I said I was too exhausted to go out and just wanted to be allowed to unpack in peace – in my own single bedroom. Actually I wouldn't have minded being able to relax for a while. Even though Oscar and I had stayed the night with some friends of his near the Loire and hadn't spent so much time travelling today, I was still uncomfortably tired and would have appreciated washing away the grime of the journey by having a swim. But since I was already heading for the Miss Unpopularity prize, I decided not to make myself a runaway winner. Besides, even post pneumonia, I wasn't so feeble as to willingly turn down a social invitation and a chance to see what a genuine château was like from close quarters.

'Fine,' I said, and gestured at the cotton dress that had looked so fresh and pretty this morning and now resembled the cheaper sort of dishcloth, 'but I'm going to need more than a few minutes to get ready.'

'Janey and Tom aren't at all formal. You don't have to get *dressed up*,' Maggie said airily, managing to imply both that I was the sort of person who didn't know what to wear and also that it wouldn't make any improvement even if I did. I ignored her, and took my time over choosing the least crushed garment out of my suitcase and putting on enough makeup to ensure I no longer looked as if I'd just come off the set of the Addams Family. Anyway, I was brought up to believe that it's the height of bad manners to arrive dead on time. I've been caught at the bra-and-knickers-and-no-makeup-on stage on several occasions by early birds, so I *never* do it to anyone else. That's my excuse for constantly being late anyway. (Another of George's complaints.)

Maggie was obviously one of those who believes that punctuality is the politeness of kings and PR executives. When I finally emerged, having done my change and titivate in what I thought was very reasonable time, she muttered something about having agreed to allow me five minutes and I'd taken nearer twenty (neither statement was true actually) and herded us out of the cottage and on to the road through the vineyard to the château almost at a jog. We'd probably have been whipped on to an even faster pace if Charlie hadn't said firmly that he was damned if he was going to arrive dripping in sweat and defiantly slowed down to a normal walk. I began to think that Charlie might be my sort of person. Maggie still marched on ahead, but the rest of us took the opportunity, now the landscape wasn't rushing by in a blur, to look around. The cottage, small and square with a roof that dipped almost down to ground level on one side, was only a few hundred yards from the château if you took the short cut through the rows of immaculately tended vines that stretched away over the hillside like neatly combed hair, but it meant going the whole way in the full heat of the sun, still uncomfortably strong even at this hour.

Instead we went via a narrow road, so rarely used that it had grass growing up the middle, with a magnificent avenue of welcoming shady chestnut trees along it. I'd been hoping we'd make a grand entrance via the front of the château, which was a long, low building of ivy-covered honey-coloured stone with dark red shutters at the windows and turrets with pointed roofs like witches' hats at either end. Instead, Maggie was waiting, almost visibly tapping her foot, by the entrance to a cobbled courtyard. 'The winery,' she said importantly, waving a hand at a row of buildings jutting out of the back of the château. Two men who were closing a huge pair of double doors with elegantly curved tops on some impressively technical machinery, turned at the sound of her voice and bade us a courteous '*Bonsoir*', then made a lengthy examination of her legs as if they were committing them to memory.

'This is a proper working château, you know,' she went on. 'Tom will probably give you a tour if you're interested.' Her tone implied that we'd all better be. The two men disappeared through another large set of doors, leaving the courtyard quiet and still in the evening heat. The only movement came from a pair of fat fantail pigeons pecking lazily at the ground, who were being watched idly by a black and white cat, comfortably stretched out on the top of a disused well half covered by a rampant honeysuckle.

The pigeons raised their heads and eyed us as if they were wondering whether they could be bothered to move at all before very slowly launching themselves into the air to go and perch on the top of a stone *pigeonnier* shaped like a beehive in one corner of the courtyard.

It was wonderfully quiet, wonderfully peaceful. I began to think that perhaps there might be some good things to be said for being here, after all. As Oscar had pointed out, a change was as good as a rest and even if I insisted on being a good girl and doing lots of resting, south-west France was a damn sight less boring than Chatham. Difficult to dispute that. I breathed in deeply as a distinctly vinous smell wafted out of a couple of open doors. What's more, I realised, making a determined effort to look on the bright side and finding it quite easy in this atmospheric spot, Maggie might not be my personal flavour of the month, but at least she wasn't going to drive me up the wall by constantly asking if I shouldn't go and have a little lie-down. *And* I'd kept my own room, I thought in satisfaction. So really, things weren't going to be too bad, were they?

CHAPTER 2

'I knew you'd like it here,' said Oscar in a self-satisfied tone, accurately reading my expression and sounding a tad relieved. He'd probably been imagining he was going to spend the next fortnight getting it in one ear from Maggie and in the other from me. At least one ear was safe now.

Maggie marched us back out of the courtyard again, saying she had just been letting us have a little peep. Skirting what she informed us was the barrel store, she opened an iron gate in an outside wall and herded us through a neatly tended vegetable garden. A middle-aged woman, wearing a print apron around a figure that suggested she was fond of *la bonne cuisine*, nodded politely to us and continued to carefully select green beans, putting the satisfactory ones into a bucket by her side. Maggie clicked her tongue impatiently at our slow pace and strode off down a paved path as Phil closed the gate setting the antique latch clattering. A baying that would have done justice to the Hound of the Baskervilles started up from somewhere and she jumped back with a loud shriek of alarm as two dogs, making enough noise for a whole pack of Great Danes, rounded the corner of the house and charged at us. One of them was an overweight and elderly Labrador; the other was a Dalmatian, which was roaring along simultaneously barking, wrinkling up its lips and snorting in the most extraordinary fashion. 'Help! It's coming for me! It's showing its teeth! And snarling! It's about to bite!' she cried, turning tail and dodging behind Phil for protection. 'Get away from me, you vicious animal!' Phil didn't look particularly thrilled at being thrown into this manly role.

The Labrador was snuffling round our feet in an arthritic manner, wagging its tail enthusiastically. Maggie moaned as it sniffed at her bare toes. 'It's not going to bite you. Come on, you must have met these animals before,' Phil said impatiently as she grabbed onto him as if she was planning to leap into his arms out of harm's way. 'How long would your precious Morrisons be able to go on letting their cottage if the dogs got in the habit of eating the visitors?' he demanded rather hoarsely, prising her arms from their stranglehold grip around his neck.

'The only way this old thing is going to be able to bite anyone is if somebody stumps up for a pair of dentures first,' said Charlie, hooking his fingers in the Labrador's collar and pulling it away from its dangerous investigation of Maggie's feet.

'And you're just pleased to see us, aren't you, my beautiful?' Oscar bent down to stroke the Dalmatian which was weaving around his legs and threatening to trip him up at any moment. 'My parents had a terrier who used to smile like this,' he added, rubbing his hand along the dog's back. In reply it wrinkled its nose up so much in a grin it made itself sneeze, and there was a series of explosions which seemed to excite it even more.

It should have been obvious to anyone that the two dogs belonged to the lick-'em-to-death category but all the same Maggie still stayed behind the safety of Phil's not very broad back, ignoring his commands to stop making such a godawful exhibition of herself, until a dark-haired woman, dressed in a baggy white collarless man's shirt and shorts, came tearing around the corner, spilling over with apologies. 'I'm so sorry, I didn't hear you coming in. I hope they didn't scare you to death,' she said breathlessly. 'I try to get Lily shut up before visitors arrive – she's still young and hasn't copped on yet that most people don't enjoy seeing a grinning dog coming at them at high speed, but I forgot the time. Here!' She snapped her fingers, and the Dalmatian ambled back to her side, then turned around to give us another unrepentant grin and sneezed explosively yet again.

'No, no, we weren't frightened at all. Anyone can see the dogs are friendly,' said Maggie airily, stepping out from behind Phil. I had to hand it to her: from the gracious way she introduced us all to Janey Morrison, you'd have thought that she'd spent the whole afternoon at a garden party, rather than the last few minutes clinging onto her boyfriend for dear life.

Janey kissed Oscar, saying it was lovely to see him again, and looked the rest of us over with a friendly smile. 'How nice to meet you all. Welcome to Château du Pré.' She was a tall, deep-bosomed woman in her early thirties, with a slight snub nose and the sort of strong-boned face that really comes into its own as you get older, and large, brown eyes, half hidden behind a pair of zebra-striped sunglasses. There was something vaguely familiar about her; maddeningly I had no idea whether it was her face or her name that had rung the bell. She turned to Oscar to ask him how he was and they moved off, flanked on either side by a wagging tail, while the rest of us followed.

I trailed behind, partly because it was still obvious that neither Maggie nor Sally had forgiven me for disobeying orders and partly because I wanted to be able to have a look at what was around me. And this was well worth looking at. One of my work-mates had said, somewhat witheringly, that this part of France was downright boring, it was all vines, vines and more vines. True, there were a whole load of them, but the squares of vines were broken up by copses of trees and fields of livestock so it was hardly as if this was some sort of vine prairie. And the low hills all around were enough to satisfy any romantic's heart, especially as a distant summit had been crowned by a ruined castle with only half a tower. I wondered if I'd be able to go and explore it. Maggie, who was already halfway down a flagstoned terrace lined with huge stone urns packed with geraniums and petunias in vivid pinks, reds and oranges, turned around to frown at me. Obediently, I speeded up a little, pausing only to sniff at the glorious scent rising from a bed of dark red roses.

A pair of tousle-headed little boys, pink, plump and stark naked, just like a pair of Raphael's cherubim, were industriously excavating the earth between the roots of a venerable cedar tree at the end of a large, beautifully kept lawn. A dark-haired girl, with long brown legs and the shortest pair of shorts this side of decent, lay stretched out on the grass improving her tan at the same time as keeping a watchful eye on the twins. Janey leaned over a splendid baroque balustrade and called something to her. The girl sat up to reply, showing that not a lot of material had gone into the making of her top either. Phil, who was patently uninterested in the beauties of nature, was so entranced by this view that he walked into a flower pot, setting it rattling in a very obvious fashion, and got a ferocious scowl from Maggie for his clumsiness.

Janey giggled. 'Somehow I have a feeling it wasn't Adam and Miles who made his eyes pop out like that,' she murmured to me.

'It's unlikely,' I agreed. 'Phil has a reputation as the fastest pair of hands in West London, and from what I hear there's something about girls in shorts that just brings out that old roamin' instinct in him.'

'Really?' asked Janey. 'I hadn't noticed.' She looked down at her own shorts, made a slight face and said, 'But then if he were to get excited by these, he'd have a *serious* problem!'

I wouldn't put it past him, and she had good legs too. Phil was a legs man. Phil was an *everything* man, according to what Oscar had told me in a warning voice. Oscar takes my welfare very seriously, though quite why he thinks I've reached the grand old age of twenty-eight without being able to recognise a man who makes passes at every female who crosses his path is quite beyond me.

One of the little boys turned around, saw Janey and

began waving a plump arm. 'Aren't they gorgeous!' I said, gaining myself a pleased smile. I wasn't being merely polite – at a distance they looked quite enchanting – though from my experiences with my godson and his brother I knew this angelic impression might not last once we got to a closer acquaintance. 'Are they yours?'

'The twins? Afraid so,' she said, her dismissive tone doing nothing to conceal buckets of maternal pride. 'The junior demolition team, Tom calls them.' So I was probably right about their general behaviour, I decided, reckoning it was fortunate that as a paying guest I was unlikely to be called on to babysit. Maggie and Sally were virtually frog-marching their respective partners away from the dangerously enticing view, though I couldn't help noticing Phil taking another quick look sideways before he was led inexorably towards the table and chairs set out next to the swimming pool at the far end of the terrace.

It was then that the vague little niggle that had been playing at the back of my mind exploded into a horrible certainty. I turned to Janey and said hesitantly, 'This Jed who's coming to stay in the cottage . . . is that his real name, or is it some sort of nickname?'

She looked at me in surprise. 'No, his name really *is* Jed. Jed Conway, in fact. He's a journalist – we worked together years ago.'

'Thank God!' I breathed. For a horrible moment I had been absolutely convinced that Janey was going to say Jed was a nickname for George Edward Delaney. A long shot maybe, but there had been stranger coincidences, you saw them in the tabloids every week. And with

Oscar around it wouldn't even have been a coincidence. For some reason he'd thought George and I were ideally suited – still did think so, in fact, even though I'd told him on several occasions that there were many things I was prepared to do for love but handwashing was not one of them. Oscar and I had come to verbal blows before over the way he occasionally tried to manipulate events for me so I'd been suspicious from the moment he'd casually suggested I spend my convalescence in a cottage in France. I'd made him swear George wasn't going to be a member of our party, but having him staying up at the château was exactly the sort of scenario that would delight Oscar's Machiavellian mind.

Janey cast me an amused glance. 'Afraid Jed might have been an ex-boyfriend?'

I nodded ruefully.

She laughed. 'Gosh, talk about a holiday wrecker. I've found myself in some pretty sticky situations, but none to match that. Though I had a spectacular break-up with one boyfriend in the middle of the Nullabor Plain in Australia. We were on a packed bus and we couldn't get anyone to swap seats with us, so we were forced to sit next to each other, glowering in silence for three days and nights. I didn't dare go to sleep in case my head slipped sideways and I ended up accidentally touching him, and he took it as meaning I wanted to make up. I was virtually hallucinating from sleep deprivation by the time we reached Sydney. Probably why I weakened and agreed to give it another go,' she added thoughtfully.

'How long did the reconciliation last?' I asked.

'Until the flight back to England. It was half empty so

23

I moved down a few rows to stretch out across a row of seats. When I woke up I saw the stewardess sitting on his lap and giving an *entirely* new meaning to the words "cabin service". Needless to say, we didn't make up again,' she said with a grin, pushing her sunglasses back up her nose. 'The last I heard of him, he was living on a small-holding with no sanitation on a Welsh hillside, so all things considered I reckon I had a lucky escape, even if he was very good-looking.' She waved for a last time to the twins and said, 'We'd better go and meet the others, not that there are many of our lot around at the moment, I'm afraid. Rob, Venetia's man, has gone off to meet a friend who's doing a wine tour around here, and Tom and Jed are in the tasting room with a couple of tourists, but I don't expect they'll be long. I do hope you don't mind putting Jed up? I was wondering if Maggie was just assuming that everyone would agree . . .'

She was observant then. I cleared my throat as we walked off down the terrace and said, 'No, I don't mind at all, but Maggie made a bit of a mistake. I hope Jed won't object to the sofa bed because Oscar and I aren't actually sharing a room.'

'I did wonder about that.' Janey didn't look in the least bit surprised. 'From the moment I saw you it didn't seem as if you were really Oscar's type, if you know what I mean.'

A recumbent figure lying on a steamer chair by the pool idly leafing through a magazine looked up, and seeing Janey and I were still talking got to her feet, pulling down a skirt almost as minimal as the nanny's shorts, and sauntered over to a teak table, large enough to seat at least ten people, laid with long-stemmed wine glasses, bowls of olives and thinly sliced *saucisson*. She picked a bottle of rosé from where it was keeping cool in a pottery wine cooler and handed it and a corkscrew to Phil. He seemed to be having problems connecting the screw with the cork. Maybe because his eyes weren't on the job but on the woman's lean, long-legged figure which seemed to be the result of a fortuitous combination of the right genes and a taste for going to the gym. She looked over her shoulder as we approached, tossing back an enviable quantity of superbly cut pale red hair over her shoulders, and said in a pointed tone, 'I hope you don't mind me taking over your role as hostess, Janey, but I know what you're like when you get chatting. I thought I'd better give everyone a drink before our guests began to think this was a drought area!'

I saw Janey's shoulders tense for a second under the big white shirt, then she said expressionlessly, 'Thank you, Venetia. That's kind of you.'

Venetia shrugged and handed a glass of white wine to Sally. 'It's nothing,' she said. 'Now, has everyone got what they want?' she asked the group cheerily and turned towards me, her delicately sculpted brows rising in query.

So that was what had been bothering me, I realised with a flicker of relief. The name Morrison had triggered off a distant memory. I hadn't thought about Venetia Morrison for years, but now it all came flooding back. I could even recall her telling me about her father's place in France. But she hadn't had a stepmother then so Janey must be quite recently married. 'Hello, Venetia,' I said. 'How are you?'

She looked at me blankly, obviously not having the slightest clue who I was. I was about to give her a hint when her green eyes widened behind tortoiseshell sunglasses and she exclaimed, 'Good Lord! It's Nella, isn't it? Nella Bowden. What on earth are you doing renting my father's cottage? Heavens, it's *years* since I've seen you. I wouldn't have recognised you – you've changed so much.' Even Venetia, who had never been particularly tactful, must have realised that she was rapidly heading into muddy waters here, for she visibly floundered. 'It's not surprising really,' she said finally. 'You look so different now you've lost so much weight.'

Thanks, Venetia. Everyone turned around as if they were attached to a single eye and looked at me, wondering what I must have looked like hidden under a mountain of blubber. 'I would have known *you* anywhere. You haven't changed one bit!' I said evenly. She hadn't either. As I said, she's always been a dab hand at the tactless remark.

Oscar said with loyal indignation, 'I can't believe you were ever fat, Nella!'

'No, she wasn't, not when I knew her,' Venetia said earnestly. 'But she told me herself her brother nicknamed her Nellie the elephant, though that was some time ago. That's why everyone calls her Nella, rather than Eleanor.'

I began to wonder about the other skeletons which I'd thought were safely hidden at the back of cupboards. Were they going to find themselves being taken out for an airing over the next week or so? But surely I'd never been much in the habit of confiding in Venetia during the brief time in which we shared a flat, had I? We were so completely different in every way that we'd maintained a cool and rather uncomprehending distance. (Except that my feelings about Venetia were not in the least frigid when I discovered that on departing from the flat she had also taken with her half the kitchen equipment, bought by me.) But there must have been the inevitable evenings that happen in every flat when we were both in and there was nothing to watch on the box. There's no accounting for what secrets come spilling out between flatmates when you're whiling away your boredom by working your way down the better part of a bottle of Spanish red. And, afterwards, you can never remember exactly what you've been indiscreet about until your confidante, who's been sworn to utter secrecy, tells a whole roomful of people.

Venetia yawned delicately like a cat and said, 'We shared a flat ages ago, but not for long. It was a madhouse – a complete tip, wasn't it, Nella?' Largely because Venetia didn't understand one of the basic principles of housework – that sadly for all of us there is no house elf who comes out and does it while we're all asleep. 'And Lucy or Katie were always stumping around complaining that somebody had hogged the bathroom for hours' (Venetia), 'used all the hot water' (Venetia again), 'forgotten it was her turn to buy loo paper and milk' (Venetia), 'or had borrowed their best top and not returned it.' (Never Venetia. None of us had stylish enough wardrobes for her to nick things from.) 'And Lucy was so grumpy about anyone using the telephone, wasn't she?' she asked me. The first phone bill after Venetia moved in went up from the normal £100 to £550. She couldn't understand it, she said, as she was absolutely scrupulous about making her calls to the States in cheap time.

She smiled around at the assembled company. 'I only stayed for a couple of months, then I got the offer of a really nice flat in Hampstead.' With a really nice company director with a really nice bank account. Venetia had always followed the old adage about loving where money was. We'd all been distinctly miffed that the gilt-edged wedding invitation had failed to arrive but maybe we'd done her an injustice, I thought, seeing that her perfectly manicured hand, with immaculately painted nails, was bare of any engagement or wedding rings.

'How long did you stick at that place?' she asked me.

'About a year after you left, then we got compulsorily purchased and I moved to where I am now.' Her eyebrows went up to indicate her astonishment that anyone could have lasted that long. Well, it hadn't exactly been Venetia's style. There wasn't a single item of designer furniture in the flat, not even a Dualit toaster.

'I'm so glad you're here! It's going to be *so* nice having someone around I can talk to,' she said expansively, with a keenness for my company that I couldn't remember her ever showing before and which I couldn't help feeling was a deliberate dig at her stepmother.

Certainly Janey gave her stepdaughter a distinctly old-fashioned look as she helped herself to a glass of wine, while Venetia told us all to sit down in a hostessy manner. Two men stepped out of French windows from the house and the dogs leaped up from where they'd been lying under the table, crashing into the legs and making the wine in our glasses splash around violently.

'Really, it's about time Lily was given some proper training,' Venetia muttered, dabbing at a small splash of white wine on her T-shirt. 'Look what she's done. This is probably ruined.'

'It'll wash out,' Janey said peaceably. 'Unless it's one of your designer dry clean only numbers, in which case it'll dry clean.'

Both men were looking very pleased with themselves. The tourists had had very well-filled pockets, apparently. Tom had persuaded Monsieur to take the red and the rosé, while Jed had charmed Madame into tasting and then buying the second-string white. 'There's nothing like getting our guests to work for their supper,' Tom said in a satisfied voice, adding that he hoped the tourists had good suspension on their car because they were going to need it. He walked around the table, saying his hellos and shaking hands. Maggie got a double kiss too, which seemed to please her no end. And no wonder, for even though he must have been in his early fifties, Tom Morrison was a very attractive man indeed. He wasn't particularly tall, and though he still had a lot of hair it was iron grey, but he looked fit and tough and his tanned face was deeply scored with laughter lines around a wide mouth and green eyes that were exactly the same as Venetia's but held infinitely more humour and life. I suspected when he told me how nice it was to meet an old friend of Venetia's, with a sideways look that made me believe he really meant it, that he was also a very accomplished flirt indeed. I've never been into older men but as I sat back in my chair, undoubtedly with exactly the same sort of silly expression as Maggie had on her face, I thought that for the first time I could see the point of them. Lucky Janey.

Actually his companion was a bit of all right too. Sod's law would normally have it that any man who is foisted on your sofa bed is going to look like he rightly belongs under a stone, but this one was going to be a definite decorative addition. Maggie was giving him the full eyelash-fluttering routine – to the barely concealed displeasure of Phil who was not, apparently, a believer in sauce for both geese and ganders – and even Oscar was treating him to the connoisseur's once-over. Jed had those Californian-style good looks which come from good nutrition, excellent dentistry and hours spent surfing – except that he spoke with one of those mid-Atlantic accents that meant he could have come from almost anywhere, even Salford. It was going to be no hardship having to meet him before breakfast, I decided. He'd even been decent enough to declare he'd positively enjoy sleeping on the sofa bed.

'Don't mention it. I'm just grateful for the way you've helped Janey out by offering to put me up at all,' Jed said in response to Maggie's repeated apologies about the sofa bed.

Offer? Maggie had the grace to colour under several accusing glances and wisely said nothing, taking a sip from her glass instead and turning to Tom to make a fulsome compliment on how good it was and ask what grape varieties he used to make his wine. An hour later there was a general feeling that we'd better make our farewells before we outstayed our welcome and we'd all got to our feet, when the dogs who had been peacefully asleep under the table, leaped up again and dashed off down the terrace giving joyous voice. 'Oh, that must be Rob back at last,' said Janey. 'Don't go before you've had a chance to say hello to him. I'm sure you'll like him.'

My heart hit my sandalled feet long before anybody came into sight. I could hear him as he fended off enthusiastic, canine attentions and even after all these years, it only took a couple of words for me to recognise that voice. And I'd been afraid Jed might be George . . . I laughed hollowly. Oscar and Sally looked at me as if I'd gone quite mad. Not surprising really; most people don't find a half-empty dish of olives particularly amusing. To think I'd wasted a single moment worrying about what Venetia might let out. All around me I could feel cupboard doors being flung open and skeletons catapulting out by the dozen. If only I could sneak off and find another gate out of the garden while everyone was busy with introductions – but the high box hedge looked depressingly impenetrable.

It's all very well deciding to face the music, but that doesn't stop you trying to put off the evil moment. I shrank into the rear of the group, wondering if there was any chance he might not recognise me. The designer sunglasses I'd treated myself to in London were absolutely enormous and covered at least half of my face. Surely they should be as effective as a slouch hat, shouldn't they? And then if I got away scot free I could spend the rest of the holiday in my bedroom.

I peeped cautiously around the protective screen of Oscar's head as Tom was introducing Robert to Maggie and Phil. He'd hardly changed at all. There were a few lines around his slash of a mouth that hadn't been there before, but they could hardly be blamed on what I'd done to him, as he was in his thirties now. He still had loads of dark tousled hair that never seemed to lie flat, a problem exacerbated by his habit of running his fingers through it whenever he was thinking about something, and he was as lankily slim as ever. In fact he looked pretty good, better than he had before, now that he had a touch of maturity, I thought, feeling more depressed by the second. Not even Oscar could pretend that *I* looked better than I did nine years ago. And if you've got to have an excruciatingly embarrassing encounter, it does absolutely nothing to boost your courage when you realise his first reaction on seeing you will be profound relief that he got out of *that* one when he did.

'And Ellie even shared a flat with Venetia at one time,' Tom said expansively. 'How's that for a coincidence?'

'Considering the number of flats Venetia's lived in, she must have shared with enough people to populate a small town,' said Robert with a smile, turning his head in my direction as Oscar began to obligingly move sideways to give him an uninterrupted view. 'I got into a couchette in Paris once with five strangers and discovered that I had friends in common with everyone, so I know how small a world it is.'

Tom put his hand on my arm. 'This is Ellie.'

'Nella,' Janey corrected him.

The new sunglasses were obviously bog-all use as a disguise for it took only one glance for Robert's eyes, clear grey like winter water, to harden into chips of granite. 'I don't need introducing to Nella,' he interrupted flatly. 'We already know each other.'

'Hello, Robert,' I said weakly. I hadn't really expected him to sound as if he was pleased to see me again, but it would have been nice. I'd have settled for indifference even. Actually he sounded as if he would have preferred to find a tarantula on his pillow than have me within his sightline. But since, if it hadn't been for me landing him in jail, he'd now be streaking his way up through the layers of the law, on the fast track to success, vast fees and no doubt an eventual judgeship, I suppose you couldn't really blame him.

CHAPTER 3

To my amazement, the only person who appeared to notice the icicles dropping off Robert's tongue was Janey, who gave me a very surprised look, obviously putting two and two together and coming up with a fairly accurate four. Even the normally quick-witted Oscar was far too busy marvelling at this coincidence to have noticed that, instead of catching up with years of gossip like the normal run of old university friends, Robert and I were keeping as great a distance between us as was possible without one of us actually falling off the edge of the terrace into the swimming pool.

Tom insisted on opening another bottle so we could celebrate the reunion of old friends. Luckily for my peace of mind there were several amongst the gathering who got restless if they weren't centre-stage so I was able to sit back pretending I wasn't there. I knew the awkward questions would come eventually, but I needed time to prepare myself. I knew, too, that I was going to have to talk to Robert sometime, and I didn't relish the prospect. My heart sank as Tom suggested that we stay for supper; it was only going to be something on the barbecue so he knew Janey wouldn't mind. Maggie was looking danger-ously ready to accept for all of us, even though we'd already been informed, with a slightly martyrish air, that she'd made a special journey to the Sunday market in the local town to buy something absolutely fresh for our dinner. Fortunately, before I expired through nervous tension, Jed took a quick look at Janey's set face and said, 'Say, Tom, don't you think Janey needs a little more notice about having six extra to cater for?'

She gratefully murmured something about how she had been planning on cooking trout – and they were a little difficult to stretch. 'Let's make it tomorrow,' Tom said firmly. There was a chorus of we'd all love it and were looking forward to it, including a somewhat insincere echo from myself. Perhaps I could develop acute appendicitis in the next twenty-four hours, I thought hopefully. I'd heard that French hospitals weren't too bad and even served you wine with your meals. But Robert might feel obliged to pay me a hospital visit and I didn't like to think what he might do if I were lying helpless in front of him. Though he might have calmed down a bit in nine years. It didn't look like it though, I thought, shooting him a cautious glance, unless someone else around the table had produced those rigid lines at the corner of his mouth.

'So how do you know Robert?' asked Charlie as we were walking back to the cottage. 'You weren't in the same year at uni, surely?'

'No, he was in his final year when I arrived,' I answered with admirable casualness. There's nothing like having your story prepared and I hadn't been a Girl Guide for nothing. 'I got to know him when we were both involved in a student panto – it was great fun.'

There isn't a person around who doesn't secretly wish that they'd had a chance to stand on the edge of the stage going, 'Oh yes it *is*!' while the audience roars back, 'Oh *no* it isn't!' or even to chant, 'Oompa, oompa, stuff it up your jumper.' As I'd hoped, every one of my listeners promptly lost all interest in Robert and me and started demanding to know which pantomime it had been and if I remembered any of the jokes. Panto stories carried me all the way back to the cottage and through the preparations for supper. Before it could belatedly occur to anyone to wonder why Robert and I hadn't been exchanging panto stories too I claimed I was tired and shot off to the safety of my single room. The excuse was even true, for once – nervous tension *is* exhausting.

Thank God I'd stuck to my guns and refused to share with Oscar, I thought as I sat down wearily on the bed. Quite apart from being forced to keep it tidy, since he's fussy about that sort of thing, I was fairly sure that his antennae had already begun to twitch. He has an ability approaching genius for knowing when his friends are holding out on him, and he'd been eyeing me closely. I reckon I could have held out for about three minutes in an after lights-out probing session before I spilt all the beans. It wasn't so much that I minded him knowing about it – well, about some of it – but I was pretty sure Oscar wouldn't be able to resist the temptation to try to do something to clear the air, mend a few fences, mop up some spilt milk et cetera, and the result would *not* have been Robert and me falling on each other's necks swearing undying friendship. I've experienced Oscar's attempts to organise my life for me before. All I can say is that he means well.

I woke up early, to what looked like a glorious day. The sky was a sheet of duck-egg blue, flecked with the tiniest wispiest clouds being moved about by a faint breeze that would prove very welcome as the temperature rose. But I doubted the other occupants of the cottage would be so thrilled by the beauties of the early morning so I tiptoed cautiously down the narrow wooden stairs to the sitting room and in the direction of the kettle. I jumped with surprise when I saw a fair head almost submerged under a sheet on the sofa bed and nearly undid all my good work by knocking against a chair which slid noisily over the flagstoned floor. Luckily Jed didn't appear to be a light sleeper, but not caring to put it to the test a second time, I abandoned my original idea of opening the doors and taking my coffee out on to the terrace. Instead I opened the shutters at the kitchen window, slowly, slowly in case of noisy squeaking hinges, and sat on the kitchen table which was exactly the right height for a moody examination of the view. Resting my hand on my chin, I looked out at the still hazy vineyards stretching away in the distance, hoping that this nice peaceful scene would give me nice peaceful thoughts.

It didn't work, of course. I couldn't see the château from here, but it didn't stop my thoughts from going in that direction, and to its occupants – one occupant in particular. It was what my thoughts had been doing all night, and what had made me too restless to stay in bed. I felt as if I'd strayed into the screenplay of an updated

Casablanca. In all the châteaux, in all the vineyards, in all of France – why did he have to turn up at *this* one? Except that unlike Ingrid Bergman I hadn't acted out of nobility and self-sacrifice and, judging by his expression last night, I wasn't going to get forgiven by my Rick either. I sighed deeply, taking a swig of now rather nasty tepid coffee, too wrapped up in my troubled thoughts to be bothered to get up off the table to make some more.

During my first term at university, I'd thought I'd try to be sociable and join a few of the clubs. I tried without notable success, social or otherwise, the Madrigal Society, where I was consigned to a non-singing role after my first and only solo, the Literature Appreciation Society – I didn't have a serious enough attitude, according to the Chair, a highly intense girl who had a figure more like a Chesterfield sofa, the Ramblers – too wet, too much like hard work, the Gym Club – dry, but otherwise ditto, and the Wine Appreciation Society which, I learned, had been disbanded after a particularly uproarious tasting before I even got to attend my first session.

Then a friend pleaded with me to come along and hold her hand at the auditions for the panto being put on by one of the theatre groups. She swore faithfully that it wouldn't be the sort of affair where we'd be expected to audition for the privilege of moving the scenery, there'd be absolutely nothing in the original Greek, and the director had been heard being encouragingly politically incorrect about the sort of plays where the actors walk around with blank masks in front of their faces and are deeply meaningful. In fact, the panto was written each year by the production team and any of their friends who could come up with really corny jokes or suitably scurrilous doubles entendres about various lecturers. I made protesting noises about it not being my sort of thing until Jessica confessed that actually she didn't have a burning ambition to tread the boards either, but she *did* have a very keen interest in getting to know the producer a lot better. Mike was, in her words, a bit of all right and the sexiest thing in boxer shorts she'd seen that year. Well, she hadn't yet managed to confirm the boxer shorts, but I got her general gist.

In that case, how could I say no? You owe it to your friends to help them along in their love lives, don't you, so that meant I was obliged to go and give Jessica some moral support as she tried out for a part in *Ali Baa Baa and the Rest of the Flock*. As it happens, I too had a secret reason for allowing my arm to be twisted. When I'd said I might be going to the auditions with Jess, several girls had raised their eyebrows meaningfully and implied that my true motivation lay not with supporting the sister-hood but with getting a better look at the panto's director Robert who, by all accounts, was one of the tastier bits of talent around. My interest was definitely aroused, but after my first sight of Robert in a chilly rehearsal hall, sitting with lanky legs pushed out in front of him, head bent over a tatty and much corrected script making yet more corrections, I wondered what all the hoo-ha was about. With that long nose and wide mouth he could hardly be called good-looking and I'd never been keen on skinny men. While Jess sat beside me bursting with suppressed longing and shooting sly looks from under her eyelashes at her Mike, I fished my book out of my bag and settled down to indulge myself with a hero far more to my taste than any of those in the hall with me.

Somehow it had been automatically assumed that I was reading for a part as well, for Robert suddenly handed me a script, saying, 'It's Nella, isn't it? If you can just go from here,' and one long finger indicated the place on the page. I scanned the lines quickly, wondering if I was going to be able to read them out loud without giggling at the very corny jokes. Presumably imagining I was paralysed with stage-fright, Robert looked up and smiled at me encouragingly. My fingers promptly turned to bananas. 'Don't be nervous,' he said kindly as I scrabbled on the floor for the loose pages, trying to cram them back into order and feeling like a complete fool while his eyes, an extraordinary triangular shape and dipping down at the outside corners, glinted with amusement. A mixture of acute embarrassment and the realisation that, wow, your girlfriends were quite right, does not make for a good audition. I was amazed that I managed to get a coherent word out at all and thought that it must show a basic niceness in Robert and Mike that they didn't stop me before I even got to the end of the first page and suggest that I might be more suited to helping out in wardrobe or handing out the programmes.

All Jessica's eyelash-fluttering at Mike worked, for though she didn't get the lead, she was cast as chief harem wife which involved her wearing not much more than see-through trousers and a sparkly bra. One thing led to another and she was soon in the position of being able to inform me whether Mike really did wear boxer shorts or not. And I, amazingly enough, was given a part too. As

Daisy the cow's hindquarters.

It isn't easy to impress a man with your general desirability when he looks at you and envisages a Friesian cow's bottom, but that's probably only one of the many reasons why over the next three months Robert didn't throw so much as a thoughtful glance my way while causing general havoc amongst the members of the harem – Jessica excepted, of course. I'm not what you'd call a brown paperbag job, I've got thick, blondish hair and my mother thinks my eyes are a lovely shade of blue and a very nice shape. I've even had compliments on my figure (well some), but most of the harem could have launched a thousand ships, if not more, and Robert wasn't someone who needed to take second-best. I did wonder on several occasions whether his insistence on *quite* so many wives for the Caliph was more for his benefit than for the good of the play, but Robert blandly insisted that having the stage packed with diaphanously clad girls brought in the paying male punters – an attitude which might have annoyed the feminists in the cast but even they had to admit that more punters meant more cash for the end-of-panto party. He'd also thoughtfully provided the female section of the audience with the best part of the university rowing team (best looking, best figure, best pecs, best it's better not to ask, etc.) playing true to type as the Caliph's rowing team aka Baghdad's answer to the Chippendales – so the feminists didn't really have too much to complain about. Neither did I, for that matter. The rowing team adopted me as their unofficial mascot and I was kept far too busy to even think of pining away from unrequited lurve.

It wasn't until I was helping him with the preparations for the end-of-panto party (industrial quantities of beer and cheap wine and lots of soundproofing) that Robert finally noticed I didn't really look like a bovine backside. But by then I'd already had plenty of opportunity to realise that the other reports I'd heard about him were true; Robert and fidelity weren't two words that fitted naturally together. Not that he was the notches on the bedpost type, it was more that he thoroughly enjoyed women, all sorts of women so it seemed, and like a child in a sweetshop who has just been given its pocket money he didn't see why he shouldn't pick and mix as much as he liked. Since he didn't believe in spending too much time poring over his books and had a generous allowance from his elderly parents, he had plenty of time for his favourite activity. I gathered from some of the frankly startling conversations amongst the harem (and until then I'd never thought I'd had a particularly sheltered upbringing) that Robert's girlfriends also regarded sex as a funtime leisure activity not to be taken seriously; so there was no harm done and no particular reason why he should try to resist the lures held out to him. I doubt he tried very hard.

When he turned those incredible triangular eyes, glinting underneath heavy straight lashes, my way, I pretended I wasn't interested. I had far too strong a sense of self-preservation to become one of a long line, even though according to what I overheard (the harem seemed blissfully unaware that the cow's bottom, like walls, had ears) it would be quite some experience while it lasted. So I was well armed against him. Like hell I was. All I can say in my defence is that I didn't go down immediately like a nine-pin. Well, not *immediately*. I didn't succumb right until the end-of-panto party was broken up, and it was a memorable party by any standards, lasting for longer than the actual pantomime run itself. It might have gone on for even longer if someone hadn't had the bright idea of 'borrowing' a genuine flock for Ali Baa Baa to pose with for the photos. The farmer was very good-natured about it, all things considered.

In the ever hopeful and deluded way of women I decided to make the most of the moment and pray that Robert would decide I was enough for him. The next few months were probably the happiest in my life. I was walking on cloud nine, unable to believe that I had landed this *gorgeous* man – and I have to admit that I also thoroughly enjoyed the puzzled looks I got from better-looking women who wondered what I'd got that they hadn't. (I wondered about that, too.) And it was such fun! Robert's light-hearted enjoyment of life was completely infectious. He was going along with his parents' ambition that he should be a seriously big noise in the law, as there wasn't anything else he particularly wanted to do and he had to earn a living somehow. But that was in the future; there was plenty of time to be serious when he took up his pupillage. Right now, life was for living it up.

This was not a view shared by his parents, whom I was taken to meet one excruciatingly stiff weekend. While I didn't make any of the obvious faux pas like eating my peas off my knife or passing the port the wrong way, they made it abundantly clear that they didn't think I'd make a suitable wife for a senior lawyer. They also blamed me for distracting him from his studies, which was completely unfair. A fly walking down a windowpane was enough to distract Robert from a textbook.

All idylls have to come to an end, and mine eventually did, not for what might have been thought of as the obvious reason, my lover's roving eye, but due to a couple of very uncomfortable interviews with my tutors who informed me that unless I got my act together and started doing some work – *now* – I was going to fail my first-year exams. It was all very well for Robert who had the sort of quick agile mind that allowed him to play his way through university doing the minimum of work and still expect to get a reasonable degree – not a First, for without any work that was beyond even him – but I needed to put in a lot of solid graft to get results. That meant spending considerably less time in the large and untidy bed in Robert's flat and a lot more time studying in the library. I wondered briefly if I could be bothered. After all, what use was a degree in English really going to be? But even I wasn't so lost for love as to seriously consider chucking in my course. I got my head down, did a couple of essays that had been due a month ago, and even started doing a little revision.

It didn't take long for various concerned souls to inform me that while I was slaving over medieval texts, Robert had been idling away the afternoon under a tree with Natasha Hanson, who had been my inseparable best friend for a while and now unaccountably didn't seem very keen on my company, though she was certainly fond enough of Robert's. When I confronted him, he threw up his hands in a gesture of horrified innocence and said he'd merely been helping her with an essay. Really? And even in the interests of *al fresco* tutoring, just what did popping grapes in his mouth, followed by her fingers, have to do with work? Especially as his subject was Law and hers was Philosophy. I let that one pass – that time, particularly after a demonstration of what he hadn't been doing with Natasha. Surely, not even Robert could have the energy to do that twice in one day.

But it was difficult to go on being so sanguine when I got one description after another of Natasha in hot pursuit, and how Robert, while not precisely encouraging her, was definitely not discouraging her either. Well, most men with the normal number of hormones wouldn't have. Natasha was by any standards a knockout. He claimed there was nothing to it, they'd merely played a few games of tennis – she wore shorts that had been practically spraypainted on and he served a record number of double faults; they went for a walk along the river – she tweaked her ankle and had to be half carried back, arms clasped tightly around his neck; he'd helped her move her cupboard from one side of her room to the other – she made him a meal as a thank you and there was doubtless more hand-feeding though I didn't get any reports about that. It was strictly a dinner *à deux* and all Robert said about it was that she had a heavy hand with the basil, which would have been gratifying if I hadn't been wondering how light her hand was elsewhere. I sat in the stuffy library, bitterly wondering what on earth had induced me to think I could get to grips with Early

English while my imagination ran riot with torrid visions of Natasha getting to grips with Robert.

I retained enough sense not to start nagging him about whether he was grappling with rather more than arcane points of law when he wasn't with me, for even I knew about the stupidity of putting ideas in his head if they weren't there already, but I doubt I was anything like as discreet and stoically silent about my worries as I fondly thought I was. Cross-questioning him nearly every time we met, albeit in a deliberately casual way, about whether he'd seen Natasha recently was probably a bit of a giveaway too. But I was morbidly aware, as a couple of girls from down the passage took great delight in reminding me, that I'd already lasted longer than normal with Robert and, by the law of averages, must be due to get the big Heave Ho at any moment. I like to think that's at least a partial excuse for what I did.

And of course those three ladies, the Fates, snipping away at their cords and tangling the lines of circumstance had a lot to do with it too. Robert said once, apropos of something quite different, that no accident has only one cause, but is the result of several things happening simultaneously that just happen to converge at that particular moment. So it was then.

My mother started it. She'd had an unpleasant experience with a fitting-room mirror and decided to take advantage of my father's absence on a business trip by going on a strict diet, signing up for a gym, getting herself in trim and generally presenting him with a slimmer, more svelte model when he returned. (It was always an ambitious plan – he was only going to be away for ten days.) On her second visit to the gym she fell off the treadmill and broke her arm. I don't think it's really true that the gym refused to call the ambulance until they'd made her sign a disclaimer form, but certainly the hospital flatly refused to allow her to go home unless she had someone there to look after her, and I was the only one of her fledglings available to put in a stint as a care assistant.

I was perfectly content to answer the SOS call. I get on very well with Mum even if the maternal fuss factor drives me bonkers occasionally, and it gave me a legitimate excuse for not finishing my paper on Chaucer on time – but I would have been a lot happier if, while I was doing my Florence Nightingale bit, I'd heard from Robert occasionally. He and his flatmates had forgotten to pay the telephone bill and the one time he thought of getting to a telephone box he ran out of money almost before he started. Still at least he'd tried, I thought, and refused to give house room to the nasty little suspicion that the reason why he never had time to get to the telephone box was because he was too busy dallying elsewhere.

My father eventually returned and I got back to university one evening to find, instead of a rapturous reunion, a note telling me to hoof it over to a comedy bar on the other side of town where one of Robert's friends had been given his first ever five-minute slot as a stand-up comic. I arrived just as Chris, the would-be comic, was starting and I barely spoke to Robert, engaged as I was, like everyone else, in assuring Chris that nobody could possibly have noticed when he started to corpse, that the story about the three men on the towpath had come off brilliantly, and that generally he had done great. The management seemed to think so anyway, as he was asked to come back the next week and Chris's twenty or so supporters settled down to serious celebrating. Round about two in the morning we finally spilled out into the night and began to walk home, members of the group peeling off as they reached their various flats and lodgings, until Robert and I were the last left. We walked on a bit, arms wrapped around each other, then he steered me into a dark shadow under a tree, murmuring, 'It's nice to have you back.'

One thing led to another until we were rapidly heading for the indecency in a public place stakes. I drew back regretfully, about to point this out, when I saw a faint mark, just discernible in the dim light, on his collarbone. 'What's that?' I asked, tracing it with my fingertip.

He shrugged. 'Dunno. Must have hit it on something.'

'Doesn't look like a bruise to me,' I said.

I felt him grow tense. 'Just what are you suggesting it is?' he asked coldly.

'I don't know. What do you think I'm suggesting?' I retorted, equally frigidly. He'd been preoccupied all evening. Was it a guilty conscience or was he contemplating moving on to fresher pastures? That mark certainly looked as if it could be a love bite, and they aren't one of the things in my sexual repertoire. Deciding that it was best to know the truth, I asked, 'Does it come from Natasha?'

'So what if it does!' he snapped. So much for the benefits of the truth. Ignorance is bliss as far as I'm concerned. And I'd rather not have known Robert's opinion about my suspicious, small-minded nature, either. Things careered rapidly downhill. The most vicious row I've ever taken part in was none the less venomous for being conducted in stage whispers. Being the nicely brought up middle-class children we were, we knew better than to scream at each other in a respectable residential neighbourhood when everyone was asleep. I believe I defended my corner fairly well but I would never have guessed that Robert had such a biting edge to his tongue. I took the only option left to me before I was completely annihilated; I declared grandly that I never wanted to speak to him again and stalked off down the road.

I heard pounding feet coming after me. I spun around and hissed, 'Don't touch me!'

'I wouldn't dream of it,' he said, glaring at me with distaste. 'You've got my keys and wallet in your bag.'

So I had. He'd given them to me as we were leaving the club. Flushing with annoyance, I fished in my bag and, half fearful that if I got within handing-over distance he might give in to that temptation to throttle me as he'd earnestly declared was his ambition, I chucked them at him. I've always been a hopeless shot. With neat judgement he caught his wallet as it went past at arm's length, but his keys went sailing over a laurel hedge into the adjoining front garden. He cast me a contemptuous glance, as if he was certain I'd done it on purpose, and the last I saw of him was as he went through the gate to look for them.

I was still reeling with misery, disbelief and intense

rage when the call from the police came through about an hour and a half later. It was the Desk Sergeant from the local police station saying they'd got a Mr Robert Winwood with them; they'd picked him up trespassing in someone's garden. Could I confirm Mr Winwood's story that he was looking for his keys which had been thrown in there by his girlfriend – me. The split second before I said of course Robert was telling the truth, it hit me that I wasn't his girlfriend any longer. No doubt the moment the police let him go, courtesy of me, he'd be haring off around to Natasha's place for a bit of TLC and more. No, he bloody well wouldn't. Not tonight anyway. 'I can't think what he's talking about,' I said coldly. 'I hardly know him.' Serve him right! I thought with satisfaction as I put the phone down.

Even then I knew I'd have to ring the police in the morning just in case he hadn't managed to wriggle out of a night in the cells, but in my current mood I decided that if he hadn't, he'd only brought it on himself. But I overslept and there was no time to make a telephone call before running at full speed to my lecture. Afterwards, by now uneasily conscious that the police might take a somewhat dim view of my wasting their time by lying to them, I was quite willing to be persuaded to put off the evil moment by having coffee with a couple of mates.

'Did you hear that they've got the Bakersfield Prowler at last?' asked Val as she put down some revoltingly calorific and utterly delicious pastries on the table. 'It was on the radio this morning. Pure chance. Some householder just happened to wake up on hearing a noise and saw this bloke in his garden moving the dustbins.'

I nodded vaguely as I tucked into my bun. I hadn't had time for breakfast and I was suffering from lack of sleep and food as well as an achingly numb sense of loss. The Bakersfield Prowler was a nasty piece of work who had been hanging around a respectable residential area for a couple of years making a nuisance of himself, stealing ladies' underwear, exposing himself, peering in at couples making love, and generally terrifying the local women who understandably thought his next step could well be to move on to actual sexual assault.

'Men like him should be locked up and the key thrown away,' Val went on in fine disregard for her usual libertarian principles. 'We'll probably find that some reactionary old magistrate who believes that women ask for it will give him bail and the next thing you know he'll be back amongst us.' Her eyes widened and she leaned forward, saying in a thrilling whisper, '*Really* amongst us too. He's one of the students – can you believe it? A final year. He came up with some cock and bull story . . .'

The bit of bun I was swallowing turned to rock in my throat. I didn't need to hear any more. Oh God, what had I done? I dashed out, leaving my surprised friends with the bill, and spent a frantic hour running around the town trying to find out which police station Robert was being held at. I was too panic-stricken to think of taking the time-saving option of ringing around first. At last, on my third attempt the Desk Sergeant at Mildenhall Road station cautiously agreed that they might just have a Robert Winwood there and no, he hadn't been released yet. At first he treated my stumbling attempt to tell him what Robert had really been doing in that garden with all the contempt he thought it richly deserved. I could almost see the words forming in a thought bubble above the Sergeant's head. '*Here we go, some bint of a girlfriend faking a nice little story,*' then as I insisted on repeating it and was obviously not going to stop until he'd found someone to listen to me properly, he said in a deeply resigned tone that he'd get a WPC to come and talk to me. Considering how quickly he vanished round the back as soon as she arrived I think his desire for a tea break was probably as much of a spur as my persistence.

The WPC was a dead ringer for the biology mistress at school – the one with rippling biceps and the nose that could have carved a joint – and if I hadn't already made such a fuss I might have been tempted to leave Robert to it and do a runner. But underneath that hatchet exterior there beat a heart still female enough to be able to appreciate that there are reasons why, in a fit of temper, you might condemn your ex-boyfriend to spend a night in the cells. Such as he'd just told you he'd slept with your ex-best friend. It didn't stop the lecture about wasting police time though. I nodded meekly, agreed docilely that I'd been very stupid and assured her earnestly that I wouldn't dream of ever doing it again.

Lecture over, the WPC got quite chatty as we were waiting for my statement to be typed up, even bringing me a cup of tea and a biscuit, so once we'd had a highly interesting chat about the perfidy of men in general – either she regularly acted as a shoulder to cry on or she had an extremely lively love-life – I asked how anybody had ever managed to jump to the incredible conclusion that Robert was some sort of sex pest. She cast her eyes up to the ceiling expressively. An over-zealous Sergeant, desperate to improve the clear-up rate, had leaped on the one vague description of the Prowler – male with dark hair which wasn't terribly exclusive as far as general descriptions go – and had assumed that because Robert had moved a dustbin he must have been planning to stand on it so he could look through an upstairs window on the wild shenanigans going on inside.

The fact that it was a Victorian house with high ceilings and that Robert would have needed to have been over seven feet tall to see in a first-storey window, even when perched on a dustbin, or that the owners of the house were over seventy so the most exciting things he was likely to see were false teeth soaking in a glass, had escaped the Sergeant completely. All he was concerned about was the evident weakness of Robert's story that he had been looking for his keys when they were in his pocket all the time. Who was going to believe that nonsense about his finding them seconds before the police arrived? Then when I denied even knowing Robert, he was so sure that he had his man that he was confident enough to tip the wink to a contact he had at the local paper. And the reporter, who was no mean slouch at his job, took no time at all in finding out which particular student was banged up in the nick. As he disliked students as a whole, thinking them idle, pot-smoking, unwashed layabouts who would be better occupied in holding down a proper job, and what's more were always after his pretty daughter, he'd taken an almost gleeful delight in naming Robert as the person who was being questioned over a series of sexual offences, without troubling himself with any of the more obvious discrepancies in the theory.

It was so ludicrous it was laughable. I could imagine how Robert, with his ready sense of the ridiculous, would one day greatly enjoy retelling the story of how he'd been arrested. Perhaps not just at the moment though. 'Is he very angry with me?' I asked the WPC, slightly nervously.

She looked at me with raised brows. 'Put it this way – I'd apply for police protection if I were you,' she said with only a glimmer of a smile. 'He'd be annoyed enough about spending an unnecessary night in the cells – they aren't very comfortable – but what seems to have sent him into orbit is missing an important appointment in London this morning.'

'Appointment? This morning?' I felt the first trickling of cold horror creeping down my spine. It could only be one thing, meeting the head of chambers where he was hoping to do his pupillage. 'But he's supposed to be going on Friday, I remember him telling me.'

The date, it turned out, had been changed and in the general crush and celebrations for Chris's success last night Robert hadn't got around to telling me. At that point he probably hadn't thought it was any big deal. After all, he'd already been promised it was virtually in the bag. This meeting was merely supposed to be a final dotting of the i's and crossing of the t's session, followed by a substantial lunch at the head of chambers' club where everyone would agree that Robert was exactly the sort of rising young star they wanted for a dynamic chambers making itself fit for the twenty-first century.

Only the rising young star never turned up because he was being questioned by the police, and his name was already being splashed about as a suspected sex pest in the early edition of the local evening paper. And though as upholders of the law and defenders of the innocent, that group of eminent barristers should have known better, they still decided that there was no smoke without fire and Robert Winwood was someone they could do without. As did the other two outfits that had previously declared an ardent interest in having this fine young man on their team.

Shortly afterwards one of the few of Robert's friends who would speak to me at all informed me that Robert had declared that if the law wouldn't have him he'd be damned if he was going to bother with his degree and he'd dropped out entirely.

I hadn't needed him to add, 'It's all your fault, Nella.' I already knew that.

CHAPTER 4

The next mouthful of cold coffee was so disgusting that I had to get off my perch for a glass of water to clear the taste away. Maybe doing something useful would put me in a slightly more cheerful frame of mind and it'd probably be a good idea to try and regain some of the brownie points I'd lost yesterday. I'd got the impression that a few more had gone down the tube when I went to bed early last night. There'd been more than a hint of suspicion that I was skiving off the washing up. Maggie had muttered something about not realising that I'd had glandular fever which was the only disease that she knew of that left you apparently unable to lift a finger. So all in all it seemed a good idea to take Oscar's car and find the boulangerie for the breakfast croissants.

I crept into his room and removed the keys from his table, remembering with rare thoughtfulness to leave him a note so he'd know that his precious car hadn't been pinched, and set off. It took slightly longer than I'd anticipated to find the boulangerie, a lot longer in fact, because I set off in the wrong direction and only realised when I saw a large sign with *Paris 555km* on it. Once I was going the right way it was simple to find the centre of the little village and the boulangerie which was bang opposite the church and packed with people picking up baguettes.

I was on my way back, with the back seat piled with croissants and bread, turning on to the little side road that led to the château and the cottage when I saw a spotted dog ambling along the verge. It didn't seem very likely there could be two Dalmatians in such a small area so I slowed down and leaned out, calling 'Lily!' She stopped, then as I called again, came dashing over. Yes, it was definitely Lily. There couldn't be *two* dogs about that could smile and sneeze at the same time. I was sure she wasn't supposed to be rocketing around on her own so I opened the door and told her to get in, thinking hopefully that maybe Oscar wouldn't notice the dog hair on his charcoal grey seats. But like all well brought-up females, she refused to get in a car with a stranger and skittered back every time I tried to grab her collar – until she was offered my breakfast croissant that is, whereupon I was instantly elevated to best family friend and she jumped straight in. Oh dear, I had a nasty feeling that Oscar would definitely notice the croissant crumbs as Lily made short and messy work of her present and looked around for more. I quickly removed the bag with the rest of the croissants before she decided to help herself and wondered if I could borrow a dustpan and brush when I returned her.

I hadn't really expected the château's guest to be on butlering duty before eight in the morning, but you never know and it was still a relief to see the door opened not by Robert but a slightly heavy-eyed Janey. 'Hello, Nella, what can I do for you?' she asked, looking rather confused at my early arrival.

'I found this on the road,' I said. She seemed even more puzzled as she stared at my handbag which I was holding out towards her, then her eyes travelled downwards and she saw the strap was attached to her errant hound who was sitting down, looking as if butter wouldn't melt in her mouth.

'Oh, don't tell me she was out again!' she exclaimed in exasperation. 'I'm going to kill Venetia! She *never* bothers to shut the garden gate properly and she knows perfectly well Lily can ease it open if the latch isn't pushed right down.' She took a deep breath. 'Sorry, I should have thanked you before sounding off, shouldn't I?' she said ruefully. 'I really am grateful. Would you like to come in for coffee?' When I hesitated she went on, 'Oh do, it'd be nice to have someone to talk to. While expert at food throwing, the twins aren't exactly the greatest conversationalists.' I didn't know whether it was oblivion or supreme tact that made her add, 'Everyone else is still asleep and probably will be for hours.'

Since I strongly doubted that any of my party would be awake and demanding croissants for some time either, I accepted with pleasure. We went through a cool shadowy hall, with a stunningly elegant curving staircase with curly wrought-iron banisters and walls painted a wonderful dusty blue, to a big cheerful kitchen with French windows onto the terrace, wide open even at this early hour. On either side of the windows tall, wire-fronted cupboards filled with china, glass and very professional-looking jars of preserves went right up to a ceiling crossed with dark oak beams. A dark green cooker, rather like a French version of an Aga, nestled in an inglenook and two built-in dressers had their shelves and surfaces covered with a plethora of pots containing wooden spoons, spatulas, knives, and other useful kitchen equipment, an extensive collection of cook-books, baskets holding fruit, vegetables, nuts and eggs and little piles of things that didn't have anywhere else to go. Immaculately tidy it definitely wasn't, though you could see that there was method in the disorder. It probably didn't take any longer to find a lemon squeezer or a paring knife than it would if they had been neatly stowed away and you had to remember where. I warmed to Janey; she was definitely someone after my own heart.

On the other side of the room, near a fireplace as tall as my shoulders, was a gigantic table, large enough to seat about twelve people, surrounded by ladderback chairs with brightly coloured green and yellow cushions, but with only one place laid with an empty mug and a book lying face down next to it. The twins, securely strapped into Alcatraz versions of high chairs and messily eating breakfast, were nearby but just out of food-throwing range, while the old Labrador sat next to them, ready to dash in and mop up any spills. One end of the table was also covered with piles of papers, a telephone, a laptop and a jam jar of chewed Biros. 'My office,' said Janey with a faint grimace. 'Tom's converted one of the rooms in the outbuildings into a proper office for me, but somehow I hardly ever get around to actually transporting all my stuff out there. It's easier here.'

'And nearer the kettle,' I said.

'And the biscuits – unfortunately. That's why the weight I put on with the twins is still there, firmly on my behind.'

'Oh come on! You can't have had much of one before then,' I said. While she wasn't slim she certainly wasn't fat and her figure was the well-rounded sort with plenty of hip and bosom that most men seem to prefer to the slimmer model type. Well, that's what lots of my male friends have told me – especially when they arrive hoping to be fed and are afraid that if I'm feeling fat they might get served diet food. Unfortunately, the truth is that the adjectives normally used to describe my figure are more likely to come from the 'lumpy' part of the Thesaurus than the 'junoesque' section – which still means pretty large but at least it's supposed to be flattering. 'I know what your problem is,' I said. 'You've got an acute case of Venetia-itis. It comes from spending too long hanging around her. After a while any female starts to feel she resembles the reflection in one of those fat mirrors at a fair.'

Janey laughed. 'How right you are!' She ruffled the hair of the nearer twin. 'Oh, to be like these two, they have life so easy! Wouldn't it be nice to have everyone admiring how fat your legs are or saying how sweet your pot is?'

'Mm.' I considered them. 'But I'm quite glad to be at the age where egg in the hair isn't the latest in fashion statements.' The twin, attired only in a nappy and an ample coating of cereal and egg yolk, beamed happily at me before going back to sucking on a soggy toast soldier with obvious enjoyment.

'I think it's known as storing a snack for later,' Janey said. 'I find it's quicker and easier to wash them rather than their clothes, especially in this weather. Besides,' she pointed at an old-fashioned hip bath just outside the window on the terrace, 'they seem to think the morning routine of twenty minutes in the bath after breakfast is a wonderful game and it means their mother can have a bit of peace too. You don't get that with the washing machine.'

I refused the generous offer of a well-sucked soldier from the other twin as Janey bustled around ladling coffee grounds into a very technical-looking coffee machine, automatically wiping one face or the other each time she passed, and talking over her shoulder as she went.

'So if you aren't Oscar's girlfriend, how have you ended up at the cottage?' she asked curiously as she reached to get sunny yellow mugs out of the cupboard. 'I got the impression from what Maggie said that she knows you from work. Are you in PR too?'

I shook my head. 'Good heavens, no! Nothing so grand – well, not according to Maggie. I'm in advertising – a copywriter – and Maggie considers us advertising bods to be lower-class cousins of the superior souls in PR. You see, we might have larger budgets than she does, but we have to *pay* to get our clients publicity, while she twists arms to get it for free.'

'In the meantime charging her clients an arm and a leg for all the lunches she has to treat people to in order to get her "free" mentions,' Janey said caustically. 'But of course we hacks reckon that *we're* the top of the tree. It's Maggie and her ilk who are always chasing us to do them a favour by featuring their clients.' She smiled suddenly. 'Though I have to say that you get given some jolly nice presents by PR people sometimes. Which agency do you work for? I might know them. I did a stint as a staff reporter at *Advertising World* years ago.'

'Lassiter's.' It had started off as just being Lassiter's, then in true advertising style as Lassiter took on partners and their names went on to the letterheading the company became known by its initials, first LBDO then LBDCR (O had left after a massive boardroom row) and so on until there were nine partners, and no one could ever remember the correct pecking order, or all the names. By common consent the agency went back to being simply Lassiter's again.

'Oh *them*,' she said as she cut a butter-yellow brioche and put the slices on a place. 'Fearful bunch of slave-drivers, aren't they? No wonder you look so fragile. Oscar said you'd been ill – I'm surprised you dared to be, in that place. I thought the merest sniffle was held to be grounds for the sack, since it meant you must have lied on the application form when you said you had good general health.'

'You really *do* know them,' I said wryly. 'Except even Jim Lassiter pays enough attention to employment law not to actually threaten you with the sack for a sniffle. No, he's more subtle. In my case it went along the lines that it simply wasn't fair to my clients to have their copywriter taking so much time off for what these days isn't even a serious illness, and if I didn't get my finger out and get back to work he was very sorry but he'd have to move me sideways, probably into the charge of a pimply youth who'd only just finished a correspondence course in copywriting, while someone more reliable took my place.'

'Sounds like Jim Lassiter to me,' said Janey. 'He doesn't change. As a matter of interest, what was the non-serious illness?'

'Pneumonia, which I wouldn't have had in the first place if I hadn't gone back to work too soon after a bout of 'flu. At the time it seemed easier than staying at home fielding Jim's calls every five minutes or so.'

Janey whistled softly. 'I wouldn't have thought it possible for him to have got worse. Shows how wrong you can be. Ever thought of getting a new job?'

'Frequently,' I said. 'Especially in the pub on Friday evenings. Maybe Jim's got a point when he says I lack application, though he tends to say that to anyone who asks for a pay rise. I've never managed to get around to stopping talking about finding a new job and actually writing a letter of application, but I'm going to look around now.'

'Sounds like a good idea to me, but if you decide to stay on after all let me suggest a few extra weapons that might come in handy when demanding a pay rise . . .' Janey began. She told me a couple of old but still delightfully scurrilous stories about some of the senior staff at the agency that had been deemed too sensitive to print in the sedate pages of *Advertising World*; actually your average tabloid might have hesitated before printing the full details of what happened between the Design Director and the salesman from the paper company. I never knew you could do *that* with a packet of Letraset! And I'd thought the Design Director was such a pillar of rectitude too. I made Janey repeat the most salient details so I could be absolutely sure I'd got them right. Christian, the senior copywriter who worked opposite me, was going to love this. And as for the real story behind why we'd failed to win the pitch for Bottisford Soft Drinks . . .

A simultaneous clamour arose from both twins. One was noisily bashing his tray with his spoon while the other lobbed his bowl at us. Janey caught it just in time and got them down, speedily wiping their protesting faces yet again before putting them into the tin bath. Contented splashing sounds started up almost immediately and she sat down with a relieved sigh. 'I love them dearly, but they're exhausting. Especially at breakfast. Delphine stays overnight when we go out in the evenings, otherwise she lives with her mother in the village and there are times when I bitterly regret not having a full-time live-in nanny – most mornings at about six-thirty, in fact.'

As she picked up the coffee pot to offer me a refill, something about the angle of her head rang a bell in my memory. 'Oh, I know where I've seen you before! You used to write a column in the *Gazette*, didn't you? Janey O'Donnell. Your picture was at the top.'

'That was ages ago. Fancy you remembering that,' she said, looking pleased.

'I loved it, it was one of the best things about the paper,' I said truthfully. 'I was really sorry when you gave it up. Was that after you got married and moved out here? Oscar said something about you meeting Tom when you did a feature on him for the column.' I propped my elbows on the table in a way that my mother would have disapproved of and saw with faint dismay that while we'd been talking, most of the plate of brioche had disappeared. I couldn't remember Janey eating more than one piece either. 'It sounds frightfully romantic – lovely journalist meets dashing château-owner and, pow! Just the sort of thing you read in soppy novels.'

'Mm, and everyone lives happily ever after,' she said with a faint edge to her voice.

To cover a nasty little silence I said quickly, 'Do you still write any articles?'

She shrugged. 'I do the odd one to keep my hand in and my contacts up for if I ever need them, but being a mother of young children and living in rural France doesn't really mix with high-profile journalism. Especially as I used to specialise in interviews and you've got to do that face to face; I'd need my head examined if I went away on a regular basis and left Tom alone with Delphine! My mother thinks I must be crazy anyway. She's always telling me to get an older nanny. I think what she really means is fat and ugly,' she added and cocked her head to one side thoughtfully. 'Though I'd be much safer leaving Tom with Delphine than with an older woman, unless she was utterly hideous. Going after eighteen-year-olds has never been one of Tom's vices; like his wines, he prefers his women mature.'

She turned her head towards the door at a noise and smiled. 'Though frankly, I don't think I've got much to worry about. Even if the charms of the local Adonis with the very large motorbike ever begin to pall and Delphine starts thinking longingly about Tom, one glimpse of him looking like this and his chastity would be assured,' she said as her husband, wearing a cotton dressing gown, hair standing on end, unshaven, squinting against the light and generally looking like someone who feels that they haven't spent nearly long enough in bed, shuffled in blearily. I had to admit he wasn't a pretty sight. He smiled vaguely at me as if he wasn't quite sure who I was, I don't think he was even focusing at that distance, and headed for the coffee machine like a guided missile, pouring himself a mug and looking at it as if it was the elixir of life. Half a mugful of coffee and a glass of orange juice later he was awake enough to say, 'Morning ... um ... Nella. Nice to see you, sorry I can't stay to talk but I have to rush. I'm running late.'

Rush wasn't the word I'd have used to describe his gait but at least it wasn't sleepwalking any longer. 'He's not good in the mornings,' Janey said unnecessarily. 'He's not normally quite as bad as this, but he was up with Rob for hours last night – finishing the bottle, or more than one bottle, judging from the way he tried to brush his teeth with my eyebrow brush,' she added with wifely disapproval. 'Though I suppose I should be grateful that Tom is prepared to sit up carousing with Rob, even if they aren't a very good influence on each other.' Somewhat of an understatement in my opinion, judging by Tom's state this morning. 'Tom's normal reaction to Venetia's boyfriends is to sit in silence glowering at them. He disapproves on principle of any man who gets within touching distance of his daughter.'

'Doesn't that sort of attitude come with the paternal territory?' I said, thinking of the way my own parent had been (over)reacting ever since my elder sister was thirteen.

'I suppose so,' she admitted, 'but it doesn't make for relaxed mealtimes.' I could see that. I've sat through more than a few of those myself, particularly when I was going out with Gavin with all the tattoos. 'So I shouldn't complain, even if I do have to go out and buy a new eyebrow brush. It's such a relief not to have Tom going around behaving like a bear with indigestion!' She grinned. 'At least they didn't sing. And Rob thinks he knows a couple of people who might be interested in investing in a wine business, which definitely makes me forgive him the odd riotous evening with my husband.'

'Is that what he does now? Work with investments?' It didn't seem very Robert somehow.

'No, he's got a part share in an art gallery, and these people are regular clients of his, City whizz-kids who have enormous bonuses they're not sure what to do with. He thinks they might want the fun of being involved with a wine business without actually having to get their hands dirty, which would be ideal for us.' She sighed again. 'We've had a couple of sticky years, you see. A cash injection would be really welcome.'

I'm afraid to say I was barely concentrating on what she was saying. 'A *gallery*?' I repeated. 'When did he start doing that?'

'Goodness, you two are out of touch, aren't you?' I could almost see a fishing rod hanging over the table as Janey added, 'And I had the impression that you knew each other . . . quite well.'

I suddenly found the top of the table very interesting. 'Um, we did once, but I haven't actually spoken to him since the middle of the summer term, nine years ago.' She looked at me with an uncomfortable acuity. I suspected she was well aware I could have given her the date and actual time, let alone place, of when I'd last spoken to Robert. 'And the gallery surprised me because when I . . . knew him, Robert was all set to become a barrister.'

'A barrister?' she exclaimed. 'I can't imagine him in a wig and robes.' Neither could I, to tell the truth; I never had been able to. 'It'd be a bit like setting up a poacher as a gamekeeper,' she went on, 'not that I mean he's dishonest, but somehow you get the feeling he looks on rules as something to be bent when necessary. Not a particularly helpful attitude for a member of the legal profession. Why on earth did he think he wanted to be a barrister?'

'I don't think he ever did, not really. There's always been a Winwood making waves with the law, or has been for ages, and Robert's uncle was supposed to be the one who took on the mantle and then he was killed in a car accident. Since Robert is the only boy of his generation it was just assumed that's what he'd do.'

Janey raised her eyebrows. 'Didn't the senior Winwoods realise there have been women at the Bar for some time now?'

'I don't think they're very strong on feminism,' I giggled. 'Mr Winwood was very upset when his new bank manager turned out to be female. Said it was a well-known fact that women couldn't cope with money.'

'If it was Venetia in charge of his finances he'd have a point, but she's hardly typical of our sex. So why did Rob change his mind about doing law?'

'He didn't,' I said shamefacedly.

Janey linked her fingers under her chin and waited for me to amplify this somewhat terse statement. 'I trust you aren't intending to leave me in suspense about what happened?' she said mildly.

I was beginning to see why she had been such a good journalist. In fact, she ought to be on loan to MI6 for interrogation services; there was something about the way she led you on until you'd gone so far there was no pulling back. Oh well, there wasn't really any reason why she shouldn't know; it might even be quite useful to have one person up here who knew why Robert and I were in no hurry to get reacquainted, I thought as I began a somewhat edited story of what had happened. I traced a finger slowly around the top of my mug as I came to the end and said, 'So there you have it. That's why Robert isn't a barrister. Because of me.'

'It wasn't *all* your fault,' she said reasonably.

'No, but I was the one who started it by throwing his keys at him.'

'You might as well say the blame starts with your sports mistress for not teaching you to throw straight when you were playing rounders.' That was a good point. I'd never liked the sports mistress either – now I knew why. 'And Rob could have kept his hands off your friend as well,' she added firmly, 'though granted, most men don't expect that a bit of playing away from home is going to lead to being branded a pervert and being thrown in jail! But was last night really the first time you'd seen him since you chucked his keys over the hedge?'

I shook my head. 'I bumped into him as I was leaving the police station.' Perhaps it had occurred to the police that if they weren't careful they'd find themselves the object of a suit for wrongful arrest – from a law student. By the time I'd finished reading my statement, signed it and been allowed to go, Robert was already standing by the front desk where the tea-drinking Sergeant had emptied the contents of a brown paper bag onto the counter, and was checking them off one by one before handing them back to him. The Sergeant raised his eyes, saw me, nodded politely and said, 'Goodbye, miss,' then went back to his task. Robert swung around, eyes blazing in his pale face, unshaven, looking tired and strained. And angry. Very, very angry. I was strongly tempted to bolt out of there without another word, but something, my guilty conscience probably, made me approach him. I was so nervous I had to make several attempts before any sound would come out of my mouth. 'So they're letting you go,' I said.

He didn't reply, just looked at me in a way I didn't ever want to remember. I stepped back a pace instinctively and, if possible, his rage seemed to blaze even higher. 'I'm sorry,' I began falteringly. 'I shouldn't have . . .'

'Nella,' he interrupted in a voice of ice, 'I don't want any apologies from *you*.' I've never heard a simple pronoun loaded with such withering contempt. 'It's a damn sight too late to say sorry and just hope that makes everything better so we can forget it ever happened!'

The Sergeant made a protesting, 'calm down, Sonny' sort of noise, and Robert said without turning his head, 'Don't worry, officer. I won't give into the temptation to kill her – not in a police station. I've spent enough time enjoying your hospitality already. But I'd advise you to get out of my sight, Nella, or I might forget where we are.'

That really was the last time I'd laid eyes on him. And unfortunately that old adage about time being a great healer seemed to have got it all wrong. Certainly as far as Robert's feelings about me were concerned.

There was a long silence after I'd finished, broken only by splashing sounds coming from the tub on the terrace. 'Wow!' breathed Janey, finally putting down her mug, which she'd been holding forgotten in mid-air, back on the table.

She looked at me thoughtfully and said finally, 'Do you know, I think it might be wiser if you *didn't* come for supper tonight . . .'

CHAPTER 5

I'd fondly imagined that when I got back to the cottage I'd be met by a group filled with gratitude for my kind gesture in fetching them breakfast. Talk about wishful thinking. Instead I found just about as stroppy a collection of holidaymakers as you could expect to find. Oscar had been woken by an unwarrantedly noisy bird warbling away outside his window, then on his sleepy way to the kitchen for tea he'd glanced out at the little parking area and seen a space where his beloved car should have been. General panic ensued. Everyone had been roused from their beds to have frantic consultations on how you were supposed to report a car theft when the police don't even speak your language, and where the hell was the nearest police station anyway?

They'd just about come to the sensible conclusion that the answer was to ask Janey and Tom, when someone thought to enquire if I really was still peacefully sleeping through all this noise. I was interested to note, when being told this later, that the common opinion about my general usefulness must be so low that no one had even thought to wake me to hear my valuable contribution on how this crisis might be solved. Once my bed was discovered to be empty, this group of Sherlock Holmeses came to the logical conclusion that, as no one would bother to abduct me, it must be me who'd irresponsibly taken the car without asking. And even after my note was found on the floor by Oscar's bed where he'd knocked it off the bedside table, I was still held to be at fault for not having weighted it down properly in some more visible space.

I could have said a lot in reply, would have in fact if I hadn't been uneasily aware that if I hadn't sat around gossiping with Janey for over an hour, I'd have been back long before Oscar even woke up and caused all the rumpus. Not that my offering of croissants and bread would have soothed many troubled breasts even if it had been on time. Sally, it turned out, didn't like croissants, Phil preferred chocolatines, Maggie never ate white bread, even in baguette form, and I hadn't bought any milk. Jed didn't make any comment – probably because he was in the shower when I returned with my booty. Oscar, at least, had been happy with his croissants until he glanced in the car and discovered the crumbs all over the seat. And the dog hair. I also somehow got landed with the washing up which was a bit rich since as well as actually providing the food, the only thing I'd dirtied was one mug, but the others started muttering about how I hadn't done anything last night and then just left me to it. Given the general mood, I thought it wiser to leave breaking the news until later that Janey hadn't felt it was a good idea to have Robert, a steak-knife and me in close proximity to each other and our dinner had been cancelled – or rather put off until after he had left. No doubt I'd get blamed for that too. It didn't improve my mood to know that for once they'd be right.

Maggie and Sally had gone off with Oscar to the nearest town to stock up on essential provisions and I was about to slink away with my book and a bottle of Factor 15 to the far side of the pool in search of peace, quiet and no domestic duties, when I saw both Charlie and Phil lift their heads and look out into the distance like dogs who have just sighted a pheasant. Venetia was jogging down the track through the vines, dressed in a very small pair of running shorts and a shirt tied underneath her bust, showing off her enviably flat stomach, with her thick hair tied back in a high pony tail. Seeing us out in the garden, she waved vigorously and jogged over to join us.

'Goodness, when did the passion for running start?' I called, surprised to see that she was even on her feet at this hour. Slowly leafing through the latest copy of *Vogue* while lying on a lounger on the terrace seemed more Venetia's sort of thing. 'When you were living in the flat you refused to walk anywhere. You even used to take the car to the corner shop!'

'But what's wrong with that?' she asked, looking surprised. 'Who in their right mind would walk up a London street in Maud Frizon shoes? They might get wet – or worse. And anyway, I don't go *walking*, I run,' she said seriously. 'Power walking is so undignified, with all that swinging your arms around. It makes you look like a chicken!' She flopped down to touch her toes while Phil leaned back to give himself the best possible view of what it did to her running shorts, and continued to talk while upside down. 'Annouska, my boss, has a personal trainer who comes in each morning before the shop opens to take all the staff through a quick workout. And do you know, she's *absolutely* right!' she said from between her legs.

It looked as if, not content with putting the palms of her hands on the ground, Venetia was now going to try to get her forehead down there as well; the very thought made me feel distinctly dizzy.

'I feel so much better now I'm starting to repair the damage I was doing to my body by not exercising properly.' She began to straighten up at last. I'm sure it was just guilty conscience that made me imagine she flicked a look in my direction, for though she had many faults, Venetia had never, unlike many other startlingly good-looking women, taken pleasure in denigrating other less perfect members of her own sex. She stretched upwards to the evident appreciation of the masculine contingent and announced proudly that she worked out nearly every day in London, though when she was here she had to add an extra fifteen minutes to her run due to the general lack of gyms with state-of-the-art equipment in this area.

She pouted crossly. 'Daddy won't even get a proper rowing machine. He says he keeps quite fit enough with all the outdoor work he does, and he's not spending thousands of francs for a piece of equipment when a walk would do just as well. And Robbie's just as bad. He won't come out with me either, says he prefers to get his exercise lying flat.' Charlie smothered a laugh. Venetia went on unheedingly, 'So I thought I'd come and see how you were settling in, Nella. I didn't get much of a chance to talk to you last night.' Well, I hadn't really been talking to anyone, too apprehensive that something highly embarrassing would come spilling out, and she'd been too busy fluttering her eyelashes at Phil who'd been doing the masculine equivalent back to even glance at the other women around the table.

When I came back with her cup of herbal tea – the real thing had been shudderingly refused with a 'Don't you *know* what caffeine does to you?' – she was examining my bottle of sun tan cream with a disapproving air. 'You should use stronger sun protection, Nella.' I gathered from her expression that she didn't rate an own label brand, whatever its SPF factor, too highly. 'You must have heard all about sun damage on your face, so there's no excuse,' she scolded, insisting that I drag my chair to the shade of the large umbrella by the sitting-room windows. I could see it wasn't worth trying to plead my case that I'd only been planning ten minutes in the sun in a preliminary effort to get my face to change from its current pastry colour to the weak-tea-with-plenty-of-added-milk shade which is the nearest I ever get to a tan. Besides, it made a refreshing change to listen to someone comment on my appearance and not imply I was already way past the point of any possible repair, so I didn't mind humouring her. She arranged her own chair carefully so that none of the deadly rays fell on her pale face. Given her red hair I couldn't help wondering if she was actually more worried about the possibility of freckles than skin cancer and wrinkles, and suspected that the delicate hen's egg brown on her arms and legs came out of a bottle. If I was really nice to her, she might lend me some. I'd be prepared to bet it wasn't the sort that leaves bright orange streaks running down your legs.

'I'm just longing to catch up on everything you've been up to. It's such ages since we've seen each other – at least five years, isn't it?' she said, once we were settled down to her satisfaction. 'Goodness, I don't even know if you're married. You aren't, are you?'

I shook my head, wondering if she'd come down for a little probing about how well I'd known Robert. But I needn't have worried; he seemed to have been as offhand about me as I'd been about him and she appeared to think he was merely some casual university acquaintance. Obviously he wasn't one of the subjects I'd touched on during indiscretion sessions at the flat. I blessed my previously unknown talent for keeping my mouth closed, since it seemed to me that Venetia deserved being likened to an elephant far more than I did. Not for figure reasons of course, but for her memory which was truly prodigious. I had forgotten the details about my encounter with the drunk who was visiting the lady of the night opposite and the imaginative proposition he made me, but she hadn't. I'd really rather not have had that particular story aired in front of Charlie and Phil, who began to regard me with an entirely new look in their eyes. Those two gentlemen, drawn like moths to a lamp by the amount of Venetia on display, had decided that they too were having too much sun and had pulled up chairs under the umbrella. They were also showing none of the usual disdain that men have for female gossip sessions. I suppose they were also hoping to hear another story of the type usually only told in hushed voices in the safety of the ladies' loos. Much to their pleasure, Venetia didn't appear to be in any hurry to get back to the château. Robert was still in bed and I got the feeling she was afraid she might be pressganged into performing domestic tasks if she was seen hanging around up there with nothing obvious to do. Or she might have been worried about getting an earful from Janey for not closing the gate properly.

We had an exhaustive update on everyone we knew in common – and on quite a few we didn't – but who Venetia thought I'd be interested in hearing about. I was – about some of them, anyway. We then moved on to her working life, which seemed to have been as varied as the places she'd lived in, including stints at several firms where she was the decorative element on the front desk, and a short spell as an estate agent, although as the weekend shifts interfered with going away for house-parties she chucked it in after a few weeks. Sadly, she had much the same sort of problem in her next job as a greeter in a fashionable new restaurant: the management was very unreasonable about allowing her evenings off. She'd joined up with a friend selling luxury yachts on commission until she belatedly realised that her friend was implying to prospective clients that if they were prepared to shell out several million on a floating gin palace they might well find Venetia came with the fixtures and fittings. Venetia was quite amused, and I gathered prepared to at least take a preparatory look at the buyer before she definitely said, 'No,' (there was a lot of commission at stake), until her friend almost made a sale – to a woman.

Venetia was currently working with another friend who had just opened a shop in Soho selling very expensive costume jewellery. It was the sort of place where having a mere gold card puts you firmly at the back of the queue to be served, but it didn't seem as if the working hours were too onerous since she had already been staying with Tom and Janey for a week, and was thinking of drifting off to Cannes for a few days sometime near the end of the month, and maybe even going to Italy for a bit afterwards.

'Is Robert going with you to Cannes?' I asked.

She shrugged her shoulders. The men appeared to be fascinated by the effect on her brief shirt which looked to be so insecurely tied that it might burst asunder at any moment. It would have been mean to inform them that she was undoubtedly wearing a sturdy sports bra underneath, rather than the wisp of satin and lace they were probably fantasising about.

'Good heavens, no!' she said in a sulky voice. 'I was lucky to get him to agree to spend even a few days down here. He's a positive workaholic.' He was? He must *really* have changed. 'He says he'll have to leave tomorrow or the day after.' That was a relief, then the others wouldn't have to wait too long for dinner at the château. 'He doesn't like to be away from the gallery for too long. I can't see why not. He's got a partner and an assistant, and it's not as if he was doing something in the City which means he misses out on loads of commission if he's away from his desk.'

'Maybe he doesn't like to be away from it for too long,' Charlie said mildly. 'Owning your own business tends to take you that way.'

'But it isn't much fun for me,' she protested. 'I'd like to be able to go out with him a bit more.' From the expression on Phil's face he was quite ready to jump into the breach and help her occupy any spare time she might have. 'But perhaps once he's gone we could all get together for a day out somewhere,' she suggested. Phil nodded enthusiastically, and she looked around. 'Where's everyone else? Surely they aren't still in bed?'

'You must be kidding. No one got a chance to lie in this morning,' Phil grunted and filled Venetia in on the morning's dramas. Much to my annoyance she seemed to take the view that I had been grossly careless, in which precise way was left unstated. I had to resist a strong impulse to stamp my foot and say, 'You can jolly well go and fetch your own croissants in future, so there!' They were probably going to anyway. Maggie had been muttering about the necessity of making up a proper rota for all the chores; it was just too chaotic leaving everything to whoever felt like doing it, and I sensed I wasn't going to be allowed to have anything so responsible as croissant-fetching duty for some time, though I'd probably get plenty of putting out the rubbish.

'I'm surprised you didn't meet Jed as you came down here,' said Charlie. 'He left to walk up to the château about five minutes before you turned up. Said something about Janey promising to show him around the local town before he goes off to interview some eminent writer

Victoria Corby

who spends his summers in a farmhouse near here.'

'There won't be much to show on a Monday morning. Nearly everything is shut!' Venetia retorted. Oh dear, that wasn't going to please the shopping-party. She sniffed slightly. 'Honestly, it's a good thing my father isn't the jealous type. Most husbands wouldn't be too thrilled about their wife giving an old flame a private guided tour of the countryside like that.'

'Is Jed an old flame?' I asked. 'He doesn't seem like one.'

'Anybody with eyes can see he and Janey have got a history,' she said in a pitying tone. 'Haven't you seen the way he looks at her?' Actually, after an hour of listening to Jed last night I'd got the impression the thing he looked at most was his reflection in the mirror; where was he going to find the time to look at anyone else? 'And you might wonder why Jed's been parked down here out of the way too.'

We stared at her in faint surprise, then Charlie chuckled. 'I'm sure that if Janey was planning something clandestine with Jed she'd be able to find a slightly more discreet location than a sofa bed in full view of six paying guests!'

To do Venetia credit she laughed at having her guns so thoroughly spiked, though there was a slight delay first, and she swiftly moved the conversation onto another topic. A few minutes later she looked at her watch and announced that she really ought to be getting back. 'I'll walk a little of the way with you,' I said, reminded by the super-fit being alongside me that maybe it was time I stopped using my recent illness as an excuse for taking it easy.

We strolled up to the avenue of chestnut trees chatting companionably about various topics, most of which seemed to include Venetia, until a chance remark of hers prompted me to ask ultra-casually, 'So how long have you and Robert been going out?'

She pushed her glasses up her nose and asked sweetly, 'Digging for information, Nella?'

I shrugged. 'Of course! Wouldn't you, if you discovered I'd become an item with someone you used to know ages ago?'

She nodded, showing no interest at all in finding out exactly how I'd known Robert or why I had such a keen interest in him, but then I shouldn't think it had ever occurred to Venetia that I might lead the sort of life which could give rise to juicy gossip. Mercifully.

Anyway she was too busy telling me how she'd been taken to Robert's gallery for a viewing by her then boyfriend; it had been a case of eyes meeting across a crowded room and pee-yow! The boyfriend had been dumped, she didn't appear to know whether Robert had had a girlfriend to discard, and they'd both motored off into the sunset. Any slight feelings of chagrin I might have had over the fact that I certainly hadn't had that sort of effect on Robert were tempered by the reflection that from what I could remember, Venetia had nearly always made first contact with the man of the moment in this way. The only difference about this affair was, it was still going on six months later; her instant attractions usually fizzled out within a month or so.

'So is there a future in this?'

She shrugged. 'Don't know. Might be, I suppose. He

gets on with Daddy, which is good. You might say that it shouldn't count but it makes life a lot easier if your man isn't constantly at loggerheads with your father. Daddy likes Robbie because he doesn't suck up to him as the great château-owner,' she added with surprising shrewdness. She wrinkled her nose up. 'I just wish he'd get a proper job. That art gallery of his hardly earns him a thing – well, not what I'd call proper money – and if you suggest that he should branch out into doing something more commercial, he climbs on a very high horse. Still,' she said briskly, 'if we get married he'll have to come down to earth and stop being quite so principled about earning his money.'

'Married?' I exclaimed.

'It's about time I settled down. You really ought to get married before your thirtieth birthday, you know,' she said seriously. 'It looks pretty stupid having a really big wedding with bridesmaids and loads of white veiling when everybody knows that you're past the halfway mark for a bus pass.'

I must admit this aspect had never occurred to me before and I wondered if I should inform my sister who was getting married in a couple of months that she ought to hold the veil. 'So how long have you been engaged?'

'Well, we aren't actually,' she said offhandedly and smiled at me in a conspiratorial woman-to-woman fashion. 'We haven't got around to discussing it yet, but come on, you know it's the woman who has to make up the man's mind in most cases like this.'

I looked at her fascinated, thinking that if she could really make Robert's mind up for him he must have changed beyond all recognition, and wondering how the hell she reckoned she was going to do it. But before I could ask, a car came over the brow of the hill in a cloud of dust, and drew up alongside us. It was the shopping party back with enough carrier bags to indicate that the expedition hadn't been a complete disaster though there was a certain amount of irritation about the really good pâtisserie being closed.

They chatted for a couple of minutes, then as Oscar was about to move off again, Maggie leaned out of the window and said cheerily, 'We'll see you this evening, Venetia.'

'Er, um, you won't actually,' I began and was promptly skewered by several accusing looks. I used the cover story Janey had whipped up on the spot – that she and Tom had to go out with a visiting wine merchant (it had the advantage of containing a certain element of the truth; well, it did after she had rung him and fixed it up) – and that she was checking her diary to see what other evening we should come.

'You might have told me before I went out shopping. I'll have to go out again after lunch for food for dinner tonight,' Maggie began crossly and, I noted regretfully, with a certain amount of justice on her side. Then to my horror she brightened and said to Venetia, 'Why don't you and Robert come and have supper with us at the cottage?'

'That would be really nice,' Venetia said, pleased. I doubted her enthusiasm would be matched by Robert. For both our sakes it might be better if I had a migraine. The migraine was put on hold when her face fell and she said regretfully, 'Oh, but Camilla's ringing me tonight about Cannes so I'd better stay in.' Then, 'But just because Janey and Daddy aren't going to be there doesn't mean that I can't have you all for supper anyway. It's my home too! Otherwise it'll be just me and Robert, and it'll be much more fun to have a bit of company.' Since this was his next to last evening with his girlfriend for a while, I doubted that Robert would agree with that statement, especially if I came along. I heard a chorus of grateful acceptances and decided the migraine would have to be reinstated.

CHAPTER 6

Unfortunately, the best laid plans of mice, men and ex-girlfriends gang aft a-gley. Mine did so right from the start. Since the weather was so gorgeous, I hadn't wanted to spend the whole afternoon shut up in my bedroom with the curtains drawn so I'd waited until Maggie was handing around glasses of iced tea (very nice too) before announcing that I thought I could feel the familiar tightness across my forehead which usually presaged the onset of one of my migraines. This meant, I said, that I wouldn't be able to go out tonight. I can't say Maggie looked particularly sorry about the prospect of me missing out on socialising, but my dearest friend turned over on his long chair, propped himself up on one elbow and looked at me in surprise, saying, 'But you've *never* had a migraine, Nella. I remember you saying so.' At this everyone else also looked suspiciously at me, as if I was up to something.

'Um, that was some time ago, unfortunately,' I said quickly, deciding that if Oscar said it was only last week, I'd kick him – hard. 'I should think it's something to do with having been so ill. When I'm better, I'll probably never have another. I'll see how I feel later on,' I temporised. The problem was, I realised when I went inside and glanced at my reflection in the little mirror in the downstairs loo, I didn't look as if I was just about to come down with a migraine. I didn't know what that did look like, but I had the impression that it made you appear pretty cheesy, and I, due to sneaking an illicit half-hour in the sun after Venetia had gone, had a healthier colour than I'd had for months. I might not have been a glowing picture of health, but I no longer looked like an instant candidate for a sickbed either. Damn! I wondered if there was a convenient bag of flour in the kitchen . . .

I went back outside and lay down in a shady corner, covering my eyes with my arm in what I hoped was a suitably weak and fluttering gesture indicative of worse to come. Maggie said in a solicitous voice that if I was really feeling ill I'd better stay at home. I nodded feebly, trying my hardest not to let the others see what deep pain I was in, when to my dismay I heard Oscar saying, 'Nella doesn't normally make a fuss. If she's feeling bad enough to cancel an evening out I'd better stay behind and make sure she's all right.'

Oh bugger it! I thought crossly. If Oscar insisted on playing Florian Nightingale I was going to end up confined to a darkened room and at the very most being allowed to have one cup of weak tea. Oscar doesn't believe in feeding the sick. And I was starving too. I opened one eye to see him standing over me, hands on hips.

'Feeling better already?' he enquired sarcastically. So much for my acting abilities. 'There's nothing wrong with you at all, is there, so what's all this about?' he asked, sitting down on the end of my chair. When I said there was nothing for it to be about, he merely shrugged and said, 'OK, if you don't want to tell me I'm sure Venetia – or *Robert*,' the emphasis was unmistakable, 'can give me all the low-down.'

He bloody well would ask them too, I thought sourly. By now, Oscar must have sussed out that the love affair at university that had ended so badly and which I'd mentioned in passing to him, must have something to do with Robert. Oscar's passion for gossip comes only a narrow second to his enthusiasm for interfering in people's lives. Knowing I was beaten, I sighed and gave in. Then I threatened to tear him limb from limb if he did anything at all to promote diplomatic relations between me and Robert. Oscar's a great believer in being friends with your exes, not, I've noticed, that he's exactly on pally terms with all of his ex-boyfriends, but he doesn't reckon his own rules apply to himself.

'I've never known someone for getting into messes like you do, Nella,' he said, once I'd given him a highly edited and abridged version of why I thought the wisest course of action was to lie low and keep out of trouble. 'You don't really want Robert to think you're too scared even to be in the same room as him, do you?' he asked reproachfully. No, though it seemed a preferable option to getting within his reach. However, I knew I wouldn't be allowed to get away with that reasoning. I've often thought that contrary to his general appearance, manner and dress, Oscar must have been a Roundhead in his last incarnation. He takes an almost puritanical delight in insisting you face up to your problems, which is probably quite sound reasoning in many cases but not when it comes to facing enraged ex-boyfriends. There's nothing Oscar enjoys more than a good confrontation and clearing of the air – especially at second-hand.

Actually the evening was nothing like so bad as I'd feared, not the beginning of it anyway. Oscar had offered to help me choose something to wear so I'd look absolutely stunning, which was sweet of him but not quite as much help as you might think. He is one of those people who thinks all his friends are automatically gorgeous, which says a lot about the niceness of his character but not a lot for his dispassionate judgement over whether a dress really does make your bum look elephantine or if the hairdresser's latest attempt to put a bit of life in my straight thick hair had simply made me bear a disturbing resemblance to Worzel Gummidge. But his unfettered praise of how I looked was a useful and necessary morale booster.

When we arrived at the château, Jed and Robert were already into the first of the staggering number of bottles that Venetia had liberated from her father's cellar, and Jed was in full flow on journalistic mishaps around the world. He barely broke off to say hello to all of us and wait for us to sit down before picking up where he'd left off, seemingly almost on the same sentence. I was pretty sure that nobody could have had quite that number of misadventures and remain alive; judging by his slightly cynical expression so was Robert, but Jed was an excellent raconteur, even if a critical listener might have thought he was slightly too inclined to put himself in the starring role, and his stories made an easy topic of conversation for the first half hour or so.

Things got stickier when Venetia summoned us to come inside and eat. She'd decided that there was a wind getting up and it was going to be too chilly to spend the whole evening out of doors. Since the back of her dress consisted of about three pieces of ribbon she had reason to be worried about breezes across her bare skin, but to someone used to an English summer the temperature outside was one that would have had back gardens from Richmond to Clapham hidden under a pall of barbecue smoke while everyone said how nice it was to eat outside, and did anyone want another cardigan?

'Sit where you like,' she called, waving an airy hand as she carried through plates of pâté and wicker baskets of bread and put them down on the long dining-room table. The result was we milled around uncertainly at one end of the room, everybody waiting for someone else to take the plunge and sit down until Venetia sighed theatrically and took charge. 'Now, where shall I put you all?' I had a nasty feeling I knew what was coming next; my ever-increasing powers of prescience were proved right when she turned to me with a broad smile and said, 'You and Robbie must have loads to catch up on. I'm sure you'd like to sit next to each other.'

Needless to say I didn't have the bottle to say that actually, no we wouldn't, but at least I wasn't as hypo-critical as Robert himself, who murmured that nothing would give him greater pleasure. To wring my neck, probably, I thought as I sat down next to him, shooting an accusatory glance at Oscar, who widened his eyes in an innocent manner to indicate that no, he hadn't had anything to do with putting Venetia up to this. I thought I believed him. At least I had Jed on my other side, and since he talked quite enough for two, our end of the table wouldn't be the deep pool of silence that I'd feared. The only problem was that Maggie, on his other side, was equally determined that she shouldn't waste a burgeoning tan and a flatteringly cut dress that showed off her considerable bosom to its best advantage on Oscar, and kept laying an elegantly manicured hand on Jed's arm to gain his attention. My own much reduced endowment simply couldn't compete; by halfway through the pâté I gave up Jed's attention as a bad job and decided to concentrate on my plate instead. Better everyone thought that I was greedy rather than that no one wanted to talk to me. And it was jolly good pâté too, I thought, taking a bite.

I almost choked on it as Robert turned around to me and said, 'So, Nella, we're supposed to be catching up on old times. We'd better do just that.' It didn't sound as if he was regarding the prospect with pleasure. 'Where shall we start ...? Ah, seen the inside of any police stations recently?'

For about the first time in my life I obeyed my mother's instructions to chew my food forty times. 'Only when I had to go with George,' I said, when I couldn't put off swallowing any longer, deciding that wilful misunderstanding was the best approach.

It backfired. Robert's eyes narrowed with real interest. 'Who's George? Someone else you put in chokey?'

I could feel the colour rising up my cheeks. 'No!' I

hissed, fiercely enough to make Oscar's head swivel around. He regarded the pair of us curiously. 'A man in another car thought George had cut him up on the A40 and tried to drag him out of the car for a fight. I had to go along as a witness, that's all.'

'And George let you make a statement on his behalf? He must be a brave man, foolhardy even.' I gritted my teeth and stared straight ahead, wondering how long I could stand this before I made the sort of scene that would keep Venetia in a fund of stories for months to come. 'And where is this George? No longer around presumably, as he'd be here otherwise, so who is there in your life these days?' Robert went on, making it sound as if it was highly unlikely there was any idiot fool enough to take the position.

I hesitated, wondering whether to lie through my teeth or not. Sadly, even in these days of female empowerment it still somehow goes against the female grain to admit that you're, er, celibate. For one thing any suggestion that it's by your own choice is usually met with a resounding raspberry and a recommendation that you go and relate it to the Marines. But, for once, in my case it really was the truth. I'd given up men for Lent – the débâcle with George the weekend before Lent began made this a much more attractive choice than the normal abstentions from alcohol or chocolate, and I was pleased to say it was the first Lenten resolution that I'd ever kept during Lent itself, let alone for the three months after-wards. Admittedly pneumonia and double doses of extra powerful antibiotics do a far better job than bromide in tea in quieting any restless hormones so it hadn't been a particular hardship, but I was still able to take the moral high ground here. Except Robert was hardly likely to believe my single state hadn't been forced on me, nor that I was merely taking my time about deciding which one of the hordes of eager men hankering after me I was going to pick, was he?

I took a large swig of wine and made a dismissive gesture, trying to look the epitome of cool without, I feared, an enormous amount of success. 'Oh well, you never know. George and I might get back together again,' I said, hoping mightily that Oscar's long ears hadn't caught that particular statement. 'It's been mentioned a few times.' Not by me, but that wasn't the point. In any case the thought of George was growing steadily more attractive by the moment; we might have had the odd difference of opinion over such subjects as my unreasonable addiction to feminism, aka not agreeing with George, but it had been peaceful going out with him. He was steady, reliable and I hadn't been constantly on tenterhooks about what verbal shaft he might be about to aim at me. I usually knew what he was going to say next. And he'd been faithful too, I thought with a dark glance at my tormentor who looked as if he was preparing to launch another volley.

Luckily for my overstretched nerves, Venetia got up to check the oven and asked if someone would be kind enough to begin collecting plates. I leaped to my feet and started to clear my end of the table with a speed that would have done justice to a waitress in a fast food restaurant. I even offered to put them in the dishwasher once I'd staggered through with my heavy load. As I'd hoped, by the time I'd returned with the next course Robert's attention had been thoroughly claimed by Sally who was absolutely determined not to let it go. She looked up at him with wide eyes, just as good in her own way of playing on her femininity as Maggie was, and asked how he'd got involved in the gallery business. I sat down with my ears flapping, delighted at this opportunity to gain information without actually being seen to ask for it. He cheerfully admitted it was by chance; after he'd dropped out he'd taken any old job that came along if it paid enough to cover the rent, and had taken a temporary post with a small gallery in Chiswick. He'd discovered he had a knack for selling pictures, and more importantly a good eye, had moved on to something bigger until he was now, as he said, mortgaged up to the hilt to provide his share of the business. 'It's hardly the cutting edge of modern art. We leave "statements" to other galleries, and deal mainly in the sort of picture that won't actually frighten your auntie, even if she doesn't particularly like it. But we do, which is the important thing, even if it doesn't exactly earn us a packet.'

I wondered how long he'd be allowed to go on like this before Venetia started chipping in. Mortgaged up to the hilt wasn't her style. I expect she enjoyed 'statements' too; especially the profitable sort that got written up in the papers. It would be an interesting clash of wills. I couldn't see Robert giving up easily, yet she had the water-dripping-on-a-stone sort of persistence.

I came back into the conversation to hear Sally, who though she didn't have the obvious pzazz and forceful personality of her friend, was equally tenacious, telling Robert that what he needed to send the gallery stratospheric was a proper campaign educating the public about the longterm value of works of art. After all, the average person would happily spend £1000 on a holiday that lasted two weeks but grudged £500 on a picture that was going to last for life . . .

I thought she was making several good points, but as I knew any contribution by me would be neither sought nor welcomed by either party, I kept quiet. After five minutes or so he put up his hands in a gesture of laughing surrender and promised to speak to her about it when they were both back in London, but like any well-trained terrier with a bone she continued to keep him too occupied for him to be able to aim any more of his needle-like comments at me. I decided that Sally had a lot of good points. I talked to Jed, or rather he talked to me, but that didn't matter. I'm quite capable of eating and listening and the chicken was delicious. I didn't remember Venetia being interested in cooking and said as much when I was clearing plates again at the end of the main course.

'I'm not,' she said blithely. 'I got it out of the freezer. Was it any good? I barely tasted it, much too fatty for me. Food like that goes straight to the hips, and frankly once you start approaching thirty you can't afford even a few ounces of extra weight. It's much harder to get rid of and you've got to remember that everything starts to *sag* unless you're very careful,' she ended on a note of complete doom.

I backed up against the wirefronted dresser so that my own, no doubt heavily sagging, posterior was decently hidden and tried to smother the guilty memory of the second helping I'd had of the chicken, but then I hadn't had very much the first time round ... I hoped that Venetia hadn't seen either portion, or how much pâté I'd eaten before. I was prepared to bet she hadn't allowed more than a morsel of that to have passed her lips either. No wonder she had such a wonderful figure. 'It was still very good,' I said as I was stacking the plates. 'Did Janey do it?'

'I expect so. She's keen on cooking – usually things loaded with calories and cholesterol.' She sniffed slightly. 'Well, you can see from her figure that she's not exactly addicted to Slimfast, can't you?'

I turned around and looked at her, startled by the amount of naked venom in her voice. 'You really don't like her, do you?' I asked unnecessarily.

Venetia stared at me over the rim of her glass before saying in an offhand way, 'How would *you* like it if your father was cavorting around with someone who's only three years older than you are?'

I blinked and tried hard for a moment to consider the highly unlikely prospect of my staid and somewhat rotund parent cavorting with *anyone*, let alone a woman the age of my sister, but had to give up the task as hopeless. However I could see that having such a young stepmother wouldn't be easy and said so, which mollified Venetia a bit. Unfortunately I then blew it completely by adding, 'But your father was alone for so long after your mother died. It must be nice for him to have company.'

Venetia laughed in a very theatrical way, and had another glug of wine. 'Come on, Nella, how naïve are you?' she asked in a pitying voice. 'Daddy's never lacked for company; he's always had loads of women running after him. And it's not just because he's rich and has a nice house.' Yes, I agreed with her that there were a lot of very attractive things about Tom Morrison other than his bank balance. 'There's no way he'd have married someone like Janey if she hadn't trapped him into it.'

'Trap him?' I repeated. 'How do you trap someone into marriage these days?'

'With the oldest trick in the book, of course,' she said contemptuously. 'She got pregnant. Daddy's the old-fashioned sort, just the type who when his girlfriend gets into trouble would feel honour bound to marry her. Janey isn't stupid, she must have cottoned on to what sort of person he is and knew she wasn't going to get another chance at landing someone like him. So she flings herself at him, of course he succumbs – she's not unattractive if you like them like that – and bingo! She conveniently "forgets" to take her pill.'

'It was probably just an accident,' I said in a soothing voice. I'd already realised Venetia didn't like Janey; only someone who never looked further than their own navel could have failed to notice that, but this was something else. Was it the fallout from what presumably had been a fairly charged encounter about the gate being left open again, or was it the amount Venetia had drunk this evening that was responsible for this outburst?

'Oh come on! Don't you swallow that line too,' she said sharply. 'Women just don't have contraception accidents these days.' She swung around to face me. 'Have you ever had one?'

'Um, no,' I said.

'Me neither,' she said as if that proved it. 'Of course the moment Janey told Daddy she was pregnant and keeping the baby, he said he'd marry her – as she knew he would. And they didn't even do it quietly; they insisted on having a big do and by that time Janey was five months' gone. You should see the wedding photographs – she's absolutely *enormous*! It was really embarrassing. I don't know what people must have thought.'

The masculine viewpoint had probably run along the lines that Tom must be some sort of super-stud to have scored so obviously with a pretty woman twenty years younger than himself, and what had he got that they hadn't? Except this wasn't something I could say to his daughter. I shifted uncomfortably from foot to foot and wished I could think of a nice innocuous change of subject that wouldn't be too obvious when the door swung open and Robert came in, saying we'd been rather a long time and asking if we needed any help.

'Just coming, we've been waiting for the sorbets to soften up,' said Venetia airily, picking them up from the side. 'We got to gossiping about . . . cooking, didn't we, Nella?'

I nodded and she smiled in relief, though Robert looked fairly surprised. Presumably cooking wasn't a normal topic of conversation with Venetia. She walked through to the dining room carrying the sorbets and putting one foot in front of the other with enormous care. I noticed that she stuck to water for the rest of the evening.

We were on the point of leaving, hanging around in the

hall with the dogs milling about our feet, waiting for Sally who'd gone to the loo. Everyone was looking at the ornaments and photographs on the huge oak table along one wall and eyeing up the pictures on the walls.

'Oh, isn't this pretty!' exclaimed Maggie, pointing to a small oil painting of two children playing on a beach under a sky so brilliantly blue that it couldn't have been England. A small boy in the background was closely examining something in the sand; to the front, an exquisitely pretty girl in the white pinafore of a well-brought-up Edwardian child was holding up a delicately whorled shell in triumph. Her broad-brimmed hat had been pushed right back and from underneath it, her hair, a distinctive light red, streamed down her back in windblown disarray. 'The girl – it could almost be Venetia!'

'It's her grandmother, I think. I remember her telling me about this,' I said and called her over.

'Actually, it's Great Granny and her brother on the beach near Le Touquet. Fancy you remembering,' Venetia said, looking pleased.

She had banged on about it at some length, on more than one occasion, so it was hardly surprising actually. 'It's lovely,' I said, taking another look. 'No wonder you're so fond of it. It's a . . . Sydney, isn't it?'

Venetia nodded earnestly. 'You'll have heard of Willard Sydney, of course,' she said to Charlie and Phil who had wandered over to join us. They both tried to look as if they had, but she told them anyway. 'He was one of the leading English Post-Impressionists, a member of the Camden Town Group for a while,' everybody nodded knowledgeably, 'and his pictures are very sought after. But there aren't many, as he had consumption and was too ill most of the time to be able to paint.' She pointed at the picture proudly. 'This is one of the few left in private hands. He was on holiday and supposed to be having a complete rest, and used to see two children playing on the beach when he went there in his invalid chair for a breath of sea air. He never spoke to them or found out their names, but he thought he'd never seen such an enchanting child as Great Granny.' Venetia looked slightly self-conscious, well aware how much of a dead ringer she was for her granny. 'Anyway, he did a whole series of sketches of her and Great Uncle Ozzie in secret; his wife didn't even know he'd got his sketchbook with him. He painted this picture from memory when he got home and exhibited it at the Summer Exhibition, where Great Granny's aunt saw it and recognised the children. Once he was introduced to Great Granny he gave her the picture and promised he'd paint her again when she was presented at court.' Venetia made a face. 'But he died before he could do it.'

'What a tragic story,' said Maggie. 'No wonder you treasure it so much.'

'Are you leaving it here until you have a proper place of your own for it?' I asked, and when Maggie turned to look at me as if I was completely mad, I explained: 'Venetia's grandmother gave it to her ages ago because she's so like the little girl.'

'No, she didn't,' Venetia said shortly, her face setting like stone. 'She always *said* it was mine, but when she died two years ago it turned out that she'd left everything

101

outright to Daddy, though I'm sure she still intended he should pass it on to me. But Daddy said it wouldn't be fair to Janey, it's too valuable.'

Oops. Nil points to Tom for tactfulness there. How to make your daughter loathe your new wife in one easy step. I was prepared to bet that Venetia also thought it had been Janey's idea to hang onto the picture and if it had been left up to her doting father, he would have handed it over calmly as anything.

'Mm, too pretty-pretty for my taste, but I can see it suits Venetia perfectly,' Charlie muttered in my ear and said out loud, 'Shouldn't a Willard Sydney be in a gallery somewhere, guarded by a seriously sophisticated security system? Isn't it an enormous risk having it hanging in a private house?'

'Daddy says it's one of the advantages of living in France,' Venetia said lightly. 'French burglars don't rate English Post-Impressionists very highly – same sort of snobbishness about our art as they have about our food. Besides, our alarm system is pretty good and it even works most of the time, though it goes a bit funny if there are too many powercuts and then someone from Bordeaux has to come out and fix it. And the dogs bark like mad whenever someone they don't know comes to the house. They had the alarm engineer trapped in his van for about half an hour last time he came, so all in all they're probably a much more effective security system than the alarm.'

'Much better, since the alarm system doesn't bite,' Robert said.

'Neither do those two.' Oscar looked at the two dogs,

peacefully curled up in their baskets in a corner of the hall. 'All Lily knows how to do is smile, and Solomon couldn't bite, he's got no teeth.'

The old Labrador gave proof of this as on hearing his name he looked up and yawned.

'You never know,' said Robert. 'He could always give a nasty suck.'

CHAPTER 7

The next afternoon, I was alone in the cottage, poodling around and clearing up after lunch. 'As you won't be doing anything you won't mind doing the little bits and pieces, will you, Nella?' Maggie had said sweetly. As a matter of fact, I did mind very much, but I was too chicken to say so. My book had just got to the exciting bit and was screaming out for me to finish it in one galloping session, which ruled out any domestic duties.

Maggie was in a vindictive enough mood already without my adding fuel to the embers. She had announced at lunch that she'd organised a culture vulture tour around no fewer than three of the local châteaux, each of which was in its own way a little architectural gem with many fascinating pictures and pieces of furniture. Two of the châteaux even did guided tours lasting forty minutes each – some of it in English too! The male contingent of the party looked underwhelmed at the treat in store, but wise men that they were, they knew better than to argue – especially after the earbashing they'd had about sitting up last night after we got back from supper with Venetia and polishing off the best part of a bottle of armagnac with

Jed. It wouldn't have mattered so much if on their way to their respective beds they hadn't managed to trip over, loudly, just about every piece of furniture in the cottage. As if any of them had needed *more* to drink, Maggie had declared in a ringing voice, no doubt relishing the collective masculine wince at her decibel level. It was no excuse, she said, to say they were on holiday and entitled to let their hair down a little, though they made a valiant attempt to pursue this line of excuse until they realised that arguing was doing nothing for their headaches.

Oscar accepted his punishment with good grace. He enjoys a bit of rubbernecking and since he doesn't like armagnac very much it wasn't going to hurt his head anything like as much as it would Charlie and Phil's to tilt it backwards to admire a finely painted ceiling. These two remained looking thoroughly depressed until Oscar produced the guidebook he'd bought in the local town yesterday. Since it was written for the French it naturally listed vital information about feeding the stomach as well as the eyes and soul; all three châteaux, it turned out, had vineyards, one of them very good. They sold direct to the public and all offered *dégustations* of their produce in specially designed tasting rooms. Phil and Charlie cheered up immediately.

I had declined the not very warm invitation to join everyone on this cultural trip, claiming I was obeying doctor's orders and was going to rest. Quite why Maggie thought resting included the washing up was beyond me. I like sightseeing, within reason, but I felt three châteaux in one afternoon might result in a severe case of mental indigestion, not to mention the distinct possibility of me saying something stupid about the architecture which would result in my being put firmly in my place by the head prefect.

I washed everything up and put it all away, too – something I don't bother with at home and hadn't been instructed to do either so I gave my halo a quick burnish at the same time – changed into my swimsuit and wandered over to the pool with a cushion, a long drink and my book and prepared for an extended session of peace. I was half aware of a car going past the cottage as I flopped down on my stomach – the road was so small that only about three locals used it as a short cut, or when they had reason to avoid the police checks for papers and insurance that were frequently held on the main road, so Tom had told me.

I'd just begun the first paragraph when there was a squeal of brakes, a loud crunch and that sound of breaking glass so familiar to everyone who lives in London – the one where you usually discover that your car radio has been nicked. A deathly silence followed. Just as I was scrambling to my feet to see what had happened, the air was split by a terrible squealing sound. I flew to the gates and looked around. A car was half slewed across the road a few yards away, the bonnet inches from demolishing the last vine in a row. The car appeared to be empty though the engine was still running, but I didn't have any time to wonder where the driver had gone for all I could do was follow the unearthly howls that were coming from further down the road. My heart clenched with fear as I saw Lily lying on the narrow verge, moaning piteously.

Hardly daring to breathe, I approached her. It was

obvious that she had been hit by the car for there was a dark mark where it must have clipped her on her shoulder. She looked up and thumped her tail weakly though she continued to whimper and howl as I knelt down alongside her and gingerly ran my hands over her body, trying to find out how badly she'd been hurt. How on earth did you tell if there were internal injuries? Well, there were no obvious broken bones, and surely all the noise she was making was a good sign. If she was seriously injured, wouldn't she be conserving her energy? But in films didn't the mortally wounded usually have blood coming out of their mouths? I peered cautiously, remembering too late as she opened her jaws hugely, showing a fine display of large white teeth and an interestingly spotted roof to her mouth, that perhaps it wasn't the most sensible thing in the world to be probing around an injured dog's mouth. A big tongue came out and licked my face wetly. Well, at least she'd stopped the ear-piercing shrieks, I thought as I tried to wipe the worst off, and wondered how long it would be before my hearing returned to normal. My heart seemed to still as she flopped back inert and I wondered if this was it. Then she opened her eyes, looking at me with a mercifully alert expression and lifted her head. She struggled upright, wincing as she put her weight on her front leg and sat down promptly, holding the paw in the air.

I patted her head, telling her what a good, brave dog she was, and to stay there while I checked to see what had happened to the driver of the car. It was a bit late maybe, but any vague fears that I might find a corpse had already been allayed by the muffled sounds of swearing coming from the other side of the car. Great-Aunt Gwyneth, who had seventeen cats, would have approved mightily of my decision to administer first aid to an animal before a person. Since she was married to the uncle who was such a favourite with the bookies, her belief that animals were vastly superior to humans, especially men, was perhaps understandable. I approached the car with some trepidation, fearing that the driver might not share her opinion.

I couldn't tell whether the look Robert gave me as he was levering himself up from the ground was general loathing for my presence or disapproval of my sense of priorities. 'Oh, it's you,' he said as he saw me and shrugged off my offer to help him up. It was a bit late, I suppose. 'What's happened to Lily?' he demanded, his face a curious bleached shade of brown. 'She's gone all quiet. Is she dead?'

'Very much alive, if you ask me,' I said as Lily looked around with an aggrieved air at no longer being the centre of attention and got up, hobbling over to the car to give the wheel a good sniffing. 'She's hurt her leg where the car hit it, but it doesn't seem broken. Otherwise she looks as if she's escaped pretty lightly.'

'Are you sure?' he asked, then as Lily limped around to his side and presented her living breathing self for inspection he seemed to lose about ten years in fewer seconds. 'Thank God!' he breathed. 'I was sure that I'd done something really bad to her, broken her leg at the very least. That noise . . .'

'It was probably just shock. If you ask me, our Lily is just a teeny bit of a drama queen.'

He nodded slightly, looking a little better. He was still pale but at least he didn't look as if someone had just rubbed his face in a bucket of ashes. 'All the same, Janey ought to get her to the vet straight away for a proper check-up. You never know what unseen injuries she might have.' Not many, judging by the way Lily was snuffling at something in the grass but I saw his point. 'I'd take her myself except,' he gestured to the bonnet, 'this car won't be going anywhere except the workshop.'

In swerving to try to avoid Lily he'd had the bad luck to hit just about the only serious obstacle for about a mile along this section of road, the remains of an old stone gatepost that stood in the middle of an almost entirely demolished wall. The headlight was hanging out of its socket in a sorry manner and the front wing had been bent right in over the wheel. 'My mobile's in the door pocket on your side of the car. Can you get it out and ring Janey to tell her what's happened?'

Was he so worried about Janey's reaction to the news that he'd nearly killed her dog that he didn't feel up to facing the flak? His mouth twisted. 'I fell over one of those sodding stones as I got out of the car,' he said, pointing at the few blocks that were all that was left of the ancient wall. 'I was in such a hurry to see what I'd done to Lily that I didn't notice it and went flying.'

'Oh Lord! Have you hurt yourself? Do you need a doctor?'

'I banged my knee, that's all.' He held up a hand as if to ward off an onslaught of female fussing. 'It's fine.'

Oh yeah? 'In that case, why aren't you prancing around the car to fetch the mobile yourself?'

'Because,' he said through gritted teeth, 'if you must know, right now it hurts like hell. But it'll be OK soon – providing I don't have to jerk it around too much in the next few minutes.'

I took the hint and fished his mobile out but couldn't help glancing over at him, wondering if we had an extreme case of stiff upper lip here. He was looking distinctly pale, but I know better than to argue with men when they're being brave. Besides, he'd already made it quite clear he didn't want to risk submitting himself to my hamfisted nursing skills. In the circumstances it wasn't such an unreasonable attitude. Last time he'd asked me for an alibi he'd ended up in jail for the night; if I so much as glanced at his knee, he might end up in the amputations section of the local hospital.

'Janey's got to hand the twins over to Delphine and she'll be on her way – in about ten minutes, she thinks,' I reported a couple of minutes later, after repeatedly assuring her that her dog wasn't lying in pieces on the road and listening to a few choice words about Venetia leaving the gate open *again* which I thought more tactful not to pass on. 'And she's very worried about your knee too.'

'That's decent of her considering that I've just nearly killed her dog,' he said gloomily.

'I thought so too,' I agreed, and after a slightly startled glance at me, he laughed.

'She said she'd take a look at you when she got down here and see if you needed to go to the doctor. You might have broken something, and if you've cut your knee you'll have to have a tetanus injection.'

'There's no need for any of that,' he said in a throwaway

manner. 'Nothing's broken and I certainly don't need a tetanus booster. All I need is to rest my knee.'

To me it definitely sounded as if the gentleman was protesting a little too much. 'Did you hit your head when you pranged the car?' I asked anxiously, as another possible reason for that green tinge to his face occurred to me. 'You did! I can see a mark on your forehead. You might have concussion, Robert! You'd better go to hospital and have an X-ray.'

'Don't be so stupid. I don't need one,' he said sourly.

'You can't be too careful with head injuries,' I said, trying to remember what I'd been taught when I'd done that St John's Ambulance course. The man taking the course had an enormous and mobile Adam's apple and I'd tried not to make it too obvious that I was staring at it going up and down when he spoke. That was probably why I'd hardly absorbed anything about first aid. 'Ah!' I said in triumph. 'Double vision! If you've got it you definitely need to go to hospital. How many of me can you see?'

'One,' he said, sounding heartily relieved. 'Look, Nella – I don't need an X-ray, I don't need a doctor, I definitely do *not* need a tetanus injection. Got that?'

'Don't worry, injections don't hurt much these days. I'm sure the doctor will use a nice thin needle, you'll hardly feel it going in at all . . .'

'Will you just shut up, Nella?' he demanded in a voice that suggested he did not want to hear another word about needles.

'OK,' I said amiably. Always indulge the wounded. 'But you'll be much more comfortable if you sit down.

Let's wait in the cottage until Janey arrives.'

'It's all right, I'm fine here.'

I glared at him, wondering if he was simply being bloody-minded or really thought leaning on his car out here in the middle of the road was preferable to being confined in a room with me. 'You may be all right, but I'm not!' I snapped. 'You may be able to stay out in the sun for hours without turning a hair but I can't. In fact, I'm already starting to burn. And no, I'm not going to leave you out here alone, playing the macho male idiot who can't bring himself to admit that he's hurt himself falling over a stone. So, if you don't want me to drag you inside you'd better make up your mind to come with me. Now.'

'Your bedside manner doesn't last for long, does it?' he asked shakily. I think my remark about macho posturing had struck a sore point, if that wasn't too much of a pun. He eyed me speculatively. 'And I wonder if you could drag me . . .' I hoped fervently he wasn't going to put it to the test.

Just as I was starting to get worried he gave in and said, 'OK, let's go inside. Frankly, I'm getting too hot out here too.' His sharp intake of breath as he took his first step showed that he'd hurt his knee a lot more than he wanted to admit, and I had to get him to lean, heavily, on my shoulder so that we could make it the few yards to inside the cottage. By the time he was sitting on the sofa he was back to being ashy pale again with beads of perspiration on his forehead.

'The doctor definitely needs to see that knee,' I said, stating the obvious. It was swollen and already bruised the most alarmingly Technicolor shades of red and purple; he must have caught it a terrific bang, though surprisingly he hadn't cut it, just grazed it a little. I put a tentative hand out to feel how hot it was. 'Just checking to see if I need to put something on it in the meantime,' I said quickly, in case he thought I was doing a bit of surreptitious touching up. 'I'll see what I can find to act as a cold compress.'

I remembered reading somewhere that bags of frozen peas are ideal for minor injuries, except the Napoleon of our kitchen (Oscar, who takes cookery very seriously indeed) would have downed his *batterie de cuisine* immediately had anyone dared import frozen vegetables, and all the little freezer on top of the fridge contained was ice cubes, one of those gel-filled wine sleeves and a bottle of Charlie's vodka. I didn't think that Robert would appreciate a tea towel of ice cubes being dumped on his sore knee but, after a moment's hesitation, for I wasn't sure who it belonged to, I took the wine sleeve and slit it down one side.

'Unusual,' Robert said as he took it from me and wrapped it around his knee, 'but effective. Thanks.'

He even smiled at me. It was the first time he'd looked at me with even a vaguely friendly expression since we'd met again. Well, there's nothing like needing to be looked after to make a man feel slightly kinder about his nurse. And this nurse was wearing a very Barbara Windsor-ish sort of costume for the job too, I realised belatedly. I shot into my room and, lacking a crackling white dress and a starched bosom, pulled on my largest T-shirt, hoping that I'd look as if I'd found it a little chilly.

Janey arrived in a flurry a minute or two later, any worries she might have had that I had been drawing a tactful gloss over the extent of Lily's injuries immediately soothed by the way her dog hopped around her, smiling maniacally in pleasure and still chewing the biscuit she'd wheedled out of me. 'Of course Rob's got to see the doctor. Do tell him to stop making such a fuss about it – or perhaps you'd better not,' she amended. 'I know Dr Dupont will be on her rounds in the village now so I expect she could pop in and see him quite soon.' She hesitated, biting her lip. 'Would you mind if she came to see him here? I'd take him back to the château except that the vet closes in half an hour and everyone's out except for Delphine. If it wouldn't be too trying for you . . .'

'No problem,' I assured her. 'He's being positively nice towards me at the moment – probably afraid I might suggest tapping his knee to test his reflexes if he steps out of line.'

'Let's hope it lasts,' she said as she went to ring the doctor. I don't know if she was naturally more authoritative than me or if Robert was just more prepared to accept her word about something, but he took her announcement that he could complain as much as he liked but he was still seeing the doctor, and what's more he was being left to my tender mercies until the doctor arrived, like a lamb – if anyone who scowls so ferociously can be described as lamblike. That's what he did when I asked him if he wanted a drink and he said a very large whisky and got given a cup of tea.

'Honestly, Nella, talk about clichés,' he grumbled. 'Any minor crisis and you get the great British panacea poured down your throat.' He took a sip and made a face. 'Sugared, too.'

'It's good for shock,' I said primly.

'I'm not in shock,' he snarled.

'And bad temper,' I added.

He glared at me, then reluctantly laughed. 'I suppose it wouldn't be tactful to breathe alcohol fumes over Janey when she comes back with that wretched hound.'

'And you shouldn't drink after you've hit your head either,' I said, dredging up another remnant of that long-ago first aid course.

'I didn't hit my head, it's a dirt mark,' he said in a remarkably even tone, 'and even if I had, I was going so slowly that it would only have been a light tap. Why else do you think that stupid dog is still alive after I hit her full on?' His face set in strained lines. 'She came out of the vines like a rocket – she was after a pheasant – and I didn't see her until it was too late. It was entirely my fault. I wasn't concentrating. I was looking at the cottage and wondering what it was like inside.'

'Well, now you know,' I said cheerily, trying to divert an imminent case of self-flagellation. 'You'll have to wait a while before you can do the grand tour upstairs, as the steps are pretty steep, but it's just as nice as it is down here. And, given the number of times Lily's been getting out recently,' no need to point out whose fault that was, he'd probably get an earful when Janey next met Venetia, 'the only surprising thing is that she hasn't had a prang with a car before now.'

Fortunately the doctor chose that moment to rap on the door, and he quickly changed his *mea culpa* expression for the tense look of someone who is afraid that what's coming is about to hurt. It relaxed as he realised Dr Dupont was a shapely brunette in her early thirties who must have been the pin-up of her year at medical school. As she came closer we both noticed that instead of smelling of disinfectant like your average doctor she moved around in a waft of expensive and distinctly un-medical scent. Much to my relief she spoke fluent, if strongly accented, English. Even if Robert's French was good enough to tell her what the matter was, mine was certainly not up to following medical speak and I had a feeling I'd be for it from Janey unless I was able to give her a full report.

Dr Dupont sat down beside Robert, inviting him to tell her how he'd injured himself, feeling his knee gently with slim, perfectly kept hands. When he winced slightly she warned him she might have to hurt him a little more, though she'd try her best not to, and advised him to concentrate on something else to take his mind off any pain. So he did – focusing on the highly impressive cleavage that was revealed as her loose linen jacket fell open while she bent over him. It was probably her patent method for distracting her male patients, though I trusted she kept the buttons done up if they suffered from high blood pressure.

A couple of minutes later she finished her examination and announced that in her opinion there was no need for him to have an X-ray; the knee was badly bruised but nothing seemed to be broken. If it didn't start to improve in two days he was to come and see her again. And how long ago had he had his last tetanus injection?

'Er,' Robert hesitated, obviously wondering if he could risk a blatant lie. 'About three years ago, I think.'

She shrugged charmingly. 'No need for another, then.' From the look of intense relief on his face I suspected Robert had a needle allergy, the sort that ends up with an increasingly short-tempered doctor pursuing you down the corridor as you back away from the fearsome instrument he brandishes in his hand. I speak from experience.

The doctor issued a prescription for heavy duty painkillers and two different unguents to deal with the swelling and the bruising, instructed him to rest his knee as much as possible, to use a stick if he had to walk about and not to even think of driving back to England for the time being. He said she must have passed his car on her way in and she admitted that in the circumstances this last instruction was probably unnecessary. Oh, and could we ask Monsieur Morrison if she could have another case of red wine. If he would drop it off at her surgery when he was passing it would be very kind.

She departed in a blazing whirl of energy to go and dazzle some other patient. Robert gazed after her. 'I've got a lady GP in London but she doesn't look like that. Doesn't smell so good either.'

'Nor does mine,' I agreed, 'which is rather a relief since he's sixty if he's a day with a large moustache. His patients might start to wonder if he were to begin drifting around in a cloud of Diorissimo.'

I went off to make Robert another cup of tea, refusing to allow him any alcohol, though I think this second request was made more for form's sake than because he was really desperate for a strong drink. 'Thanks, Nella,' he said as I came back. 'I really appreciate all this.'

'What else did you expect me to do?' I demanded, only half joking. 'Leave you draped over your car unable to move in the hope that some other vehicle might just happen to come down the road and rescue you, while I fed Lily biscuits and finished my book? Anyway, I thought that if I made you feel really grateful you might feel slightly less like decking me each time you see me.'

His eyebrows shot upwards. 'I can't think what you mean,' he said in a haughty voice. 'I never hit women.'

'Only threaten to,' I muttered. 'Several times.'

He shrugged. 'Can you blame me? After what you'd done?'

I looked away and fidgeted about uncertainly. 'At the time no, but what makes me nervous is that you *still* look as if you want to strangle me.'

'Do I?' he asked, looking startled. 'I don't, not any longer, so perhaps the expression's just habit. In all honesty I can't say you're top of my list of favourite people, but really, I suppose I ought to thank you.' His tone didn't make it sound as if he was overflowing with gratitude though. 'If it wasn't for you I'd be at the Bar, and I'd have made a lousy barrister. My heart wasn't in it.'

'Hence the reason why you never did any work?'

'Precisely,' he said, unsmiling, 'but I'd been headed for the law for so long it seemed stupid to jack it all in at the last moment. And only someone off their head, or with a one-way ticket to Australia, would have voluntarily faced my mother's weeping and wailing once she realised the law courts were going to have to do without a Winwood for the foreseeable future.'

I thought of Mrs Winwood, all fluttering draperies and a delicate constitution that always took a turn for the worse whenever she was crossed. Funny how she got better the moment you did what she wanted. The first person who ever spoke of the tyranny of the weak must have been thinking of Robert's mother.

'So all in all an enforced career change was undoubtedly a good thing, though I'd have appreciated it happening another way.'

In nine years I really should have got over cringing every time I thought of what I'd done to him but at the acid tone in his voice I could feel the flush rising in my cheeks. 'You don't think I'd have undone it if I could?' I demanded in a low voice. 'You knew I was sorry—'

'Yes, well, that's known as repenting after the event,' he said coldly.

'I could hardly do it *before*, could I?' I snapped, realising a little too late that this was hardly a concilia-tory way to behave. But as they say, in for a penny in for a pound. Besides, I was getting a bit fed up with having to do all the self-abasement. 'As things turned out, you didn't do too badly, did you? You said yourself it was all for the best. So isn't it about time you started doing a bit of forgiving and forgetting?' Judging from his expression he had absolutely no intention of doing either. I took a deep breath and said in a slightly less heated voice, 'Yes, I agree that I was deeply at fault, behaved like a cow, call it what you will, but damn it, Robert, you bear some responsibility for what happened too!'

'How come?' he asked in a frosty voice.

'You kicked off the whole chain of events by sleeping with my best friend.'

'She wasn't your best friend,' he corrected me. 'She wasn't a friend of yours at all, in fact, unless your friends normally try to pull your boyfriends.'

'So that makes sleeping with her while you were going out with me all right?'

'No,' he said calmly. 'It doesn't. And I didn't.'

I could feel my mouth falling open like a goldfish's as he added, 'But I did afterwards. What was the point of refusing what was on offer? You'd had your revenge, so I thought I might as well have my pleasure.'

'It wasn't revenge,' I said weakly, still trying to get my head around what he'd just told me. 'I had no idea that you were supposed to be going to London the next day.'

'Didn't you?' he asked sharply.

'No! You never told me.' He stared at me as if trying to read my mind and see if I was really telling the truth. After a fraction of a second I saw him nod slightly. I took a deep breath. 'I thought you were going straight round to see Natasha—'

'So you decided to put a spoke in my wheel,' he said with an unamused smile.

'Something like that,' I admitted. 'Not very clever or nice but I was so upset and furious I couldn't think straight.'

'Going to claim mitigating circumstances due to acting while of unsound mind?' he asked with raised brows.

'So all that law study didn't go to waste after all. I suppose I could, but I'd rather go for provocation.'

He eyed me with an expression that suggested bad

knee or no bad knee he wasn't going to stay immobilised for long if I went on in this way. 'Funny,' he said. 'Provocation will be my defence too – when your lifeless body is found at my feet.'

So much for trying to clear the air, I thought. Maybe in another nine years Robert might be ready to consider forgiving and forgetting. It didn't seem very likely though. Then to my surprise he said, 'Since it appears I'm going to have to stay here for God knows how long until this bloody knee gets back into driving condition, it's going to be pretty unfair on Janey and Venetia if I'm constantly at loggerheads with you. They appear to like you.' It sounded as if he thought this was highly eccentric of them. 'And so perhaps we ought to have a . . .' He seemed to be having a problem finding the exact words he was looking for. I doubted somehow they were 'loving friendship'.

'Armed neutrality?' I suggested helpfully after a few seconds.

'I was going to suggest something a little more cordial, like peace.'

OK, so it was naïve of me to feel a pang of disappointment that any making up Robert was doing was for Janey and Venetia's sake and not mine. But beggars can't be choosers so I smiled and said, 'Fine. That's even better. Peace it is.'

CHAPTER 8

Janey arrived back only a few minutes after Robert and I agreed our momentous peace accord and looked distinctly relieved to see that her rash gesture in leaving her guest alone with me hadn't resulted in having to clear body parts up off the floor. She reported that Lily was fine; in fact Lily had recovered so well that she'd taken one look at the vet, whom she'd encountered before and obviously remembered, turned a double somersault, slipped her collar and shot out of the door. She had a remarkable turn of speed for someone operating one leg short and it had taken the vet, Janey and both assistants several minutes before they could catch her.

Unfortunately the news on Robert's car wasn't quite so good. Monsieur Carreau from the garage arrived at about the same time as Janey came back. He walked solemnly and slowly around the car with an 'it's only good for scrap' expression, sighing in such a gloomy manner that it could be heard in the cottage. Robert's face grew steadily more depressed as each hearty gust seemed to put another thousand francs on the bill. Just as I thought he was going to expire with tension Monsieur Carreau appeared at the door, refusing to come in because he was wearing his overalls, and announced that while it would only take hours to beat out the damaged wing and realign the wheel, repairing the headlight was quite another matter.

Lots of head-shaking and tutting followed. The whole thing had to be replaced, and as it was a foreign make of car, and not a new one either – more tutting – he doubted he could get a new headlight locally, maybe not even in the *département*. He sucked in air through the gap in his teeth saying that he might even have to send to Paris for the new part, and we all knew what they were like up there. He cast his eyes up to heaven expressively; it might take weeks, years even before the spare part arrived. Now if only Monsieur was driving a sensible French car he'd be able to get a new headlight without any problem, this afternoon even; in fact, he had a very nice Renault in the garage if Monsieur was interested in doing a part exchange . . . Monsieur made it quite clear that he wasn't and forced the garage owner to admit it was perfectly possible to get a new headlight by the weekend, even if it did have to come from Paris. As the garage was closed on Mondays (judging by the size of the stomach under his overalls this was so its owner could sleep off a substantial Sunday lunch), Monsieur could pick his car up on Tuesday.

Robert didn't look as thrilled as Monsieur Carreau evidently expected him to be by this news and started muttering about needing to be in London by the week-end which produced a whole volley of Gallic shrugs and 'Bof!'s and 'Bah!'s.

'Remember what the doctor said about resting your knee,' I put in. 'There's no way you'll be fit enough to do that long drive back to England until well after the weekend, so you might as well stop grumbling and accept it.'

The look Robert gave me was a reminder that our newfound *entente* wasn't all that *cordiale*, though his voice was mild enough when he spoke. 'I haven't started grumbling – yet,' and turned to extract a commitment that the car really would be ready on Tuesday, and not on Wednesday, or even Friday. Monsieur Carreau didn't appear to be willing to be pinned down; he expostulated, shrugged, protested at speed and volume in an almost impenetrable accent, waved his hands in the air, then when Robert didn't back down, shrugged again and with a broad smile swore the car would be back in perfect working order by Tuesday lunchtime at the very latest. To show he had no hard feelings about being pushed into a corner he even offered Robert a lift back to the château as his car was larger than Madame's Twingo and easier for someone with long legs and a bad knee to get into. As they left I heard Monsieur Carreau expansively suggesting that maybe a diversion for a '*petit Ricard*' at the bar in the village would be a good idea.

I was overflowing with that virtuous feeling you get when you've been up and about and engaged in healthful pursuits while everyone else is still festering in bed. I'd woken up early yet again, and instead of lying around as usual, I'd been spurred by thoughts of Venetia and her fantastic figure to get up and do some serious exercise to try to get my own, considerably less fantastic figure, into shape. Swimming, even if it's a leisurely breaststroke in a sunwarmed pool the temperature of tepid milk, is supposed to be one of the best exercises around. And floating counts as winding down and relaxation – that's good for you as well. All before breakfast too.

I must be turning over a new leaf, I thought as I hung my costume out on the line to dry, my mind full of pleasant visions such as going to the gym and actually working out rather than gossiping with my mates Liz and Jackie. A loud toot from the road behind me interrupted this unlikely fantasy and I turned to see Janey leaning out of the window of a black Twingo and waving frantically. 'I'm just off to the market. Do you want to come with me and have a look around?' she called.

'Love to,' I said. 'Hang on a moment while I get my shoes.' I dashed in, told a sleepy Maggie and Phil, who were morosely sipping coffee in the kitchen, where I was going, grabbed my handbag and departed at high speed saying over my shoulder that Janey was waiting so I didn't have the time for a lengthy shopping list, though I did hear something about 'melons' floating after me.

Janey was staring out of the car window, frowning at nothing in particular. She jumped as I opened the door, turning with a startled expression as if she expected to see the local axe murderer rather than someone she'd just invited to come along for the ride. 'Is everything all right?' I asked cautiously as I got in. 'You look as if you've woken up with all the worries of the world on your shoulders.'

'I haven't. Tom takes care of all of those,' she said

tersely as she started the car.

It wasn't the sort of tone that invited you to go on and ask a few invitingly nosy questions. I wondered what they'd had a flaming row about and decided to change the subject. Tact, that's my middle name. 'So how's your patient?'

'Which one?' she asked with a grimace. 'The spotted one is doing a massive amount of lead swinging, holding up her paw, whimpering every time anyone looks at her, and generally implying that the only thing to take her mind off the pain is a constant flow of dog treats. The two-legged one is being *hideously* tough, refusing to accept any help and making us all feel acutely uncomfortable even to be near such stoicism. However, the most affected and least stoical is Venetia who has been completely prostrated by an acute case of guilty conscience over not latching the gate properly. She bursts into tears at every possible opportunity, wailing that she can never forgive herself for so nearly causing Rob's death. This despite him telling her, several times, that he was never anywhere near being killed. However, if she doesn't shut up soon *she* will be.'

I laughed. 'Oh dear, no wonder you're making an early escape to the market!'

'Not kidding,' she said in heartfelt tones. 'Breakfast was altogether too much. I merely asked Venetia if she'd had a good run – I wasn't really that interested in the answer, you appreciate – and she began to gulp in the most ominous way saying that, thanks to her, Rob wouldn't be able to have a run for ages.'

'But he doesn't go for runs,' I said.

'Why should a little matter like that make any difference when you're wallowing in gallons of guilt? And Rob's nearly as bad. When he isn't being noble and brave he constantly apologises for nearly squashing Lily and landing himself on me for another week. It's driving me bonkers!'

She slowed down, pulling over to the verge to allow a high-wheeled vine tractor that looked like some sort of lunar buggy to pass by on the other side and said, 'Luckily, it doesn't seem to have occurred to him yet that he might find himself stuck here for considerably longer than a week.'

'Why?' I asked curiously.

She swung out again. 'I'm no doctor, but you saw how he could hardly walk yesterday. Is he really going to be fit in under a week for a ten-hour drive to Dover?'

'Oh gosh, I see what you mean.' I contemplated the dire prospect of having to play hostess to the caged lion Robert would become if his departure for England was delayed yet again. I was unworthily relieved that it was Janey and not me who would have to live with it. 'Couldn't he fly, or go by train – and come back for his car later?'

'I suppose so, except he's got some canvases he picked up from an artist in Toulouse last week. What would he do with them?'

'Couldn't you pack him off to Cannes with Venetia until he's fit to travel? At least you wouldn't have to suffer his bad moods that way. I know!' I exclaimed. 'Get Venetia to drive him back on Tuesday. If her conscience is really that troubled, I'm sure you can get her to agree . . .'

There was a long silence, then Janey turned to me with a wide smile. 'What a brilliant idea!' She looked as if all her Sundays had come at once. 'Of course it wouldn't be worth Venetia coming back to us before she went off to stay with her friends in Cannes . . .' she went on thoughtfully, her smile widening further. 'You're a genius, Nella.'

'Always glad to be of service,' I said modestly as we reached the outskirts of the little market town that dated back to the Middle Ages and was still encircled by high defensive ramparts. There was a large square tower in the middle of one wall where, Janey announced with gory relish, the seigneur of the town used to amuse himself by throwing malcontents off the top in 1376 or some time like that.

We went underneath a massive archway to a narrow road of tall houses, several of them with half-timbered walls out of kilter, shutters thrown open to allow a tantalising glimpse of shadowy interiors. I walked along, my head swivelling this way and that, feeling as if I'd walked into a time warp. It seemed as if the most modern additions to the buildings in the last five hundred years had been glass in the windows and the occasional lick of paint. Then I glanced in through an open doorway and saw a large woman putting something into a microwave. So progress had reached this far, after all.

Halfway up the street we had to slow down and start threading our way past the clothes, shoe and fabric stalls on both sides of the road, making frequent detours around groups of people greeting each other, kissing, slapping backs and gossiping. Obviously shopping was a secondary motive for coming to the market, the principal one was social. We stopped at a stall which seemed to have about a thousand different hats laid out in neat piles, from panamas to flat caps to baby's bonnets with animal ears, so Janey could replace the sunhats which the twins had buried somewhere in the garden. It seemed only reasonable to while away my time by trying on a few hats myself while she was making her selection. I walked away with a very fetching little number in straw with the most deliciously upturned brim on one side, telling myself that it wasn't really an extravagance. As Venetia had told me so pointedly, I needed to protect my skin from the sun.

The arcaded main square was devoted mainly to food stalls and was even more crowded than the side streets. We must have spent at least an hour wandering around in the cool shade under the medieval arcades, drooling over incredibly delicious-looking fruit and vegetables which, it seemed, had been arranged to please the eye as much as tantalise the taste buds. Gleaming tomatoes were piled in enormous curved straw baskets, a green pepper placed just here or there for colour contrast, aubergines and courgettes next to each other, so vivid they could have come off an Impressionist's palette, set off by pink, red and white radishes of all shapes and sizes, and doubtless all grades of pepperyness too. Then there were the local farmers who had laid out their surplus produce on trestle tables, lettuces so fresh they still smelt of earth, tomatoes, onions, garlic and shallots arranged in neat piles on little plates, great bunches of parsley, tarragon and basil heaped on wicker trays, and on the ground in front, buckets of brilliantly coloured flowers.

Janey was being just as fussy as all the Frenchwomen around us about the quality of her foodstuffs; she picked up this, sniffed that, prodded these, squeezed those and accepted small tastes before she made her decisions about what was going in her straw shopping basket. She chose for me as I hovered over a stall selling nothing but melons piled high in gorgeous disarray, my capacity to make a decision undermined by their intoxicatingly sweet smell. Then I got waylaid by the strawberries, which had a scent nearly as strong as the melons . . . I had to leave her holding my purchases while I found the man who sold baskets as I'd run out of carrying capacity. On the way back I couldn't resist buying a huge bunch of sunflowers, heads almost the size of dinner plates.

'I think I'm going to have to admit defeat,' I said as I added some very smelly Brie and a cheese I'd been assured was made locally to the heap in my basket. 'I can't carry any more.'

Janey grinned and glanced down at her own bulging bag. 'No matter how restrained you promise you're going to be, greed gets you every time! Shall we grab a coffee and rest our arms before we go back to the car?'

We found places at a tiny round table outside a crowded café and settled down for a bit of people-watching while we waited for one or other of the waiters to notice that we were there. I was watching a small child solemnly tasting small pieces of *saucisson* from the charcuterie stall and informing her mother which one she favoured, when Janey turned around with a sudden exclamation. 'Hell! There's one person I don't want to see – Solange Bradley-Cook, wife of a friend of Tom's

131

who has a château a few kilometres from us,' she muttered out of the side of her mouth and making a great show of looking for something in her basket so her face was hidden. 'Blast it! Too late, she's seen me.'

I turned and looked curiously at the blonde woman who was pushing her way round the tables towards us, a wide smile on her scarlet lips. A few years older than Janey, she was very good-looking in that highly polished, well-cared-for manner that only the French seem to be able to get away with. Exactly the sort of woman who makes me acutely conscious of my own shortcomings, but then anyone who matches their accessories and puts on lipstick just to go shopping tends to do that, I find. More than one person was following her progress with his eyes; from the little smile on her lips I got the idea she was well aware of it and enjoyed it thoroughly.

'Janee, 'ow lovely to see you!' she cried, planting air kisses on either side of Janey's rigid face, giving me a brief and impersonal smile as if she'd already summed me up and decided I wasn't worth bothering with. 'I 'ave been on the telephone to that 'usband of yours. What a wicked man he is! The things he says!' She trilled with laughter. I got the impression Janey didn't find this anything like as amusing as Solange did.

'Did you have any reason to ring Tom other than to hear him saying sweet nothings to you?' asked Janey calmly.

Solange's glossy red lips tightened a little. 'Why yes, I ring Tom about this cricket match. 'E says he has not 'is team yet. *Quelle dommage* that your Davide is away, and he cannot decide who is to be in 'is place.'

'I didn't think that sort of thing interested you very much. Surely it's Napier who normally goes over the teams with Tom, not you,' said Janey.

Solange looked at her pityingly. 'But it is I who have to make the arrangements for the day. I must discuss them with Tom.'

Janey raised her eyebrows. 'You aren't going to get very far if you discuss the catering for a lunch for more than thirty people with Tom, Solange. The only thing you can rely on him to do is to make sure there's an adequate supply of corkscrews.'

'That is what he say,' Solange reported with a little smirk, looking just like the cat that's found the largest cushion. 'He said we would talk about it over dinner this evening.'

'Dinner. This evening,' Janey repeated woodenly. 'Has Tom invited you for dinner?' she asked in a tone that didn't bode well for her husband.

'Why yes, as I say,' Solange said blandly. 'It is only the four of us so you mustn't put yourself out.'

'The four.'

'Napier's stepbrother is here with a friend. Tom says it is all right to bring them too.'

'I'm sure he did,' said Janey in an even voice. She looked as if she was having considerable effort forcing a smile to her lips. 'We'll look forward to seeing you all this evening then, Solange.'

Her hands were clenched in such tight fists that her knuckles were white. 'God, I *detest* that woman!' she said somewhat unnecessarily once Solange had left, with more air kissing and lots of waggling of fingers in au revoir.

133

'She's always making up to Tom. He loves it, of course, won't hear a word against her, especially as she's just the sort of woman he really likes – glossy, sophisticated, well polished, insincere. He says that she's just being French and they all indulge in a bit of harmless flirting. With her it's not harmless though,' she stated flatly. 'She leads poor old Napier by the nose. He's a nice old stick even if he is a bit dull, but he certainly doesn't deserve to have his wife sleeping with half the men around here.' She broke off as a snake-hipped waiter with a smile guaranteed to win forgiveness for any slow service from his female clientèle appeared at last and took our order.

He glided away and Janey went on saying with barely suppressed rage, 'And what I detest about her almost as much as the way she's constantly trying to lure my husband into bed is that fake accent of hers! She's perfectly capable of speaking without one if it suits her, but she puts it on because Englishmen, particularly Tom, find it sexy.'

She looked up and curtly thanked the waiter as he placed two tiny cups of coffee in front of us. He looked rather surprised she hadn't swooned with gratitude. 'And then Tom invites her to dinner without even asking me first.'

'I got the impression that inviting people to dinner without asking you was a habit of his,' I said.

She looked at me and smiled. 'It is, and it drives me mad. One of his fond delusions about the differences between the sexes is that the little woman is always ready and willing to rustle up a delicious meal for God knows how many at a minute's notice. And I really don't see why I should have to spend all afternoon slaving away to cook something that Solange will pick at. She claims she never eats very much, but Delphine's sister who occasionally cooks there says that when she comes back from going out to dinner, Madame makes herself a bacon sandwich!'

I must have looked more than usually blank for she said in a cod French accent, 'But eet is so feminine to 'ave a tiny appetite.'

'I always knew I was missing something in the super femininity stakes – it's probably that,' I said.

'Me too. But if Tom wants to make sheep's eyes at Solange while she pushes food around her plate looking as if something under her nose smells bad, he can do the cooking himself,' she said with sudden determination. 'Tonight is going to be barbecue night. Another of Tom's theories about *la différence* is that women are completely incompetent when it comes to burning meat over charcoal.' Her eyes lit up. 'It'll keep him away from Solange, too. She won't risk the heat spoiling her makeup. In fact,' she looked at me speculatively, 'it would be even better if I kept him really busy, with lots and lots and *lots* of cooking. How about all of you coming to dinner?'

'How much is my life worth if I give you a collective refusal?' I asked and she grinned. I added more seriously, 'But surely that's far too many people for you to cater for, even if Tom is on punishment detail.'

She shrugged. 'Our friends often bring their guests so we're used to large numbers, especially in the summer. It's a doddle when you can eat outside.' Her face sparkled with mischief. 'And it'll serve Tom right if he hardly gets a chance to sit down. He's done it to me often enough! You don't really think I'll mind if my husband's too busy with his chef's duties to even look at Solange, let alone have her snuggling up to murmur little secrets in his ear, do you? I'll put you and Maggie next to him during dinner, and perhaps Solange should go next to Oscar – right at the other end of the table, naturally. I'll let you have Napier's stepbrother on your other side – no, perhaps not,' she said reflectively. 'He's very nice, but he bears a distinct resemblance to a sheep. I'm not prejudiced against sheep, I like them, especially the ones with curly horns, but sadly his brains match and you have to admit sheep don't make very entertaining dinner companions. You'd better have his friend. Unless you'd prefer to have Rob, of course.' She glanced at me speculatively. 'I gather that friendship is now the order of the day. You must have an *excellent* bedside manner.'

She drained her coffee, dropped some coins in the saucer in front of us and stood up. 'We'll have to stop off at the butcher on the way to the car. I would never have thought I'd be thankful for bumping into Solange, but if I'd gone home and then heard I had to come all the way back, I'd probably be in prison tonight on a charge of crowning my husband with his own grill pan!'

The butcher's was quite unlike any other butcher's shop I'd ever been into. There was a vast vase of sunflowers in one corner and another packed with roses placed squarely in the window. No one seemed to have noticed or objected to the woman in front of us who had her poodle in her shopping basket, and the butcher's wife was standing behind one counter chopping up a huge pile of meat into neat squares and threading the pieces onto kebab sticks with long lacquered fingernails. She wasn't in the traditional hat and overalls more normally seen on those who work with meat either; instead she sported an elaborate chignon with two jewelled combs sticking out of it, immaculate makeup including shiny blue eyeshadow and a beaded T-shirt. Her sole concession to her work was a small apron tied with a very large bow at the back. 'How on earth does she manage to keep clean?' I whispered.

'You should see her in the winter,' said Janey. 'She wears dinky embroidered angora sweaters in pastel colours – and doesn't even get a mark on the cuffs.'

'What's this cricket match Solange was ringing Tom about?' I asked as we moved to the front of the queue. The butcher was asking the poodle lady what she was planning to do with the pork chops she'd asked for and they'd got on to discussing whether it was really necessary to throw thyme into the hot coals before starting the meat so it seemed as if it might be a few minutes yet before we got served.

Janey sighed in a slightly exasperated fashion, casting her eyes up to heaven in a way indicative of her opinion of men and their passions. 'It's a longstanding tradition, going back all of five years or so, and they play for a stuffed sanglier's head – a wild boar – which they found in an antique shop after a particularly good lunch. *Don't* ask me how it came to be used as the trophy in a cricket match, please!' she added. 'From the amount of fuss Napier and Tom make about it you'd think they were playing for the ruddy Ashes! They get up scratch teams – very scratch sometimes, *I* had to play one year – and they, or to be accurate Solange and I, take it in turns to host a slap-up lunch with a match afterwards. Tom's lot have won for the last two years and rumour has it that Napier is so keen to get the sanglier back that he's even been seen having batting practice with his star player – a winemaker from Bordeaux – which he denies completely. But then he would, as it's completely against the spirit of the match. Rank amateurism rules OK in this case, though for some reason it's considered perfectly sporting for the host to try and pour as much of his wine as he can down the visiting team so they're incapable of running in a straight line.' She grinned. 'Which goes to show you that these two fine upstanding English gents don't always play quite as fair as they pretend to!'

Several chops were held up for the poodle lady's inspection and she shook her head decisively. The butcher sighed slightly and suggested that in that case she might prefer lamb, and she bent over the counter to take a closer look. 'Tom's in a deep gloom about the match this year. Our star player is in South Africa for the next six weeks getting married. Even Tom didn't feel he could ask him to delay his wedding for a cricket match, and nearly everyone else who usually plays with us is away as well.'

'Couldn't Tom have delayed the match until later?' I asked.

'The host gets to choose the date – when his star players are available, of course, and usually when he's got a guest who knows one end of a bat from the other and who might be a useful boost to the team.'

'So who gets to play?'

'Anyone who's available and allows their arm to be twisted. The only rule is neither Napier nor Tom are allowed to poach each other's guests or their workers. Friends are fair game and booked well in advance.'

'Tom could always ask Oscar if he's short of a player,' I said as the poodle lady inclined her head graciously over the cutlets that were being held up for her inspection. 'He plays regularly and is quite good.'

'Really?' asked Janey with a gleam in her eye that showed perhaps she wasn't quite so blasé about who won the match as she pretended. The poodle lady departed carrying a parcel neatly wrapped in waxed paper and tied with string; her dog was still comfortably sitting in the basket. Janey moved up and started her own lengthy negotiations with the butcher, turning around to me after a few seconds. 'Madame is going to make me some of her special kebabs, but she can't do them right away. Would you mind hanging around in town for another half hour or so?'

'Not at all, providing I don't have to carry these bags all the time.'

'We'll go and dump them in the car.' Janey turned back to the butcher and put in a large order for sausages and steaks to be picked up at the same time. 'None of your lot are vegetarian, are they?' she asked in sudden anxiety as we left the shop.

'Put it this way,' I said, 'nobody told Oscar last night that they weren't going to eat his spiced lamb. Of course he was holding the carving knife at the time, but even so I don't think you're going to have to get Tom to rustle up any veggie burgers.'

Relieved of our burdens, we were wandering along peering in shop windows when Janey stopped outside a small hairdresser's saying she needed some more of her shampoo.

'Do you get your hair cut here?' I asked in surprise. I would have imagined that her glossy bob came from somewhere very *haute coiffure*, not a little backstreet salon.

'Marie-Hélène was chief stylist at one of the top salons in Paris before she got married,' said Janey with that smug air of someone who knows that they have made a real and unexpected discovery. 'Even Venetia comes here sometimes.'

'Goodness!' I said, impressed. 'Do you think she could do something about mine sometime?' I'd just caught sight of my reflection in the glass and it hadn't been a happy experience. The new hat might have been sublime but its very glamour just highlighted the Worzel Gummidge effect of my hair. A girl with straight hair so glossy it looked as if it had been French polished opened the door of the salon and went in. If she thought she needed anything doing to her hair, what hope did I have, I thought and wondered how much it would cost to buy a decent wig.

'Let's go and ask,' said Janey practically before I could start wallowing in having a *really* bad hair day.

It turned out that Marie-Hélène could indeed do something about it, and right now too. Her eleven-thirty client had booked in for a major restyle and then had a major attack of nerves and settled for having her fringe trimmed. With the best will in the world, Marie-Hélène hadn't been able to spin it out for longer than five minutes. She was a tiny, round woman, with hair dyed an eyeball-searing scarlet and pulled back in an untidy ponytail on the top of her head. She fizzed with energy as she danced around me, picking up tendrils of hair and clicking her tongue disapprovingly. It seemed that, 'Who on earth was the butcher with the blunt scissors who did *this*? You must have been *out of your mind* to let them anywhere near you,' or some similar sentiment is universal in every culture. At least she was decent enough to admit that my hair was in adequate condition, though she recommended something to brighten up the colour. I didn't need the agonised shaking of Janey's head to be able to suss out that subtle coloration wasn't Marie-Hélène's strong point and hastily declined.

The hairdresser was a wizard with the scissors though. She snipped here and there, not appearing to take off very much, but when she'd finished I'd been transformed from scarecrow lookalike to someone who could have modelled hats. Well, that was a bit of an exaggeration maybe, but that wasn't her fault, it was the raw material. At least I no longer positively shamed my new hat. I could even see properly as she'd done something magic to the heavy hank of hair that used to fall like net curtains across my face every time I moved my head so that it now stayed obediently to one side.

'That looks fantastic,' said Janey approvingly as I was paying the eye-wateringly enormous bill. Marie-Hélène had taken advantage of my starstruck admiration of my new improved reflection in the mirror to sell me several products which she said contained the rarest and most marvellous ingredients and were absolutely essential to keep my hair looking its very best. Judging by the prices they must contain powdered pearls, I thought handing over a wad of francs and wondering if the sign that you've finally grown up is when you start paying as much for your shampoo as you used to spend on a pair of shoes.

'You might have warned me that the Parisian stylist charges Parisian prices,' I said, half grumbling.

'Worth every centime,' Janey said airily.

Everyone back at the cottage seemed to agree with her, which was nice. I was even told how pretty my new hairdo made me look. Though I had the feeling that some of the flattery was prompted by the goodies I'd brought back from the market and a fear that if I started to feel unattractive, I might refuse to hand them around. A move was made to bring lunch forward and Maggie had a hard time restoring order, saying that according to the rota she'd drawn up, it was *her* turn to do lunch and *she'd* decide what time we'd have it. On the other hand, she did need some help with laying the table and washing the salads . . .

Like magic the starving hordes remembered urgent things to do and slipped away like smoke.

CHAPTER 9

I hadn't even needed to hint to Maggie that for once her hostess would welcome it if she were to vamp her host this evening. Maggie had been well on the case from the moment I mentioned that another local château-owner was going to be there too, and she disappeared into her bedroom halfway through the afternoon to start lengthy beautifying preparations – during which she used all the hot water, as Sally and I discovered later.

Phil looked singularly unworried about the way his girlfriend was dolling herself up for another man and I wondered if, contrary to all appearances, he allowed his women the same degree of licentiousness that he appeared to think was acceptable in himself. Except that it seemed unlikely that a man who disappeared to have a bath every time there was some domestic duty like laying the table to do would have cutting-edge beliefs about sexual equality. He didn't.

When Charlie made a remark about his tolerance he smiled complacently and said, 'She's only drumming up new business for this agency of hers.' Sally made some protesting noise and he waved his cigarette at her. 'Come on, everybody knows by now that Maggie's going it alone, don't they?' I hadn't, but then I wasn't surprised at not being taken into her confidence. 'She reckons that the English-owned châteaux around here should do a joint promotion and that if she plays her cards right and wears something from Agent Provocateur Tom and his mate'll be so busy staring down her cleavage that they won't even notice that they've signed on the dotted until it's too late!'

No wonder Maggie had been so keen to butter up Janey, and therefore Tom, by offering to have Jed to stay, I thought as Sally said loyally, but not very convincingly, that Maggie never tried to use cheap tricks like that to get what she wanted.

'Are you going in with Maggie too, Sally?' I asked, thinking of how she'd been talking to Robert and rather admiring the way both of them were prepared to seize any business opportunity that crossed their paths. The fact that I don't is no doubt one of the reasons I tend to have unpleasant conversations with my bank manager. 'I hope you'll think of me when you need some brochures written,' I said half seriously.

'Oh no, I don't think so!' said Sally with unflattering speed, then to do her credit she blushed furiously. 'I mean, we'll have our own in-house copywriter, we won't need to use freelances,' she stammered.

'If you ever do, Nella's very good,' said Oscar, who also has an eye for the main chance, though in his case it isn't always for himself. Then, when Sally didn't look particularly convinced: 'She got shortlisted for an *Advertising News* award last year.'

'Did you really?' Sally looked ludicrously surprised. I decided not to tell her that my contribution had been a single strapline to a stunning visual done by my partner, and that we'd been up for a prize for artistic excellence.

It seemed that Janey's plans had gone slightly awry, for when we arrived in the garden later that evening, all done up in our glad rags, it was Jed who was bent industriously over the barbecue basting away while Tom was on the terrace chatting to a vision wrapped in a slim column of peacock-blue silk. At least Janey had armed Tom with a bottle so the opportunities for a tête-à-tête were going to be limited by the siren calls of glasses waiting to be refilled, though judging by the way Solange had a hand placed on his wrist she was happy to see everyone else go thirsty for a while. Delphine, wearing a sundress apparently made from three handker-chiefs and a very small scarf, was handing around a plate of little bits and pieces, while her two small charges were also doing their bit. This consisted of carrying around bowls of crisps which they thrust imperiously at guests and whisked away before any could be taken, then helping themselves to a handful as a reward for their labours. Lily, still a bit dot and carry, was following one of the twins around, hoovering up the inevitable spills almost before they hit the ground. Solomon, the old Labrador, was doing the same with the other. All four of them were getting under everybody's feet on a regular basis.

Lacking a staircase to come down, Maggie stopped about ten feet away from the party, and resting one hand on the edge of the balustrade, delicately wriggled her feet into a pair of vertigo-inducing mules she'd had to carry on the walk here. Then, just to ensure that the maximum number of eyes were upon her, she straightened her devastatingly simple little floral dress, which had probably cost a bomb and which did absolutely nothing to hide her good figure. Or to hide the fact that her underwear was minimal. Sadly for her, Tom had his back turned so he missed her grand entrance, though she still had the satisfaction of seeing the man who was talking to Venetia do a double-take. Janey was right, his curly hair and long face really did give him a distinct resemblance to a sheep, I thought with secret amusement. Then all desire to laugh fled as I realised I knew that sheep. It was Hugh Cavendish. And if Hugh was here ... I looked grimly down the terrace, ignoring Janey's wave, my forebodings spot on. There was Robert, leaning on a stick, talking to a fair-haired man with a large nose.

Where was Oscar? I was going to *kill* him. But alerted by some sixth sense, Oscar had stopped nattering to Sally and looked around, his face falling with almost comical dismay as he too saw Robert's companion. He glanced sideways at me, then ever so casually started to put a safe distance between us. 'Oh no you don't!' I hissed in my best pantomime whisper as I grabbed his arm and made it quite clear that I was prepared to hang on for dear life no matter what, so there was no point in struggling.

He looked at me in a hunted fashion, then decided to tough it out. 'What's the matter, Nella? You seem a little – upset – about something.'

'A little upset?' I echoed. 'Oh no, Oscar, I'm not a little upset, I'm *incandescent*! And you, you snake in the grass, you lying toad, you know perfectly well what I'm upset about!'

'Hey, come on, Nella, whatever it is can't be that bad,' protested Phil, hovering with an interested air and eyeing my clenched fist uneasily. I daresay he thought it was shortly about to connect with Oscar's nose. Judging by his expression, so did Oscar.

I smiled as nastily as I could. 'It's going to get a whole lot worse, for Oscar.' At this Oscar froze like a rabbit in headlights. 'This is nothing to do with you, Phil, so if you don't want to get hurt I suggest you leave us alone,' I said, still glaring at my prey. I was just getting nicely into my stride.

Phil hesitated, obviously torn between a desire to get away from an enraged female and sheer nosiness. The fear factor beat curiosity and male solidarity hands down. Muttering that I should remember that I'd got witnesses, he hightailed it off down the terrace.

I took a deep breath, trying to calm myself down a little, and looked Oscar straight in the eye. 'Just *what* is George doing here?'

Oscar widened his eyes. 'I haven't the faintest clue. I had no idea he was going to be here, I promise you,' he said with an irreproachable air of innocence.

I regarded him in silence for a moment. 'All right, I'll give you that,' I said grudgingly. 'If you'd known George was coming tonight you'd have spent most of the afternoon either trying to persuade me that I didn't want to come or telling me what a nice bloke he is. But you do remember our conversation when you suggested that I come here to France?'

'Of course. I said you needed to get away for a really good rest and I was right. You look a million times better already!'

'Don't try to get around me by flattery,' I said severely.

'It's not flattery, it's the truth.'

'Shut up, Oscar, and listen. What you *also* said was that George would definitely not be joining us – remember? I do, for I had a feeling your devious little mind might come up with a trick like this one. You absolutely *swore* this was going to be a George-free zone, Oscar, George-*free*, not maybe-a-little-bit-of-George-from-time-to-time, but no George *at all*. Does that ring any bells? You made a solemn promise about it, on your grandmother's grave too,' I added bitterly. 'Which grandmother was that? The one who goes line dancing every week?'

'No, the one buried in Great Eastby churchyard,' he said promptly. 'And I promised that I wouldn't introduce George into the cottage by some ruse. You should know I wouldn't play a trick like that on you.' He took note of my silence and moved hastily on. 'But I couldn't promise that he wouldn't happen to be in the area – how could I? I'm not his keeper. How was I supposed to know that his friend's brother just happens to live near Tom and Janey?' He might just have convinced someone who didn't know him better.

'So it's just some coincidence, is it?' I asked with deep sarcasm. 'Of course it is. Even though the two of you work in the same building—'

'For different companies,' Oscar interrupted.

'You still meet in the lift and have a drink together at least once a fortnight,' I snapped. 'And you really expect me to believe that you were both too busy discussing cricket to even think of mentioning where you were going on holiday? Pull the other one, Oscar!' Then I thought of something else. 'And just how do you happen to know that it's Hugh's brother George is staying with?'

Oscar was caught between a rock and an exceptionally hard place. He began to stammer out some excuse but I snarled over it: 'Of all the conniving, deceitful, unscrupulous *bastards*!' I was strongly tempted to take him by the throat and shake him, hard, never mind if it had terminal results or not, but that wouldn't be fair on Janey. A minor row provides a party with a useful talking point for those sticky moments when conversation is flagging, but a row that involves the police being called is another matter. But I could always get my own back in some other way, couldn't I? For instance, back home there was Felicity from the flat upstairs who had developed a most improbable tendre for Oscar and was always asking me when she could meet him again. Never mind that she was a lady wrestler and scared him witless, it was *my* turn to do a little matchmaking . . . I'd have them both around for a candlelit dinner as soon as I got back.

I began to feel much better, since thoughts of revenge are very restoring, and decided to try one last time to get Oscar to see sense. 'George and I are over, finished, kaput, wound up, finito. In other words, Oscar, can't you get it into your thick head that we aren't *ever* going to get back together again?'

He relaxed slightly as he realised that retribution

wasn't imminent. Didn't he know the old adage about revenge being a dish best eaten cold?

'I know George probably said some very hurtful things to you, but you should give him a second chance, Nella,' he said persuasively. He glanced at my grim expression but still went on gallantly. 'Come on, you've got to admit that as far as your last few boyfriends went, George was quite the pick of the bunch.'

This was absolutely true, but considering that his pred-ecessors had been a New Wave performance poet who considered that his art freed him from mundane matters like baths, and a stockbroker who had unaccountably forgotten to mention that he had a wife, this didn't cut much ice. Encouraged by my reluctant nod, Oscar went on eagerly, 'He's a decent sort, reliable, earns lots of money, has got a nice house—'

'From the way you bang on about him I'll start to think you're in love with him yourself,' I said snidely.

'No, he's not my type,' he said seriously. 'But he *is* yours.' I opened my mouth to deny this heresy but he forestalled me. 'I distinctly remember you telling me that you liked tall men who had plenty to say for themselves.'

'I also like being allowed to participate in the conver-sation myself, from time to time!' Before Oscar could point out the undeniable truth that at least George was tall I said, 'You're forgetting one thing, that irrespective of what I feel, George dumped me.'

'He regrets that. Really he does.'

Oh yes? This was bound to be another case of Oscar deciding that he knew what someone was thinking better than they did themselves. 'Even if he does, *I* don't regret our breaking up.'

Oscar ignored this trifling hindrance to his grand scheme of reuniting two distinctly un-star-crossed lovers. 'You were so good together, it was such fun having supper with the pair of you.' He waved away my protest that the evenings usually involved at least one argument because George's nanny never 'mucked up' food like I did. 'OK, I know he can be a little overbearing at times, and occasionally he can be a trifle stuffy, but both of you need to learn to be a bit more tolerant of each other's foibles.'

'I don't have any foibles,' I said loftily and untruthfully. 'And as for George's – do you expect your lovers to do all your washing for you, Oscar?'

He looked astonished. 'Of course not. I do it for both of us.'

I gave up. Oscar was going to go on believing George and I were a match made in heaven until one or other of us shacked up with someone else. I just hoped George would do it soon. Nor was there any point in my trying to extract a promise that there wouldn't be any more 'accidental' meetings between George and myself. As had already been amply proved this evening, when Oscar thinks he's doing something for someone's good he doesn't allow little things like promises, or even the spirit of promises, to stand in his way.

I let Oscar go and noted with grim amusement that he virtually did 100 metres in under ten seconds in his desire to put as large a distance as possible between us. Tom had been prised away from Solange for long enough to start wandering around offering refills, though I couldn't help noticing that he seemed to have come to a halt at Maggie's cleavage. I looked around for a glass. I needed a drink after that little session – besides, I was going to have to talk to George some time. Indeed, I was even prepared to go and be all things civilised with my ex – providing I'd got a good slug of alcohol inside me first. Well perhaps all things civilised was a bit much, but I'd be civil at least.

Janey, wearing a red dress that did wonders for her dark colouring, materialised at my side. 'You looked like you were having a bit of a ding-dong with Oscar there,' she said invitingly.

'Nosy, aren't you?' I said with a smile.

'If you don't ask, you don't find out – first motto of a journalist.'

'And the second motto is to go on asking questions until your victim caves in, I suppose?' She grinned. 'Oscar, not for the first time, has been interfering. Match-making to be precise, or rather trying to mend very broken fences.'

She almost dropped her glass in shock. 'Surely he doesn't imagine you and Robert—' she exclaimed, her face a mask of comical incredulity. I felt my sense of humour beginning to return.

'Even Oscar wouldn't dream of trying to reunite Robert and me,' I said, relishing the thought of the comeuppance he'd get if he even tried. 'This is much nearer home. That,' I gestured with my thumb, 'is George. George who is Oscar's friend. George who I *don't* go out with any more and who I was afraid might be sleeping on our sofa bed.' Janey spluttered into her drink. 'George who Oscar *knew* was staying at Napier and Solange's when he suggested I come to the cottage. Does that answer your question about why I don't love Oscar very much right now?' I asked.

'Oh lor!' Janey said when she could speak again. 'Why did you break up with *him*?' she asked, as if she was worried that she was treading on very thin ice and sounding a long way from a tough professional investigative journalist.

'Laundry,' I said. 'I don't do handwashing,' I amplified. She nodded in a way of someone who has been down that particular road herself. 'Officially, it was my refusal to do normal female domestic tasks that was the last straw for George, but to be honest I think it was because I was no good at the more personal things.'

'Like what?' she breathed eagerly.

'Intimate massages.'

'What?' she exclaimed, eyes widening pleasurably, and loudly enough for Venetia and the sheep to turn around and look curiously at us.

'Of the ego.'

She giggled, obviously recognising that one too, and gave George a speculative glance. 'He's not very like Rob, is he?' she asked in a leading way.

'Maybe that's the reason I went out with him,' I said, cursing myself as I saw her suddenly attentive look. The last thing I needed was someone else thinking I was still holding a candle for an ex-boyfriend. 'Look, I stopped comparing boyfriends to Robert years ago.' Janey still looked sceptical. I sighed. 'If you must know why I went out with George . . .'

'I must.'

'Well, look at him.' She did. 'He's decent-looking, he's got no obvious faults like picking his nose in public, he washes regularly and he isn't married.' A slow grin began to creep across her face at my list of minimum requirements in a man – I don't think they're that eccentric actually. '*And* he seemed to like me. And I liked him, quite. I began to think that maybe all those people,' namely my mother and Oscar, 'who kept on telling me I'm far too fussy about men and any reasonable man is better than no man at all might be right, and that I'd be crazy to let a chance like that slip through my fingers.' I paused. 'I tried, really I did, but the problem is you can't make yourself fancy someone rotten, can you?'

'So why did you let him dump you?' asked Janey in a puzzled voice.

'Bad timing,' I said with an effort to keep a light tone. Even after several months I was still furious with myself for letting George upstage me. 'I was going to chuck him – but not until after my brother's thirtieth birthday bash so I'd have someone to go with. George got in and did it first. *Before* Nick's party. And everyone knew about it too. I had to go alone and suffer all those bloody commiserations over my supposedly broken heart and I couldn't say a damn thing because they'd have just thought I was suffering from a bad case of sour grapes.'

'Mmm, maybe you'd better not sit next to him during dinner, after all . . .' Janey began, then was interrupted by a shove somewhere near knee-level. One of the twins pulled at her hem so sharply that it was a good thing she wasn't wearing a skirt with an elasticated waist and said in an imperious voice, 'Pick up.'

She gave him a quick inspection to see if there was anything on his hands or body that might get transferred to her dress, and getting satisfactory results scooped him up. He put plump arms around her neck and gave her an enthusiastic kiss which would have been enough to make any mother go quite soggy at the knees. However, even mother love gets rather tried by a stranglehold and several splodgy kisses applied with a liberal helping of second-hand crisp. Murmuring that it was about time she started the twins on the going to bed bit, Janey told him to say 'night-night' to me and bore him off in search of his brother and Delphine.

'About time too,' Venetia muttered as she beckoned me over. 'When I was that age my mother always had me in bed by six o'clock. It can't be good for the twins to stay up so late.'

It was the first time I'd been aware of Venetia showing any interest in child-rearing. 'Maybe Janey's trying to make sure that she doesn't get woken up at the crack of dawn,' I suggested.

Venetia's 'humph' would have done justice to an old-fashioned nanny passing comment on the dangerously liberal tendencies of some modern mothers.

'Hello, Nella, nice to see you,' said Hugh in a surprisingly welcoming voice. We'd only met a couple of times and I'd always got the impression he was so tied up with his girlfriend, a pearl-wearing Sloane with a blackboard scraper laugh, that I'd barely registered with him. George couldn't stand the frightful Camilla either (one of the few topics on which we were in complete agreement), so he usually arranged to see Hugh in places where she wouldn't be welcome, like his club or the men's night at the Turkish baths. I cocked my head listening for a few seconds but there was no screech periodically punctuating the buzz of conversation that hung over the terrace so I presumed that Camilla wasn't here.

Hugh's enthusiasm for my presence was explained as he said in apparent surprise, 'But you haven't got a drink – I'll go and find you one.' He sped off without waiting to ask what I wanted. His route to the glasses of wine took him in a big loop that went past Maggie and as soon as he got within a five-foot radius it looked as if his feet had hit a patch of quicksand. Since George had frequently commented on Hugh's regrettable tendency for fidelity, this must mean that even old Hugh had grown tired of Camilla's laugh. Shame he couldn't have had this revelation at some time other than when he was fetching me a drink. Oh well, no doubt it would do my liver good to hold off on the alcohol for a while, I thought with resignation.

CHAPTER 10

'Really!' commented Venetia, watching Hugh goggling as Maggie made an expansive gesture and several interesting bits jiggled. 'I don't believe any man has ever been *quite* so eager to leave me.' She didn't sound too offended so I gathered she didn't really care either way if she had one sheep more or less to add to her list of followers.

She turned around, her eyebrows rising slightly. 'Mm, *like* your hair. Cunning old you. I wouldn't have thought you were that calculating.' I stared at her, wondering what she was on about and she smiled conspiratorially. 'Come on, Nella, we all know why you went off and got a complete makeover. Hugh's been telling me all about you and George.'

'Oh no,' I interrupted quickly. 'I had no idea George was going to be here, I promise.' I felt the colour rising in my cheeks under Venetia's 'don't give me that' gaze.

'Well, if you say so...' she murmured. 'But it's a funny old coincidence, isn't it? And there's got to be something that's put the sparkle in your eyes. I mean, no one would have guessed seeing you at the beginning of the week that you could brush up so well.' Thanks,

Venetia, I thought as her eyes swept restlessly around the terrace. 'Honestly, would you look at that,' she murmured, pointing to the barbecue where Jed was conscientiously turning bits of meat. Janey was next to him, leaning forward to say something in his ear. 'Couldn't she at least avoid touching him up in public!'

It looked to me as if Janey had merely touched Jed's arm to gain his attention and not because she couldn't bear to keep her hands off him, but Venetia wasn't having any of that. She tossed her head saying, 'I don't know what Daddy must think, it's so blatant. And I sent Jed off there to keep him out of the way of Janey, too.'

'Thus releasing your father for that,' I said with a nod in Tom's direction to where, far from merely touching his arm, Solange looked as if she were about to climb onto Tom's lap. He was standing up too.

Venetia's eyes widened in indignation. 'The way that woman behaves is disgusting. She should know better at her age, too – she's much too old for that sort of thing.' I doubted Solange would ever be too old for 'that sort of thing'. 'I can't stand her!' Venetia declared vehemently. So though she didn't know it, she had at least some common ground with her stepmother. 'I can't think how poor Napier puts up with it; it must be so humiliating for him to see his wife draped like an octopus over every single man who comes along. And the married ones too,' she added with another furious look towards her father. 'Look, you can see Napier's upset, and you can't blame him either. He's so loyal to her, won't say a word against her, more's the pity. But then that shows you what a decent sort of person he is. I'd better go and talk to him, see if I can't distract him a little from the way his wife is carrying on.'

With that she click-clacked her way off in heels nearly as high as Maggie's and seconds later was doling out consolation and distraction to Napier, a less ovine-looking version of his younger brother. I stood for a moment gazing out over the garden and thinking that even without the benefit of some alcoholic fortification I couldn't put off saying hello to George for much longer. The problem was, I couldn't be certain that he wasn't still bearing a grudge over what I'd said in our last row. Most of it was true, but nearly all of it was also the sort of thing it's unwise to say unless you plan to spend the rest of your life protecting your back. And George was good at bearing grudges, too; he was rather proud of it, claimed that it came with his Scottish ancestry like tartan and deep pockets.

But George was still talking to Robert, and I wasn't sure I could cope with both of them at the same time. They were talking about the gallery, too. George's voice could be heard easily across three fields. That was another reason to leave them in peace. George had plenty of money, he might put some business Robert's way. Except it didn't sound as if he was going to.

'Well, one doesn't *buy* pictures, does one?' he was saying. 'Or hardly ever. One inherits them from relations. I've picked up a couple of attractive hunting prints in antique shops of course, but I never buy modern art. One can't. No offence, old chap, I'm sure you've got some very nice pictures in your place, if you like that sort of thing, but with furniture like mine you've got to have the pictures to match. I mean, a collage of newspaper and cow dung just wouldn't go with a Sheraton sideboard, would it?'

George chortled at his own joke. I could almost hear Robert grind his teeth as he retorted, 'It might look a damn sight more attractive than the normal gloomy portrait of Great Uncle Roger that seems to hang over most sideboards.' There was a slightly startled grunt from George. It was actually his great grandmother who hung there, but despite the most flattering efforts of the artist she could easily have passed for a Roger. 'I can't recall that we've ever handled a cow-dung picture,' Robert went on thoughtfully, 'and I certainly wouldn't recommend it for a dining room. *Not* very hygienic. So what would you prefer over your sideboard? A nice Monet? I can get you one if you really want, except I must warn you that most of our clients prefer artists who are less well known.'

'Eh?' George asked blankly.

'Unless you appear regularly on the *Sunday Times Rich List* it's a bit obvious that *The Garden at Giverny* on your wall isn't likely to be genuine, isn't it?'

There was a startled silence, then, 'You deal in forgeries?'

'Reproductions,' Robert said firmly, 'all painted to order. We've got a woman who does a wonderful Constable if you'd rather have something more English. I should warn you though, that they don't come cheap.' George looked highly offended at this implication that he might not have the readies for a mere copy. 'And I'm afraid they aren't an easy route to making a few million either. They all contain a microchip so they can't ever be sold on as the real thing.'

'I would never try to pass a fake off as genuine!' George expostulated indignantly. 'In fact I wouldn't dream of giving house room to a reproduction!'

Oh dear. I had a nasty feeling that Robert's next comment would be along the lines of how could George be so sure his sideboard was genuine since Sheraton wouldn't have had time to eat, let alone sleep, if he'd really made everything that was attributed to him. It might be nine years but I still knew how Robert's mind worked in some ways. I was wondering if I shouldn't go in and try to smooth things over a little. Except, given my past relationships with both men, I was hardly the obvious choice for oil pouring on troubled waters. The matter was decided by Tom who was wandering around, doing his duty with the bottle. Seeing I was alone he seized me by the arm and interrupted Robert in the middle of saying something about the authenticity of sideboards. 'Let me introduce you all—'

'It's all right, Tom, I already know George,' I said.

He looked at me in faint surprise. 'Do you? You seem to know a lot of people. You must be the sort of girl who gets around a lot.'

I laughed. 'I don't think you meant that to come out that way.'

He thought for a moment. 'No, I don't think I did,' he agreed apologetically, then feeling that his social duty was done he wandered off in the direction of the barbecue saying he must go and see if Jed needed a hand. He probably felt that his hormones needed a breather before they returned to the high activity stimulation provided by at least two of his female guests.

The boredom had disappeared from Robert's face and he was glancing from me to George with a knowing look in his eyes. 'George,' he murmured. 'Oh, I *see*. Is this the George you were talking about the other night?'

'Yes,' I said shortly, thinking that if he started to go on in the same way that Venetia had I'd kick him – on his bad leg. I didn't normally have these violent impulses; it must be something in the air tonight, I thought, as George smirked slightly, sure that whatever I'd said must be complimentary. Perhaps my memories of the part of our epic row where I'd got *really* personal were the result of after-the-event wishful thinking. Or maybe not. George probably hadn't believed it was possible any female could think that about him.

Robert's bright eyes rested on my new hairstyle. 'Nice cut. Had it done on an impulse, did you?'

I glared at him – he was *worse* than bloody Venetia – and turned my attention to George. 'Hello, George, how are you?' I said with a smile that was much warmer than I intended it to be.

He kissed my cheek. 'All the better for seeing you, Nella,' he said with a gallantry that had been quite absent from his manner when we'd been going out. 'I must say you look very nice indeed.'

I smiled and thanked him, though I didn't return the compliment. I was prepared to be civil but drew the line at flattery. Besides, absence hadn't made me any fonder of the blackberry-coloured shirt he was wearing.

George was looking me up and down assessingly as if I was a heifer in the local fatstock show. 'Really, you look very good indeed,' he said with an unflattering degree of surprise. 'Much better than when I last saw you. How did you manage to lose so much weight? Been using the gym at last?'

I bared my teeth. 'No, I've been ill. I'm sure that Oscar must have told you.'

George looked slightly uncomfortable. His fear of catching my germs had been so acute that not only had he not come to visit me – a good thing as my feelings about him at that point were so strong the very sight of him would have given me a relapse – but I hadn't had a Get Well card either. Perhaps he was afraid I might feel obliged to thank him, and you never know what infection can rest on a stamp. 'Well, it's certainly brought good results!' he said with a slightly forced laugh.

'Do you think so?' Robert asked. I was subjected to another of those fatstock assessments. 'I disagree,' he said coolly, after a few seconds. 'Nella's much too thin now. Of course she looks nice, but she's always been pretty whatever her weight and she looks better with a few curves.'

I'd have been a damn sight more grateful for these compliments if I hadn't felt that they had very little to do with me and a lot to do with a simple desire to disagree with George on every possible topic. And he'd just managed to make me feel that I'd got all the sex appeal of a broom handle too, I thought crossly as George said, 'So you've known Nella for some time have you, old chap?'

Robert's jaw tightened slightly. 'Nine years.'

'Oh university,' said George, enlightened. 'That explains you being in the art world. It was that sort of place, Nella said. I haven't met many of her friends from those days, she doesn't seem to keep up with them. Of course, it's easier for me. I was at Oxford. Lots of people of one's own type there.'

'Mm.' Robert nodded his agreement. 'But I met quite enough people of my own type at school. I thought it'd be interesting to meet some different ones. That's why I turned my place down.'

George stared at him for a moment as if not sure whether to believe that anyone, no matter how bohemian, could possibly turn down a place at Oxford. 'My father would never have allowed me to do anything quite so rash. I daresay he'd have threatened to disinherit me if I'd even thought of it,' he chuckled, looking extremely proud of having a parent who could act with such firmness.

Robert smiled thinly. 'My father didn't threaten. He did it.' His eyes flickered sideways in my direction. 'But not over which university I was going to.'

Oh God! Yet another black mark chalked up to my account. I swallowed nervously. 'Um, did he re-inherit you later?'

'No,' Robert said flatly. My heart sank even further. 'He didn't believe in going back on his word, but it didn't actually make much difference. He'd always intended to leave nearly everything to my mother. The only thing which had been earmarked for me were the Winwood spoons – great bulbous things from the sixteenth century – and they went to my eldest sister as she was deemed to be a more fitting custodian of family treasures. Frankly she's welcome to them. They're hideous, cost a fortune to insure and she can't even get rid of them. Family legend has it that whoever sells the spoons will see their teeth go green and their nails go yellow, or something of the sort. No one's dared put it to the test yet. But as you can see, I didn't miss out on much.'

'It can't have been very nice for you though,' I said.

I got a very hard look from under his eyelashes. 'None of what happened around then was very *nice*,' he said with emphasis.

Ouch! I was wishing the flagstones under my feet would open and swallow me up when my persecutor looked at me, and murmured, completely unapologetically, 'Sorry. I forgot I wasn't supposed to say that sort of thing any more.'

I glared at him, but before I could reply my attention was distracted by the glass of wine that was being thrust at me. Hugh had managed at last to tear himself away from Maggie's charms. 'Afraid I took a bit longer than I meant to,' he mumbled, then looked rather surprised at the way I almost snatched it from him and took a large gulp immediately. My jangled nerves needed it.

Robert looked on the point of making his escape when he was forestalled by Hugh who turned to him with an amiable smile. 'I heard about your knee – bad luck. Shame you won't be able to play in the match on Sunday.'

Robert shrugged. 'I'm not a brilliant player so I won't be any great loss, but I'm going to umpire instead. Tom's dug me out a few old copies of *Wisden* to refresh my memory and Janey's trying to find me a white coat. The best she's come up with so far is an old lab coat Delphine used for chemistry, which is so tight that I can't move my arms.'

'I thought it was only the refs in football who needed to wave their arms around,' I said, gaining myself a pitying stare from all three males for my abysmal ignorance. 'What about one of Janey's big white cook's aprons? I'm sure she can spare you one and it wouldn't restrict your arm movements at all, would it?'

'Really, Nella! We can't have the umpire looking as if he's come off the lunch shift at the local restaurant,' George said in a repressive voice.

'Can't think why that should make a cricket match played in the middle of a vineyard for a stuffed boar's head seem any more eccentric,' I said sweetly.

George frowned at me. Cricket was not a subject for levity in his opinion. 'If you're worried about not remembering all the rules, you don't have to bother with *Wisden*, Robert,' I went on. 'All you have to do is ask George here. He knows everything about cricket, don't you, George? I'm sure that he can give you lots of advice.'

'Glad to,' my ex said genially. 'Any time you want.'

'Thank you,' Robert said through gritted teeth, looking at me in a way that promised retribution later. I smiled blandly at him and, thinking that perhaps it would be wiser to get away while I was still on a winning streak, muttered that I'd go and see if I could help Janey. Twenty minutes later when Janey asked me to go around telling all the stragglers that they should come to the table I was delighted to hear George still explaining some of the more arcane rules of cricket to a stony-faced Robert.

To seat all of us, Janey had pushed three of her teak tables together, covering the joins with a long piece of yellow and white cotton, to make one enormously long table. 'The seating's been absolute *hell*,' she grumbled in an undertone as she wandered up the length of the table placing slips of paper with names on at each place, 'and it's mostly been your fault!'

'*Mine?*' I exclaimed.

'You appear to be on non-speaks with half the men here,' she said unfairly. 'I've got a few ex-boyfriends myself, but I've always had the sense not to gather them together in one place. First I had to move George from next to you, then I was going to put Phil next to Solange, they're two of a kind and deserve each other, but that meant having Oscar on your left. I thought that in your present mood you'd probably kill him, so what about Rob? You two are getting on better now . . .'

'Er . . . it'd probably be wiser to let him recover from his intensive cricket instruction before he comes in close contact with me again,' I said and explained what I meant.

'And I was thinking of putting George on his other side too!' she said with a giggle. ' Oh well, Rob can sit next to Solange. He'll be quite safe from being lectured about cricket there. She pretends she knows nothing about it and likes to say it's all some Anglo-Saxon madness of her husband's.'

Solange must have been one of the few people around the table who wasn't talking about cricket. Actually Hugh wasn't talking cricket either, but that was because he was next to Maggie and her bosomy presence seemed to have robbed him of the powers of speech. It was a bit unfair on the poor man to keep on leaning forward and pressing her arms together like that. But otherwise I could hear batting averages being discussed all around the table, even between Tom and Maggie. Maggie was surprisingly knowledgeable; she took a party of her more cricket-mad clients to Lord's a couple of times a year, and had offered to be scorer for the match.

'Janey tells me that Oscar's quite a useful batsman,' said Tom, turning to me, when Hugh had at last managed to find enough voice to grab Maggie's attention for a few minutes. 'What number does he go in at, do you know?'

'Afraid I don't,' I said guiltily. The only way I'd managed to get through being taken to a cricket match virtually every weekend last summer was by setting myself *War and Peace* as match reading. I was on the last chapter when George got a hat trick in the final game of the season. He hadn't been too pleased that I had been so absorbed in what was happening to Pierre and Natasha that I hadn't noticed he'd just saved the match. It was probably around then that it began to occur to him that we didn't really have very much in common.

Tom glanced quickly at Hugh as if checking he was still so mesmerised by Maggie's curves that he couldn't pay attention to anything else, and leaned forward. 'Tell me,' he hissed. 'You know George, don't you? Napier says he's quite a reasonable player, was in his school First Eleven. He's a bowler, isn't he? Is he actually any good? Napier's pretty keen to get the sanglier back, it hasn't seen the inside of Château Vielleroche for some years I can tell you,' he smirked slightly, 'and I was wondering if maybe Napier's hoping to take me unawares by boosting his team with a really good player or two.'

'He's done that all right,' I said without thinking. Damn your big mouth, Nella, I thought in dismay as Tom jerked to full attention. There are certain things you ought to keep until someone has finished eating – that is, if you don't want him to have indigestion. This was one of them. It was too late now. I sighed and said, 'I don't know about the First Eleven – he was probably in that – but I do know George had a trial for the county.'

Tom looked as if he was about to choke on his marinated trout salad. 'What happened?' he asked hoarsely.

According to George, he'd decided his future lay in making a packet in the City and not in making runs at Lord's, but I suspected he'd thought he might not be quite good enough to make it to the first rank and had decided that if he wasn't going to the top it wasn't worth making it his career. All the same, a near professional cricketer was going to be a formidable addition to Napier's team.

Tom sat in silence for a moment. 'I'd never have expected Napier to possess that degree of low cunning. Well, well, well. The crafty bastard! I wonder how long he's been setting this up. So your George,' I hastily denied he was my George but Tom ignored me, 'is a ringer. *Quite* a useful player indeed!' He leaned forward confidentially. 'Let's keep this to ourselves for the moment. Napier thinks he's going to wipe the field on Sunday, but now his star player has been outed, he's lost the surprise factor, hasn't he?'

He steepled his fingers together and rested his chin on

them, deep in thought. 'We've still got time to prepare ourselves. We're going to have a real fight for the sanglier this year, aren't we?' he asked in a voice full of gleeful anticipation. 'I wonder what surprises we can spring on Napier next Sunday . . .'

CHAPTER 11

Janey's impromptu dinner party had turned into a rip-roaring success. At one time it seemed as if the sole topic of conversation was going to be cricket but fortunately, round about the time the fruits of Jed's labours were brought to the table, even Tom and Napier had run out of things to say about bats, balls and stuffed sangliers' heads and had turned to subjects more congenial to their neighbours. Napier was too far down the other end of the table for me to be able to hear what he was talking about, but judging by the rapt expression on Venetia's face, he wasn't wittering on about batting averages any longer either. Solange, who had been distinctly sulky about not sitting next to her host, had recovered no end when she discovered that Oscar could and would match all her most flirtatious moves. She was now practising every one of her wiles on Robert who was lapping them all up, one by one.

George and Sally seemed to have hit it off too. I'd never heard Sally so giggly. When George looked up and saw me glancing at him, he smirked slightly. Damn it! I was prepared to bet he reckoned all he had to do to

resume our relationship was decide if he could be bothered with a female who wouldn't sort his socks. The last
thing I wanted was for George to get diverted when he
was getting on so well with Sally. It'd be perfect for me.
Even Oscar would have to shut up if George started
going out with someone else, and Sally would suit him
so much better than I ever had. She was a far more
disciplined country type than me. I was sure she
wouldn't jib at doing cricket teas and she'd leave the
men to enjoy their port alone after dinner without
insisting on having some, too. She probably even knew
how to pluck a pheasant – another of my rank failures.
You never know, she might even be prepared to do
laundry. Or maybe that was going a bit too far. Sally
certainly wasn't a complete push-over. I glanced towards
Oscar, hoping he had noticed how well George and Sally
were getting on, but he had his head turned away and
was talking to Janey and Charlie at the end of the table.

Of course that was a problem. What a shame Sally was
already going out with Charlie, especially as they didn't
seem a particularly well-matched pair. They didn't argue
or anything, there just wasn't that spark there usually is
between lovers. For instance, he never bent towards her
when he was saying something in the way he was doing
now with Janey. Her eyes widened, then she giggled,
made some quick retort and he threw his head back,
laughing with an abandonment that made everyone
around him smile as well. He didn't do that with Sally
either. He was certainly on good form tonight. Had he
just heard he had won the lottery or was this the real
Charlie that he kept hidden for some reason under the

rather quiet persona he usually presented to the world? I'd already realised that with Charlie, quiet didn't necessarily mean spineless or dull. He had a nicely subversive sense of humour which I appreciated, particularly when it was aimed at Maggie, but I hadn't seen him being as outgoing as this. I like men who laugh so wholeheartedly.

The only people around the table who didn't appear to be having a good time were Jed and me. Jed, because he was sitting between Hugh, who didn't find him nearly as attractive as Maggie, and Sally, who couldn't take her eyes off George, so the conversation wasn't exactly flowing around him. To add insult to injury, it was obvious that he really wanted to be next to his hostess. Judging from the way his eyes narrowed jealously as Janey capped one of Oscar's jokes, Venetia hadn't been exaggerating about his feelings for her stepmother. Tom noticed, too. I saw him glance at Jed, follow his look and frown slightly before returning to talk to Maggie and Hugh.

And I wasn't having such a good time because, lacking better quarry, Phil was playing footsie with me, 'accidentally' putting his hand on my thigh, dropping his napkin and managing to stroke the length of my leg as he picked it up and so on. I felt sure that it was almost a reflex action whenever he had a female next to him, whatever her age, and was prepared to bet he'd even have stroked my granny's knee if she were in my place.

I don't appreciate uninvited strokes at the best of times, particularly not when the stroker's girlfriend is sitting dead opposite. Sooner or later Maggie was going to notice something – and guess who was going to get blamed?

'Stop it!' I hissed as his hand found its way to my thigh yet again. 'If you do that once more I'll jab you with this.' I waved my fork menacingly in the air.

Phil looked at it and then at me as if convinced I couldn't possibly be serious and stroked my knee again. I let the fork fall into my lap and while picking it up jabbed his thigh, not as hard as I would have liked. He bit his lip, more from shock than from pain, it hadn't been *that* hard, but didn't make a sound. I suspected he was as keen as I to make sure Maggie didn't discover what he'd been up to. 'You're a hard woman, Nella, but it's your loss,' he gasped.

'In your opinion!' I retorted, and in an ostentatious display of virtue he put both hands on the table where I could see them. He was actually okay once he dropped the Phil the Philanderer act. I was quite enjoying myself until I intercepted a venomous glare from the other side of the table and I realised that Maggie was no keener on me talking to her man than she would have been on me doing anything considerably more intimate. A few minutes later I felt something warm stroking my thigh through my skirt yet again. I jumped and said sharply through gritted teeth, 'Phil! I won't warn you again. It'll really hurt next time.' He held up both hands with an innocent expression and I looked down to see Lily's head resting on my lap. She fixed her eyes on mine and told me as clearly as she could that the one thing missing in her life was a piece of cheese. Like the bit on my plate.

Long after darkness had fallen and Janey had lit fat candles in painted covers that threw flattering flickering lights on everyone's faces, we were still sitting around the table, finishing coffees and last glasses of wine and gossiping. Even though the stars were glittering out of a cloudless inky sky, the air was so warm it was like sitting in a thermal bath, just the right temperature to make you feel that you would really rather not move, thank you. Then Solange came back from the loo and tapped me on the shoulder. 'I'm sure you will not mind if I change places with you, er . . . Nettie. I 'ave barely spoken to Tom.' The smile she flashed was certainly not aimed at me.

Oh hell! That meant I was going to end up next to Robert and directly opposite George. The only way I could avoid catching the wrong eye would be to spend the rest of the evening gazing at my lap. But what else could I do? Hang on to my chair seat with both hands and refuse to move? The idea was tempting. But like the nice girl I am, I smiled mechanically, and said, 'Of course – Salomé.'

I got a very old-fashioned look as she sat down. I didn't feel that I'd made a friend.

'Ah, musical chairs, is it?' murmured Robert as I took my place beside him. 'But you've ended up next to the wrong person. I'd offer to swap with your George but Sally might protest. She appears to be enjoying herself.'

Under the cover of a peal of laughter from Sally that seemed to prove his point I muttered, 'He isn't my George.'

'But he might be again. You told me so yourself,' he reminded me.

Oh blast it! So I had, I remembered ruefully and resolved never, ever to tell a face-saving half-truth again.

Not to Robert anyway. Well, at least, not again tonight.

'What is it with that man that he has both you and Sally eating out of his hand?' he said thoughtfully, leaning back in his chair and glancing across the table. 'It must be something in his aftershave for I certainly can't think of anything else. Maybe I should ask him what he's using.'

'What, you mean that you want to have Sally and me eating out of *your* hand?' I asked before I could stop myself.

He looked at me measuringly. 'Not really.' I'd laid myself wide open to that, I thought in resignation. Didn't make it any nicer though. 'Sorry, Nella, didn't mean to hurt your feelings,' he said with patent insincerity. 'Shall I make it up to you by incurring Sally's displeasure and changing places with George?'

'I'd rather you didn't,' I said. 'I've heard enough about cricket tonight to last me a lifetime.'

'And you think *I* haven't?' Oops. I'd forgotten about setting George on him. To my relief I thought I could just see the faintest twitch at the corners of his mouth. 'That's another score I'm going to have to settle with you one of these days, Nella. The tally sheet seems to be growing day by day.'

'A tally sheet?' I asked, startled. 'I thought we'd agreed that all scores had been settled already.'

'What makes you think that?'

'Well, when you said it was unfair on Janey . . .'

'I said it was unfair on Janey for us to keep sniping at each other, and it is. But if you've got some idea that we can just become kissy kissy ex-lovers and friends, I have to warn you there's a lot of unfinished business to be sorted out first.'

His eyes locked onto mine and I felt a shiver go down my spine as I tried to work out what on earth he meant. I could only assume that he felt that my disastrous exit from his life hadn't been properly explained. I hadn't been that long on detail, true, but what more did he want? He already knew how sorry I was. Did he want to know if I'd bounced back from losing him as easily as he'd apparently done with me? I hadn't. Or how long it had been before I stopped crying about it every night? Months. Or when I began to find other men attractive again? A long time. But I wasn't going to tell him any of that. No matter how guilty I felt, and frankly my guilt was beginning to wear a bit thin with all the hoops he was gleefully putting me through, I didn't feel guilty enough to reveal things like that.

'We could sort out the whole problem of world peace and the state of the environment and you'd still be saying it was too soon to be on kissy kissy terms with me,' I retorted.

He laughed. 'Perhaps,' he agreed cheerfully.

Just then, Phil tapped him on the shoulder to ask him if he could name three of Alan Ladd's films and he turned away from me, getting embroiled in a discussion on which were the best westerns ever made, which probably would have lasted right until the small hours of the morning if someone, quite possibly Solange who was patently uninterested in westerns or any subject that didn't include her in it somewhere, hadn't suggested that it was a lovely night for dancing under the stars.

With great enthusiasm chairs and tables were pushed back against the wall, flowerpots which couldn't be easily seen under the soft light from the candles were put safely where they couldn't be tripped over, and Solomon who was sleeping the sleep of the old and deaf in the middle of the terrace was persuaded to go and lie somewhere slightly more convenient. Janey deliberately chose tracks on the fast and lively side, saying out of the corner of her mouth as she passed me that she bloody well wasn't giving Solange a chance to do a cheek-to-cheek number with Tom, not that anyone with any sense tried to dance with him unless they were wearing protective footgear. Her grand plan backfired when Tom, who really did seem to have the proverbial two left feet, unwisely attempted an ambitious rock and roll move and stamped on Solange's lightly shod foot. It went without saying that she had to sit down in a secluded corner to recover from this appalling injury and it was necessary for Tom to absolve his conscience by sitting next to her, holding her hand, repeating how incredibly sorry he was and, as Janey said wrathfully, doing everything short of promising to kiss the poor wounded toe better.

Maybe he was, but if you ask me he was also keeping a discreet eye on his wife. I'd been talking to her while Charlie and Oscar were arguing in a good-natured way about which one of them was first in line to have a bop with her, when Jed nipped in with some nifty footwork. The next moment, he was leading her out into the middle of the terrace while Charlie and Oscar looked at each other with raised eyebrows and knowing smiles. Tom, who had been listening attentively while Solange pouted attractively in his ear, raised his head, mouth set in a straight line as he watched the pair of them give a far more skilful display of disco dancing than he had done with his partner. Seconds later his attention was back on Solange as if she was the chocolate he'd most like to find on his pillow that evening. I was the lucky recipient of the fallout from Jed's speedy manoeuvre as Charlie promptly turned to me. In the circumstances it would have been churlish to get all offended about being so obviously Charlie's second choice, especially as he went to great lengths to ham it up and assure me that he'd been dreadfully torn about who to dance with, but of course I had to understand manners insisted he asked his hostess first . . .

One of the things I had liked about George was that, unlike most of the men of my acquaintance, he enjoyed dancing as much as propping up the bar having another drink. He was always happy to take to the floor to bop around with admirable unselfconsciousness, if not an enormous amount of skill. But Charlie was in another league altogether. He was the sort of partner who can make anyone feel that she really has got a sense of rhythm and that one of these days she could even be twirling around in clouds of feathers and sequins on *Come Dancing*, showing off her fancy footwork. He modestly denied having any great skill, merely saying that he'd had a girlfriend who'd been into all forms of modern and ballroom dancing and out of necessity he'd been forced to learn how to do it properly otherwise he'd never have seen her at all. 'Or had much to talk to her about either,' he said reflectively and smiled. 'She didn't have much of a brain, but wow, did she have wonderful muscle tone!' He could also, unlike many men, dance and talk at the same time and to my pleasure it wasn't just Janey who seemed to be able to bring out his lighter side. That laugh was definitely very attractive, I told myself, as he was good-mannered enough to laugh at a weak joke of mine rather more than it could possibly have warranted.

Much too soon, and much to my irritation, my shoulder was tapped firmly by Phil who was demanding a dance as Maggie had been borne off by Hugh. I reluctantly let go of Charlie, reminding myself that he was already bagged by Sally – even if she was still hanging on George's every word.

'If you're wondering who to bestow your talents on next, you'd be doing Janey a real favour if you could amuse Solange for a while,' I said over my shoulder as Phil bore me off.

'Right, I get your message,' Charlie said cheerfully. 'But I'll see to the music first, I'm getting rather bored with this.' Minutes later an unmistakable Latin-American beat throbbed out from the speakers and he shimmied up to Solange with his hand held out invitingly, as if he wasn't prepared to take no for an answer. She looked surprised and amused but after a quick glance at Tom, maybe to check he could support the prospect of her absence, she gave Charlie her hand and got to her feet.

From the moment she and Charlie stood facing each other, his hand curled around her waist, you got the feeling that we were about to see something different here. We did. You would never have guessed that they were moving over flagstones instead of the best waxed, perfectly sprung wood, their steps were so fluid and seamless, nor that they were merely amusing themselves after dinner on a terrace in France instead of engaging in a battle of sexual wits and dalliance in some smoky dive in downtown Buenos Aires. Gradually, everyone else stopped dancing and stood back to watch as Charlie and Solange slid, slunk and slithered up and down in a tango, their steps and bodies in perfect unison.

'Wow!' said Janey as Charlie bent Solange over backwards like a piece of rubber, her legs sliding fluidly between his. 'She might be a cow but you've got to admit she can dance! So can he, for that matter,' she murmured appreciatively. 'I had no idea that Charlie could be so sexy. Will you look at *that*!' she breathed as they turned and Solange ran her knee up Charlie's thigh and smouldered into him as if a fire blanket might be needed at any moment.

'Granny used to tell me that her mother wouldn't allow her to dance the tango because it was unsuitable for young gels, might give them strange ideas,' Venetia said, her eyes almost as wide as ours. 'I can see what Great-Granny meant now!'

The three of us settled back to enjoy the spectacle, but I got the feeling that not everyone was enjoying it quite as much as we did. Sally had a slight frown between her brows, as if she couldn't quite believe what she was seeing, Phil was openly bored and was occupying himself looking for a bottle with something in it while Napier simply looked deeply displeased. Well, I suppose if it had been my wife rubbing herself up against another man like that I wouldn't have been too thrilled either.

Eventually the CD came to an end amidst a spontane-
ous burst of applause. Hugh was too busy gazing sheep-
like at Maggie to even notice the music had stopped and
Napier's fingers were flexing in a way that suggested he
could think of other ways of using his hands, possibly
around Charlie's throat. Charlie bowed over Solange's
hand, kissing it with a splendidly theatrical gesture that
brought another black frown to Napier's brow, and
laughingly refused to give us another demonstration of
his skill. 'Not that I wouldn't give almost anything for
another chance to dance with this beautiful lady,' he said
with a look at Solange, who preened in a way that wasn't
entirely suitable for a woman of her age, 'but I'm completely knackered. Couldn't do another step! Yes, Tom, a
drink would be very welcome indeed,' he added, stretching out his hand.

Naturally after a virtuoso display like that, nobody else
felt inclined to risk looking like a flat-footed fool so from
then on the dancing was a complete non-starter. But there
seemed to be a mutual feeling that it would just be too
boring to simply say our goodnights and make our way
back to our respective beds and so nobody objected
when Tom grandiloquently suggested we should all have
a nightcap to see us on our way home.

That was the problem really. If Phil hadn't had that
extra glass or two he might just have realised that while
flirting was one thing, and even a bit of surreptitious
knee-stroking could be held to be comparatively harmless, trying to kiss another woman while his girlfriend
was only a few feet in front of him was another matter
entirely. And if my mind hadn't been so dreamily full of

other things, the beat of the tango still reverberating through my pulse, I might have had the nous to realise that someone like Phil wasn't going to be put off by a fork, and I wouldn't have allowed him to give me an impromptu lesson in star-gazing. At least he held himself in check until we'd left the château and were weaving our way slowly home through the vines, so Janey and Tom weren't there to hear the flaming row that ensued when Maggie turned to see Phil lunging at me.

CHAPTER 12

I was sitting on the kitchen table with my feet comfortably propped up on a chair staring out of the window, finding for once absolutely no charm in the view, and thinking that in the circumstances it might be a good idea if I made myself scarce for a while. There was always a faint chance that if I wasn't around to rub salt into the wound, Maggie might calm down a bit, although that seemed optimistic, judging from the way she'd been going on last night.

Where could I go? The château was out. For one thing they'd all seen rather a lot of me recently; more importantly, I didn't feel up to explaining why I was currently *persona non grata* at the cottage. Especially not to Venetia, who definitely knew a good story and when to run with it. For that matter I wasn't too keen on Robert finding out that I'd been stupid enough to let myself be caught in a clinch with Phil. This wasn't the sort of countryside where you could pack a few sandwiches and a drink and take yourself off for a walk. Too hot, not enough shade. Those same factors, plus the number of hills locally and my distinctly unmuscley legs, ruled out using the elderly bicycle stored in a shed at the back of the cottage. There was always the bar in the village, but I gathered from a brief glance in at its smoky interior that it was not a place respectable women went on their own.

The door opened slowly and Oscar's fair head popped around, cautiously surveying the terrain. As he saw who was sitting on the table, he hesitated for a moment and then said in a painfully polite voice, 'Do you mind if I come in?'

'Why should I?' I asked, slightly taken aback.

He cleared his throat. 'I thought you might still be angry with me, and you know that I've never been able to face rows before I've had my first cup of tea in the morning.'

Oscar always dodges out of rows if he can help it, whatever time of day it is. Judging by his pallid face he was in greater need of Disprin than the tea pot but, as he always indignantly denies he ever has hangovers, I didn't say anything, just pushed the packet into the middle of the table where he could see it. I'd already had to use it myself, though I put my headache down to entirely justified nervous tension after the events of last night.

'Don't be silly!' I scoffed and showed I meant it by getting up off my perch and putting the kettle on for him. He was still at that hungover stage where it's difficult to hold the kettle under the tap and turn it on at the same time. 'How could I be angry with you after the way you defended me last night?'

I had been on the verge of really losing my temper, for there is only so much you can take of being accused of being the next best thing to the Whore of Babylon, when

Oscar waded in. He told Maggie to stop making so much fuss. It didn't matter whose fault it was and we should all forget about it. Phil, standing behind her looking cowed, nodded vigorously in agreement. Needless to say, Maggie had no intention of forgetting about any of it and Oscar ended up getting a torrent of abuse dumped on his own head, largely to do with his total lack of judgement in being friends with me. How could you go on bearing a grudge against someone when he's shown such bravery on your behalf; impossible when you've heard him tell Maggie that she was making more fuss than a maiden aunt at an orgy. It was after the explosion that followed that he'd felt it necessary to retire for a restorative drink or three with Jed.

I tactfully kept my back turned ladling tea into the pot while the rustling sounds of pills being emptied from their packet went on behind me. I smiled reassuringly as I put the milk jug, sugar bowl and a large gaily painted mug in the middle of the table. 'Come on, Oscar, you're my knight in shining armour! What maiden in distress ever starts banging on to her saviour about a few of his past transgressions? It'd hardly be grateful, would it?'

Oscar brightened immediately. 'I'm so glad. I hate having you cross with me, Nella.'

Yet I noticed he didn't promise not to transgress again where George and I were concerned. Maybe he had decided he couldn't go on making promises he had no intention of keeping.

'I wonder how long it'll be until I'm forgiven in other places,' he remarked, as he drained a mug of disgustingly sweet tea. He didn't look too worried about it, he knows perfectly well that no one stays angry with him for very long, but in the meantime the atmosphere wasn't going to be very pleasant. He poured out a second mug of tea, adding enough sugar to keep a dentist in Ferraris for months, then sat in silence for a few moments stirring absently. 'I've been thinking,' he said slowly. 'It's a shame to be so near the sea and never go to the beach. The Atlantic coast is supposed to be lovely too. Today looks like it might be a good day to go ... just the two of us. What do you think?'

'That's a brilliant idea!' I said fervently. 'You really are the answer to a maiden's prayer, Oscar.' He preened modestly. 'Can I call on you if I need any other dragons dealing with?'

'Now, now, Nella,' he said reprovingly. 'It's not nice to call Maggie a dragon.'

I stuck my tongue out at him. 'When do you want to leave?'

'Before she wakes up?' he asked hopefully.

I have never got ready for a trip to the beach so quickly or so silently before. It was only a matter of minutes before we were tiptoeing towards the car with a basket full of all the paraphernalia you need. 'Phew!' said Oscar once we'd put a safe distance between ourselves and the cottage. I was amused to notice that he'd driven at a faster speed than was strictly necessary for the first few kilometres. 'It feels rather like bunking off double maths at school, doesn't it?'

'Double domestic science actually,' I corrected him. 'You and I were down on the rota to do lunch today.'

The car wobbled as Oscar gave a horrified groan.

'Want to go back and do your detention?' I asked.

'Certainly not,' he said promptly. 'But it might not be such a bad idea to send you back to do yours. I'd never have asked you to join us if I'd had any idea what trouble you were going to get me into. Honestly, Nella, you *know* what Phil's like. What on earth induced you to dally around with him in the dark?'

'I wasn't dallying with him!' I said indignantly. 'He was showing me where the Great Bear is.' Oscar made a pull-the-other-one snorting noise. 'Really, I promise you. He had a telescope when he was a boy, so he knows all about the stars. It was just unfortunate he seemed to think it necessary to put his arm around my shoulders to point me in the right direction. OK, maybe I should have known with Phil what was coming,' I admitted, 'but I had this strange idea that even if he assumed the fork I dug into his thigh earlier was some form of weird come-on, he'd find his girlfriend being only five feet away a blight on any thoughts of combining star-gazing with a little slap and tickle.'

'Except you didn't slap him.'

Yeah, that had been pointed out to me, at length, by Maggie, as conclusive proof that I must have been leading poor Phil astray.

'I was trying not to draw her attention to what was happening,' I said a little sourly.

'I'm glad it was merely an error of judgement.' Oscar slowed down to let an elderly woman and her prancing miniature poodle cross the road in front of us. I stared at him in surprise. Surely he didn't really think I would have been that close to Phil from choice? 'I did wonder if

189

Maggie had got up your nose so much that you decided to tease her by flirting with her boyfriend.'

'No way!' I exclaimed. 'Even if I was careless enough of my own life to think of nicking Maggie's man, I wouldn't go near anyone who runs after everything in a skirt! You don't know where he's been, do you? I can't think how she puts up with it.'

. 'She loves him,' Oscar said simply. 'And don't ask me why someone as beautiful as her is besotted with such a slime bag, but she is. You'll put up with a lot when you love someone. You should know after Robert.'

'Robert wasn't like that,' I said. 'I admit he didn't score very high marks on the fidelity front, but he didn't have a compulsion to try and pull every woman who crossed his path. And as he only ever had one bit on the side at a time, rather than a whole crowd of them, I suppose you could say it was serial infidelity rather than multiple infidelity. Besides, it's normal to play the field in your early twenties. Phil's getting too old to go on behaving like a teenager with a testosterone overload. And he spoilt everything too,' I added with a sigh. 'It had been such a nice evening up until then.'

'Do you really think so?' asked Oscar in an offhand voice.

'Discovering what you'd been up to with George was not one of the nicer parts.'

He glanced sideways at me. 'I didn't plan it. Not really,' he amended with rare honesty. 'I admit that Hugh knew we were going to be at the cottage; in fact, he arranged his and George's own trip to coincide with it.' He raised his eyebrows. 'I gather he finds Solange altogether a bit much, and thought we'd be a tactful bolthole when he'd had enough of her. I didn't tell you because you bit my head off every time I mentioned George's name.'

'Because you insisted on going on about his good points, and George's good points are enough to make anyone have a relapse!'

Oscar ignored me. 'I was thinking what a shame it was that you weren't going to be with us, then Maggie's sister dropped out. It seemed like serendipity and too good an opportunity to pass up – that's all.'

'Seren-*you're*-quite-dipity, if you ask me,' I said. 'That's all, indeed. And it never occurred to you while you were singing the praises of the cottage and the other people I was going to meet that it might just be sensible to point out who one of those nice people was?'

He busied himself with a lot of unnecessary gear-changing. I laughed. 'It was never going to work. You should have known what my reaction would be.'

'Mmm.' He sighed mournfully. 'I'm beginning to think that George isn't the man for you after all.'

I turned to look at him in surprise. Never before have I known Oscar to voluntarily drop one of the bees in his particular bonnet. 'I suppose he is a bit staid for you, really.'

Pompous was the word I would have used, but George was Oscar's friend so I didn't. 'Well, please don't even *think* of finding me someone a little less staid,' I said in genuine alarm. 'You might not believe this, Oscar, but I'm having a really good time at the moment. I get to keep the duvet to myself, I watch the classic serial whenever I want to, I can have cornflakes for supper and there's no one sighing impatiently when I'm on the phone to my friends. There's a lot to be said for being a man-free zone and I'm in no hurry to change it.'

'I enjoy it myself sometimes,' he agreed, 'but it's nice to have someone to hold your hand at a scary movie.'

'I can do that with you,' I said, wilfully misunderstanding.

'That wasn't what I meant.'

I grinned and changed the subject. Well, sort of. 'Funny how well Sally and George got on, wasn't it?' I said in a casual voice. 'They're just perfect together, aren't they?'

'Which is a combination that would suit you perfectly,' Oscar said slyly.

'I don't know what you mean.' I spoilt my air of haughty nonchalance by saying, 'I only had a couple of dances with Charlie. He's amazingly good, isn't he? I would never have believed he could be as uninhibited as that. He seemed like a completely different person last night.'

'Mm, his moods do go up and down a bit, don't they?' Oscar murmured enigmatically, peering at a road sign. 'Can you check the map? I don't want to have to bother with the motorway the whole way and if we're going cross-country I think we need to take the next turning.'

For the next hour I was kept fully occupied with map reading. Oscar is one of those people who never willingly take the direct route from A to B, and as the vast expanse of pine forest we were traversing seemed to have masses of roads not even marked on the ruddy map my skills were stretched to their limits. And beyond. Luckily he doesn't mind getting lost occasionally; he says it adds colour to the journey.

Eventually we arrived at what Oscar had decided was to be our first port of call, a semi-mountain of sand which he informed me was the largest sand dune in Europe. Looking up at it I could well believe it. I admired it, bought a postcard to send to my mother and asked where we were going next. 'Up there,' said Oscar, pointing to the top where I could just see some ant-like figures walking around.

When I protested that I still had a slight hangover and thought it would be wiser to sit in that nice café at the bottom and have a drink while I watched him do the climb for both of us, he told me a 400-foot climb up shifting sand was exactly what the doctor ordered for convalescents, to strengthen their poor wasted limbs.

It's probably best not to describe my feelings about that climb. There were several occasions when I felt that death would be preferable to struggling on with my aching legs and heaving chest. I seriously thought about mugging a six-year-old child for her Labrador which was bounding ahead of her on its lead as if it did this climb every day and offering a very useful tow. Whenever I had the breath I rained down curses on Oscar's head; he merely took advantage of my weakened state to point out that if I kept myself fitter I wouldn't be in such trouble now. Actually I noticed that despite his regular workouts he wasn't exactly leaping up the dune-side like a mountain goat either but I didn't have the energy to say it. At long, long last we got to the top and I collapsed on the sand in an exhausted heap. Oscar patted my head indulgently and promised to buy me an *I climbed the Dune de Pyla* T-shirt as a reward for my efforts. I growled at him.

When my legs stopped feeling like jelly and I could breathe again I had to agree with a smirking Oscar, who was looking infuriatingly pleased with himself, that yes, the view over an enormous sweeping bay, dotted with sandy islands and fringed by Atlantic rollers breaking and foaming over lines of sandbanks, was absolutely spectacular. I was even large-minded enough to admit that it probably *was* worth the climb, though I refused point blank to explore a tiny little seaweed-covered beach we could just see directly below us. It was obvious even from up here that there wasn't a way around the bottom of the dune back to where the car was parked. Oscar gave in with surprisingly good grace; I suspected that he hadn't been too keen on a double climb himself.

He'd been commenting in an ominous way on the bicycle paths that went, he said admiringly, for literally hundreds of kilometres through the forest all about here. Unfortunately every second sign seemed to be a large *Location de vélos* so the, 'What a nice idea but shame we don't have any bicycles, otherwise I would have *loved* to do it' excuse was stymied before it even began. I was greatly relieved when he told me he'd heard there was a nice beach just up the road with two or three good fish restaurants, so how about a spot of lunch? Oh, and what did I think about hiring some bikes this afternoon?

Luckily even Oscar found the allure of strenuous exercise palled after a leisurely swim in the surprisingly cold sea and a lengthy lunch eating local mussels and freshly cooked crabs, and we passed the bike hire shop without a second glance as we took a post-prandial walk along the sea front.

'I wonder if Maggie's calmed down yet,' I said as I picked up a pretty ridged shell from the sand and jumped back as a larger than expected wave came rushing in towards me.

'Doubt it,' said Oscar. 'She's a girl of pretty fixed opinions. I'd give it until tomorrow at least.'

'I was afraid of that,' I said. 'Do you think we ought to have supper somewhere around here as well?'

'Can't. I'm meeting Hugh and George in Festras this evening to listen to some band who are brilliant, so Solange's daily's daughter says.'

I noted the lack of an invitation for me and turned to him with deep reproach in my eyes. How could one of my best friends think of leaving me to face Maggie on my own?

'You can always join us,' he said after a pause. 'I'd have asked you before except that I knew I'd get an earful about trying to push you and George back together, so I didn't.'

He knew perfectly well that in the circumstances I'd forgive him for sending me off in a boat down the Tunnel of Love with George – if it meant I could get out of spending the evening with Maggie. I wondered if his declaration about George not being the perfect man for me was so much hogwash and this was the beginning of an infinitely more subtle campaign. Step one; get Nella to *ask* if she might be allowed to come out and spend an evening with her supposed Mr Right.

'Can I sit between you and Hugh?' I said after a few seconds and he laughed.

At my insistence we went back to the cottage for a shower and a change of clothes, even though Oscar assured me that I looked perfectly nice and why waste time on changing. It was all right for him. He's one of those infuriating people who suit a bit of dishevelment. After a brisk sea bathe, his hair goes into a mass of fetchingly windswept curls; *my* non curls go into crusty hanks, a different matter altogether. Appearing in public looking like a barnacle-encrusted piece of rope is not one of my secret ambitions. I was feeling considerably stronger in the spirit area than I had been this morning, but all the same it was still a relief that when we got back the others were down the far end of the garden, pointedly ignoring our return. We sneaked in, washed and changed with mouse-like discretion, and were creeping out again when Charlie came in with a tray of empty glasses. Keeping my voice low, I explained that Oscar and I were going out for the evening.

'Enjoy yourselves,' he said, grinning at me conspiratorially. Charlie's smile was just as nice as his laugh, I thought, and wondered why I hadn't noticed it before. 'Going somewhere fun? You certainly look super,' he added approvingly, eyes fixed on my legs. Funny how it didn't annoy me like it did when Phil ogled me. He wagged a reproving finger. 'But watch out. You and Oscar mustn't even think of going anywhere else for the next few days. You've both been put on double kitchen duties to make up for skiving off today!'

The bar where we were meeting Hugh and George was

the same one where Janey and I had had our coffee, but there was an entirely different clientèle tonight from the housewives with shopping baskets and beret-clad farmers who had packed it on market day – had it really only been yesterday morning? This evening it was crowded with young music lovers, and not quite so young music lovers; a couple of leather-clad ex-rockers who might well have seen the Beatles in concert were just settling down with a carafe of red. Hugh and George were standing at the bar talking to two young neighbours of Napier's and looking as if they were trying hard to meld into the local scene and not stand out as tourists. Bit difficult really, what with Hugh's near-Scandinavian fairness and height and George's penetratingly English accent.

Hugh was too deep in conversation with the pretty Virginie to take much notice of our arrival, but George looked up when he saw me, kissed my cheek and said, 'I've just got to discuss something with Oscar then I'll be able to concentrate on you,' as if he was giving me the answer to every maiden's prayer. I began to wonder if I shouldn't have stayed to face Maggie after all. But Virginie's husband Etienne, who had blue eyes, a ready smile and an advanced line in flirting which entirely made up for his English being only marginally better than my French, was an excellent antidote for the sort of high blood pressure caused by your ex's delusions that you're in hot pursuit. I was distinctly sorry when he and Virginie had to rejoin their own friends, especially as George had finished whatever he had to 'discuss' with Oscar. Judging from Oscar's round eyes and attentive stance the topic hadn't been global warming or even the current state of the stock exchange.

Then Oscar, who has the knack of talking to everyone, fell into conversation with the man next to him and within seconds it seemed we'd been drawn into a group of Australian winemakers and their girlfriends who had come from Bordeaux for the music and were ready to have a thoroughly good time. As far as they were concerned, the more the merrier so I doubt we could have avoided spending the evening with them even if we'd wanted to. One of them managed to grab a table outside in the square from under the noses of all the other punters who had been hovering around like vultures waiting for the moment it became empty, and before I knew it I was squashed between a large rugby player from Queensland visiting his brother and a perpetual student from Perth dossing his way around the world for the second time.

George, looking as if he wasn't at all sure about our new friends, had vainly tried to get alongside me and had to be satisfied with a seat opposite where he could keep a watchful eye on my companions. Hugh had been appropriated by a female winemaker with a predatory expression called Kerry and led firmly down to the far end of the table. He didn't look absolutely certain whether he should be prepared to defend his honour or lie back and enjoy what was coming, but after a few minutes or so seemed to have decided the latter was the better option.

Solange's daily's daughter had been right about the music. The band, three men and a dark gypsyish-looking girl with an astonishingly throaty contralto, was very good indeed. According to the resident know-it-all who always seems to pop up amongst groups of more than eight, the band was on the verge of signing a major record contract and would soon be much too grand to play at small venues like this one. The bar's proprietor looked a very happy man as he dashed around filling orders, while in the square, people on first- and second-floor balconies leaned on wrought-iron rails and listened to the music. They didn't really have much choice. The glass doors at the front of the bar had been thrown open to allow in some cool evening air and the amplification was so loud you could probably hear the music on the ramparts.

The band wound down and took a much-needed break while the tables began to heave with those making a dash to the bar to replenish drinks. Carlton, one of the winemakers and the rugby player's brother, was taking an extensive order when he froze. 'Jeez, will you take a look at that!' he exclaimed, looking over my head at the far side of the square. 'Is that a great-looking girl, or what? Nah, not the one with the bandy legs, you great pom,' he said to Oscar, who had twisted around and was apparently looking in the wrong direction. 'Haven't you got eyes? The leggy one with all the ginger hair and the great tits,' he went on loudly, accompanying his words with some expressive gestures just in case we hadn't understood exactly what he'd meant.

Needless to say every male head swivelled as if on a single stalk. Somehow I wasn't surprised to see Venetia, wearing a short dress that indeed showed off her legs, and her tits admirably, on the far side of all the tables. She and Robert could have only just arrived, for they both had searching-for-somewhere-to-sit expressions on their faces and Venetia's bottom lip was starting to poke out sulkily as it began to dawn on her that they might have to stand.

Amid a rumble of appreciative remarks, all of which were extremely politically incorrect not to say obscene, I said, 'Do you want to meet her?'

'You *know* her?' Carlton exclaimed, looking as if all his Sundays had come at once. 'Sure thing. I've gotta see if she's as good close up!'

The next time Venetia's eyes strayed over our part of the crowd I waved vigorously. Seeing who it was, her face lightened and she began to push her way towards us, Robert following, still limping noticeably. By the time he reached us Venetia had already been appropriated by Carlton who must have decided that she *was* as good close up, and with typical Aussie resourcefulness had found another two chairs from somewhere, squeezing them in at the far end of the table in such a snug spot that when they sat down Venetia was virtually in his lap. She didn't appear to object unduly, probably because Carlton was very good-looking in a blond, blue-eyed Australian way though Robert didn't look too thrilled about his girlfriend being appropriated like this. He looked even less thrilled when he saw that the only spare chair was between George and Carlton's cousin who had little conversation but a startling ability to down prodigious quantities of lager without apparently turning a hair.

'Hello, Nella.' He glanced at me, then at George, in a maddeningly meaningful way, and said, 'I didn't think you were a fan of live music.'

'I just didn't like those terrible jazz bands you used to be so keen on,' I said, refusing to rise to the bait.

He laughed. 'They were an acquired taste, weren't they? One which I seem to have lost, I have to admit.' He looked up with thanks as a bottle of beer was thrust at him and then said, 'I hear you had an adventurous walk back to the cottage last night. Jed was telling us all about it.'

Oh bloody hell, I'd forgotten about Jed. So much for my fanciful ideas of being able to keep such a red-hot piece of scandal away from everyone at the château. But instead of smirking knowingly Robert said, 'Phil was really out of order last night. I could see what he was doing – I even got *my* leg stroked a couple of times! I'm sure it was an accident,' he added hastily, 'but it was bloody awkward to know what to do about it with Maggie sitting opposite. She'd have been even more furious if she thought Phil was after me, than she was about you! Jed says she's being pretty unpleasant.' Jed must believe in understatements. 'If she gets too bad I'm sure Janey could manage to put you up at the château.'

'I doubt it'll come to that, but thanks for the thought,' I said, feeling rather touched. Just then, George leaned forward, demanding to know in a proprietorial manner what all this was about. It took the whole time until the next set started, and part of the following interval to inform him I didn't need him to do a Tarzan act and 'deal' with Phil. I was quite capable of doing it for myself. To my annoyance neither of the males looked convinced by this.

I was in danger of becoming what George calls 'strident'

when luckily the attention was taken off me by Venetia, who came bustling up. Leaning over my shoulder, she said with great excitement, 'You'll never guess what I've just heard, Robbie! It seems that Solange—'

'Venetia, do you really think Hugh wants everyone knowing about his family business?' George interrupted.

'If it was such a secret why would Hugh have told me?' she asked reasonably. 'And anyway, you've already told Oscar, I heard him saying so!'

George suddenly found something very interesting in his glass of beer.

'Anyway,' Venetia went on, glancing at Robert and me to make sure we were attending properly, 'Hugh was saying he and George were going to have lunch at the Auberge de Vieux Chêne today – it's a lovely old place, all kitsch rococo decorations with lots of swags and mirrors and a very good cook, we should go sometime – and when they went into the dining room, who should they see sitting on one of the secluded banquettes in the corner but Solange and a companion!'

She waited expectantly. 'Surely she's allowed to go out to lunch with people, isn't she?' asked Robert.

'Sweetie, you don't lunch on one of those banquettes!' said Venetia pityingly. 'They're the sort where you can draw the curtains around the table to hide you from view if you want to be very *à deux* – if you know what I mean. Hugh said, from what he could see, the waiters were going to have to do that at any minute to spare the blushes of the other diners.'

Robert laughed. 'I find it difficult to believe that there's anything you could get up to over a dining table that would make a Frenchman blush.'

Venetia opened her mouth to reply and I intervened hastily before she could spell out exactly what could make the French blush, earning myself reproachful looks from several listening Australians. 'Maybe she was having lunch with Napier? Women do go out with their husbands sometimes.'

'Hugh couldn't see who it was, just a leg and a man's hand stroking her ... well anyway, that doesn't matter,' she said to the disappointment of a large part of her audience who obviously reckoned that even if it didn't they'd still like to know. 'But it definitely wasn't Napier. They'd left him at the château working out some figures and he'd have needed to break the land speed record to get there in front of them, let alone to quite that stage with Solange! Napier's always turned a blind eye to what she gets up to before, since he seems to think that if he allows her a bit of leeway she'll stop short at flirting, but it sounds as if she's gone too far this time. She's making a laughing stock of him, and he's too nice to be made a fool of like this,' she said furiously. 'Do you think Hugh should say something to Napier about it?'

'It's up to him, but if he goes on passing the word around like this he won't have to,' Robert said dryly.

Venetia stared at him for a moment then nodded thoughtfully. 'You're probably right. And it doesn't really matter either. Napier would never kick Solange out, more's the pity. I wonder who the man was?' Her face fell. 'You don't think it might have been Daddy, do you?' she asked in a small voice. 'I thought he just mucks around with Solange, nothing more, but he was out to lunch today too.'

Robert's eyes met mine. 'Of course it wasn't. Your father was out on business, and don't even hint to Janey that he might not have been. He'll be absolutely furious with you.'

Venetia nodded obediently. 'OK, I won't say anything to her then.'

CHAPTER 13

I got a steely look from Maggie as I stumbled downstairs for breakfast a couple of days later, but at least she didn't look on the verge of name calling so I gathered that time had done some of its healing stuff. All the same I thought it wiser to retire for the morning to the other side of the swimming pool and conceal myself behind the border of lavender bushes well away from any roving male gaze.

I'd been waylaid yesterday by Janey who informed me that Miles and Adam had decided to help by doing the washing up. Unfortunately this included all of Tom's post which had just been placed on the table next to his plate. She'd decided the best way of improving the twins' chances of surviving until sundown would be to get them out of Daddy's reach so she was going to take them for a picnic on the edges of a nearby lake. Would I like to go with them? It was a really nice place and she'd love some company . . . When I said I reckoned that, as it was Delphine's day off, she was actually looking for another warder to help keep control of the boys, she unblushingly agreed there was an element of that too. We had lain in the shade of a pine tree nattering while the twins played on a small sandy beach and didn't get into too much trouble, all things considered. They only fell in a couple of times. The water wasn't very deep so it hadn't been difficult to fish them out, and as they weren't wearing anything all we had to do was shake the drops off and let them loose again.

It occurred to me as I settled down behind the lavender with my book that, one way and another, this holiday had hardly been the peaceful type that's usually recommended for convalescents. I rolled over on my back and closed my eyes for a moment, thinking that at least it hadn't been boring.

I jumped as a shadow fell across my face and my eyes flew open to see a black silhouette against the bright blue sky. God, what now? 'Oh, it's you!' I said in relief as I saw it was Charlie.

'Sorry if I startled you,' he said. 'I just came to tell you Venetia's been down to say that Tom's got the bit between his teeth about this match tomorrow and has summoned the others for an hour's cricket practice.'

I propped myself up on my elbows. 'I thought Tom reckoned it went against the essential amateur nature of the match to do anything so serious as practice.'

'Yeah, but Maggie's offered to do the scoring and as she's never done it before, Tom wants to give her a run-through before the big day.' Charlie grinned. 'That was his excuse for getting in a sneaky bit of practice, and he's sticking to it.'

Now he'd delivered his message, I expected him to take his leave and join the cricketing party, but he glanced down and said, 'I don't feel like walking all the way up to the château. It'd be much nicer to stay here and chat to you – if you don't mind being disturbed from your book.'

Of course I didn't. Not by him anyway. 'The book isn't even very interesting,' I said untruthfully, 'but aren't you an essential part of the team?'

He shook his head. 'God no! I went to one of those progressive schools where competitive sport is thought to be bad for the juvenile psyche, so the nearest I've ever got to playing cricket is throwing balls for my eight-year-old godson to practise his batting. Unfortunately the staff seemed to think it would be bad for *their* psyches if they did anything so strenuous as actually teach us anything, so I left after seven very expensive years a happy well-adjusted chap without any of the basic qualifications that you need to get a decent job these days.'

I was startled by the bitter tone in his voice. 'But Sally said that you've just started something new which could really lead somewhere,' I said.

'Sal's in PR. She's conditioned to putting the best spin on everything,' he said with a wry smile as he pulled off his T-shirt and flopped down on the grass beside me. 'My last job promised me great things and went precisely nowhere, but this one might turn out OK, I suppose. I hope so. It'd be nice to earn more than my girlfriend for once.'

I was prepared to bet anything that he earned more than me, I thought, eyeing him covertly and noting how brown his torso was, a result of the olive-tinged skin that went with his dark eyes and hair. No matter how hard the pundits try to push pale skin as the newest fashion statement there's no denying that a brown stomach is considerably more attractive than a white one. And his stomach was a good one too, not a six-pack or anything, just nice and firm . . . This sort of thought was leading me precisely nowhere, I told myself sternly. I might be merely taking an appreciative look, the sort of thing men do all the time, but wasn't I already in enough trouble with the female duo who ruled this cottage without laying myself open to accusations of making a play for *both* their boyfriends in turn? Besides, I was coming to rather like Sally, who had proved that she wasn't entirely under Maggie's thumb by hissing that if Maggie remained daggers drawn with every woman Phil had tried to kiss since they had been going out, she would soon be on non-speaks with most of the female population of London.

'Are we the only two in the cottage who don't have an official role to play in this great event tomorrow?' I asked, forcing my eyes away from Charlie's physique to contemplate a much less interesting small climbing rose on the cottage wall.

'Well, I understand Jed's being put on as eleventh man if Tom gets really, really desperate – he's planning to try Lily out first – but otherwise it looks to me as if the only thing Jed's doing is casting longing looks at Janey. Mind you, improving the morale of the team captain's lady is a very important role indeed.'

'Do you think it really *does* improve her morale?' I asked.

'I doubt it somehow,' he said slowly. 'I wouldn't like to make a comment on the state of Tom and Janey's marriage, but I reckon Janey's far too astute to import a lover, if she actually had one, right under her husband's nose. And she certainly wouldn't be insane enough to do it when Venetia was here!'

I laughed and he added, 'Of course, the reason Venetia thinks Janey might do that is because it's exactly the sort of cock-eyed thing she'd do herself! Long on looks, that girl, but short on brains. Just the way I like 'em,' he said in such a deadpan voice that for a moment I was taken in – until I saw the little smile on his mouth. 'As for the others, Sal's keeping Maggie company, otherwise known as a chance to yak, and Oscar's supposed to be showing Tom how good he is, once he stops fussing about whether he can play in his white jeans. He thinks they might be too tight for strenuous exercise.'

I thought of Oscar's white jeans. 'Well, he could wear them – it just depends on how keen he is to keep his options open as far as fathering children is concerned. He'd better borrow something from Tom and risk the fit not being absolutely perfect.' I picked a couple of daisies off the lawn beside me and started slitting the stems to make a daisy chain. 'I didn't know that Phil was going to play.'

'He isn't – he's just tethered to Maggie's right ankle,' Charlie said cheerfully and with a mischievous look at me. 'For some strange reason she didn't feel like leaving him here when she wasn't around to watch over him.'

I groaned. 'Oh God! Is she still furious with me?'

He thought for a moment. 'Not furious precisely,' he said carefully, which didn't do an awful lot to cheer me up. 'I just wouldn't suggest having another cuddle with

Phil in her presence, that's all.'

I sent him a dirty look and he grinned. 'Don't worry, she'll get over it.' I noticed that he hadn't cared to put a time limit on this statement. 'But listen, when I was getting the bread this morning I saw a poster for a *foire de broccante* -you know, an antiques fair – in Roaillac. Shall we go this afternoon?'

'What, just the two of us?' I asked, the words slipping out before I could stop myself. God, I sounded like a gauche teenager, I thought in disgust, bending my head to concentrate furiously on my daisy chain so he couldn't see my red face.

'I doubt Sal will want to come, it's not her sort of thing,' he said easily. Was I imagining the unspoken 'we don't really have that much in common'? He went on, 'And if you're not here, Phil won't be forced to come along and watch cricket practice, so if you're feeling generous you could look on it as an act of kindness.'

So this invitation was just a form of male solidarity, I thought, feeling slightly disappointed. It didn't stop me accepting though. I fancied spending an afternoon wandering around with Charlie, and I like antique fairs too. I might even find a wedding present there for my sister who was getting married in the autumn. Both Min and her intended had got houses so they were already well stocked up with the normal wedding-present fodder of china, blankets and quiche dishes, so finding something wasn't easy, especially as Min had waved an airy hand and said, 'Something beautiful' when I asked her what she'd like. An amusing little *quelque chose* picked up from an antiques fair in France could be just the ticket.

Maggie, Phil and Oscar arrived back in time for lunch, full of horror stories about Tom's mood and congratulations for Charlie on having the sense to stay out of the firing line. At least Phil and Oscar were; Maggie was too busy checking Charlie for lipstick marks and preparing a report for later.

Apparently Tom had had a phone call to say his fifth best batsman had a poisoned finger and couldn't play, the third best had received a non-refusable summons from his mother-in-law to attend a family lunch tomorrow, and Tom had seen any hopes he might have had of getting even with Napier for trying to pass George off as a 'reasonable' player fading inexorably away. Besides himself, his only decent batsman was Oscar; he was gloomily afraid he was going to have to include Jed in his team – Janey had already been co-opted – and had even been driven to making enquiries along the lines of was I any good at fielding and could I throw a ball? With admirable self-restraint Robert said he could personally assure him that my throwing skills were zero.

It was best to draw a veil over what Tom said when he discovered Phil didn't play cricket at all. 'A waste of space' was the only repeatable one, Phil sniggered. As for Tom's reaction when he'd yelled for Venetia to come out and help field and she'd retorted that she'd just done her nails and didn't want to smudge her varnish ... Things went downhill a little more when Maggie thought Robert was swotting at a mosquito rather than signalling four runs, and Tom had bawled that she should bloody well know it was far too early in the day for mosquitoes to come out; besides, they didn't have ruddy mosquitoes up here anyway! The final straw had been when Solomon had waddled deafly onto the pitch, obeyed his Labrador instincts by retrieving the ball and had made off with it at a remarkable pace for someone so old and arthritic. Phil said he and Oscar had been laughing so much they had failed to give chase until Solomon was well away in the laurel hedge. That hadn't done anything for the team captain's blood pressure either.

Tom had only been saved from an explosive coronary by the arrival, just in time for a pre-lunch drink, of a carload of Australians; *cricket-playing* Australians. In between whispering sweet nothings in Venetia's ear, Carlton had let slip that he was a bit of a cracker at the old bat and ball, as were a couple of his mates. With commendable initiative Venetia had promptly invited them all to come over and try out their paces though she'd forgotten to tell her father and thus save everybody a very trying morning. She had also forgotten to inform Janey that she'd invited an unknown quantity of beer-drinking Aussies for lunch. Sally had offered to help Janey do a loaves and fishes act at five minutes' notice while Maggie and Oscar were allowed to leave, albeit under strict orders to return for more intensive training this afternoon.

Maggie hung around making one excuse after another to delay returning to her lesson in scoring until she was absolutely sure that Charlie and I really were going to be out for most of the afternoon. She'd been pretty pointed in her questions about how long we were going to be, though these were disguised as queries about whether we'd be back in time to bring home some decent pâtisseries for tea.

Fortunately the first stall we saw was selling home-made cakes and 'things' made of flying leaves of pastry interleaved with some gooey paste or other. They looked very good so, even though I didn't have a clue what they were, I bought one, hoping this offering would take me another step on the road to social rehabilitation. Charlie was more taken with the next-door stand, which was selling nineteen different sorts of armagnac of varying vintages, all of them made at home by the producer who was extremely generous about offering tastes. Somewhat reluctantly Charlie agreed it probably wouldn't be a good idea to sample all nineteen, and allowed himself to be steered away from such temptation. Not before he'd bought two of the nineteen varieties though.

The main part of the fair had been set up in a large market square dominated by a magnificent twin-towered and flying-buttressed church and was already packed with people moving slowly between the long lines of stalls. The really superior traders with the serious antiques, with serious prices to match, were in a long green and white tent in front of the church. We didn't spend too long in there as the prices made me wince, even more so when I imagined tripping over the uneven flooring and taking a pearler onto one of the tables laden with Chinese porcelain. I didn't breathe properly again until we were in the safety of the outdoors. The stalls outside, sheltered from the sun by awnings, were much more my sort of thing. Their contents ranged from the frankly junk-like, such as rusty pans or bent spoons that someone was hoping to pass off as 'antique', to second-hand and antiquarian books, old dolls and children's toys in various states of disrepair to stacks of pictures of very varied styles and quality. It was a junk-shop junkie's paradise.

We meandered around, rifling through boxes of old postcards and seeing if we could find one of the château, turning up our noses at frankly dreadful collections of china, stopping to look at hundreds of old doorhandles jumbled together in a great big heap before we gave up our place to a man who had taken a handle out of his pocket and was trying to find a pair for it. I didn't see anything that might do for Min and Francis, though I fell in love with a large wooden pig that had once advertised a charcuterie and Charlie was particularly keen on a fine old armoire that he said would look marvellous in his high-ceilinged flat. Sadly, even with the best will in the world, it was much too large to go in the back of his car.

We had seen nearly everything, had a drink and I'd got to that object-blind stage where a swim in the pool seems infinitely more enticing than any amount of fine china when Charlie, who seemed to have an inexhaustible appetite for going through boxes filled with mystery objects, pointed at a line of stalls we hadn't investigated yet and said, 'Shall we just take a butchers at this lot before we go?'

'OK,' I said slightly wearily, and while he began to examine a pile of leather-bound books, I started to sort through a stack of pictures resting haphazardly against a wall. I knew the moment I saw the pair of watercolours in heavy old ornate gold frames, one of vinepickers returning home after a day's work, the other of an extremely congenial *fête du vin* to celebrate all the grapes being in, that they were exactly what Min would like. I knew because our tastes are very similar – in art, not in men – and I wanted them for myself. I sat back on my heels, considering the little price tag stuck to the top of one and doing a conversion from francs to pounds, wondering if I could afford them. I couldn't, not even if I bargained the stall-owner down, but I knew my brother wouldn't have got Min a present yet. Nick always leaves everything to the last minute, so if we went halves . . .

I havered nervously, and got Charlie's attention for long enough to ask what he thought of them.

He pursed his lips. 'Not my taste,' he said frankly. 'Too pretty-pretty and the frames are in terrible condition. Look,' he touched a place where the ornate gilding had flaked off to show the plaster underneath, 'and there,' indicating a curling acanthus leaf that had lost its tip.

'But the frames are still lovely even if they are worn, and anyway that's one of the things Min will like about them,' I protested, wondering if I had no taste or if it was just that his taste ran to minimally furnished loft apartments and uncluttered brick walls. 'She's a great fan of the Miss Havisham style of interior design; the more tatty and distressed the better, though she draws the line at actual dirt.'

He shrugged. 'You know your sister's taste. They'll certainly make a different sort of wedding present.' It didn't sound as if he thought this was entirely a good thing. 'But if you don't mind me asking, have you thought of how you're going to pay for them?' He bent down to look at the price. 'Even if you manage to knock that down a bit it's still one hell of a lot of money to get out on your credit card, unless you've got a gold one.'

Of course I didn't. And I had a nasty feeling that if I did try to make a withdrawal of that size on my long-suffering credit card, the machine would first make an embarrassingly loud raspberry, audible over the whole square, before saying something along the lines of: 'You are already over your limit. Would you like to pay in for once rather than take out?'

Since I'd heard Charlie refer more than once to how little his new job paid him, it wasn't likely that he would be able to advance me anything. I was wondering whether it would be pushing my friendship with him too far to ask if he'd drive me back to the château so that I could beg Oscar for a loan when I heard a cheerful voice say, 'Hello, Nella. I wondered if we were going to meet up with you. Oscar said you'd gone antique hunting.'

I turned to see Janey, wearing a soft pastel printed sundress with a hat pushed on the back of her head, and looking uncannily as if she were on her way to a garden party; except that the accepted accessory for a garden party isn't usually a pushchair containing a small and grubby child beaming seraphically through a thick covering of ice cream. She was missing something though. 'Um, aren't you supposed to have two of those,' I asked, pointing at the filthy face.

'She used to, but she gave the other up for adoption,' said Robert from behind her.

Janey made a face. 'I was tempted, I promise you, but I wouldn't have stuck with just giving away the one. We had to separate them for a while. They started an ice-cream fight,' she said meaningfully. So that explained

216

why there was liquid strawberry ice cream dripping off the twin's ear. 'Jed was noble enough to take Miles off to look at something else on the other side of the square.'

'I note that you don't appear to possess the same degree of nobility,' I said to Robert.

'Unfortunately I just don't have Jed's way with children,' he said with a solemn face. 'And Adam prefers to stay with his mother.'

Adam's mother didn't look as if she thought Adam's opinion in the matter should be taken into account. 'But aren't you supposed to be clad in top-to-toe white and standing ready to catch a cricket ball?' I asked her. 'How come you've been given leave to attend anything so frivolous as a *foire de broccante*?'

'Alas!' Janey heaved an unconvincing sigh. 'My place in the team was given to one of the Australians and I was so broken-hearted that I simply had to get away. In other words, I reckoned if I had to hear *another* word about cricket I'd have hysterics so I took the opportunity to hoof it while Tom's back was turned. Have you seen anything you like yet?'

'Mm, I'm thinking about those,' I said, pointing at the two pictures.

'Oh, aren't they pretty! You are clever to have found them!' she exclaimed and called Robert to come over and see.

'I know they're only the sort of thing that ladies who liked to amuse themselves with a little light sketching used to turn out by the dozen,' I said defensively as he bent down to have a closer look, 'but they'd make a perfect wedding present for my sister.'

'They're very nice,' he said as he straightened up. 'If they were really done by an amateur lady artist she had a good deal of talent. The drawing is superb. You've got a good eye, Nella. I'd snap them up if I were you.'

'I'm still making up my mind if I can afford them,' I said, delighted that my taste had been approved. Robert and I seemed to have come a long way in civility terms since the beginning of the week. Had he decided at last that all the scores really were settled? I wondered hopefully.

'What's the problem?' asked Janey, and when I told her she said, 'Easy as pie. I'll pay for them and you can give me a cheque to put in my English bank account.' Then, when I hesitated; 'Go on – I wouldn't offer if I didn't mean it.'

So I approached the stall-owner to ask him in my rather indifferent French if that was his best price, my fluency, or lack of it, not helped by the three listeners to my atrocious accent. The stallholder must have been a very bad judge of character, or unduly influenced by Janey's garden-party attire, for he decided in spite of all evidence to the contrary that I must be a feelthy riche Anglaise, and unblushingly put the price up. Well, I suppose it was a better price for him. Ten minutes later I'd managed to convince him that I wasn't a dot com millionairess, or that even if I was my pockets were sewn up very tightly, and the price began to inch down slowly. When we eventually agreed an amount he began to address Charlie in a torrent of machine-gun-like French of which I could only understand a few words, but the gist was that Charlie's girlfriend was a hard woman and that he hoped for Charlie's sake she was as efficient in the kitchen as she was in depriving a poor working man of his right to a modest profit. Charlie and I looked suitably unmoved by this pathetic tale and the stallholder sighed dramatically, grinned hugely and shook my hand, so I gathered that he hadn't made such a disastrous loss after all.

'But Oscar said you're going back on the train,' said Janey. 'How on earth are you going to manage with those?' The stallholder was wrapping the pictures up in several sheets of the local free paper and making two unwieldy parcels that wouldn't be easy to carry comfortably.

'I'm sure Oscar won't mind taking them back for me,' I said with a little more certainty than I actually felt. The pictures were quite large and Oscar's car, though fast, was small and he'd already agreed to take the suitcase I didn't need at the party for me, so he might not appreciate a whole lot of extra luggage. However, Janey's attention had been seized by the stallholder who was trying to convince her that as she was paying by cheque he was obliged to add VAT to the price.

'What's this about leaving early?' Charlie demanded in a low voice and with a flattering degree of regret. 'It's not anything to do with Phil, is it?'

I laughed. 'You don't really think I'm spineless enough to let myself be driven away by him, do you?'

He smiled. 'Not Phil, no. Maggie, possibly? Are you getting out of the line of fire?'

'No, it's nothing to do with that. It's my grandparents' diamond wedding anniversary, and they'd be terribly hurt if I didn't make it back for the party.'

'At least you're cutting your holiday short for a fun reason, not for something like a pressing problem at work.'

'If I'd obeyed instructions and furnished myself with a mobile so I could be contacted "just in case", I daresay I'd have been told to hotfoot it back to London already,' I retorted. 'My boss doesn't approve of his subordinates going on holiday.'

'Sounds like exactly the same reason I don't check my messages,' said Charlie with a smile of shared complicity. 'So when are you leaving – Friday?'

'Thursday. The party's in the Lake District and as it's such a long way to go we're making a real weekend of it. I'm going straight to my parents', and then we'll drive up together on Friday morning.'

Charlie touched my arm softly. 'What a shame,' he said. 'I've been really enjoying myself and—'

Whatever else he was going to say was cut short by Janey turning around and telling me I could now take possession of my purchases. The VAT question had been sorted out to her satisfaction and she'd also successfully fielded an attempt to put an extra 2 per cent on the price for bank charges when cashing the cheque. She fixed the stallholder with a stern eye and suggested he change banks since hers didn't charge for cheques. Unabashed, he grinned and pressed his card into her hands, telling her to come and see him at his shop where he had many more beautiful things and what a pleasure it was doing business with two such lovely ladies. She nodded somewhat perfunctorily, muttering that Jed had said he'd only take Miles off for five minutes and they'd been gone for much longer than that. 'I don't normally find anybody keen to hang on to either of the twins longer than strictly necessary,' she said, looking worried. 'I hope nothing's happened.'

'Doubt it,' Robert said easily. 'They're probably laying waste to the sweetie stall, the one with the saucer-sized lollipops over there.' He turned to look with professional disapproval at my untidily wrapped packages and said, 'Those frames are much too fragile to be wrapped just in newspaper. I've got some spare cardboard sleeves for transporting pictures in the back of my car. You can have a couple if you like.'

'Thanks, that's really kind of you.'

He shrugged, eyes wandering around the crowd. 'I hate to see nice things being damaged,' he said in an offhand voice as he waved vigorously, and Jed, on the other side of the square, lifted a hand in response.

True to Robert's predictions Janey's missing fledgling was returned sucking a lollipop half the size of his face. Jed can't have been as ignorant of children as he claimed for he'd avoided war breaking out by buying a similar one for Adam. Janey celebrated his safe return by buying a jug shaped like a duck which made a glugging sound when the water was poured out. 'Though I'd better not tell Tom I've bought it just yet,' she said to me as the jug was being wrapped up in layers of paper. 'He's being really tiresome about money at the moment. I hope it's just taking this wretched cricket match too seriously that's the matter and not something to do with the bank. Not that he'd tell me if it was,' she added in such a sour voice that I couldn't help staring at her in surprise.

'One of the problems of marrying a man with a daughter virtually your age is that he tends to treat you both the same when it comes to doling out the pocket money! And he's about as informative about the mechanics of the business as he would be to a six year old too. "Don't bother your little head about this, darling. Leave the hard stuff to the grown-ups." What makes it even more annoying is that I know considerably more about basic finance than he does. I filled in my own tax returns for years, so at the very least I could take an intelligent interest in what's going on, if not actually offer him a bit of advice.' The stallholder touched her arm handing over the parcel, and she smiled ruefully. 'Still, all things considered, I infinitely prefer a man who is over-protective to one who thinks he ought to stay in bed all day while I earn the money, like Tom's predecessor did.' She looked around. 'I wonder where the men have got to? The beer stall, I daresay.'

She was right, though as they'd had the consideration to take the twins with them she declared they were forgiven. 'The final straw which drove Tom's stress levels to the point where I was about to ring Dr Dupont and demand valium – for me, though I might have allowed him some too – was when Delphine announced this morning that she thought she might not be able to work tomorrow. Some family crisis or the other. I thought Tom was going to explode! Luckily it's all been sorted out. I couldn't cope with having to take the twins to Solange's – it isn't a child-friendly sort of place. You'll see what I mean tomorrow.'

'I still don't think I should be going,' I said. I had a

nasty feeling that Oscar had done nothing to disabuse George from his mistaken notion that I was desperate to get my mitts back on his person again. Turning up to watch him do his bowling magic certainly wasn't going to help throw cold water on that particular idea. And as far as entertainment went I'd rather watch a lawn-mowing contest than cricket, though I had sense enough not to mention this to Tom, or Oscar, or any of the other cricket fanatics who had recently emerged from the woodwork. The final niggle was that I felt sure that, with two cricket teams and their partners to feed, Solange had quite enough guests already without adding extraneous hangers-on.

That particular objection was ignored completely by Janey, who wasn't in the *least* troubled about the thought of Solange being put to any extra trouble. I could see I was on a losing wicket here, and said so.

Janey aimed a mock punch at me. 'That was a terrible pun! For that you're definitely coming – and no excuses!'

CHAPTER 14

Venetia had given us instructions for her special route to Château Vielleroche which she swore was much quicker than the one shown on Oscar's touring map of France. Perhaps it would have been – if she hadn't neglected to say we were supposed to turn right by the church with the separate bell tower instead of going straight on. We were already late because Oscar had caught sight of his reflection kitted out in Tom's second-best cricketing trousers, and had a sartorial crisis of an intensity that would have done justice to any teenager going to her first proper party. With a skill honed by several years in advertising, I'd lied through my teeth and eventually managed to persuade him he looked fine, though I'd had to threaten Charlie and Jed with disembowelling if they dared to mention that the trousers were also too short as well as being too wide – a detail that seemed to have escaped Oscar's attention so far.

Thanks to Venetia's instructions we'd ended up by going on and on down a road that gradually became narrower and narrower, then turned into a semi-rutted track before it ended in the back entrance to a farmyard and some very surprised-looking chickens. Naturally the back-seat passengers knew much better than either the official map reader (me) or the driver (Oscar) how to retrace our steps and find Château Vielleroche, and tempers were beginning to get just a little frayed by the time an elderly lady on an even older bicycle was able to give us proper directions.

Venetia had begged us not to be late. Daddy's nerves wouldn't be able to stand it, she reported, nor hers for that matter, given the mood he was in. The advent of the Australians hadn't been an unalloyed success. Carlton, who was supposed to be such a cracker at cricket, had been suffering from co-ordination problems due to the number of tinnies he'd necked the night before and had not acquitted himself with honour, though Tom had grudgingly admitted that at least he knew how to hold the bat properly. Matt, the perpetual student, just wasn't terribly good and Carlton's rugby-playing brother Oz's game was ... rugby. But at least they were better than Janey, and it meant that Tom could field a full side, even if we all wondered whether this match was going to be a defeat, a walk-over or a complete rout.

According to Janey and Tom, there had been a battle royal when Napier and Solange started looking for somewhere to buy. Napier, who took the making of wine very seriously indeed, had concentrated on finding a superb vineyard and reckoned the living accommodation didn't really matter as long as it was weatherproof. He had been particularly taken with a magnificent property that produced world-renowned wine, had absolutely up-to-the-minute wine-making facilities –

and a modern four-bedroom bungalow with white tiled floors for the *patron* and his missis. Solange had put her elegant size 5 foot down firmly and declared that Napier needn't think she was living in some hovel, even a modern one with electric blinds; she wanted a decent house. And Madame got one.

The château was as exquisite and well cared for as Solange herself, straight out of a fairy tale with its pointy roof, mullioned windows and double set of stone steps that curled up to a huge black oak front door. At any moment you expected to see Rapunzel lean out of a window at the top of one of the towers and let her hair down to her waiting prince, and even the high hedge on either side of the elaborately curlicued iron gates could have been the one that kept Sleeping Beauty safe from all those predatory suitors until the right prince came along.

We followed the noise around to an immaculately tended garden at the back, and I could see straight away why Janey had been nervous about letting the twins loose in such perfection. The garden was so immaculate that even the weeds looked as if they'd been pruned into shape. About thirty people stood around on the grass chatting; the men, naturally far outnumbering the women, wore a variety of clothing that at times bore only the vaguest resemblance to normal cricketing gear. Oscar looked positively immaculate compared to one man whose stomach attested to his love of good food and stuck out proudly over a pair of originally white Bermudas, or to Carlton and Oz, sporting garments more suited to surfing at Bondi than cricket at a château in France.

While Jed went off to take photographs for the story he was doing on the match for one of the colour supplements, George bounded forward to give me an unwanted kiss on the mouth and Napier followed, saying in a genial voice, 'Glad to see you all at last. Tom was getting quite worried, you know. Thought you might be a no-show and I gather he certainly can't afford to be without *you*, Oscar.' Napier smirked with the air of someone who knows he's already got everything sewn up. That probably meant the man in the Bermudas was on our team. (He was and, as he told me later, had never yet managed to hit the ball, though he claimed to be quite useful as a fielder.)

'Poor old Tom. He's had a bit of a problem getting a team together this year, so I'm glad he's got at least one player he can rely on,' Napier went on insincerely, grinning like a crocodile as he doled out glasses of wine to Charlie and Phil who fell on them as if hairs of the dog were going out of fashion. They'd been a little over-enthusiastic last night about sampling Charlie's liquid purchases from the *foire*. It would have been positively unfriendly, they claimed, not to have had a farewell drink with Jed who was leaving for somewhere on the Loire right after the cricket match.

Napier looked slightly startled when their two glasses were held out for refills before he'd even finished handing out the firsts. The wine was much better than Tom's rather liverish comments had led us to expect, but I daresay those two would have downed it in one even if it had tasted of petrol. 'Well well, you two aren't playing so I don't suppose Tom can accuse me of trying to nobble his team,' he said with a chuckle that clearly implied he didn't need to bother and wandered off to attend to some of his other guests.

'Presumably Hugh decided against telling Napier that Solange was having an off-the-menu appetiser at lunch the other day?' I said as she touched Napier's arm in the time-honoured way of the wife who has absolutely nothing to hide.

'Well, of course,' George said seriously. 'You can't worry the captain just before a match. It might put him off his stroke.'

Mm, well, I could think of a few other good reasons not to tell a husband about his wife's misbehaviour but there you are. The result was the same. Napier was wandering around as if he didn't have a care in the world and distributing bonhomie like a man who reckons that he's already got the match in the bag. Meanwhile, Solange flitted around like a bird of paradise in a vividly printed dress that clung to every one of her well-maintained curves like a second skin, though it was noticeable to everyone, except apparently her husband, that the perch she chose to alight on most frequently was Tom's. For once Tom had his mind on more important matters than flirting and was keener to discuss the final batting order with his number two bat than to whisper sweet nothings in Solange's ear. Eventually she flounced off, and could be heard a few minutes later venting her frustration on one of her army of helpers who were streaming like a line of soldier ants from the kitchen to the tables with dishes for the first course.

You had to hand it to her; she might be the fastest off

the blocks when it came to snuggling up to someone else's husband, but she certainly knew how to put on a good spread. She had set up four or five long tables under the shade of a row of chestnut trees. The tables were wonderfully laid out with intricately folded napkins and tiny little flower arrangements, but what I found most impressive was that Solange appeared to have a set of matching china and napkins for more than forty people and hadn't had to resort to begging, borrowing or stealing anything. Even the chairs were a matching set. She had turned down Janey's offer to help with the food, apart from requesting a couple of her special puddings. Janey was *so* talented at desserts, Solange had cooed, unlike her, but of course she didn't really know what went into making a good dessert since she never touched sweet things. This information was accompanied, Janey later reported, by a meaningful look at her waistline.

Solange clapped her hands and announced that lunch was served and we should sit where we liked. Despite this apparent spontaneity I couldn't help noticing the masterly way she peeled off all the most entertaining men to come and sit at her own table. She'd included Tom in that number but punished him for his former neglect by sending him down to the Siberia at the bottom of the table while a heavy-featured *négociant* from Bordeaux and Robert were assigned the favoured places on either side of her. I'd had my elbow firmly grasped by George who bore me off to sit by him, though I was amused to see that Sally had been just as quick off the mark in claiming the place on his other side. She was looking very pretty today, too; the sun had brought out red lights in her hair and dusted a light smattering of freckles over her nose and chest like a sprinkling of that exorbitantly expensive gold sparkle stuff that gets sold at Christmas each year. When I caught George giving her a quick sideways look, I decided that it wouldn't be long before he reverted to his belief that we were not the perfect couple and realise that there were plenty of more suitable fish in the sea.

At a particularly loud burst of laughter from the table behind us he asked me with a slightly superior air, 'Aren't those men sitting with Venetia two of the Australians who latched on to us the other night?' I was surprised he hadn't realised before. Carlton's idea of the right things to say when chatting up a Sheila must have been audible to half the garden. Luckily Venetia didn't appear to mind being compared to a wombat. 'Tom must be really desperate if he's had to resort to using her casual pick-ups in his team,' he said with a hearty laugh.

'He is. Solomon's better at fielding – or should I say retrieving the ball – but Tom thought that Carlton just made it on the batting,' I said, dead pan. George looked at me as if I was quite mad, and turned to talk to Sally.

When the last cups of inky strong coffee in tiny cups had been served and cleared away, Napier announced that the fun part of the afternoon was about to begin. Actually a good proportion of the party, including some of the players, looked as if they would infinitely prefer to stretch out on a long chair and sleep off Solange's immaculately presented lunch rather than watch leather hitting willow (or missing it as the case might be). No one had the courage to admit it so we all dutifully removed ourselves to the cricket pitch, a field that was normally used for sheep, and arranged ourselves beneath the trees along one side of it. Napier's gardener had been on tractor-mowing duty every day for the last fortnight, hence the grass was in an immaculate condition, but some of the other accoutrements were not of the type usually seen at top-class cricket matches. For a scoreboard they were using a blackboard and easel pinched off Napier's opening batsman's five-year-old daughter. Since it was too small to see easily, every so often Sally had to walk around the spectators holding up cards marked with the runs and wickets taken as if she were a bellhop in a hotel foyer.

I can't honestly say that I paid much attention to the progress of the cricket match, even though I knew I was undoubtedly going to be asked by more than one person if I'd seen the brilliant way he'd hit this or bowled that. Fortunately, I had gained enough experience of making equivocal answers to questions of this sort last season while not watching George's genius at work to be fairly confident that I could manage to conceal that I'd spent most of this titanic match stretched out peacefully under a tree chatting to various like-minded souls. Even so, there were times when I couldn't avoid noticing what was going on, like when Oscar and the man with the large stomach were both running to get the ball; the fat man had a surprising turn of speed which was where Oscar made his mistake. He nearly got steamrollered. Or when, just as Hugh was about to go in to bat, Janey leaned forward and whispered something in Kerry's ear. With much giggling Kerry moved forward to a sunny spot on the edge of the pitch and took off her blouse, before slowly anointing herself with suntan cream. Even from this distance we could see Hugh's head swivel around and his eyes goggle frantically.

Hugh didn't get a very high score.

'We should have got you to do that too, but it's too late now,' said Sally as George, all padded up and raring to go, strode purposefully onto the pitch.

'Wouldn't have worked. George takes the game far too seriously to be sidetracked by a mere woman. And even if he could be distracted, it wouldn't be me who could do it.' I paused deliberately. 'Far more likely to be you.'

'Me?' she said, and stared out at the pitch as if she was committing every detail of how George was holding his bat to memory. Maybe she was.

'Judging by the way he was eyeing you up during lunch, yes, you.'

'Oh,' she said. 'I'm sorry.'

'Why should I mind?' I asked cheerfully. 'Has Oscar been filling you in on how George and I go together as naturally as Astaire and Rogers?'

'Well, sort of.'

'Just remember they broke up. And *didn't* get back together again.'

She raised her head and looked at me with a conspiratorial grin. Then she sort of shook herself and said in a prim little voice, 'Not that it matters of course who George is or isn't going out with, though it's very flattering if he really does fancy me. I've got my hands full with Charlie.'

That was a strange way of putting it. 'Mm, sure,' I agreed, 'but it's always nice to know you can still wow the odd man, isn't it? Not that George is odd of course,' I added hastily. 'In fact, he's positively . . .' I'd been about to say conventional, but decided another adjective would be more appealing. I floundered around. 'Normal,' I ended up with, thinking that didn't seem very satisfactory either.

Luckily Sally didn't appear to notice for Maggie was waving frantically for her to come over and she got up with a vague, 'See you later, Nella.' But it was said in a much more cordial tone than usual. I watched her go hoping that I'd managed to throw some seeds on fertile ground anyway. At least she was perfectly placed as a cry of 'Howzat!' arose and Robert raised his arm to indicate that George was out. George looked pretty peeved about it too and I thought for a moment that he was about to commit the unpardonable sin of arguing with the umpire. Instead he stumped off, looking martyred. I hope he found the consolatory hand Sally laid on his arm as he left the pitch some balm to his wounded feelings.

Despite George's early dismissal the Château du Pré team had a formidable score to beat when they took to the pitch after tea. Tom looked determined to do his best but already bore a defeated air, especially after his first two batsmen fell victim to George's lethal bowling.

'You're in for a gloomy dinner tonight,' I said to Venetia who was stretched out on the grass beside me, chin resting on her hands and apparently paying attention to what was going on in front of us. In fact she'd been burbling on about driving back to London with Robert on Tuesday and wondering if there was going to be anyone around in Town for her to see. By luck I just happened to be looking when Oscar was bowled out; at least I'd be able to make some sympathetic noises and say, truthfully for once, that I'd actually seen it. 'This is beginning to look like a massacre,' I whistled as Matt trudged off the pitch after achieving the grand total of six. Considering how his predecessors had done, it wasn't too bad.

'There's still Carlton. He might be on better form than he was yesterday,' Venetia said, then as Tom began to look around with an increasingly frantic air, she added, 'but where is he? Or Oz? Carl was saying they didn't get to bed until six this morning. I hope they aren't catching up on their kip somewhere. Oh God, if they don't turn up I'm going to stay with you lot at the cottage tonight. In fact, you'll have to do my packing for me, Nella. I'm certainly not going anywhere near Daddy. I know exactly who'll get the blame for this!' she wailed as Tom gave an exasperated sigh and called to the fat man in the Bermudas to get up from the deck chair where he'd been relaxing with a newspaper over his face and come and get the pads on.

The fat man opened his eyes and looked at Tom in horror. Tom shrugged with a 'there's nothing I can do about it' expression. George stood in the middle of the pitch like a white-flannelled Nemesis, rubbing the ball on his arm in a meaningful manner. Idly I wondered if there was a 'stomach before wicket' rule as well as an LBW.

Just then, a bellow came from off the pitch and Carlton belted into view, wearing nothing more than a pair of baggy bright blue swimming trunks and a smear of sun block on his nose, shaking water off his shaggy hair as he ran. 'Sorry, mate, I was in the pool, forgot the time,' he panted as the fat man ripped off the pads and handed them over with every expression of relief.

Venetia giggled as Carlton hastily did up the pads over his bare legs. 'He's much easier on the eye than dear fat old Fred Barlow, isn't he?' she murmured. Carlton stripped down very nicely indeed, as we all had plenty of opportunity to observe. He tied his hair back in a pony tail with what looked like one of Venetia's scrunchies, shoved bare feet into his shoes, and picked up the bat. George smirked at this apparition and began shifting from side to side like a Spanish bull preparing to charge – one quick strike and it would all be over.

'I can't bear to look!' moaned Venetia, fingers laced across her eyes as George started his run. There was an almighty crack and her head shot up to see the ball fly off the field like a rocket, nearly clipping Hugh's ear as it whizzed past. His attention had once more been fatally distracted by Kerry, who was carefully applying more suntan cream – this time to her thighs, her skirt bunched right up to hip level. He missed catching it by about an inch.

As he disappeared red-faced into the vines to retrieve the ball, Venetia said faintly, 'Gosh! I might escape being disinherited after all. He *said* he played a beaut game of cricket when his eye was in, didn't he? Let's pray it lasts.'

It appeared it was going to. Carlton continued to slam a steady stream of balls in every direction and the gradual rising of spirits from the Château du Pré team was almost visible as first they realised it wasn't going to be an ignominious walk-over after all; then, that their score might be respectable; then, as a four made it over the boundary, that it was just possible we were talking of a close run thing – perhaps even a draw. Even I began to pay attention. Janey looked as if all her fingernails had been sacrificed to tension a long time ago, Maggie was gripping herself with excitement at every run and Sally was looking distinctly torn.

Venetia sighed happily. 'He's really *very* good-looking, isn't he?' she said. For a moment I wasn't sure who she was talking about, then realised it must be Robert. 'Money isn't everything, is it?' she went on. 'I mean, I know love in a garret is infinitely more difficult than love in a mansion, but there is a happy medium, isn't there? It's not as if we'd be stony broke and I suppose he could always start earning a packet some time in the future.'

'You could always start earning a packet,' I pointed out in the interests of equality.

'Oh, I doubt it. Not unless some kind person wants to pay me for being decorative and useless,' she said frankly. 'But there are some people you just wouldn't mind being poor with, aren't there?'

'Um, yes,' I agreed, not quite sure why I was feeling so uncomfortable with the way this conversation was going. I was also dead certain that Venetia and I had two completely different definitions of what 'poor' meant.

'Ooh look!' she exclaimed as Sally walked around, holding the latest score aloft. 'We're only ten runs short! Eleven and we've won! *Oh no!*'

Oz, who had proved to be much better than he'd claimed, had been caught behind. 'That's it then,' said Venetia despondently. 'The only man Daddy's got left is

Fred and he's never stayed in longer than second ball, that's why he's always last man.'

Fred Barlow looked just as appalled to be pulled out of his deck chair again as were the rest of his team-mates. Then Venetia brightened. 'But look, as it's a new over Carlton's getting the ball. We might still do it.'

She was biting her knuckles with tension, hardly able to speak as Carlton slammed the ball again for another four. 'Careful,' she pleaded. 'Don't get over-confident and get caught! Careful... careful... well done... pity... oh nearly... oh no! We lose by one run.'

The prospect of the match slipping out of his grasp had lent wings to Napier's heels and he'd raced for the ball, returning it to George so quickly that Carlton had made only a single run instead of the two he'd been expecting. An apprehensive Fred Barlow was left to face George and the last ball of the match.

George roared up to his mark like an express train and let fly. Fred closed his eyes and hit out at random. The ball snicked off the bat and flew over the wicket-keeper's head. Fred stared at it in total disbelief until Carlton yelled, '*Move it*!' and charged down the pitch. Fred wound himself up and began lumbering towards the bowler's end as Hugh scooped up the ball and threw it at George.

'*Run*!' screamed Venetia above the shouts of both teams and the spectators.

'Come on, Fred!' yelled Janey, jumping up and down with excitement.

'He'll never make it,' muttered someone behind me in a tone of gloom. Then suddenly Fred was airborne, diving full length like a mighty torpedo, bat held out in front of him. The ball hit the stumps, sending the bails cartwheeling into the air, at exactly the same moment that Fred hit the ground like half a ton of nutty slack.

There was a terrible silence, broken only by a wheezy groan from the prostrate batsman as everyone looked at the umpire. He shook his head slowly and grinned broadly – not out.

'It's a draw!' cried Janey ecstatically and raced onto the pitch, dragging Fred to his feet, which says something about the strengthening powers of delight, before giving him a smacking kiss of congratulation. Within seconds, the still-winded Fred was surrounded by a crowd of cheering players and spectators.

To do him credit it took Napier only a few seconds to force a smile to his lips and go over and clap a gleeful Tom on the back. 'Well done, old chap! Never thought you'd do it.'

'Neither did I,' Tom said candidly.

'Well, you might not have done if there hadn't been one or two rather tough calls from the umpire,' said Napier, turning to give Robert a very hard stare. 'Particularly with some of the no ball calls on George's bowling.'

Robert smiled in a particularly shark-like manner. 'Tough, but just, Napier. George was kind enough to think of the good of the game the other night and tell me some of the lesser known rules. He's too much of a good sport to have wanted me to bend the rules in his favour.'

Napier looked as if he was going to dispute the point, especially about the time when Oscar had been bowled out, but Solange, who had been all over the Bordeaux *négociant* a few minutes ago, now slipped in between the two team captains and linked her arms through theirs, though her hand rested lightly on Napier's arm and it might just have been possible to run a knife through the gap separating her from Tom, though I doubted it. 'Now, now, there is nothing more boring than undertaking a match like this,' she announced brightly.

Not surprisingly this statement was met with a certain amount of surprise and blank misunderstanding. After a pause Janey said, 'I think that what Solange means is endless post mortems. I agree with her,' she added, though she looked as if the effort of agreeing with Solange was akin to sucking a lemon.

'Yes, yes, that is what I mean,' Solange said. 'The only thing we 'ave to discuss is that sanglier. You can't both 'ave it so 'oo will?' She cuddled even closer, if that were possible, to Tom and turned a winning smile up towards him.

'Ruddy hell,' muttered Janey, who had been watching this display with intense disfavour. 'As if Tom would really part with that blessed sanglier for a few dropped h's! Tell you what,' she called over, 'as it's a draw, why don't you both have it for six months each?'

Tom nodded while Solange pouted prettily. 'And as Napier hasn't seen much of it in recent years,' he sent his rival a very self-satisfied smile, 'he can have it for the first six months.'

Napier quite properly ignored the first part of this remark and merely said, 'Very decent of you, old chap. Now shall we all have a drink to celebrate a very good match?'

It seemed that he had been quite prepared to celebrate a not so good match too, for the moment we all appeared outside the house Solange's army of helpers began to stream out with trays of glasses and ready chilled bottles of champagne for us to toast the players, most especially the man of the match – Fred Barlow, still looking stunned by his achievement. I think we would have been there 'undertaking the match', as Solange would have it, and generally gossiping for hours if the sky hadn't begun to darken in an ominous way, presaging one of the violent summer storms so common in the area and we all decided to leave before it broke.

Tom had asked the Australians back to Château du Pré for a slap-up supper and a general wallowing in the brilliance of their performance.

'We must try to get together tomorrow, it's our last day,' Venetia called, leaning out of the car window as she drove off, narrowly missing a large antique stone planter packed with white trailing geraniums on the edge of the drive. I saw Robert, sitting next to her in the front, wince and wondered if he was about to decide that, come what may, his knee was sufficiently recovered for him to do all the driving.

The storm hung around on the edges of the horizon, crowning all the distant hills with dark purple and grey, occasionally rumbling to let us know it was there and hadn't actually gone away but never moving close enough to obscure the patch of blue sky above the cottage. It made for some very strange light effects and Oscar, who fancies himself as a bit of a nifty photographer when he's not earning a fortune manipulating the money markets, dashed inside the moment we got back to change into shorts and went out again with some highly expensive equipment to see if he could capture it all on film. Somewhat to my surprise, Phil elected to go with him.

'Good,' said Maggie as the two men left. 'At least it means Phil will have a chance to work off some of the booze he's consumed today before he starts all over again this evening.'

I murmured to Sally, 'It also gives him an excuse to get out of helping with supper.'

To my horror Maggie heard. She turned around and there was a pause while I wondered if the salad bowl she was holding was about to be cracked over my head for impertinence, then to my utter amazement she laughed. 'Phil isn't the most shining example of a new man, is he? Here, can you chop up these herbs for the salad dressing, Nella? You always do them nice and fine.'

Was she on happy pills or something, I wondered, or maybe that old holiday magic was beginning to kick in at last. Whatever, Maggie's sunny mood set the tone for the most relaxed evening we'd had since we'd arrived. We didn't tempt Fate by eating outside and sat around the old oak table at one end of the sitting room, staying there long after we'd all finished eating while the shadows lengthened and the sky began to darken.

The thunder was coming closer. Maggie jumped slightly at one louder rumble and I wondered if that was her one weakness, a fear of storms. But it was still some way away and we were settling down to playing poker for matchsticks with a pack of cards Sally had found at the back of a cupboard when we heard a car pulling up outside and Venetia came in, followed by Robert and Oz. 'Janey thought you might not know how to reset the electricity if it goes off – and it usually does during thunderstorms. She didn't come herself as she's gone to bed – she's not feeling very well, she says. She certainly didn't look too good, I must say,' Venetia added with cheerful unconcern, 'so I thought I'd better come down and show you myself.'

'And Oz and I decided we could do with a break from a run-by-run reprise of the greatest match since W.G. Grace first laid his mitts on a bat,' said Robert with feeling. I wasn't surprised Janey had strategically retired to bed.

Our visitors didn't appear to be in a hurry to return to the château. Oz said he had a nasty feeling Tom and Carlton would have moved onto the Bodyline tour by now. At this Phil pricked up his ears – until Maggie informed him that Bodyline had nothing to do with underwear. While Oscar found clean glasses and Phil and Charlie dealt with the serious masculine business of finding out what they were supposed to do in a power cut – this largely consisted of watching Venetia while she opened the door to the fuse box, I just hoped they took their eyes off her behind for long enough to take note of which button she was pointing to – I was sent off to the kitchen to make coffee. Even I, who fondly likes to imagine I have nerves of steel, jumped at the next crack of thunder which was so loud it felt as if the bang was about two feet above my head. I swore as the tin of coffee slipped from my fingers, bounced off the edge of the draining board and fell in the sink, though the genie in charge of kitchen mishaps must have been distracted for a moment, since the tin didn't promptly burst open as they usually do when there's lots of nice difficult-to-clear-up powdery stuff inside.

'Are you all right, Nella?' asked Charlie, poking his head around the door.

'Fine, just dropped the coffee,' I said, trying to dry the tin with the tea towel. The kitchen genie had made sure the sink was full of tepid washing-up water. I had a feeling my newfound accord with Maggie wouldn't last long if she discovered that I'd given her special coffee, bought from an exclusive specialist shop in a hard-to-find backstreet, a nice bath.

'That all?' he asked, rolling his eyes. 'From the noise I thought you must have smashed the pot at the very least.'

'I didn't,' said Robert from behind him. 'Nella used to make a devil of a racket even when she dropped a pencil. It's nice to know that some things don't change in this uncertain world.'

'Have you two come in solely to make smart alec remarks or are you going to actually be of some use?' I demanded. 'I could do with that tray being carried out for starters.'

'She's still bossy too,' Robert remarked in an aside.

I might have thrown something at him, not Maggie's precious coffee, when the darkness outside the window was lit up by a searing flash, the room seemed to shake with a simultaneous crash of thunder and the lights flickered a couple of times, then went out. I had just picked up the full pot and stood uncertainly, not daring to move too quickly in case I slopped coffee over myself or Charlie, who I could hear feeling his way into the kitchen in search of the box of matches by the cooker. 'Have we got any candles in here?' he asked.

'There's a box in one of the drawers I think, but I'm not sure which one. Maggie took most of them through to the sitting room,' I said as I inched my way towards the table, feeling for the surface with my free hand.

'Maggie says she's just lighting her candles and will bring one straight through for you,' said Robert, his voice sounding unusually deep in the darkness. My fingers met wood and I set the pot down cautiously, amazed at what should be such a mundane task becoming so difficult when you literally can't see anything.

I squeaked with surprise as my fingers brushed something warm and moving. 'It's only me,' murmured Charlie, who must have been able to move with a cat-like speed and silence, not to say cat-like ability to see in the dark for I'd thought he was still over the other side of the kitchen.

'You're lucky you didn't get hot coffee tipped all over you,' I said a bit indistinctly, for in the darkness I could feel a hand, I presumed it was his, curl over mine and pull me towards him until I was near enough to feel his breath playing on my face. His other hand cupped my cheek, a circling thumb tracing little movements at the corner of my mouth and sending delicious little shivers through me. It was all so unexpected that I couldn't move, not that I wanted to, frankly. I was enjoying this little adventure in the dark very much indeed.

There was a shout of triumph from Phil as the lights

came on, flooding the kitchen with dazzling brightness. I could only hope that Robert's eyes were still adjusting to the light as I shot backwards, but I had a nasty feeling from his expression that he'd had all too good a view.

We hadn't actually been *doing* anything, I told myself, though anybody who walked in would have presumed that we had from the ridiculously guilty expressions on our faces. At least I imagined that mine was mirroring Charlie's. And of course it would have to be Maggie who appeared with a candle seconds later, though her view of the tableau was impeded by Robert, who was blocking the doorway, muttering apologies that his knee had gone into spasm and he couldn't move for the moment.

Mustering all my acting ability, I said as calmly as I could, 'Thanks for the candle, Maggie, I wasn't sure where they were.' I smiled weakly at Charlie, avoiding direct eye contact. 'We'd better take this through while we can still see. If you'll do the tray I'll bring the pot.'

Somewhat to my surprise, since acting isn't my forte, Maggie's suspicious look didn't fade completely, but she didn't leap in with the immediate denunciations that I feared either. Charlie picked up the tray and walked out without giving me a second glance.

I might have put the whole incident down to my over-active imagination if it hadn't been for Robert, who said quietly as I passed, 'Into bloodsports, Nella?' I looked at him curiously and he added grimly, 'Because there'll definitely be blood spilt if you're seen to go after another of the boyfriends in this cottage.'

'Hey, come on,' I protested quietly so my words didn't carry down the passage. 'I did *not* go after Phil.'

He shrugged. 'OK. I'll give you that,' and whatever else he was going to say was lost as Phil, sounding very pleased with himself, shouted, 'Those of us who bring light to the needy are thirsty. Where's that coffee, wench?'

'Coming!' I called as with perfect timing the lights went out again.

CHAPTER 15

Robert, Venetia and Oz had been pulled into the poker game and ended up by not leaving until the small hours of the morning, by which time nearly everyone around the table had lost millions in matchstick currency, the biggest losses being mine. I was told kindly by Oscar as he was raking in the last of my 'cash' that I just didn't have the right sort of face for poker. Maybe I am a bit transparent but I suspected he could see my cards as well; he was doing a suspicious amount of leaning back in his chair. I then had immense satisfaction in seeing him wiped out by Charlie, an intense player who took the most outrageous risks and was always teetering either on the brink of enormous matchstick riches or bankruptcy, but the biggest surprise of all was Venetia whose instinct of when to raise or throw in was uncanny. She merely smiled when we complimented her and said, 'Do you remember Jack who had the private gambling club, Nella? I worked for him as a croupier for a while.' Aha, we all nodded wisely. Inside knowledge – that explained it.

The storm had blown itself out with much crashing

and banging during the night. Fortunately the electricity was back on again otherwise the Dunkirk spirit so much in evidence last night might have failed miserably if everyone had got up to find the kettle wasn't working. It was such a beautiful morning that I decided to duck out of bread-buying duty and go for a walk while it was still cool enough to be a real pleasure.

That was my intention, except it wasn't nearly so cool out in the middle of the vineyard as it had seemed in the shade of the kitchen, and after about ten minutes I discovered an annoying hedge, just too wide to climb over, blocking my way down to the little river in the valley where I'd been planning to go. I got to that hot, cross stage where you wonder if you can really be bothered to go on and if returning home for a cup of coffee wouldn't be a far more pleasurable option. I had sat down under a tree to rest when a whirling mass of spotted energy burst into view and started cavorting around me smiling and sneezing, followed closely by Solomon who had his nose so intently to the ground that he ran right into my outstretched legs.

I patted both dogs, hoping it wasn't the smell of my feet Solomon had been tracking so keenly. My plimsolls were old but I had washed them twice before I packed them.

Janey appeared at the end of a row of vines a couple of seconds later, head sunk low on her shoulders, hands stuck in the pockets of her shorts, feet scuffing up little clouds of dirt as she went. The only resemblance she bore to the person who had been having such fun at the cricket match dreaming up naughty little tricks to put the opposing team off their swing was in hair colour and a certain similarity in feature, though everything else seemed to have sagged and aged infinitely overnight. She was so lost in what were obviously deeply gloomy thoughts that she visibly jumped when I said hello.

'Sorry,' she said, forcing a smile. 'I wasn't concentrating. You're up early.'

'I couldn't sleep.'

'No, neither could I,' she said. That was obvious to anyone from her waxy pallor and the deep shadows under her eyes. For a moment it seemed as if she was going to plod on by then she flopped down alongside me under the tree and put her arms around her knees. 'What was your problem?' she asked. 'Or was it just the storm?'

'Sort of,' I said evasively. 'And I think I may have got on the wrong side of Maggie again.'

'Really,' she said dully, so unlike her normal curious self that I began to feel alarmed. And she had been in such high spirits yesterday. Had she received some bad news when she got home? But surely Venetia, the arch gossip and information gatherer, would have known if she had, and would certainly have passed on some hint, not just said she'd gone to bed early.

'Are you feeling any better this morning?' I asked as she returned to staring blankly into the distance.

'No,' she said flatly, pushing Lily's head away as she tried to lick her ear. 'That business about you'll feel much better after a good night's rest is utter balls.'

'I think you're supposed to sleep, not just go to bed,' I offered, fending Lily off my ear this time.

'Mm, perhaps. But how the hell do you go to sleep

when your whole life has fallen apart?' Slow tears started to well out of her eyes, rolling down her cheeks. She made no movement to wipe them away, just sat motionless as they dripped one by one into her lap. I dithered uselessly. I didn't have anything practical on me like a clean tissue, or even a dirty one for that matter, and I wasn't sure if I spoke whether it would be an unwelcome intrusion into whatever was troubling her so deeply or even if she'd rather I left her alone. My uncertainty was mirrored by the dog who looked at her mistress anxiously, whined and then when that got no response put a paw firmly on Janey's bare arm.

'Ow!' Janey exclaimed, pushing the paw away, then ruffled Lily's ears. Lily's nails were obviously enough to break through any degree of abstraction. 'Sorry about that,' she said, wiping the tears away with the flat of her hand. 'I'm not fond of thunderstorms at the best of times and I had a bad go of middle-of-the-night fears. I let them get on top of me which was silly because things are always better in the daylight. It's been a bit difficult to shake them off this time, but they'll go soon.' The words were brave but it didn't look as if she believed them.

Rather belatedly I put two and two together and for once managed to add up correctly. 'Oh Lord! Someone told you about Solange's lunch, didn't they?'

'So you know too,' she said in an accusatory tone.

I shrugged. 'George told me, he was there. But why on earth do you think it might be Tom she was dining off?' I asked, ignoring the doubts I'd had on the same subject myself.

'It stands to reason,' she said. 'You know ignorance

really is bliss. I'd never have known anything about it if Raoul the bottlemaker hadn't rung on Thursday saying he needed to get in touch with Tom urgently and that his mobile was turned off. Tom told me he had a meeting in Bordeaux but when I checked his diary to get his number there wasn't anything written down. He *always* notes his appointments. I asked him about it when he got back, and he hummed and haa-ed, then said he'd been looking for my birthday present.' She smiled sadly. 'My birthday isn't for three weeks and every year up to now he's started looking for a present for me about an hour before the shops close on the evening before, so why should he alter a well-established habit? But then I thought maybe he was actually getting me something that needed a little planning in advance. I thought it was rather sweet of him – that is, until Oz mentioned in passing how it was common gossip that Solange had been seen sharing a lot more than asparagus with a man who definitely wasn't her husband on the very day that *my* husband hadn't been where he said he was going to be.' She laughed, a horrid grating sound, completely devoid of any humour. 'Funny how clichés always turn out to be true, isn't it? The one about the wife being the last to know. Husband too in this case, I should think.'

Oh Lord, this sounded bad. 'You know, Janey, things aren't always the way they appear to be,' I said eventually. 'Look at me and Robert. I was convinced he was sleeping with Natasha, and he wasn't. Well, not then anyway. That's what he says, and I believe him.'

'But you still broke up,' Janey said dismally. 'And anyway, I doubt Tom is actually having an affair with

Solange.' I gaped at her, wondering what the problem was then. 'Even at the height of my besottedness I did retain just enough sense to wonder about the wisdom of marrying a man who had had quite so many ladyfriends, but he swore he'd never be unfaithful,' she went on. 'Venetia's mother had a serious problem keeping her knickers up so Tom knows very well what it does to you to always be wondering whose bed your spouse is in.'

She rested her chin on her knees, deep in thought, then said, 'I'm sure that as far as Tom is concerned, he really thinks he's a loving, faithful father and husband, and he is – in the literal sense, since he doesn't break his promises. I expect he also thinks that it won't matter if he wants to go to bed with Solange, providing he doesn't actually do it. But it does matter – to me,' she whispered. 'It shrivels something inside me to know that he's so restless that he's got to go out for risky lunches with other women, and play with fire, even if he draws back from actually putting his hand in it.'

Except that wanting to go to bed with a woman and actually doing it if she gave you the green light was the normal procedure as far as most men were concerned. Was Tom so very different?

'I daresay Venetia's already told you Tom only married me because I was pregnant,' Janey went on, looking at me. I nodded, feeling embarrassed. 'Oh don't worry, it's perfectly true, except that contrary to what Venetia thinks, I didn't deliberately trap him into marriage. I wasn't capable of being so calculating. All I could think of was if and when I was going to see him next. Everything else went to the wall – work, social life, commonsense – and taking my pills at the proper time. I doubt he'd even thought of our fling going beyond the summer and he'd certainly not contemplated becoming a father again at over fifty, but the moment he knew I was keeping the baby he insisted on marrying me. He even said it was what he'd wanted all along but thought it was too soon to say so . . .'

And she'd believed him because she wanted to, because she loved him so much she couldn't bear not to marry him. But there was always a nasty little niggle of doubt that remained, not too well buried, and which was dug up on a regular basis by Venetia, who could not come to terms with her father remarrying at all, let alone to some-one of nearly her own age. Janey's confidence in Tom's love for her, never rock solid, had started to dwindle and was now hurtling downwards at an incredible rate.

She had started to sense that something was really wrong about a year ago. Tom had seemed to withdraw from her then. She caught him staring blankly into space as if there was something preying on his mind, yet he always denied that there was anything the matter. She'd walked in on him a couple of times when he was on the telephone and he'd dropped his voice suddenly in the most painfully obvious attempt at concealment. She'd even sneaked in once and pressed the *voir appels* button to see who had been calling him, she admitted in a shamefaced voice, but she couldn't get it to work prop-erly. However, it didn't take a genius to work out that something was going on, and that something must be connected with Solange.

'I tried to make myself believe it was money that was

the problem,' she said sadly. 'God knows he's worried enough about that, but when I offered to sell my flat he just thanked me and said I ought to keep a bolt-hole in London. It's not worth much, to be honest.' She absently stroked Lily with one hand. 'I just don't know what to do. I'm not noble enough to tell Tom to work Solange out of his system – I'm well aware there's only one way a man ever does *that* – yet I can't bear to think he's feeling trapped. It's going to poison everything. I'll always be wondering if he's hankering to be off, if he really wants to be somewhere else, if he's going to look at me and start resenting me for restricting his freedom like this.' She pushed Lily away gently. 'Maybe I ought to go off for a couple of months, take the twins to stay with my parents for a while, they're always saying how they miss seeing their grandchildren on a regular basis. Though a couple of months of the twins' company will no doubt cure them for ever. Anyway I ought to do something that gives Tom a bit of space. What do you think?'

'That you're completely bonkers!' I said frankly. 'And you said you weren't being noble. So what are you trying to be, then? Another Patient Griselda?'

She frowned. 'I don't think so. What use would sitting on a monument be in this situation?'

'That was Patience, silly! Griselda was one of those depressing medieval woman who proved what wonderful wives they were by putting up with everything their husbands did. Hers was a particularly unpleasant specimen who, amongst other things, divorced her and turned her out of the house stark naked. She still went on thinking he was really a nice bloke.'

'More fool her. What happened? Did she marry someone else and live happily ever after?'

'Nope. The husband said he'd just been putting her
through a few tests to make sure she loved him, and that
she could come back now. So she did.'

'Tom might have his faults but at least he's never tried
to do anything like that,' Janey said, smiling through her
tears. 'And he'd think it very bad form to turf his wife
out of the house in the buff.'

'What – you mean he'd allow you to keep your bra and
pants on?' I said. 'I think you've really got your wires
crossed here, Janey. I don't know Tom very well, but if
you ask me, he adores you. You should have seen his face
the other night when he saw Jed casting you languishing
looks . . .'

'That's only because Venetia's been banging on about
old flames ready to be relit,' she said dismissively. 'She
couldn't be more wrong too. If Jed was casting languishing looks at anyone, it would have been at Oscar.'

'No!' I exclaimed. 'Jed can't be gay.'

'He isn't exactly gay – his closet door is locked, bolted
and has a chain on for good measure – but he certainly
isn't one for chasing skirts either.' She wrinkled up her
nose. 'Actually I'm not sure he's terribly interested in sex
per se. I reckon he's what they used to call a confirmed
bachelor, but if he does lean in any direction it's towards
men.'

'Rather like Oscar,' I said. 'He seems to prefer friends
to lovers too.'

'The perfect couple,' Janey said with a faint smile.
'Perhaps we ought to try and bring them together.'

'Mm, could do,' I said. 'It'd serve Oscar right to be dosed with his own medicine for once, except I've got a hot date with a female wrestler to arrange for him first.' I told her about my plans for revenge, pleased to hear her giggle when I described how, when Oscar first met Felicity at a barbecue given by my flatmate and me last summer, he'd been so alarmed by her that he'd started backing away and had ended up impaled on a rose bush. He'd then had a terrible choice between carefully extricating himself and staying in Felicity's frightening company for another ten minutes, or making a quick break for it, and ruining the new silk sweater he'd bought only that morning.

The final credit for making Janey cheer up didn't go to me but to Solomon, who burst through a row of vines, sending small marble-like unripe grapes scattering everywhere and came heavily to a halt in front of us, looking very pleased with himself. It was not such a delight to us since within about five seconds it was all too apparent that he had found something to roll in, something very dead, probably a fish that hadn't seen water for weeks. We jumped up with a shriek, dodging behind the tree before he could come any closer and actually touch us.

'You'd better take him home and bath him,' I said faintly.

'*Bath* him?' she exclaimed. 'You don't seriously think I'm going to get close enough to do that, do you? No, it's the other end of the courtyard with a hosepipe aimed at you, old man. Luckily he's a real water hound, he enjoys being soaked, but I'd better deal with him before he decides to do it for himself by jumping in the pool. I don't think even the amount of chlorine Tom uses could cope with that smell. Thanks for listening, Nella.' She hesitated, then said shyly, 'Did Tom really mind about Jed?'

'Yes, he did,' I said firmly. 'And think of this, Janey. Hugh didn't know who Solange was lunching with. If it had been Tom, don't you think he would have recognised him, even if it wasn't a very good view?'

'I hadn't thought of that,' she said slowly and walked off, keeping carefully upwind of Solomon, looking a lot happier than she had done a few minutes ago.

By the time I was back at the cottage, it was already clouding over again. By mid-morning it was raining in a steady, depressing drizzle that was distinctly uninviting, yet made you feel lacking in spirit for not doing something hearty and English like having a picnic under an umbrella. It was the sort of weather that regularly turns up in England for every public holiday, and in some ways it was reassuring to know that things weren't so very different on the continent. Everybody in the cottage was acting as if the rain was a personal affront, specifically intended to ruin his or her plans for the day. Maggie had been thinking in terms of the beach, Sally of doing what was supposed to be a rather spectacular ten-kilometre walk along the riverbank, and the men of investigating a fair in the local town. Perhaps, all things considered, it was a good thing that the rain prevented any decisions having to be made; we tried the fair, but all the rides with the exception of a children's roundabout were closed up and covered in tarpaulins. The French were far too sensible to come out in weather like this. We returned to the cottage for a desultory and bad-tempered game of Monopoly; Charlie was accused of swiping money from the bank, Phil of gassing everybody by chainsmoking, Sally of being stupid, me of being a wicked landlady and Oscar of conducting underhand deals with just about everyone, then refusing to pay up. Your average game of Monopoly really.

So all in all, we were rather pleased when a rap on the door broke up a severe bout of cottage fever. I even stayed pleased when it turned out to be a damp George, though I gave Oscar an old-fashioned look. 'Nothing to do with me, I promise,' he said, hands held up defensively in case I felt like lobbing my silver top hat at him.

George's excuse for turning up out of the blue was that the atmosphere at Château Vielleroche was such that he'd felt distinctly *de trop* and had thought it would be more tactful to absent himself for a while. I suspected that the real reason was that, despite his frequent claims that he was completely uninterested in gossip, he was big with news and wanted the exquisite delight of being the first to tell us. The balloon had gone up at Château Vielleroche in the biggest possible way, not because anyone had seen fit to tell Napier how his wife spent her lunch hours, but by sheer mischance. Solange had knocked her handbag over, spilling the contents on the floor, and while Napier was helping her pick everything up he'd happened to glance idly at a little note and read it without thinking. It had a date and time on it; Solange might have got away with her claim that it was just her next appointment at the hairdresser except that even the most conveniently blind husband knows there's something fishy going on when the hairdresser signs his appointment card with *I want to kiss you all over*. The actual phrase was probably something considerably more fruity given Napier's reaction, but disappointingly George was too much of a gentleman to tell us what.

The subsequent row had raged all over the château from top to bottom, and still wasn't resolved. What had made Napier really go into orbit was that the note came from the expert who oversaw the making of his red wine; this added an extra, completely unacceptable dimension to Solange's disloyalty since he couldn't possibly continue to employ someone who was making his wife as well as his wine, and a winemaker wasn't someone who could be replaced easily. So far she hadn't admitted that there had been anything going on other than a bit of surreptitious handholding, which had resulted in a rather unfortunate exchange where Napier had asked wearily, 'Come on, do you think I'm stupid enough to believe that?' and she'd replied, '*Oui*.'

At that point, George had decided it would be wiser to get out of the firing range, though most of us felt this was a bit poor-spirited of him. He might at least have waited to see if there were further developments. Sally was so concerned about the terrible strain on him of witnessing such a scene that she was virtually wiping his forehead with a handkerchief dipped in cologne. I didn't tell her George always claimed he had more important things to think about – such as the rate of the yen against the dollar or the next three-day international – than silly emotional nonsense. This was usually said when I had something I wanted to discuss. My subsequent reaction would just go to prove another of his deeply held beliefs, that women were at the mercy of their hormones.

It was inevitable that George would be deemed too fragile to go back and face the atmosphere at Château Vielleroche yet, so he was invited to stay for supper, though I told Oscar under my breath that I thought George ought to do the decent thing and go back to support his friend. 'He couldn't possibly!' said Oscar, shocked. 'It would be terribly insensitive to intrude on a family problem like that.'

It had never occurred to me before that George was bothered about matters of sensitivity – but there you are. I merely warned Oscar that if he even thought about pandering to George's delicate emotions by offering him the newly vacated sofa bed, I was moving out. But perhaps before I went, everyone would be interested in seeing the photograph of Oscar after he'd had the accident with the lobster . . .

'You haven't really got it with you, have you?' he asked in alarm. 'You *promised* me you'd destroyed it!'

I smiled sweetly. 'Of course I did – I do keep my promises, Oscar. But I didn't say anything about destroying any copies I might have, did I?' I'd never actually made any but what does the literal truth matter when you're fighting to keep the sofa bed free? Besides, I'd learned the art of half-truths, or virtually no truths at all, off a master.

Oscar knew that old adage about liars always being the ones to look the most virtuous, but he didn't press the point. He really didn't want to risk anyone seeing that photograph. Frankly, I didn't blame him. I waggled my fingers at him, and as it was his turn for making the dinner left him to work his magic in the kitchen. I was down on the rota to be general kitchen skivvy but Oscar was trying out something new. I knew this would entail some chef-like displays of temperament and banging of pans, so I decided to keep out of the way and take advantage of the others being distracted to have a bath and nick all the hot water for myself for once.

Maggie said in a martyred voice later that she'd had to lay the table as I hadn't been there to do it, but I didn't care. It was so nice to feel for once that I was the one with the nice clean shiny hair, even if I could have done without George smirking and obviously thinking it had been washed just for him. It was even nicer to feel that for once an expensive purchase really was money well spent. Marie-Hélène's exorbitant haircut was still falling back into place so perfectly that I began to wonder if it wouldn't be worth popping out here every so often just to have a trim. Investment hairdressing you could call it, except perhaps not in the hearing of my bank manager.

CHAPTER 16

A mild wind blew away the last of the clouds, and the rain had gone completely by the end of a surprisingly pleasant dinner. Oscar's new dish had worked so there were no creative sulks, and Maggie had punished me for my selfishness by commandeering George and taking him to sit at the other end of the table. As a ploy for engendering remorse it backfired splendidly.

When we had all finished, Phil took a perfunctory look at the spectacular sunset outside and said that as the rain had stopped, the fair might have got going. Did anyone fancy challenging him on the dodgems? He got an enthusiastic response from the sophisticated and cool grown ups present. In that case, he declared, we'd better start out now and leave the clearing up until later.

Sally grinned at me from the other side of the table. Guess whose turn it was to do the washing up?

The fair, which had been set up around the square where the old men usually played their boules, had indeed got going. We could hear the thump of music played at top volume, and each ride seemed to be playing something different, combined with the rumble from the generators powering the rides from about half a mile away. At first George and Oscar, who had been to Alton Towers with their nephews and nieces, were a bit sniffy about a fair that didn't have any futuristic monster rides, let alone a proper roller-coaster that subjected you to some massive G force as you shot almost vertically downwards, but they soon succumbed to the lure of the dodgems and were buying five tokens at a time for their cars before going on the attack. There was nearly a row between Phil and Maggie when she chickened out of ramming Oscar head on, and Phil told her that her driving was thoroughly girly. I thought he was being rather unfair; she wasn't being girly so much as having problems using the pedals with such high heels. Sally, on the other hand, was determined to annihilate the opposition. When she had crushed the men of our party into submission she set about charging various spotty French youths who were delighted to be the subject of such aggression and appeared to think it was a particularly English form of flirting. When she had to give up her dodgem she was almost swamped in the rush of offers to buy her a plastic glass of wine from the *buvette*.

Oscar was dying to go on an octopus affair with little pods like inverted teacups on long arms, saying that it was perfectly safe, didn't tip you upside down and the iron bar that went over your lap was just there because of over-cautious EC regulations. Like a complete idiot I fell for it and agreed to go with him. I should have known that nothing has quite that number of fairy lights dotted all over it if it's perfectly harmless and the music was

266

deliberately loud to drown out the terrified screams of those within.

'Shame it didn't go faster. It was a bit on the tame side, wasn't it?' said Oscar as we got out, me on legs that were shaking so much I didn't know if I'd ever be able to walk properly again. 'Fancy another go?'

I looked at him with loathing and wondered if dropping a plastic beaker of red wine down the front of his precious new cream linen trousers was revenge enough, then decided it wouldn't be. Besides, I was going to need every drop of alcohol for myself to soothe my shattered nerves.

George had dropped all pretensions about being too grand for such a small affair and insisted I watch him while he demonstrated his prowess at the shooting gallery. It was that or go on the teacup again so I chose the lesser of two evils. Not content with scoring the bull three times with three pellets, he decided to have a go at winning the main prize – an exceptionally large teddy bear made of some shiny synthetic pink plush. He was getting dangerously close to winning the beastly thing. I could just see Oscar's face when he realised he was going to have to drive the whole way through France – and up our street – with an almost life-sized pink teddy in his front passenger seat.

Thank heavens Venetia bounced up just as George was rooting through his pocket for enough change to buy the final three pellets and said, 'I thought it was you two! Are the others here as well? Oh good, it's going to be like a real party then. Robbie's just over there. Come on, join us, do!' While George hesitated, torn between the teddy and Venetia, she made up his mind for him by linking her arm through his and leading him off, chattering nineteen to the dozen and wanting to know everything about Solange and Napier's epic row. Napier had rung Tom earlier that evening but, she reported, her father had been unsportingly closemouthed about what Napier had actually said.

Robert was standing by the dodgems. 'Well, well, well, what a surprise,' he said as he turned around and saw who it was, then he leaned over to kiss my cheek. I blinked, wondering what had prompted him to this unexpected show of warmth. Probably the thought that he wouldn't be seeing me again. 'Are you all here?' he asked, then spotted Venetia still animatedly questioning George. 'Our George gets around a lot, doesn't he? Like sand. Gets into everything and is downright irritating.' There was a pause, then, 'Sorry, Nella. I forgot he was a friend of yours,' he said insincerely.

The teacup was disgorging its latest load of victims. I was pleased to note that even Oscar looked as if he'd had enough of being whirled around at some terrible rate and was a little pale about the gills. There was a general feeling as we gathered around the *buvette* that we'd experienced just about everything the fair had to offer, and more importantly, we were running low on ready cash though Charlie was making a brave attempt to regain our general fortunes with the money sweep machine. So far he'd lost about thirty francs and won two but he was still hopeful. Venetia was complaining about leaving, saying she was enjoying herself and wasn't there somewhere we could go on to, while Robert turned to me and said, 'I never got around to giving you the sleeves for your pictures, but if we don't see you before we go tomorrow I'll leave them with Janey.'

'Why don't you come and get them now? Otherwise you might forget,' said Venetia, cheering up instantly. 'And you can all stay for a drink, too. It is our last evening,' she added before Robert could say anything. 'It'd be nice to be able to say a proper goodbye.'

He shrugged. 'If you can see to say goodbye.'

'Yes, there is that,' she admitted. 'We don't have any electricity. Daddy thinks a branch must have come down on the line to the house and we're short of candles after the dinner on the terrace last week.' She smiled guiltily. 'Janey asked me to get some more but I forgot. Anyway, you're all coming, aren't you?' She looked at George hopefully, ignoring a frown from Robert, but he shook his head and said he really ought to be getting back to Château Vielleroche. 'What a shame, but give my love to Napier, won't you?' she said. 'Tell him I'll be in touch in the morning to see if there is anything I can do.' Considering she and Robert were supposed to be leaving at midday, this was cutting things a bit fine; maybe she was planning to get up very early.

Tom was already asleep when we got to Château du Pré but Janey was still up and was decent enough to look delighted that her house had just been invaded by a large party when she was on the point of going to bed herself. Actually she was in such an incandescently good mood that I don't think she'd have been too bothered if Venetia had brought the local Hell's Angels with her for a Chapter meeting around the pool. Telling Venetia to get the glasses, she shooed everyone into the drawing room and hijacked me to hold the candle while we went down to the cellar to fetch a couple of bottles.

'Who would have guessed it. Solange and *Gaetan*!' she said over her shoulder as we went carefully down the cellar steps, avoiding a spider dangling from the ceiling. 'I promise you, Nella, he's got bow legs and looks just like a monkey. Solange isn't his only conquest either. He's got a pretty fearsome reputation as a ladykiller, and you've really got to work at it to get one of *those* around here, and that's despite his looks and the amount of aftershave he wears, so he must have something that isn't immediately obvious.'

'Hidden assets, perhaps?' I suggested.

'Very large hidden assets,' Janey said with a remarkably dirty chuckle, then immediately looked conscience-stricken. 'Oh dear, I shouldn't laugh, not when you think of what poor old Napier must be feeling. It's all very well saying he should have had the nous to guess why Solange suddenly took an interest in polishing the wine tanks, but he isn't the first spouse to look the other way.' She selected two bottles, put them under her arm, hesitated, then took two more. 'This morning I'd have given anything to be able to go on believing that all Tom ever did with Solange was flirt with her in a highly public and obvious way.'

'Surely you do now, don't you?' I asked, startled.

She laughed. 'I don't think even Solange could cope with Gaetan *and* my husband at the same time. Though I'd still like to know what's on Tom's mind,' she said in a more sober voice. 'Never mind – as long as it isn't Madame Bradley-Cook! She's gone, you know. Napier gave her an either or, and she chose the or. I wonder if she's moved in with Gaetan? I can't think he'll be very pleased if she has. It'll put a considerable restriction on his activities.'

'Poor Napier, he must be terribly upset,' I said as we started back up the steps again.

Janey thought for a moment. 'Well, judging from what Tom says, of course Napier isn't exactly *happy* about what's happened, he was very proud of having such a glamorous wife, but he appears to be more concerned about not having a winemaker, especially this close to the harvest, than he is about his wife doing a bunk. That's what he rang Tom about – the winemaker, not Solange,' she added hastily. 'Tom suggested he have a word with Carlton. He's worked in a couple of pretty high-class châteaux so he must be quite good, and he's just gone freelance.'

Robert was waiting at the top of the steps to take the bottles from Janey. He smiled wickedly. 'Do you think it's occurred to Tom yet that he's just given his top scoring batsman to the other side?'

'Oh God, I'm sure it hasn't!' Janey looked horrified. 'Maybe I'll take the twins to stay with my parents after all. We'll leave at first light.'

One quick drink lengthened into two, then three . . . as everyone got their hands firmly around their glasses and Venetia kept on blithely refilling them. At some point I decided to clear my head with a little fresh air, using the excuse that I'd better put the picture cases Robert was giving me into the car lest I forgot them later. Janey, who was distinctly tight, the first time I'd seen her so, said she'd come with me as the dogs would appreciate going out for a few minutes.

I went out to the courtyard and stashed the cases in the boot of Oscar's car, while Lily and Solomon ran out to snuffle around the grass along the drive. They were still at it when I came back. Janey didn't want to shout at them in case she woke Tom so we decided to hang around until their dogships were good enough to come inside again.

It was distinctly cool outside with a nippy little breeze, so we'd retreated to the shelter of the hall, romantically dim and gloomy in the flickering candlelight. I picked up a guttering candle stuffed in the neck of an empty bottle of Château du Pré rosé and held it up, admiring the oil painting on the wall; the colours of the beach scene at Le Touquet by Willard Sydney were very vivid even in this dim light. 'It really is very pretty, isn't it?'

'Depends if you like being reminded of Venetia every time you go through the hall,' Janey said dourly, enunciating her words with excruciating care and not always succeeding. ''S nothing but trouble as far as I'm consherned. Costs a fortune to insure, but every member of Tom's family would turn over in their graves if he even thought of selling it, no matter how much we need the money. It's an heirloom, you see,' she pronounced solemnly, the effort to get the word out properly almost making her eyes cross. 'An' just about every time Venetia comes here there's an arg... agr... row between her and Tom because she says it's morally hers,' she reported gloomily. 'They had one this mornin'. Frankly, we'd be much better off if we could get rid of it. Trouble is, I don' know how to do it without hordes of outraged Morrisons descending on our heads.'

'Someone might always steal it,' I said lightly. 'Then no one could possibly blame Tom for trousering the money and singing all the way to the bank.'

'If only!' she said feelingly. "Cept how would I arrange it? The insurance might play up if I left the front door open too many times with a large sign saying *valuable painting here, free to first comer.*' She laughed and waggled a finger at me. 'But since you like it so much, why don' you take it?'

'Because I'd set the alarm off the moment I touched it, and I don't really fancy trying out a French jail.'

She rolled her eyes. 'But this is a real onesh-in-a-lifetime offer, never to be repeated. There's supposed to be a battery back-up so the alarm works even when the electricity's off, but there's a fault and it kept going off, so we've had to switch it off.' She tapped the side of her nose. 'Big secret, only known to you, so just for tonight you can lift the picture straight off the wall and I can promish you won't find yourself being met by a poshee of gendarmes before you even get out of the door. So go on, why don't you have it?'

'There's a place just above the fireplace where it would look perfect,' I said thoughtfully, eyeing it. 'Sure you don't want it? OK, I'll relieve you of your unwanted picture then, Mrs Morrison. Name's Nella Bowden-Raffles, you know, house-breaking a speciality, not breaking in even more of one. Glad to be of service. Do you want me to take it off your hands now?' I looked at the picture through the flickering candlelight. 'Except

I'm not sure if I could face having to take it down and hide it behind the sofa every time Venetia popped in for a mineral water. Tell you what, I'll make up my mind later and if you see it's gone you'll know who's got it.'

A door swung to in the draught as the front door was pushed open and Solomon lumbered in, pausing to run a cold wet nose up our legs before waddling off to see if the patron saint of dogs had been nice enough to put something in his bowl since he last looked. Janey clicked her tongue impatiently. 'Where's that other bloody dog of mine? Prob'ly halfway to the village after a rabbit. I'll have to go out and get her,' she said grumpily. 'No, don't come, Nella. There's no point in both of us getting cold.' She stumped out and I returned to the drawing room where the party was still in full swing, though Robert had retired to bed and Sally was curled up in a corner of the sofa, closing her eyes, while Charlie leaned forward holding his glass out.

Oscar looked up with a smile as I sat down next to him. 'You've been ages. What have you been up to?'

'Working out how to steal that nice picture of the beach at Le Touquet.' I picked up my empty glass and held it out for a refill too. 'It's not going to be too difficult. All I'll have to do is give the dogs a treat so they don't bark and the alarm won't be any problem because . . .'

Oscar whisked the glass out of my hand. 'I think you've had enough of that.'

'You sound like a founder member of the Temperance Movement,' I said crossly, 'and the fact that I can say temperance without slurring proves I *haven't* had too much to drink!'

He just grinned and put a companionable arm around me, drawing me against his shoulder and thus ensuring that I was physically unable to get at my glass. Deciding that a tussle to free myself would be undignified, probably what he was counting on, I relaxed and listened to Venetia and Maggie busily climbing the ladders of social one-upmanship over which was the smartest and most exclusive of the Caribbean islands. I lost track after Maggie countered Venetia's B-list movie star spied in the distance on the beach with a famously reclusive, but prestigious author a mere two tables away in a restaurant, and since Oscar is very comfortable, I drifted off. I don't recall much of what happened after that, except for taking my clothes off in my room and letting them fall anyhow on the floor (nothing unusual, to be honest) before I climbed into bed and went back to sleep again.

The next morning we discovered one of the disadvantages of an idyllic little cottage in the middle of the vines. The machines for spraying the vines are very noisy, especially at eight o'clock in the morning, and whoever was operating this one seemed to take a fiendish delight in working around the cottage for just long enough to wake us so thoroughly there was no chance of going back to sleep again, and then taking his infernal machine right over to the other side of the vineyard where it was merely a muffled rumble in the distance.

The atmosphere around the breakfast table was distinctly muted, though compared to the others I seemed to have escaped pretty lightly since I was just tired.

Maybe I did have something to thank Oscar and his strong-arm tactics for after all, though it gave me a certain amount of satisfaction to see that he didn't appear to have taken his own advice and was downing tea and aspirin like there was no tomorrow. Sally hadn't said a single word so far, Charlie looked as if he felt that birdsong should be one of the tortures banned under various human rights charters, Phil hadn't been able to get up at all and was lying in bed groaning and declaring he'd never drink a single thing, ever again; even Maggie was skulking around wearing a pair of dark glasses against the fierce glare of the light creeping in through nearly closed shutters.

I was sitting in the garden wondering if I could muster the energy for a swim when the decision was taken out of my hands by Oscar, resplendent in a blue silk dressing gown with a natty emerald green lining, wandering out and blinking blearily at me. 'Nella, Delphine's just dropped by on the way to taking the twins somewhere,' he said, rubbing a slightly stubbly chin. 'I couldn't really understand what she was on about, but it seems that Janey needs to see you. Well, I think that's what it was, anyway. She was banging on about Madame, so you'd better go up and see what it is. I gathered it was pretty urgent,' he added, as I showed no signs of moving.

What on earth could it be now? I wondered as I got dressed. Could Janey have discovered something else about Tom, something that meant that she needed a shoulder to cry on again? Oh God, I hoped not – she'd looked so happy last night.

As I was crossing the courtyard at the Château the

back door was flung open and Tom marched out, followed by Robert. When Tom saw me, he slammed to a halt and glared. 'What are you doing here, Nella?' he demanded with a curtness quite at variance with his normal friendly politeness.

'I've ... er ... um ... come to see Janey,' I stammered.

'She's busy at the moment, so if it's just a social call perhaps you could come back later.'

I was about to say Janey had asked to see me when some sixth sense warned me it might not be a good idea. 'I've got something for her, something she asked me to give her,' I said, hoping he wasn't going to ask what it was.

He sighed impatiently. 'You'd better go and give it to her then. You'll find her in the kitchen. Are you coming, Robert?' he demanded, and without waiting for an answer strode off across the courtyard towards his office, nearly trampling an idle pigeon that wasn't quick enough to fly out of his way.

'It must be something very small,' murmured Robert with a pointed look at my empty hands. He touched my shoulder lightly. 'But I'm glad you're here. Try and get Janey to calm down, will you? She seems to imagine that Tom's going to blame her for it and it really isn't her fault.'

Then he went after Tom, leaving me wondering what on earth he was on about. The only scenario that could explain why Tom was in a flaming rage with both Janey and Robert was completely out of the question. Wasn't it?

Janey was pacing around the kitchen, more ashy pale

than any hangover could warrant, looking as if she had literally fallen out of bed and into the first garments she came across, whether they were hers or not. I found out later it was the truth, those were Tom's shorts. It was also the first time I'd ever seen anybody really wringing their hands.

'Oh thank God you're here!' she exclaimed, skittering to a halt. 'I thought you were never coming.'

'I only got your message ten minutes ago,' I protested. 'What's the matter?'

'Hush!' She held up her hand and cocked her head, listening. 'Did you meet Tom in the courtyard? You didn't say anything to him, did you?' Not waiting for an answer she dropped her voice as if she was afraid we were going to be overheard and hissed, 'He'll be back in a minute so we have to be quick. Last night – did I *really* tell you that you'd be doing me a favour if you pinched the Willard Sydney?'

'Yes, you did,' I said with a grin. 'At some length too.'

Her face fell. 'I thought I had,' she said in a voice of doom. She ran her fingers through already untidy hair, bit her lip, then said in a rush, 'Did you actually er . . . er . . . *do* it?'

CHAPTER 17

'Well, naturally, I pinched it,' I retorted. 'I said I was going to, didn't I? Though I had a bit of a problem explaining to Oscar why I was walking out with one of your pictures under my arm . . .' My voice petered out as I realised she was in deadly earnest. 'Oh my God!' I exclaimed, catching on at last. 'Has it really gone?'

White-faced, Janey nodded.

No wonder Tom had looked so displeased to see me. The last thing he needed at this moment was stray friends of his wife cluttering up the place. 'And you really thought I might have taken you seriously?' I asked in surprise.

She swung around, eyes widening in dismay. After all, she'd just implied that I was capable of art theft on an impressive scale. 'No, no, not *steal* it properly,' she stammered, 'but you did say if it was gone, then . . . Oh hell! Look, Nella, I was hoping, *praying* that it was going to turn out to be you who'd done it, because I knew if you had you'd give it back.'

'Well, thanks for the vote of confidence. You think that while I'm quite capable of nicking a very valuable picture, I'm still decent enough to be prepared to part with my ill-gotten gains if I'm asked nicely enough.'

She smiled weakly. 'You know what I mean. We were both under the influence, well, I certainly was, and I thought you might just have done it for a joke. After all, I told you to do it, didn't I?' She sighed heavily. 'I thought, if you had, perhaps we could have hatched up some scheme to get it back, like leaving Tom an anonymous message saying that if he goes to the ruined hut on the back road and looks on the central beam he'll discover something of interest. I had a feeling that I wouldn't be quite so lucky though.' If possible, she went even paler than she was already. 'I don't know what Tom'll do to me if he finds out that I've been going around telling people to steal his precious heirloom.'

'What, have you suggested it to anyone else?' I asked, startled.

'No, of course not! But he's going to think it bad enough that I did it once, isn't he? *And* I told you about the alarm being off, too,' she added despondently. 'I can't think what came over me. I must have been stark, raving bonkers. Well, actually I was paralytic, but he's not going to accept that as an excuse, is he? He's going to *kill* me when he finds out.'

Given the mood that Tom appeared to be in, her fears didn't seem entirely unjustified. I gave her a quick hug. 'Don't worry, he won't find out from me. Promise. And I doubt Solomon and Lily are going to spill the beans either, so I think your deadly secret is quite safe.'

She started muttering what a good friend I was, getting all misty-eyed and swaying about as if she were about to keel over at any moment. I made her sit down, and set about making her coffee and finding her something to eat as it turned out, unsurprisingly, that in all the drama no one had thought about breakfast. The bread hadn't been delivered yet and the remains of the loaf had been well seen to by the twins and looked distinctly unappetising so I dug out a packet of shortbread and half a box of chocolate biscuits, not what I'd normally recommend for breakfast but the circumstances were exceptional. Besides, Janey looked in need of a heavy-duty sugar fix.

'Does it really matter what you said to me?' I asked as I put the kettle on and found the cafetière. The electricity was back on again but I didn't feel up to coping with the terrifyingly high-tech coffee machine. Like Janey I glanced quickly out of the door and down the passage to make sure we couldn't be overheard. 'We know I didn't do it, and it's hardly likely that whoever broke in was standing in the drive listening to you give me instructions on how to take it, is it? Lily's idea of a burglar deterrent might be a good lick but surely even she would have let you know if there were intruders hanging around?'

'I wouldn't bank on it,' said Janey, as at the sound of her name the dog trotted over to see if she could cadge a biscuit. 'This animal would sell her soul for a dog treat.' Her face settled back into worried gloom as I put the coffee on the table in front of her. 'In any case, we aren't at all sure that someone did break in. If it wasn't you, then I'm afraid that Tom must be right.'

'Right about what?' I asked blankly.

'That it was Venetia who stole the picture.'

'What!' I sat down in shock. 'She can't have – I don't believe it.'

Janey smiled tiredly. 'That's what I thought, what I wanted to think too. I mean, we all know Venetia's pretty silly but I can't imagine even she would be so unbelievably stupid as to do this. God knows, there have been times when I'd have welcomed the opportunity to think she'd never come here again and I'd be free of her, but not in this way. Right now, Tom's so furious at what she's done that it hasn't really sunk in that his own daughter has made off with his most valuable possession, but when it does it's going to tear him apart. I could wring her neck!' She stirred her coffee so ferociously that it slopped over the sides of the cup onto the table. 'It's all Tom's mother's fault – silly, vain old woman. She filled Venetia's head with this idea that the Sydney was hers by right. She liked to play Lady Bountiful and used to get the members of her family to hang around her by promising to leave them this and that. There was a terrible scene at the reading of the will when both Tom's sisters and his eldest niece all discovered that they'd been promised the same diamond brooch – and Venetia really did believe that she was being left that wretched picture, even though it had been passed on to Tom years ago for tax reasons. To do my stepdaughter credit,' Janey looked as if she wasn't finding this easy, 'she really doesn't seem interested in how valuable it is, she just wants it for itself. But it still doesn't excuse what she's done.'

I shook my head. None of this felt right. 'Just because she thinks it ought to be hers doesn't automatically mean she went ahead and took it.'

Janey dabbed abstractedly at the puddle of coffee on the table. 'But it doesn't look good. For one thing she told Tom yesterday that if he wouldn't give her the picture, she was damn well going to take back her own property whether he liked it or not.'

'But you do say things in a row,' I said a bit weakly. 'It could just be unfortunate timing.'

'Very unfortunate,' she agreed. 'Especially as the picture is missing. And so is she.'

I felt my mug slip in my fingers and just managed to catch it. My poor tired brain couldn't cope with all these surprises. 'Venetia – missing? As in doing a bunk?'

'As in doing a runner, I'm afraid.' Janey nodded. 'In all the hoo-ha this morning none of us noticed she wasn't there. I just thought she was out jogging. Frankly I was too preoccupied with stopping Tom from contacting the gendarmes before I'd had a chance to speak to you, to wonder where she was, apart from being mildly grateful that she wasn't hanging around making a thorough drama out of a crisis. Then Alain, who works in the vineyard, came in and asked when Mademoiselle Venetia was going to return the farm car because he needed it to get a spare part for the spraying machine. Apparently she came belting out of the courtyard gate and nearly knocked him off his moped as he was arriving for work this morning. Of course that could be a bit of an exaggeration; according to Alain he has close encounters with manic motorists about three times a day. It never seems to occur to him that if he didn't drive in the middle of the road he wouldn't have these problems. But anyway she's gone and so has the picture. It seems reasonable to assume the two are connected.'

'She could have had some other reason for dashing off like that.' Janey waited in expectant silence for me to provide one. 'She could have been going to get the bread,' I said finally.

Janey looked at me pityingly. 'Nella, not even Venetia could take *three hours* to get the bread.'

'Doesn't Robert know where she's gone? Or does Tom suspect him of being involved in this as well?' I asked, recalling the aggressive way Tom had looked at Robert.

'I don't think so. Rob's the one who raised the alarm in the first place. He noticed there was something funny about the hall – a blank space where the picture used to hang. And he's just as much in the dark about where Venetia is as the rest of us. He hasn't seen her since last night.'

'Surely he can't be such a sound sleeper that he didn't wake up when she got up?'

Janey laughed hollowly. 'You don't really think that an old fossil like Tom would allow his daughter to share a room with her boyfriend under his roof, do you? They not only had separate rooms, but were at different ends of the house! Bloody nuisance it was for me, too. I could have had Jed up here instead of landing him on you, and if Venetia was in with Rob we might have a chance of knowing where she is now. As it is, she was able to slip out without anyone knowing anything about it.' She rested her chin on her hand and nibbled thoughtfully on a biscuit. 'I'm the last person Venetia would ever confide in, but she gets on well with you, Nella. I was wondering if she said anything to you about what might have been on her mind?'

'I don't think so,' I said doubtfully. 'At the cricket match she was talking about love in a garret and how it would be supportable with the right person.'

'She must really be in love if she's intending to live in a garret,' Janey said dryly, 'though I suppose it helps if you're providing yourself with a dowry in the form of a very expensive picture.'

'It also depends on what your definition of a garret is,' I pointed out. 'All she seemed to be able to talk about yesterday was Napier and Solange. Hey, hang on! She said she was going to ring Napier this morning . . .'

My voice tailed off as our eyes met. 'Of course! Why didn't I think of that before?' Janey jumped up. 'You're brilliant, Nella! You must have noticed this massive crush she's got on Napier, haven't you? God knows why, he's miles older than she is.' She smiled a little defensively. 'OK, OK, I know I'm hardly one to talk, but Napier's both older *and* stuffy to boot – and you certainly can't call Tom stuffy. But Venetia's always thought he's absolutely marvellous. He was very kind to her after her mother died, and she's never got over looking at him through rose-tinted spectacles. She even thinks he's one of the best-looking men she's ever met.' Goodness. Either Venetia hadn't met many good-looking men, which seemed highly unlikely, or those rose-tinted spectacles had very thick lenses indeed. 'Even if he only needed someone to help run his bath, she'd have gone haring over there to show him how without a second thought; it wouldn't occur to her to let anyone else know or watch out for poor innocent souls on their mopeds like Alain!'

'But if she's just gone over there to hold Napier's hand, why would she have taken the picture with her?' I asked.

Janey shrugged. 'Beats me, but then a lot about Venetia does. We'll just have to ask her and find out.' She dug the telephone out from under a heap of papers and began to punch out numbers, talking to me over her shoulder as she did so. 'I'd better get hold of her before Tom comes back; given the mood he's in, if he speaks to her the lines are liable to melt.'

She stuck her thumb in the air in triumph as the telephone was answered. 'Venetia! Glad to have tracked you down... You were about to ring us?... No, we didn't find your note, where did you leave it?... In your father's study? But he hasn't been in there yet. Things have been at sixes and sevens this morning,' she said with masterly understatement. 'You didn't think it would have been fair to tell Rob as well, before you left... Oh I see... you didn't know how long you were going to stay... at least today... yes, I suppose he *might* understand, I wouldn't bank on it though, because you've rather let him down, haven't you? I understand that Napier needs someone to help him entertain these wine buyers but...' Janey held the telephone slightly away from her ear as Venetia rambled on, her words reaching me where I was sitting as a mere vague tinny squeaking. At last she must have stopped to draw breath for Janey cut in quickly with, 'Yes, your father does want the farm car back. That's why it's called the farm car, because it's used on the farm... No, I don't think he'll feel like sending someone over to pick it up this afternoon . . . can't you bring it back yourself? . . . No, Venetia, given that you've apparently just jilted him for Napier I doubt Rob will really feel like ferrying over your clothes . . . it isn't like that? Really? . . . Of course I'm not passing judgement,' she said as Venetia's voice rose high in indignation. 'I think it's very kind of you to help Napier this way, but Rob might see it differently . . .' She looked up, eyes wide with alarm at the sound of voices along the corridor.

'What might I see differently?' asked Robert as he appeared in the doorway, looking rather tired and fed up. Tom, his face still set like thunder, was hard on his heels.

I made urgent shushing noises as Janey spun around, dropping her voice and cradling the telephone into her shoulder, and before either he or Tom could start asking exactly what was going on, I said loudly to mask Janey's voice, 'Would you both like some coffee? I've just made it. I'm sure you haven't had time for one so far. I'm so sorry about the picture, Tom, it must be such a shock for you. Here, have a biscuit.'

Tom took one, looking bemused to find me acting as hostess in his own kitchen, and ate it while I deliberately burbled away, clattered mugs and rattled milk jugs. 'Just what are you up to?' Robert asked quietly from behind me as I was reaching for the spoons. I jumped and dropped them on the floor.

'Keep your voice down,' I hissed. 'Janey's talking to Venetia and doesn't want Tom to know yet.'

She wouldn't have wanted Robert to know either, I realised a little too late as he stiffened. He had every reason to be livid with Venetia himself, didn't he? 'So that's why you popped up here, to tell us where she'd gone?' he asked in an icy voice.

'No. It was just a lucky guess,' I protested, but judging from the way his eyes were fixed on my face he had more than a fleeting suspicion that I was in this, right up to the neck.

In the sudden silence Janey's voice came over clear as a bell. 'Before you go, there's something I wanted to ask you.' She glanced uncertainly at Tom, took a deep breath and said rapidly, 'Um, er ... can you give the picture back? ... What picture? The Willard Sydney, of course. I know you feel you have a right to it, but this isn't the way ...'

Venetia's indignant squawk reverberated all around the kitchen. Janey listened for a few seconds, then Tom snatched the telephone from her. She looked at Robert and me and said flatly, 'She hasn't got it.' Her shoulders slumped. 'Of course, I'm pleased that she didn't steal it, but in a way I can't help wishing it *had* been her. It would have been such a relief to get it back so easily.'

'You're sure she doesn't have it?' Robert asked gently.

'Positive,' she replied. 'She's not a good enough actress to have faked that amount of outrage about Tom's carelessness in allowing it to be stolen.'

'I hope she's thought better of actually saying that to Tom,' Robert observed. 'Apparently not,' he said as Tom's face grew red with fury and his speech began to be punctuated by a series of intemperate, 'Look here, my girl's and 'Don't you speak to me like that's. We silently removed ourselves to the terrace out of earshot.

'Did she see the picture when she was leaving this morning?' Robert asked as we sat down. 'It could help us pinpoint when it was taken.'

Janey glanced at him curiously. 'I expect she went out the back like we normally do. The problem is, no one really sees the painting unless they're going out through the front door, do they?'

'So where is Venetia? Vielleroche?' It was impossible to tell from his voice whether he was deeply hurt or not, though a certain rigidity about his posture suggested he was feeling distinctly sniffy about the whole affair, and who could blame him? Perhaps that explained why he was apparently more concerned about locating the picture than his girlfriend. 'Has she given any indication of how long she's intending to administer succour to Napier?'

'She says she only went over for a couple of hours to see what she could do this morning, but things are at such sixes and sevens that she promised to stay there for at least two days to help him entertain some wine buyers who are arriving today.' She bit her lip, looking deeply embarrassed, and said in a rush, 'I'm so sorry, Rob, it's too bad of her. I don't think she really means anything by it. I'm sure that as far as she's concerned she's just helping out an old friend who's in trouble, and there's nothing more to it than that. It won't have occurred to her how it might seem to you . . .'

Her voice died away as a deeply sceptical expression settled on Robert's face and he said, 'I think what you mean, Janey, is that she didn't *care* how it might seem to me.'

There was a long silence until Tom stepped out

through the French windows. His mouth was set in a straight line, and he was in an even worse mood than before he'd had his conversation with his daughter. 'The police will be here in about half an hour,' he said, giving me a hostile look. I got up immediately, saying that I wouldn't hang around getting under their feet and that I'd be on my way. I scuttled off feeling relieved to have escaped so easily. Tom looked as if he was quite prepared to take out his blistering rage on everyone around him. Was about to, in fact, if the look of loathing he gave Robert was anything to go by.

No one believed me at first when I got back to the cottage and told them all about the art theft. Oscar accused me of having DT's, and Phil asked sceptically how anyone had managed to get past the dogs. Sally and Maggie were far more interested in what Venetia thought she was doing than in a missing picture, and began to speculate wildly whether Venetia had been concealing a torrid affair with Napier all this time. This flight of fancy fell to earth when they tried to imagine Napier being torrid, so then the two girls moved on to sympathising with Robert's heartbreak. Everyone looked pleasurably excited when I told them that Janey had said we might have to give statements as we'd all been up at the château last night. This led to a discussion of how you made a statement in a foreign language and wondering whether the gendarme interviewing us was going to look like Alain Delon.

'Probably more like Peter Sellers in *The Pink Panther*,' said Charlie.

None of them were right. Neither of the two gendarmes

who turned up in their blue Renault would have been given a part in any film, though the older fatter one, with the tummy bulging at the waistline, might have been considered as an extra playing the universal father type. His sidekick, a youth who looked as if he had only just started shaving, must have been brought along just to gain some experience on the job, for all he seemed to do was chew a pencil, look vacant and nod authoritatively when his senior made a pronouncement.

Not that either of them actually did much. The older one took our names and addresses and said that two detectives from the art squad were coming out from Bordeaux to take charge of the case. We were to present ourselves at three o'clock sharp at the local police station to be interviewed.

'You aren't accusing one of us of stealing the picture, are you?' asked Sally in a nervous voice.

Charlie put an arm around her shoulder and gave her a squeeze. 'Don't be silly, 'course he isn't!' But judging from the look on the gendarme's face, it was a distinct possibility.

Phil, who was still at that stage where a ride in a car was going to be absolute torture, protested weakly that it wouldn't be very convenient to go to the police station and couldn't our statements be taken here in the cottage.

'That is not the procedure in France, monsieur,' the older gendarme said in a severe voice, suddenly seeming a lot less avuncular. It might have been my imagination that he deliberately rested his hand on his hip to draw attention to the holster hanging from his belt, but certainly it dawned on us all simultaneously that it wasn't being used for his sandwiches but for a very large revolver.

Phil swallowed hard and said in a strangled voice that he'd be delighted to follow the French procedures. I got the impression that the junior who had been patently bored by the general lack of action felt a certain amount of regret that Phil had capitulated so easily.

'Good,' said the senior man, unsmiling. 'At three o'clock. Do not be late.'

The gendarmerie was an austere, box-shaped affair with barred windows. Oscar, as the one who spoke the best French and was therefore the least likely to annoy the guardians of the law by an execrable accent, had been elected to go and say we had arrived as ordered. The gendarme at the front desk raised his head slowly from the list he was studying and looked at him with a deadpan expression while Oscar's self-confidence began to leak out of him. The gendarme waited until it was in a puddle on the floor before he finally gestured with his head and said we were to go through that door there and wait until we were called.

Silently we filed in and sat down on a row of those plastic moulded chairs which seem to breed in any public place in any country. A vague effort had been made to brighten the room with a few out-of-date magazines heaped on a table, but their homely effect was offset by the posters on the walls of villainous-looking men, a couple of women too, who were wanted for a variety of offences from murder to armed robbery. The wordy notices which threatened us with enormous fines for breaking various laws weren't particularly cheering either since we couldn't understand them, so everybody sat in silence, knees pressed together like obedient little mice, almost too afraid to move in case we contravened some regulation or other. Even Maggie was affected by the atmosphere. I could have sworn that I saw her nibbling on a nail, and Sally said reflectively, 'I need a cigarette. Surely one in five years won't really matter, will it? Have you got one on you, Phil?'

'Wait until afterwards,' said Oscar warningly. 'It's against the law to smoke in public places and I bet that bloke behind the desk would be in here like a dose of salts the moment he smelt anything.'

'Oh,' said Sally weakly. There was a pause then she added, 'Aren't you guilty until proved innocent in this country?'

I think this thought had been lurking uneasily at the back of all our minds; it certainly had with me.

'All we're needed for is to fill in a few details about last night, not because the police believe one of us did the deed,' Oscar said rallyingly. 'Where do they imagine we could have stashed the loot? The cottage is too small; there aren't any hidey holes.'

'The kitchen's got lots of big cupboards,' I said.

'Come on,' he said scornfully. 'They're all in use. Even Charlie would have noticed several hundred thousand pounds' worth of picture propped on top of the spices as he groped inside the larder cupboard for the jam to go with his croissant.'

Sally shook her head. 'Doubt it. Charlie can't focus more than a few inches in front of himself in the mornings until he's drunk about three pints of coffee. Besides, he hasn't got his own breakfast once since we've been here,' she added with a mock ferocious glare.

Charlie made a big show of covering his head protectively and promised hastily to do it tomorrow.

Oscar looked at her adoringly and pressed his hands together. 'Wow! You make breakfast? Oh bliss! You wouldn't like to move in with me, would you, Sally? I've always thought you were something else, now I see you're quite, quite perfect!'

She laughed, her nerves fading away, and now the ice was broken we chatted, albeit in low voices, until the door opened and I was summoned. Why me first? I thought in a blind panic. Oscar leaned forward and squeezed my hand. 'Bowden – you're the first alphabetically, that's all,' he whispered.

I smiled gratefully. Afterwards I couldn't understand why I'd been so frightened. The detective from Bordeaux was a dark-haired man in his early thirties wearing jeans and an open-necked blue shirt who was going to fit every cliché Maggie and Sally might have dreamed up of what a French detective should look like, even down to his English which was fluent and idiomatic but with a marked accent. He introduced himself as Lieutenant Fournier and couldn't have been more friendly and charming, though something in his eyes made me feel that if I happened to get on his wrong side I'd see a sea change in his attitude as marked as the one in the gendarme this morning.

He'd already interviewed Janey and she'd told him that we'd stopped by the Sydney and admired it, which wasn't precisely how I would have described it but I couldn't help appreciating her careful use of language, so he wasn't particularly interested in hearing what I had to say about our conversation, which was a distinct relief. He wanted to know if I'd seen anyone lurking around in the courtyard when I put the picture cases in the car and more importantly, since Janey hadn't been wearing a watch, if I knew precisely what time it was when we'd been chatting in the hall. I didn't, to his regret.

'And you did not see the picture again, not even when you left?' he asked.

'The cars were parked in the courtyard, so we left by the back door.'

'And you went back to your friends after Madame Morrison went to look for her dog?'

I nodded, then as a man in the corner who was tapping my answers straight into the computer looked up with irritation, presumably gestures don't count, said out loud, 'Yes, I went straight back. Is that when you think the picture was taken?'

'We have not made up our minds what happened yet, Mademoiselle,' the Lieutenant said in a repressive voice. He didn't say it was his job to ask questions not mine but he might just as well have for the suddenly chill atmosphere that settled in the little interview room. Just as I was beginning to imagine that the shadow of the oubliette was looming over me, he stood up and said, 'Thank you for giving us your time, mademoiselle, you have been very helpful. You are planning to go back to London on Sunday?'

'Thursday. I've got a family party to go to.'

He hesitated, then shrugged. 'I do not expect there will

be any problems in giving you permission to leave,' he said then, as I made a sound of protest, 'but it will not help our investigation if we allow all the . . . witnesses to leave the country before we are certain we have finished questioning them.'

Since his first choice of word might have been 'suspect' I didn't protest any further and meekly went to have my fingerprints taken, a much messier procedure than I would have imagined, as the ink does not come off easily. I was then shown into another little room. I was to be segregated from the others until after they had given their statements, presumably so we couldn't cook up matching stories. Quite why we would have found it necessary to wait until we were actually in the gendarmerie to start inventing alibis for each other was beyond me but I didn't feel it would be tactful to question the police mentality in this way. I settled down to wait and amused myself by boning up on yet another selection of the local villains whose portraits were adorning the walls around me.

CHAPTER 18

Within twenty minutes of our getting back to the cottage Janey, looking tired and worn around the edges and with fingers still tinged with blue from fingerprinting ink, just 'happened' to pass by. Her excuse was that Lily needed exercising. Since she knew how nerve wracking one's first encounter with the French police system could be, she thought, in best British stiff upper lip tradition, that a brisk walk was just what I needed. Actually, I would have far rather soothed my ruffled nerves with a stiff gin and tonic but I wasn't allowed that option. We wandered off down the little road while Lily hunted for imaginary bunnies in the vines. It took only about thirty seconds once we were out of earshot to reassure Janey that I'd been thoroughly discreet with the police, and about another minute and a half to say that according to our post mortem in the gendarmerie car park, none of the others had had a particularly bad time with the detective either, though they'd kept Charlie a worryingly long time. We were beginning to get seriously concerned when he appeared, completely unfazed, saying that he had been discussing Manchestaire's chances in the European Cup with the desk gendarme.

'How's it going with you?' I asked.

She cast her eyes upwards in an expressive gesture. 'Don't ask,' she said grimly, then promptly added, 'it's absolute hell! Tom's in the most filthy mood. It's understandable, I suppose. He's incredibly embarrassed by the way Venetia's behaved to Rob and his picture's been stolen, which is enough to put even the most amenable person into a bad temper, but there's absolutely *no* need for him to take it out on poor Rob. He's even taken to growling at him about not getting out of bed early enough this morning.'

'What difference would that have made?' I asked, wondering if I was missing something.

'Don't ask me. Tom seems to be beyond logic at the moment,' Janey said in some exasperation. 'I've given up asking, I just get snapped at too! Anyway I think Rob is behaving like an absolute saint, though if things continue like this I won't blame him if he moves out to the B & B in the village until the police say he can leave. I might even join him there!' She kicked a loose stone on the road out of the way and said gruffly, 'Of course what's really on Tom's mind is the possibility that the insurance are going to refuse to pay up because we didn't have the alarm on. I'm glad to say he hasn't got around to pinning *that* on Rob's shoulders yet.'

'But if there was a fault . . .' I began.

'There's a provision in the policy for when the alarm's out of order, but if the insurance company discovers I told you it wasn't on they'd certainly use it as an excuse to wriggle out of divvying up, wouldn't they? Not that according to the police it would have made any difference.

They say it would have taken any half-competent intruder about thirty seconds to realise it wasn't on, but all the same . . .'

'No wonder you were in such a paddy this morning.'

'I hadn't even thought of it then,' she said wryly. 'I just wanted to stop Tom finding out about what we'd been doing last night. And before we can start thinking of insurance payouts we've got to see if the picture's going to be recovered, though the detective in charge doesn't seem to think there's much hope of that. He said it could already be out of the country and might well have been stolen to order.' She pushed her hair out of her face with a dispirited gesture. 'At least that's a notion we can live with, although it's not nice to think a stranger has been in your house. What's worse are the sort of questions the police have been asking us, like do we have any ideas about who might have taken it – by which they mean our friends or employees.' She laughed humourlessly. 'We've already accused Venetia of larceny once today, so we kept quiet on that.'

She jerked to attention as a spotted bottom disappeared into a half-derelict hut on the edge of the road. 'Hey, Lily, get out of there! I don't care if it is a cat you're after!' she shouted. 'Tramps doss down in there for the night sometimes and there's broken glass all over the floor from their wine bottles. She could cut herself.' We heard excited snufflings coming from inside the hut; Lily obviously wasn't going to come out. I went in, wrinkling my nose at the smell – it appeared the tramps also used it as a lavatory – and grabbing Lily's collar, pulled her away from the pile of wood she was sniffing at and dragged her out as fast as possible so that I didn't have to take a second breath.

'Thanks,' Janey said, and began scolding her dog for being a silly disobedient hound. The Dalmatian didn't show any visible signs of remorse. 'We've had the scene of crime people crawling all over the house all day as well, and the mess is unbelievable. There's so much fingerprint powder dusted around the hall it looks as if a flour lorry has had an accident in there. Josette, my *femme de ménage*, is throwing a complete wobbly over how she's ever going to clean it up again.'

I swallowed nervously. I'd been leaning backwards, resting my hands on the hall table while I was talking to Janey last night. What were the police going to think about this irrefutable evidence that placed me at the scene of the crime? Yes, they already knew I'd been there, but the sheer quantity of prints were bound to give the lie to my implication that Janey and I had merely lingered a moment or two to glance at the picture before moving on. I've read quite enough detective novels to know that the instant the police reckon you haven't been telling them the full and unvarnished truth you go straight to the top of their Most Wanted list. 'My fingerprints are all over the hall table,' I croaked.

Janey laughed. 'Oh, you don't have to worry about that. Josette saw a smear on it as she was going to unlock the front door this morning and whipped out the duster she always has in her pocket for those dusting emergencies and gave it a quick going over. The fingerprint man went ballistic, especially as Josette is a complete star at polishing and there isn't a print left anywhere except for a faint smudge at the back which may or may not belong to the thief, or could just be mine from when I was rearranging the photographs yesterday. To make it worse, Josette can't even tell them if the picture was on the wall while she was busily destroying evidence; she says she has far too much to do to waste her time by looking at *things*! She's not sure if the front door was unlocked or not either; we often get up and unlock it before she arrives so it wouldn't have struck her as unusual if it was. All she is sure of is that the loo window was open as usual, and the bunch of lavender which lives on the windowsill had been knocked on the floor, but as there aren't any marks no one can tell if it was the cat who prefers the window to his catflap for some reason, or the thief who could have wriggled in and then gone out by the front door.'

'Through the *loo window*?' I echoed. 'But it's minute.'

'I'm assured that there are some very small thieves about these days,' she said seriously. 'It could even have been a child who then opened the door for his or her accomplices.'

We contemplated this prospect in silence for a moment. 'Still doesn't explain how they got past the dogs,' I said thoughtfully.

'One of the detectives said the most likely explanation is that there was a specialist there whose sole job was to quieten the dogs while his mates lifted the picture; otherwise an opportunist could have walked in this morning while the dogs were cadging off Josette in the kitchen and failing completely in their duty of guarding the house.'

I felt a cold shiver go down my spine. 'He can't be

serious. Surely nobody would have the nerve to wander in like that?'

'You'd be surprised. The fingerprint man was telling me about a case in the Médoc where Madame got out of her bath to fetch something and wandered into her bedroom wearing only a light covering of bath bubbles to discover a strange man going through her jewel box.'

'Oh dear. What happened?' I asked.

Janey giggled. 'He took a good long look, said that with a magnificent figure like hers she'd have no problem in persuading her husband to replace everything, and stuffed the whole lot in his pocket before vamoosing out of the window!' We both laughed.

'Oh dear,' she sighed as we reached a fork in the road, 'I suppose I ought to get back and think about making something for supper, though I doubt anyone has much appetite. I will certainly get indigestion if Tom goes on glaring at Rob like that! He's even taken to muttering that if Rob had kept Venetia under better control she'd never have made a spectacle of herself in this way. Honestly – as if *anyone* has ever been able to stop Venetia doing anything she doesn't want to.'

'How is she?' I asked.

'Frankly, I don't really care,' Janey said in an exasperated voice, as we turned around and started back. 'I know it's just bad luck and bad timing that she should pull her dramatic little stunt at exactly the same time as the Sydney gets stolen, but somehow it's so typical of Venetia to find a way to hog the limelight. She's staying with Napier until the end of the week and then who knows? She rang me to ask if I thought she ought to come back, though she sounded more worried about letting Napier down than about any upsets we might be feeling, but I said that after their argument this morning, it might be better if she stayed out of Tom's way for a while.'

'And what does Robert think about it all?' I asked, trying not to seem too interested.

I got a long, measuring look. 'He isn't saying,' she said finally. 'Though he did mutter that Napier was probably something she had to get out of her system and a week or so in his company should do the trick.'

'That sounds unusually tolerant,' I said after a pause.

'Quite uncannily so,' she agreed. 'Maybe he's decided that if he makes a fuss she'll just dig her heels in, whereas if he sits it out and pretends he doesn't really care she'll come back to him eventually.'

I found I disliked this notion intensely. Not that it was any of my business. I doubted that Venetia would really be as keen to stay in contact as she claimed, once we'd both got back to London, and I certainly wouldn't be seeing Robert, but I still didn't want him to be hurt. And if he really was waiting for her to come back he almost certainly would get hurt. For if she did come back she was bound to do a runner again sometime in the future. As my father used to say about my mother's greatest friend, 'Once a bolter, always a bolter,' though to be honest Fiona used to bolt with just about anything that crossed her path in trousers (and in kilts on a couple of occasions), and Venetia hadn't gone that far, but the principle was the same.

It wasn't my affair, I reminded myself again, and concentrated on Janey's tale of a messy incident involving the twins and a fingerprint set that had been left unguarded. When we reached the gate to the cottage, I promised her I'd come up for coffee in the morning to catch up on the latest news and went in. I was so deep in thought that the blue BMW parked alongside the other cars didn't register on my consciousness and it wasn't until I was heading across the garden to where everyone was standing around a table at one end of the pool that I heard a familiar loud laugh and came to abruptly.

'What's the matter, Nella?' Oscar asked in a concerned voice at my far from *sotto voce* 'Oh bugger!'

'Um, just cricked my ankle,' I lied hastily. George was the last person I wanted to see just at this moment but there was no need to spell it out.

Oscar wasn't fooled. He gave me a distinctly wary look before saying, 'Hugh and George brought back the car Venetia borrowed from Tom,' as if to point out that for once he hadn't set this up, while George broke off his conversation with Sally and Charlie and came over to give me a kiss.

'Tom invited us to stay for a drink but we thought it would be a bit of an imposition, so we decided to come and see you,' he said, smiling down at me as if he expected me to take this visit as a personal compliment and be delighted at it too. But then sensitivity to undercurrents has never been George's forte. Nor had a well-developed sense of colour, I thought, doing my best to avoid looking at his shirt, an unpleasant shade of yellow which looked particularly ghastly against his colouring.

'Tom wasn't being all that welcoming either,' said

Hugh. 'He seems to be holding everyone at Vielleroche responsible for Venetia's behaviour, which is really unfair. To start off with, Napier didn't ask her to come; she insisted it was the least she could do to aid a family friend.'

'Really?' I asked with interest. That wasn't what she'd told Janey. 'Even so, Tom still thinks Napier's taking advantage of Venetia's good nature.'

'Tom needn't worry. Napier isn't taking advantage of anything,' Hugh said shrewdly. 'It's separate bedrooms and all that; she's even been put in the guest suite across the courtyard. Short of having a Spanish duenna sitting outside her door all night it couldn't be more proper.' He paused thoughtfully. 'Except that instead of the Spanish duenna we've got Carlton, who I doubt is anything like as keen on preserving Venetia's virtue! He turned up this afternoon to talk to Napier about taking over the wine-making, and seemed to me to be paying much more attention to Venetia's legs than to what Napier was saying about his winemaking practices.'

'Can you blame him? Her legs are well worth looking at,' Phil murmured reminiscently, then whipped around to see if Maggie had heard with such a comical look of apprehension that we all burst out laughing.

In my absence it had been decided that since none of us felt much like squaring up to domestic duties we should go out for dinner. I had no quarrel with this, especially since I was down to do the washing up (again), and the arguments were flying over where we should go. Maggie and Sally appeared to be missing the sort of haunts they frequented in London, for they wanted to try a highly recommended place with two Michelin stars where the speciality was lobster. Much to my relief, since a two-star restaurant would make my bank account implode completely, Charlie said it was too hot for rich food like lobster and foie gras. When Sally began to disagree, Oscar cut in saying he was sure somewhere as smart as that wouldn't be able to fit us in at such short notice, and why didn't we try the place in the village that Janey said was simple but good?

This was agreed to, but Maggie said in that case we must all celebrate a fantastic holiday by going out somewhere really special on our last evening. I couldn't help wondering if she was choosing that particular night for celebration because with luck, and the agreement of the gendarmes, I'd be well away in Cumbria for Granny and Grandad's anniversary. I let the restaurant talk wash over me and allowed my thoughts to drift.

I came back to earth and the conversation as George laughed abruptly and said, 'All this stuff about someone coming in through the window or a gang of thieves has got to be so much guff! Is it really likely? I'll bet you that, whatever the police are saying, the reason they aren't letting any of you leave the country yet is that their chief suspects are those who were in the château last night around the time the picture was taken.'

There was an uncomfortable silence as we looked uneasily at each other.

'Are you suggesting that one of us did it?' Charlie asked curiously. 'Me, for example?'

'Doubt it. Didn't you say you left early to take Sally back because she had fallen asleep?' asked Hugh. That was one way of putting it; other people might have used 'passed out'.

'You can't rule him out entirely, Hugh,' George said reprovingly. 'Any one of them could have stolen the picture.' He looked at us all with the confident air of the man who knows he is beyond suspicion.

Sally gazed at him reproachfully. 'None of us is a thief, George.'

'I know that. Besides, if any of you *were* you'd have to have done it while you were going to the loo, say. You wouldn't have had much time to get the thing off the wall and hidden somewhere, and it would have been incredibly risky. Someone else might have come out at any moment.'

'You've obviously really thought about this,' Phil remarked, filling up his glass as he spoke.

'Well, it's interesting to stretch your brains over a problem like this,' George said modestly. I wondered as he raised his head and looked meaningfully out over the garden if he was imagining himself as some Golden Age amateur sleuth – Lord Peter Wimsey for instance. They certainly had similar noses.

'And since Venetia's talked about virtually nothing else all day it's been difficult *not* to think about it,' Hugh said simply.

'So if it isn't one of us, who are you suggesting did it?' I asked, sure that I already knew the answer.

George steeled his fingers in best Sherlock Holmes fashion. 'Tom and Janey wouldn't have stolen their own picture, naturally.' Phil muttered in an undertone that this sort of thing wasn't entirely unknown, but George pretended not to hear him. 'Apparently Venetia's in the clear, something to do with a chap she gave a lift to the village to who was able to see that the only thing she had in the car was her handbag – it's open at the back, nowhere to stash a picture. No, it's obvious who the police must be looking at. And if they aren't, they damn well should be – that Winwood fellow.'

Just because you're expecting something doesn't make it any more palatable. 'That's an *outrageous* thing to say!'

George smiled patronisingly at me. 'I know that Robert is an old friend of yours, Nella – a *very* old friend, from what I hear.' Several heads turned to look at me in sudden interest. 'Of course you don't want to believe it, but you can't let loyalty blind you to the facts. He's probably changed a lot from the days when you knew him,' he added kindly as if I should find this some consolation. 'I've been analysing the facts and certainly they indicate that he deserves further investigation.' He began counting off on his fingers. 'Firstly, he had the opportunity, much more so than any of you. All he had to do was wait until everyone went to bed, then he'd have had all the time in the world to take the picture and conceal it somewhere.'

'Robert was the one who raised the alarm. He wouldn't have done that if he'd stolen the picture, would he,' Sally said, wrinkling her brow.

'People do that sort of thing as a smokescreen all the time,' George said authoritatively. 'You read stories in the tabloids every week about men who tearfully report their wives as missing when they've actually murdered them and buried them under the patio.'

'But you never read the tabloids, George,' I said sweetly. 'So where do you get to hear about these stories?'

He ignored me but that was nothing unusual; George never replied to inconvenient remarks. 'Secondly, we all know that it's a valuable picture but I ask you; which one of us has any idea where you can get rid of something like that without too many awkward questions being asked about its provenance? We don't know, but an art dealer would.'

To my fury I saw a couple of heads being nodded in tentative agreement.

'I suggest you don't repeat that statement in front of Adam Thirkiss from Vanden's next time we see him. He won't appreciate you inferring that he knows how to unload a dodgy picture,' Hugh said warningly, looking as if he could already see the slander suits raining down all about us.

'Of course, I don't mean people like *him*. He only deals in reputable stuff – even sold a couple of pictures belonging to my aunt once. But Winwood is another kettle of fish completely. The fellow admits quite openly that he sells fakes.'

'Reproductions are *not* fakes!' I said indignantly.

'They are in my book,' pronounced George as if this was the final word on the matter. I had a strong urge to wipe that smug expression off his face. 'He might *say* that he always tells his clients that what they are buying isn't genuine, but are you really so naïve as to believe that?' He looked around the assembled company, raising his eyebrows sceptically to show that he certainly wasn't. The urge to do something was getting even stronger. I took a few deep breaths to try and calm myself.

'There's just one problem with your theory, George,' Maggie said coolly. 'Robert isn't stupid, and as you say he's got resources we don't have. If he *had* been planning to steal the Sydney, he'd have had one of his own copies painted first so he could put it in the original's place, then no one would have realised it had gone.'

I stared at her in amazement and gratitude. It felt distinctly strange.

George looked nonplussed for a moment, then said in a voice of enormous generosity, 'I'm not saying he *planned* it; it must have been a spur of the moment thing.'

'Come on, George, be fair,' Oscar broke in. 'You don't have any real reason to suppose that Robert isn't as honest as the day is long.'

George snorted. 'What about some of those calls in the cricket match? You know as well as I do that some of them were blatantly wrong. For instance, how about when I bowled you out and he said it was a no ball? Or when he said I was LBW? I certainly *wasn't*,' he huffed, obviously still smarting about this injustice. 'Haven't you heard of the old adage that if a man cheats at cricket then you can be sure that he cheats at other things too?'

'Of all the stupid, pompous things to say!' I took a step towards him.

'Now come on, Nella, you can't get upset over the reasonable analysis of a few facts.' He stepped sideways a prudent pace or two, taking him to within a foot or so of the edge of the pool.

The temptation was just too much. I put out both hands and pushed – hard.

CHAPTER 19

There can't be many better feelings than the one you get when you've just scored a double whammy. Not only had I got George to shut up, he couldn't help it with the amount of pool water he swallowed, but at the same time I had kiboshed Oscar's matchmaking plans for once and for all. Not even *that* eternal optimist could imagine George was ever going to look on me with a kindly eye again.

I was peacefully enjoying a cup of coffee in the sun the next morning and reliving the highly satisfying moment when George hit the water with an almighty splash, when the gendarmes came back. There were three of them this time, the two who had been here yesterday and a woman whom I hadn't seen before. Oscar heaved himself up off the sun lounger where he was recovering from a brisk swim and went over to speak to them, coming back a few seconds later looking worried.

'They want to talk to you, Nella.'

'Me? What for?'

He shrugged helplessly as the woman, dressed like her colleagues in blue shirt and trousers, her hair drawn back

311

tightly in a pony tail, followed him and said slowly, 'Mees Bowden? You will come with us, please. We have questions to ask you.'

For one wild moment I thought that George must have got his own back by making a formal complaint against me for assault, then it dawned on me that George wouldn't do a thing like that. He might have his faults but he wasn't petty; his French wasn't good enough either.

'What do you want to talk to me about?' I asked in a squeaky tone. It was pretty obvious that it had to be something to do with the Sydney, but what?

'You will find that out in due course.'

Hardly reassuring, I thought nervously. I said with what I hoped was a winning smile, 'Shall we go somewhere more private to talk? Over there perhaps?'

'The interview will be conducted at the gendarmerie,' she said coldly.

'Is Nella being arrested?' Oscar asked.

The gendarme looked at him for a moment as if deciding whether to answer or not. 'Not yet,' she said finally.

'But what's it about?' he persisted, not put off in the slightest by her forbidding tone. 'What's Nella supposed to have done?'

'That I may not tell you, Monsieur.' She somehow implied that if Oscar went on badgering her he'd find himself hauled along to the gendarmerie as well and charged with something, probably annoying a member of the police force.

He opened his mouth again but I cut in, 'It's all right,

Oscar. I daresay it's nothing – just some mistake or other.' I tried hard to believe that the gendarme's expression wasn't saying 'oh no, it's not!' 'But I need to get changed out of my swimsuit first.'

She nodded gravely. 'That is permitted, but I will come with you.'

So that's why they'd brought a woman with them, I thought as I walked into the cottage on jelly legs, so I could be decently accompanied into my bedroom in case I used the excuse I was looking for clean underwear to leg it out of the window. She was scrupulously polite, standing in one corner studiously not looking as I fumbled around for the bra that didn't have the rip in the lace – I didn't think it was likely I was going to be strip-searched, the Sydney was too big for even the most ample cup size, but there was no harm in covering all eventualities – but there was no mistaking that she was on the alert for any sudden movement. Why had they settled on *me*? I thought as I brushed my hair. It couldn't be anything to do with what Janey and I had said, could it? Surely the art squad couldn't be so desperate to improve their clear-up rate that they'd resorted to snatching at straws this soon in the investigation? Particularly since if Janey had already told them about it, she'd also have told them I left the house empty-handed.

I was going to find out soon enough, wasn't I? I thought fearfully. I was about to say that I was ready to go, when the gendarme's voice rapped out: 'What are those?'

I started. 'Er what?' I asked, probably looking the very

image of trying-to-gain-a-bit-of-time guilt.

'Those!' she snapped, pointing at Min's wedding presents, now safely stowed away in the cases Robert had given me, which were leaning against the wall at the end of my bed.

'My pictures. Do you want to see them?' With a chopping motion of her hand she motioned me to stay away and whipped out a walkie-talkie affair. Within seconds, heavy footsteps pounded up the stairs and the other two gendarmes raced in, making the small room feel uncomfortably crowded.

I was taken out onto the landing and one gendarme stood guard while the other two laid the cases on the bed with expectant expressions. Whether they were disappointed with what they found or not I couldn't tell from their impassive expressions, though the man started scribbling down something in a notebook while the youth did a cursory search of all the more obvious places you might hide a picture. My heart rose into my mouth as he exclaimed in excitement and lifted up the mattress; this was all getting so surreal that I was beginning to believe there really might be a Post Impressionist hidden under there. I hadn't even realised I was holding my breath until he held up a T-shirt I must have tucked into the bed by accident when I made it, and I took in a great big relieved gulp of air.

That was probably a mistake, for the woman frowned, as if by expressing relief I'd virtually confessed to hiding something, and her face went into even more severe lines as she informed me that a team was on its way to search the cottage. 'And you will tell your friends that they may not enter the house until we are finished,' she said to Oscar who, to her open displeasure, had followed us upstairs.

'Wait!' he said as we were about to leave. She turned to him in irritation. 'When are you bringing Nella back?'

'When we have finished with her.' In the circumstances it was a reasonable enough answer, but hardly reassuring. 'Step aside, please.'

Oscar didn't move. 'Does she need a lawyer?'

'There will be time for that later on. She has not been charged with anything.' I could hear the unspoken 'yet' reverberating in my ears and wondered if it was actually true that you could pass out from sheer tension. Sadly it didn't seem to be so because I would have done almost anything to delay walking out of the house, a gendarme on either side of me, under the appalled eyes of Maggie, Sally, Charlie and Phil who were grouped uncertainly in the middle of the lawn talking in low voices. Oscar trotted alongside us, looking even more terrified than I felt, telling me not to worry, he was sure it wasn't anything, the police must have mistaken me for someone else. I'd be back in half an hour and if I wasn't he'd find me the best lawyer there was. If necessary he'd go to the consulate and get them on the case ...

'That is enough, Monsieur,' the older gendarme said, not unkindly, as I got into the back of the car.

Oscar took no notice and was still going on making reassuring noises as the door was shut and cut him off. I mouthed, 'Thanks,' and made an effort to smile, though it was all I could do not to burst into tears of apprehension as we drove away.

At the gendarmerie, I was shown straight into an interview room, a different one from yesterday. It had a barred window that looked out onto an asphalt enclosure at the back and a one-storey breeze-block building with heavily barred windows. Was it intentional that every time I looked out of the window I couldn't help seeing the cell block and the exercise yard? A sort of softening-up technique maybe? If so it certainly worked, for by the time someone came to interview me about two hours later, I was so wound up that if it was going to get me out of there any quicker, I would happily have confessed to being every single one of the armed robbers in the posters I'd memorised yesterday – even the bullet-headed one with *Maman* tattooed on his arm.

This time there were two detectives, the man from yesterday, again in jeans and open-necked shirt, and an elegant woman in her forties wearing a short-sleeved, short-skirted suit that was incredibly stylish but I bet was also practical enough to allow her to chase after and tackle any miscreant who was unwise enough to try and make a break for it.

'Thank you for coming to see us, Miss Bowden,' she said in English, making it sound as if it had really been my choice that I was here. 'I hope that we have not kept you waiting too long?'

I mumbled something. She might have smiled at me as she came in, but she looked about as user-friendly and easy to deceive as my old headmistress. She introduced herself as Capitaine Dubesset, told me to sit down at the scuffed Formica table and took the seat opposite me, while a mousy little translator, who hardly seemed necessary given how good the detectives' English was, sat on one side and Lieutenant Fournier sat at her right hand. For a minute or so there was silence while she frowned and rubbed at a scratch on the surface of the table with a fuchsia-pink fingertip which only served to remind me that I'd occupied some of the last two hours by peeling off my nail varnish. I hid my fingers in my lap as, satisfied at last, the Capitaine took out a pad and aligned it absolutely square in front of her, before looking up and beginning her questions.

Whenever I read about people being interrogated by the police they seem to be able to recall what was said to them and what they replied, virtually word for word. I can only admire their powers of recall. Most of what went on during the hours I spent in that stuffy little room has passed into a blur and only a few clear details stand out, such as when I realised that whatever it was they were suspicious about, it had nothing to do with a certain conversation I'd had about stealing pictures with Janey. I also recall glancing out of the window while I was being asked for the third time to describe to my sceptical listeners exactly what I'd done between leaving Janey to find Lily and sitting down next to Oscar on the sofa, to realise with a sinking heart how close the cell block was.

At first, it wasn't too bad. The questions were simple, easy to answer – in retrospect I can see that they were softening me up. Then the tempo began to hot up and the questions started to range all over the place, probably deliberately so to keep me off balance, from my apparent interest in buying pictures, to why I'd chosen to have my holiday in Château du Pré's gîte, to if I'd brought the

picture carriers out with me from England, to how I
knew the others in the cottage, to had I ever worked for a
dealer or one of the auction houses (thank God Sotheby's
had turned my application down), back to my interest in
pictures and what I'd personally thought of the Willard
Sydney. I tried to answer as truthfully as possible; it was
quite easy since I didn't have anything to hide. Even so I
got the distinct feeling that the two detectives were none
too impressed by some of my answers, particularly when
I denied, yet again, that my object in coming to the gîte at
Château du Pré was to renew my relationship with
Venetia.

'But you shared an *appartement* with her!' the Lieutenant exclaimed. 'You say you forgot all about her. How
is this?'

'Of course I didn't forget her entirely,' I said, flounder-
ing.

'So you change your mind – you did *not* forget her?'
he said triumphantly.

'Yes, I did. Well, not completely.' I saw them look at
each other significantly. Well done, Nella! How to
destroy your own credibility in thirty seconds, I thought,
wondering when I was going to be escorted to that cell
block. I then attempted the near-impossible task of
explaining convincingly how it is that you can almost
forget someone entirely but remember everything about
them the moment you see them again.

By the time I was told we were breaking for lunch I
was completely exhausted by trying not to incriminate
myself. I'd probably already done it, I thought gloomily.
I'd been expecting that I'd have prison fodder brought to

me on a metal tray and would be eating it under the watchful eye of a frowning gendarme, but much to my surprise I was told that I was allowed to go out and eat where I wished though I was to present myself back at the gendarmerie no later than two o'clock. I was reminded politely that I'd surrendered my passport this morning, so presumably making a dash for it was pretty pointless. I'd hoped to go to a little café just down the road but the two detectives and the translator were already in there tucking into large portions of the *plat du jour*, so I bought a can of Coke and an egg and salad baguette and went to sit on a bench and eat it in the sun.

Unfortunately my lack of foresight in not bringing my book with me meant I had nothing to occupy myself with, though in the circumstances I probably wouldn't have been able to concentrate on even the raciest thriller, so it was inevitable I fell back to worrying. Despite the random nature of their questions a clear pattern had emerged of the way my interrogators' thoughts were leading them. I had once shared a flat with Venetia, yet I hadn't mentioned this when I was being questioned yesterday. Most suspiciously of all, although I denied recalling anything specific Venetia might have told me about the Willard Sydney, I had recognised it the moment I saw it at Château du Pré. Who had told them *that*, incidentally? Had I deliberately manoeuvred myself into being included in the group renting the gîte? They were keeping an open mind on that, it seemed. I had reacquainted myself with Venetia the moment I saw her, thus making sure I was invited up to the château on several occasions and giving me the perfect opportunity to case the joint. I was intensely thankful that no one had cottoned onto the fact that I'd done History of Art at A-level, but even without that little nugget, which would have proved I had a certain amount of knowledge, as well as the opportunity, the case against me was building up in a seemingly logical manner.

There was only one thing wrong with the hypothesis. I hadn't done it. But I couldn't prove it. And, as everyone kept telling me, to get off a charge in this country I had to prove my innocence. Oh God. As the last bit of baguette turned to stone in my throat I tried to think of something cheerful, but deep dark thoughts in the sunshine are even more insidious than the ones you have somewhere gloomy. By the time I presented myself back at the gendarmerie at precisely two minutes to two I had worked myself up into such a state that I was convinced I was about to be charged with grand larceny, and was wondering how many months, years even, it would be before I saw my own homeland.

'I do not think we have many more questions to ask you,' Capitaine Dubesset said with a pleasant smile as she sat down. 'You have been very helpful, Miss Bowden, but we would like to check a few details with you before we take you back to your gîte.'

I stared at her incredulously, hardly daring to believe my good fortune. She nodded graciously in confirmation and looked at a sheet of paper in front of her, making a couple of notes while her colleague smiled at me too and asked how I'd travelled to France. I said in Oscar's car and I was going back, if allowed to, by train tomorrow. Surely even the most suspicious detective couldn't think I'd be transporting stolen property by *train*, I thought, as I explained, yet again, that my early departure was for a family celebration. Another twenty minutes of dotting i's and crossing t's in this way and the Capitaine gathered her notes into a neat pile, looked up and said in the same pleasant tone she'd just used to confirm my profession, 'Did you have an accomplice in this plan to steal Monsieur Morrison's picture, or did you do it on your own?'

For a moment I couldn't believe that I'd heard right and nearly had to ask her to repeat the question. 'Plan? What plan?' I said, jerked straight back into heart-hammering fear. 'What do you mean?'

She looked at me as if I was very stupid. No doubt compared to her I was. She'd already demonstrated that she could run rings around me as far as lulling someone into a sense of false security was concerned. 'Do not pretend with me, Miss Bowden,' she said in a voice so frigid it seemed to have icicles in it. 'We have had the information already. You were heard saying you were going to steal the picture.'

'You've had the information...?' I echoed. 'As in *denouncing* someone? Like they used to do when they were sending someone to the guillotine during the Revolution?'

'We have not had the guillotine in France for many years.' The Lieutenant sounded as if he regretted this intensely. 'Answer the question. Do you deny saying you were going to steal the picture?'

I stared at the two implacable faces in front of me, feeling sicker by the moment. I'd always heard that when you're being interviewed like this there's a Mr Nice and a Ms Nasty or whatever. It seemed that I'd landed up with both Monsieur and Madame Nasty. My mouth was so dry it seemed as if my tongue had cleaved to its roof, and my heart was racing so fast I began to have a panicky feeling that shortly I wasn't going to be able to breathe.

I used to fantasise when I was a child about being a brave, derring-do sort of spy stoically bearing all sorts of horrid things and refusing to give up my secrets no matter what was done to me. Now I know I'd be completely useless; the first sight of an implement of torture and I'd be spilling the beans all over the place. It only took the Capitaine to say she was entitled to hold me for forty-eight hours without charge and I caved in. She tapped her pen pointedly on the table top, waiting for my answer. I looked over her shoulder through the window. The cell block seemed even more prominent. Sorry, Janey, I thought miserably as I shook my head.

'Out loud, *si'l vous plait*,' she snapped.

'Yes, I said I'd been working out how to steal it,' I whispered. 'But it was only a joke.'

'A joke?' she repeated. 'You think it is a *joke* to take the picture that belongs to your friend?'

'But I *didn't* steal it! I was just larking about with Janey.'

Whatever she was expecting me to say it wasn't that. Her face froze into disbelief. 'Janey? You mean Madame Morrison?' Her pen scribbled furiously over her pad as she made notes. She leaned forward, eyes glittering. 'Madame Morrison is planning to take the picture of her own husband?' she asked, grammatical English deserting her in the excitement of such a spectacular coup. 'Why is this? What reason has she?'

'No, no,' I cried, seeing this getting worse and worse. God, they'd be arresting Janey next. 'Look, I'll tell you what happened . . .' Well, I did, sort of. I just didn't get around to telling them that Janey had told me that the burglar alarm was off. After all, it wasn't really relevant. I hadn't made use of the information, had I? But I did include most of the rest.

The two detectives listened to me in impassive silence, only breaking in once or twice to clarify parts of my narrative, heads nodding occasionally, glancing at each other a couple of times. I didn't have a clue whether they believed me or not, and I could feel my heartbeat accelerating again as I came to the part where I'd sat down next to Oscar, and presumably whoever had split on me had heard me announce I was thinking of stealing the picture.

There was a long silence then the Lieutenant said, 'Yesterday when I asked you how long you had looked at the picture with Madame Morrison you said only a few seconds. Why did you not tell me you spent several minutes talking about it with her?'

I swallowed uncomfortably, wondering what the penalties were in this country for deliberately misleading a police officer. Judging from the icy way he was looking at me, he was in the mood to exact every single one of them. 'Because I promised her I wouldn't,' I said eventually. 'She doesn't want her husband to know she even joked about wanting his picture to be stolen.'

The Capitaine's iron façade cracked a little as she

nodded slightly, looking as if she understood that sort of feeling all too well. It made me wonder what on earth Monsieur Dubesset was like.

After that, though it was like swimming uphill through treacle, I began to get the sense as I went over my movements that evening again and again that my version of events was winning through and they were starting to believe me. The Lieutenant fetched a pile of statements which had been taken yesterday, and the two detectives leafed through them, asking me a question from time to time, ticking off something in the margin, then asking another. They seemed particularly interested in my relations with everyone in the cottage and wanted to know if there had been any rows, so I shamefacedly admitted to my grapple with Phil and the little incident in the kitchen with Charlie. Lieutenant Fournier looked at me with interest and a certain degree of puzzlement, as if trying to work out how this frazzled creature in front of him who hadn't been allowed any time for putting on makeup this morning could possibly have created so much havoc. He shook his head slightly as if this confirmed everything he'd heard about the English male. They got up and retired discreetly to one corner of the room to have a whispered conversation, glancing frequently over at me and from time to time making portentous nods.

It was getting late; presumably they were going to pack up for the day soon. I was trying to convince myself that I wasn't going to be the first person in my family to find out what the inside of a French cell, any cell, was like when they left their corner and came back to their seats. My heart was in my mouth, my cautious optimism evaporating as the moment for hearing what they were planning to do with me approached. 'I think we have finished with you, Miss Bowden,' Capitaine Dubesset said as she sat down.

It took a moment or two for this to sink in. 'You mean you're letting me go?' I asked incredulously. 'You don't believe I did it?'

'We always keep the open mind in the French police,' she said serenely, 'but it does not look likely. We could tell you were not telling us all the truth,' she looked at me very severely and I gathered I was lucky to escape a lecture about the folly of misleading an officer of the law, but perhaps she thought I had already been punished enough, 'and the information here was worth the investigation.' She tapped a statement in front of her. I did my best to read who had made it, but reading things upside down has never been a particular forte of mine, especially not when they are in French. 'But I think maybe you have had the trouble made for you. It is not unknown,' she added reflectively.

'You remember that I was supposed to be leaving tomorrow for my grandparents' party? Am I going to be able to go?'

She frowned. 'There are procedures to be followed. We must speak to Madame Morrison tomorrow.' As my face fell, she showed that really she was quite a decent sort after all for she said, 'I think it will be possible. Make sure you leave us your address in England.'

I was so grateful that I would have given her the contents of the whole of my address book if she'd wanted it, but she seemed to be quite happy with the flat and my grandparents' in Cumbria for good measure. We shook hands and I turned down the offer to sit in a waiting room while she arranged for a car and driver to take me back to the cottage. I said I'd rather wait in the blessed, free, open air, and be on my own for a while. Outside, I let it slowly sink in that a key wasn't about to turn on me, and revelled in the absence of that rather acrid smell of the gendarmerie – disinfectant mixed with something else. I sat on a wall flanking the car park, leaning back against a conveniently placed tree trunk and closed my eyes, just letting myself be and not wanting to think about what had happened today.

'Nella! I thought it might be you! Have they let you go?'

I opened my eyes to see Robert, wearing a tatty pair of cut-off shorts and an elderly T-shirt, standing over me, beaming from ear to ear and looking so pleased to see me that I felt my heart skip for a moment.

I nodded. 'Completely and utterly, and they don't want to see me again, fingers crossed.'

'Thank God!' he said as he sat down beside me. 'We were beginning to worry that they might be going to keep you in overnight.'

'You can't have worried half as much as I did,' I retorted, smiling back at him, then felt my face freeze. I'm not quite sure why the reaction chose to hit me at that particular moment; maybe because it was the first time since I'd left the cottage this morning that anyone had looked at me without suspicion.

'Are you all right?' he asked, frowning. 'You're very pale.'

'I'm fine,' I whispered through the lump in my throat and began to tremble violently.

'Are you feeling faint?'

'No, and don't you dare try to put my head between my knees, it makes me feel sick,' I warned through gritted teeth as I buried my face in my hands so that he couldn't see the way my mouth was wobbling.

'Wouldn't dream of it,' he said hastily, putting an arm around me instead, which was much more to my taste. He smelt nice too, I thought as he began to murmur in my ear, 'Hey, it's all right, it's all over, you're safe now. Don't worry . . .' I rested my head against his shoulder, revelling in friendly contact, while he muttered soothing platitudes and ran his hand up and down my back until the urge to burst into weak tears over my near escape from a French prison left me. 'Are you OK now?' he asked as I stopped sniffing quite so frequently, and to my regret gently released me. There are times when even the most liberated woman wants to feel protected, and just after you've finished being questioned by the French police is definitely one of them.

I was tempted to say I wasn't so I could have that arm back. 'Yes, thanks,' I said instead, with what was probably a very watery smile. 'Sorry about that. It was just . . . I was so *scared*.'

'Gets to you, doesn't it?' he said flatly.

I looked at him quickly, but he was staring straight ahead so I couldn't see his expression. 'Yes, you know all about it too, don't you?' I said quietly.

There was a slight pause then he said, 'I don't think being interrogated by the police is ever a pleasant experience, but at least in my case it was in my own country, and I might have done as little work as possible for my degree but I did know something about the law. I knew they simply didn't have the grounds or the right to detain me for long. Compared to what you've just been through, it was a doddle.'

I sighed heavily. 'You're being very generous.'

He squeezed my shoulder again in a friendly, impersonal manner. 'It's true,' he said and smiled, his eyes lighting up. 'Besides, whoever tipped off that bloke from the newspaper inadvertently did me a real favour; sadly for you, I doubt your encounter with the police is going to have the same career benefits that mine did.'

'It might do.' I felt immeasurably heartened by his friendliness. Maybe I'd been forgiven at last. 'If I point out to my bosses that I've managed to talk my way out of being investigated for art theft by the French police, they might think I've enough of a talent for flannelling to allow me to work on one of the big accounts – like soap powder, for instance. There's a lot of money to be made if you can be interesting about enzymes.'

'If you can make enzymes fascinating, you deserve every penny – but I thought it was all about personal stains these days.'

'Those too,' I admitted, 'but enzymes are the real test.' We sat in a companionable silence for a few moments then I said, 'How come you happened to turn up just as they decided to release me? I can't believe you make a habit of hanging around police stations.'

'I avoid close contact with them if I can,' he agreed. 'We've been ringing the gendarmerie for news all day; of course they wouldn't say a thing, merely said they'd inform Tom of the progress of their investigations in due course – so Oscar and I decided to see if we had better luck trying to get some information in person. You must have just missed him, he's inside.'

Informing Tom of the progress of the investigations? Oh God, I had no idea if the police regarded what was taken down in a statement as sacrosanct, rather like the confessional, unless the details were needed in court of course, or if they passed on some of the vital bits to the owner of the property. It didn't seem very likely. On the other hand, with a case like this where there was a large insurance pay-out to be made . . .

'We couldn't really have timed it better, could we?' Robert went on heartily. 'Now what would you prefer, to go out for a drink to celebrate your release, or to go back to the cottage first?'

No, I definitely didn't want to go back to the cottage. Not yet. Call me a weed if you like, but that sick feeling about someone deliberately landing me in this was still much too strong. 'What I'd really like is to see Janey. There's something I need to talk to her about.'

'OK,' said Robert, looking at me curiously, as well he might. 'We'll just wait until Oscar comes out. I can't think what's keeping him but he shouldn't be long.'

True to his words the door to the gendarmerie swung open and Oscar came out. He must have lost one of his contact lenses again, I thought, seeing his vague expression as he looked rather blindly around; he's far too vain to ever wear his back-up glasses. I waved to get his attention. His face broke into the most enormous grin and he raced over, seizing me in a bear hug and squeezing until I had to beg for mercy.

'I have *never* been so worried in my life!' he declared, words falling out over themselves as he hugged me again, though more gently this time. 'What *has* been going on? It was the most ridiculous idea that you might have stolen the picture, no matter what you said to me – and how come you told them about that?' he asked reprovingly. 'Honestly, you should have known the police don't have a sense of humour when people make jokes about stealing pictures.' Robert started and stared at me.

'They were pretty sniffy with me for not telling them about it yesterday,' Oscar went on, 'but, as I said, I knew you hadn't done it so I didn't see the point in bringing it up. That fearsome woman with the face like granite said it was up to her to decide what was to the point or not and I could have been in serious trouble for withholding evidence. Honestly, I thought *I* was going to be the one thrown in clink next!' He looked as if he'd really thought this was a possibility. 'I told her we all knew the picture was still on the wall when you came back to the drawing room and you spent the rest of the evening leaning on my shoulder, very heavy you were too, so I would *certainly* have noticed if you'd popped out for a few minutes to do a bit of pilfering. She seemed to think I wasn't taking the matter seriously enough.

'Were they absolutely beastly to you?' he asked, looking concerned. 'I've been in twice already to get news. I was beginning to be afraid they would never let you go! I was about to start threatening them with lawyers, the Consul – the lot; I just couldn't believe it when they said they'd already let you go without charge!' I got hugged again. 'Of course they didn't bother to say so until they'd taken the second statement from me,' he added in disgust at this evidence of police brutality. 'But what made them change their minds? It should have been obvious to anyone that it was just drink talking.'

'I hadn't had as much as you thought I had,' I said mildly, taking advantage of his running out of breath just for a second or two to get a couple of my own words in sideways.

'Come on, Nella. Sober people don't go around planning to pinch their host's property! Well, not people like you.'

'I wasn't planning to!' I said indignantly. 'We were only joking.'

'We?' queried Robert, eyeing me thoughtfully. 'So that's why you need to talk to Janey.'

They both looked at me expectantly. I reluctantly filled them in.

'Unfortunate timing in the circumstances,' Robert said when I'd finished, 'but nothing heinous. If everybody who ever hoped out loud for a nice burglary to clean up on the insurance was locked up it'd be standing room only in your average jail.' He shook his head in bemusement. 'But you're supposed to be intelligent, Nella. What were you thinking of, telling the police you'd even played with the idea of going into the art-theft business? You must have known that they'd turn up with the handcuffs within minutes.'

'Of course I didn't tell them about it,' I said crossly. 'For one thing, I swore to Janey I wouldn't. She didn't want Tom to find out.'

'Given his present mood I'm not surprised,' he said. 'Then how did they find out?'

'Someone decided to make trouble for me.'

There was a silence. Robert asked in a tense voice, 'Who do you think it was?'

I couldn't pretend that I didn't know what he was asking, nor that I hadn't thought of it myself. I sighed. 'It would have been the perfect payback, wouldn't it? But it wasn't you.'

'How can you be sure?' he asked, eyes fixed intently on my face.

I shrugged. 'I can't, can I? But I think if you were going to get back at me in that sort of way you'd have done it ages ago while you were still in a red-hot rage. And I can't believe that you'd land me in the soup, then come along to give me a cuddle and let me sob on your shoulder, either. You aren't that devious.'

'I could have changed,' he said, then smiled suddenly. 'But thanks for believing that I haven't,' he said as he bent down to give me a quick kiss.

'Then who did it?' Oscar asked.

I wrenched my attention back from Robert. 'There's only one person who's got it in for me – two now, I suppose – but denunciation isn't George's style. So it must have been Maggie, mustn't it?'

CHAPTER 20

Oscar immediately protested that it couldn't possibly be Maggie. One of his friends would never do something like that. But he was forced to concede eventually that everything pointed to her as the culprit; for one thing, she had been the only one sitting near enough to us to have heard what I'd said. 'But you can't be sure,' he said firmly. I was, actually, but was prepared to leave a small margin of doubt if that made him feel happier. 'Look, if she did drop you in it, I'm certain all she thought she was doing was giving you an unpleasant half hour or so. She couldn't have known it would get out of hand like it did,' he said unhappily. Robert and I both looked at him rather sceptically, and he shrugged. 'Come on, Maggie knew Nella was due to leave tomorrow. Do you really think she'd have risked having her hanging around Phil for a second longer than strictly necessary?'

Rather reluctantly, for it would have been far more satisfactory to be able to dump all the responsibility for today's traumas on a single set of shoulders, I had to admit that he was probably right. I also doubted Maggie would have been prepared to chance Phil seizing on me as a poor little thing in need of masculine protection. 'He can't know you very well if he thinks that,' commented Robert.

It seemed that once the police antennae had been set twitching by the information that I'd openly declared I was going to steal the picture, they started picking up on random statements made by the others, all harmless in themselves, and wove them into a seamless theory that implicated me completely. So it wasn't *all* Maggie's fault – not entirely. But it still didn't mean that I had to like her.

Oscar suggested that he and I went out for dinner this evening, and since I wanted to see Janey anyway he said he'd save time by fetching me a change of clothes from the cottage while I was talking to her. As I had no more wish to see Maggie than Oscar had to referee the blood bath that would undoubtedly ensue, I was quite happy to fall in with the idea. As it happened it wasn't necessary to warn Janey that I'd been forced to break my promise. Lieutenant Fournier had already rung her for a quick telephone interview and she knew I'd been released – and why I'd been taken in for questioning in the first place.

'Really, Nella, you should have told the police all about our conversation straight away,' she scolded as she took me out on to the terrace to have a welcome glass of wine.

'I didn't realise that was what they wanted to know,' I said tiredly. I'd already heard far too much on this subject on the way here. It had taken the two men a remarkably short time to go from delight at my narrow escape to carping along the lines of had I been *completely* mad to imagine even for one minute that I was going to get away with concealing anything from the French police, and did I have any idea how lucky I was . . . etc. Yes, I did, and I didn't need anybody spelling it out for me. The conversation had gone rapidly downhill and by the time we reached the château the atmosphere was so heated, on my part anyway, that Robert promptly decided the decent thing was to give Oscar a lift to the cottage while I was left to talk to Janey alone.

She glanced at me and probably wisely decided that it was better not to go on with this line of conversation. Instead she handed me my drink which was a much better idea. 'I feel so guilty,' she said quietly. 'You spent the last day of your holiday banged up in the nick. And all because of me.'

'Because of Maggie actually,' I corrected her, my hands curling into fists. 'Whatever Oscar might think.' It was lucky for the others in the cottage I was leaving tomorrow, all things considered. I did my best to summon a smile. 'But just think of when I'm back at the office next week. Nobody, but *nobody* is going to be able to better my holiday stories, are they?'

'Don't add murder to your list of holiday exploits, please!' Janey begged and then with rare understanding helped me to work off my residual bad mood by speculating on how I could get even with Maggie – in ways that didn't involve a prison sentence. She had some very hilarious and inventive suggestions. By the time Robert appeared, swinging a carrier bag from one hand and accompanied by the usual canine cacophony, I was by no means reconciled to what had happened but at least I no longer wanted to rip someone's head off.

'Shame you couldn't have made that row with the burglar,' he said severely to the dogs and put the bag down on a chair. 'Clean clothes, Nella. Oscar's choice, so if you don't like them blame him, not me.'

I had a horrid vision of what my room must look like after the police had finished going through it, all upended drawers and the mattress on the floor. Or was I mixing up police searches with burglaries? Either way it wasn't very nice to think someone had been going through all your things and noting where you'd been too lazy to do an actual mend and had cobbled something together with safety pins and Sellotape. 'Is it a terrible mess?' I asked apprehensively.

'It doesn't look too bad to me. Oscar says they were very careful about putting it all back, and your room is actually tidier than before they searched it. Nice to know that you've gained something out of the day, isn't it?'

Yeah, well, I could think of less stressful ways of getting my room tidied. Like doing it myself. I'd have to think of that in future.

'Apparently the woman gendarme searching Sally's room was fascinated by her Floris talcum powder,' he said, propping himself comfortably against the terrace wall and holding out his hand for a glass of wine with a smile of thanks. 'Sally isn't sure if the gendarme was particularly fond of Wild Hyacinth or if she imagines that scented cocaine is the latest thing on the London PR circuit.'

Janey grinned. 'Charlie must have been having kittens.'

'What do you mean?' I asked.

She raised her eyebrows meaningfully. 'Haven't you

noticed that way he goes from being really quiet to the life and soul of the party? It makes me wonder if he's not on the happy powder.'

Robert nodded. 'That's occurred to me too. There were a couple of guys at university who sometimes never said a word, then at others behaved as if they thought they were invincible. It turned out they had a major habit. You must have known people like that, Nella.'

'We obviously moved in different circles. My friends were pushed to buy a pint, let alone a line of cocaine. Look, I'm sure you're wrong,' I said uneasily. 'He's just one of those people who go up and down a lot.'

'Maybe,' he said equably, then turned to Janey. 'You'll have to tell Tom why the police were so keen to interview Nella.'

'I can't!' she said immediately. 'You've seen the mood he's in, Rob. I don't dare.'

He looked at her steadily. 'And if he finds out from someone else? Then he'll think you've really got something to hide.'

She sighed heavily. 'Oh God, I suppose you're right. Problem is, I don't know when I can do it. We've got a duty dinner this evening with a couple he finds dead bores – I do, too – so he's not going to be inclined towards forgiveness or understanding.'

'What about tomorrow?' Robert suggested. 'He'll be so delighted to have the house – and you – to himself at last that he'll be ready to forgive you anything. Maybe not eloping with Jed, but just about anything else.'

Janey smiled. 'Frankly, that's a choice I'd rather not give him. I'd hate to find out that he values his picture more than his wife. So you're really going?'

He nodded. 'I've got to. I've been away far too long. And you have to admit that as far as Tom is concerned, I've definitely outstayed my welcome.'

She didn't bother to deny it. 'Are you sure you're up to it? I still can't believe that your knee is recovered enough to do all that driving. You know you can stay here for as long as it takes.'

He put his arm around her and squeezed her shoulder. 'Don't fuss. I'm absolutely fine, though I appreciate the thought very much indeed,' he said and kissed her cheek.

Lily sat up with a woof as Tom stepped out from the kitchen. He came to a stop, his brows snapping together at the sight of his guest's hand resting on Janey's waist. 'May I ask what you're doing?' he demanded.

Robert smiled at him, completely unabashed. 'Kissing your wife. You don't mind, do you?' he asked as he let Janey go, though without any undue haste.

Tom looked as if he did mind, very much indeed. His mouth tightened and his eyes swept around the table. 'Oh it's you, Nella,' he said in a voice that was only marginally more friendly than the one he had used with Robert. I could see his next question was going to be why had the police thought it necessary to question me all day about the theft of his picture, and I agreed completely with Janey that right now was not the time to begin telling Tom how I'd agreed to steal his picture. Fortunately Delphine chose that moment to bring the twins out onto the terrace to say '*Bonne nuit*'. Adam, I thought it was Adam, it was difficult to tell, hurled himself at his father in a frenzy of affection, chanting, 'Papa, Papa,

Papa,' in a tuneless and loud monotone, while his brother grabbed hold of one of Tom's legs thus rendering him entirely immobile.

'Have a drink, darling, I'm sure you need one,' Janey said, placing a glass in his hand so he had to concentrate on not having it knocked flying by one of his over-affectionate brood. 'Goodness, Nella, you've got to hurry if you're going to have time for that shower before you go out,' she said in a bright voice, putting a hand on my arm and almost hauling me towards the door. Tom managed to put the glass down, used both hands to free his leg and told the leg-holder in a don't-even-think-of-disobeying-me voice to go to Mummy, then silenced the chanter by picking him up.

Janey flashed a nervous smile at Tom and burbled hurriedly on before he could ask why I was having a shower in his house rather than using the facilities in the very well-appointed bathroom at the cottage. 'Naturally Robert didn't want to be here on his own on his last evening, so he's going out for dinner with Nella and Oscar.' Robert looked as surprised at this news as I was. 'They've got a table booked for . . .' she glanced at her watch, 'for er . . . eight o'clock – quite soon really, and you know what it's like at this time of year. You can't afford to be late or they'll give your table to someone else.'

'You're leaving tomorrow?' Tom asked, turning towards Robert, with a considerable degree of inhospitable pleasure.

'It makes sense, you see,' Janey carried on, unheeding. She broke off to scoop Miles up, settling him on her hip.

'Makes sense how exactly?' Tom asked after a few seconds when it seemed as if she'd lost the thread of what she was about to say. Probably because she didn't know what was supposed to be coming next.

Her face went blank, then as he cleared his throat she looked around and said rapidly, 'Um ... er ... well, as Nella's got to leave tomorrow anyway, she's going with Rob and sharing the driving!' She beamed at all of us. 'So much better for Rob's knee.'

Bloody hell. What in blazes do you think you're doing, Janey? I thought furiously as Tom nodded, seeing the logic of this. Well, it *was* perfectly logical, it made sense in every way – except for one thing. Robert might be a lot friendlier towards me than he'd been just over a week ago, actually it would have been pretty difficult for him to have been any less friendly without risking grievous bodily harm, but if he had wanted my company over 700 miles and twelve hours of driving he would have said so himself. And, frankly, my nerves had been rattled enough without spending most of tomorrow in a tin can with someone who'd far rather be alone. Even if by some chance he didn't object to having me as a co-driver we had wildly different driving styles – about fifty miles an hour to be precise, Also, my being in such close contact with Robert for so long might have unexpected ramifications. What about those scores he'd said he still had to settle with me? I might fondly imagine that my own close brush with the law had wiped them out, but I couldn't be sure. It was best to play safe, let discretion be the better part of valour for once. In other words take the coward's way out.

'But it's right out of Robert's way to drop me off at my parents' house,' I disagreed. 'It'd be best all round if I went back by train like I originally planned.'

Robert turned to Tom in a confidential manner. 'Actually Nella's parents are only about ten minutes off the motorway, so it's hardly as if I was being asked to go to London via Basingstoke, but she's always had a problem with maps,' he said in a man-to-man voice. I was about to protest indignantly when I realised crossly this wasn't the place for a session of one-upmanship, as Robert knew perfectly well. A smirk flashed over his face before he said firmly, 'So that's settled.'

I couldn't think how he'd ever had the nerve to suggest that *I* was bossy, though of course in men it's called being decisive, assertive – all excellent and desirable personality traits. I contemplated fighting back, except poor Janey's nerves were already tattered enough without adding a public spat. So what else could I do other than smile and thank him? I kept my pride intact at being steam-rollered, and my options open, by saying we'd talk about it later but that I had to get changed now.

Tom turned back to me with an enquiring expression but Janey seized my arm, muttering about baths over-flowing and, still with a child attached limpet-like to one hip, towed me into the safety of the house before he could get any words out.

'That's the second time in so many minutes you've mentioned the need for me to have a wash,' I said mildly as we went up the stairs. 'Is it a hint?'

She grinned at me over one shoulder. 'No, just expedient. You don't have to have one if you don't want to.'

'Actually I'd love one,' I said frankly. 'I can still smell the gendarmerie on me and it isn't one of my favourite scents.'

She sniffed. 'Now you mention it . . . I prefer Contradiction myself.' She showed me into a sleekly equipped bathroom with a double row of white painted shelves at one end of the bath packed with more bottles of bath potions, shampoos, conditioners, body scrubs, face masks and gels than I'd ever seen outside the cosmetic department at Harrods. 'Venetia likes to keep a few things here,' she explained with a straight face.

Goodness. 'Help yourself to whatever you want. She never minds if we borrow some of her stuff,' Janey said airily, 'though I doubt she'd notice, even if she did!' She waved her free hand towards the door. 'Dressing gown over there, towels here, hairdryer next door in her room if you need it, mirror with good light ditto. Is there anything else you need?' she asked rapidly, already edging back out towards the corridor.

'My clean clothes. You hustled me out so quickly I didn't have time to pick them up.'

'I'll bring them up in a few minutes, after I've got this,' she jiggled the child on her hip, 'into bed. See you later.'

'Hang on, Janey!' If she continued to bolt out of the door every time anyone wanted to say something to her, she was going to run out of people she could talk to pretty soon. She stopped and looked at me with a slightly apprehensive expression. 'Just what did you think you were playing at just now?'

She looked at me as if she didn't understand what I was talking about, then must have realised that playing dumb wasn't going to work. 'I'm sorry, Nella, it just sort of slipped out. We were going to suggest it later—'

'We?' I interrupted. I was pretty sure I already knew who 'we' were.

I was right. 'Me and Oscar. He said he was going to bring it up over dinner.' There was another guilty little half-smile as she remembered that she'd arranged for Robert to go out for dinner with me as well as have me as his travelling companion. 'Honestly, Nella, I don't think Oscar's up to anything this time, really I don't,' she said anxiously. 'Not like with you and George.'

'Oh, I'm sure about that. Even Oscar isn't certifiable enough to imagine that there's any sort of shared rosy future for me and Robert,' I said with confidence. 'And even if he was,' for you never knew exactly what bees Oscar might get in his particular bonnet, 'he'd realise the moment to start matchmaking for Robert is not just after Venetia's publicly dumped him for an older and fatter man! On the other hand, Oscar does believe in being friends with your ex. I can just see him thinking what a good idea it would be to promote a new understanding between Robert and me by sending us off on a long journey together. It's exactly the sort of half-witted, crackpot idea he gets into his head sometimes.' I shook my head in disbelief. 'Doesn't he realise that even Romeo and Juliet would be at each other's throats after an hour or so of going around the Périphérique? So just what does he think it's going to do to Robert's and my shaky accord?'

Janey's face fell. 'We didn't think of that.' *We?* She looked at me defiantly. 'Come on, Nella, it just seemed so stupid to have both of you going back to the UK on the same day and doing it separately. You get to save the train fare and Rob gets an assistant driver. I can't think why no one thought of it before.'

Maybe because up until today Robert had been giving a strong impression that he'd rather walk over knives than spend too long in my company. He might still feel that way, except that a certain ironic sympathy for my predicament had made him rather better at hiding it. Oh well, I'd give him the chance to back out later. In the meantime I would try out some of Venetia's bath stuff.

There's no doubt that the trials of even the most traumatic day can be eased considerably by twenty minutes soaking in a bath perfumed, with a very liberal hand indeed, by bath oil that comes from the sort of shop where if you have to ask the price it's assumed you aren't going to be able to afford it. I got out reluctantly when I realised I was soon going to bear a close resemblance to a prune, albeit an exotically scented prune. Just in time really, for I was wandering around in Venetia's dressing gown, a brightly coloured silk kimono affair, which even if I say so myself suited me down to a T, sniffing at the bottles lined up on the kidney-shaped dressing table in her bedroom and wondering if she had a scent that matched her bath oil when there was a knock at the door and, instead of Janey as I'd expected, Robert walked in with my bag of clothes.

He glanced at me and remarked that I looked better for a bath. I wasn't quite sure how to take that. 'Oscar's already downstairs so it might be a good idea if you don't take too long getting ready,' he said. 'Tom's just gone up

– with a lot of grumbling – to change, and Janey reckons the coast will be clear for at least twenty minutes.'

I nodded my agreement and he turned to go, then stopped, one hand on the handle. 'Nella,' he began, 'there's something I want to—'

Here it comes, I thought. He's about to tell me he'd rather not have me in his car tomorrow. Oh hell, and once I'd got over my irritation at being pushed around by seemingly *everybody* today, I'd decided I was really rather looking forward to it. For one thing, Robert's elderly Saab was a much more comfortable way of travelling than a train packed to the gills with tourists.

I forced myself to smile. 'It's all right, I quite understand,' I said as evenly as possible. 'Janey should never have landed it on you like that. I mean, you didn't have any other option but to say you'd be glad to have me.'

'What are you talking about?' he interrupted. 'Of course I don't mind giving you a lift. It's the most sensible option for both of us.' He looked as if he meant it even though I'd have appreciated a little more enthusiasm about the prospect. 'In fact, I'd have mentioned it myself if Janey had given me the chance,' he added with a grin. 'All I wanted to know was if you've got a clean licence, otherwise I'll have to ring the insurance people in the morning.'

'My licence is as clean as if I was sponsored by Persil,' I said loftily. 'I haven't even had a speeding ticket.'

'Neither have I,' he retorted in an equally superior voice as he walked out.

Either he'd had a ball and chain attached to the back of his car since he last drove me or he'd made a pact with the devil. I knew which answer I favoured.

CHAPTER 21

'Morning, Nella. You're an early bird,' yawned Charlie, rubbing his eyes blearily as he stumbled into the kitchen. 'Too early, if you ask me. Those suitcases in the hall are a danger to decent clean-living members of the public. I nearly did an A over T with one just now. Is that coffee? Be an angel and give me a cup.'

I watched with interest as he ladled several spoonfuls of sugar into his mug and drank it, becoming more alive with every mouthful until by the time he was halfway down the mug his eyes had snapped open properly and he no longer looked as if all he wanted to do was curl up amongst the breadcrumbs and the butter dish on the table and go back to sleep.

'That's better,' he said, holding out the mug for a refill. 'I can't tell you how good it is to see you safe and sound again.' He yawned again. 'Sorry.'

'Good evening, was it?' I asked. 'You must have got back pretty late for I didn't hear anyone come in. Where did you go in the end? Oscar said everybody was still arguing about it when he left. By the way, did you know that you forgot to lock up? We found the door on the latch when we came back.'

Charlie looked as if he was finding it hard to cope with more than one question at a time. 'It's OK. I didn't go out with the others as I wasn't feeling a hundred per cent.' He looked at me slightly guiltily. 'But I did have one or two toddies to make myself feel better.' Yes, well, that was obvious. 'They said they were going to try the Auberge de Vieux Chêne – you know, the place where Solange was seen doing naughty things with the asparagus.'

'Shame you couldn't go. It sounded nice.'

'With or without the extra entertainment?' he asked, with a sly look. 'We've already been out once this week, and Maggie and Sal are planning another beano for tomorrow night – the grand finale. Frankly, I find going out this often pretty hard both on the liver and the pocket, especially as neither Maggie nor Sal are the sort of girls who are content with the hundred-franc menu and a bottle of the house red. Besides,' he glanced at me sideways, 'I didn't think the atmosphere was going to be a bundle of laughs after the bollocking your friend Robert gave Maggie.'

'Robert did *what*?' I asked in amazement. He hadn't said a word about doing anything of the sort. Neither had that arch gossip Oscar, for that matter. We'd had a very convivial meal in the little restaurant in the village where you basically got what Madame felt like cooking that evening, talking about just about everything. Or so it had seemed. There hadn't been a single word about a topic both men must have known would have been very dear to my heart. Actually I wouldn't have minded knowing what Robert felt about Venetia as well, but a chance would have been a fine thing. He was infuriatingly close-mouthed when it suited him.

'What did he say to her?' I asked, trying to hide my eagerness.

'Couldn't really hear,' Charlie said to my acute disappointment, 'though she was looking pretty subdued by the end of it. She was rabbiting on about how it wasn't really her fault and he couldn't put all the blame on her.' I didn't see why not. 'What really seems to have upset her is that, as Robert pointed out, she's lost any chance of getting Tom signed up for her new agency. Can you see Janey allowing it? And of course Sal's hard work in trying to land his gallery business has gone for a burton too, so she isn't too thrilled with Maggie either. Frankly,' he looked at me apologetically, 'I think Maggie minds far more about all that than about what happened to you.'

Now, why didn't that surprise me?

He put his mug down on the table looking like a fully signed up member of the human race at last. 'Though it beats me why the police ever listened to her in the first place. The whole idea that *you* could ever steal off a friend is ludicrous!'

I smiled my thanks as a distant church clock chimed the hour, reminding me I still had several things to do. Robert had said he'd be here to pick me up at nine sharp, implying there would be dire penalties if I was so much as one minute late. I got up and started rinsing my cup and plate, thinking in a White Rabbit-ish sort of way, 'Must hurry, must hurry.'

'I've been thinking,' Charlie said casually as he emptied the last of the carafe into his mug. 'The boot on Oscar's car is pretty small, isn't it? I know he wants to buy a few cases of wine off Tom, but he's not going to have much room for them if he's taking all your luggage as well as those pictures. You know, there's loads of space in Sal's car. Why don't we take your stuff back? I could drop it off at your flat on Monday night.'

'Oh, that's kind of you,' I said with real gratitude, 'but it's not necessary. I'm not going on the train now. Robert's giving me a lift so I'm taking everything with me.'

'But won't that mean you'll have to lug everything to your grandparents' and back down to London again? It's one hell of a hassle.'

'Not as much as it would be for you. You live north of the river, don't you? The last thing you'd want to do is cross half of London to do a delivery on a weekday evening.'

'I wouldn't mind.'

'Really, I couldn't let you go to so much trouble,' I said as I gave the plate a cursory wipe with the tea towel. 'But thank you very much indeed.'

'You're sure?' he asked in such a despondent voice that I swung around to look at him, surprised he was so put out at me turning down his offer like this. It would have been a terrible nuisance for him.

He met my eyes and smiled slightly crookedly. 'Come on, Nella, haven't you ever heard of inventing an excuse to see someone again? I didn't want to push things too much, but I reckoned if I had some of your stuff you couldn't turn me down flat. You'd have to see me at least once.'

'Oh,' I said, lost for anything more eloquent to say. For one thing I'm not used to receiving this sort of declaration at breakfast, actually I'm not really used to getting them at any time of day, and my brain doesn't seem to operate terribly well at this hour of the morning. For another, I might have played with the idea of how attractive I found Charlie, OK, let's be honest about it, I'd indulged in more than a few misty-edged fantasies in which he'd played a starring role, but this transition from makebelieve to reality was a bit sudden. I looked away and said weakly, 'What about Sally? I like her.'

'So do I,' he said, 'but you must have seen how things are between us. It's nothing specific, we've just drifted apart, and I certainly wouldn't do anything to hurt her if I can help it, but I don't think she's going to mind much about me finding someone else. After all, she has.' He glanced at me pointedly. 'Or haven't you noticed the way she hangs over your George?'

'He isn't my George,' I said automatically.

Charlie laughed. 'Certainly not any longer. So how about it? Fancy having a drink with me when we're both back in London?'

'I'd really like that,' I said honestly.

'Great!' he said with a flashing smile as if I'd just presented him with the Crown Jewels. 'Now – would you like me to take your pictures back for you? Those cases don't look very strong and there'd be less risk of them getting damaged in a single journey than if they're being transferred from one car boot to the other.'

I hesitated. There was a lot of truth in what he had said, but what was Sally going to say about having her car filled with my property? 'Well . . .' I began.

The door swung open and Oscar marched in, still in his dressing gown, clicking his tongue reprovingly. '*There* you are, Nella. I've been looking all over the place for you.'

'Not very hard. I've been in here for the last twenty minutes.'

'I thought you might be having a last swim,' he said blandly. 'Robert's here. Are you ready?'

'Help!' I exclaimed, shooting out of the kitchen while he called after me that he'd start putting my things in the car.

By the time I'd looked under the bed, in the back of the wardrobe, made two separate journeys to confirm that I hadn't left my toothbrush in the bathroom, retrieved my book from the bookcase by the loo and put on an extra coating of mascara because my eyelashes were looking unwarrantedly thin and stubby, Oscar had already packed all my stuff, including the pictures, into Robert's Saab. I shrugged at Charlie who by now was alert enough to have changed his dressing gown for T-shirt and shorts. 'Seems my mind was made up for me. But thanks again for offering.'

'Shame,' he said with a slight frown, then smiled. 'Well, you've still promised to have a drink with me. I'm holding you to that, all right?'

'Of course,' I said, still rather startled at this sudden ardour.

It seemed he was *really* keen. 'How about Monday?'

Of course I was flattered. But half of me was saying that only a man would suggest meeting up the evening after you've all come back from two weeks' holiday. I was about to suggest sometime later in the week when an impatient throat-clearing from the direction of the car told me that my chauffeur was getting fed up with hanging around. Robert was standing with his arms propped on the roof, tapping his foot, sending pointed looks my way and generally giving an impression of a pressure cooker getting to danger point, so I said hastily, 'Yes, that'd be really nice,' and scribbled down my address and phone number on a piece of paper.

'Sure you don't want to go back and have a bath, Nella?' Robert asked nastily as I came out, checking my bag for the umpteenth time just to make sure my passport hadn't disappeared since the last time I looked. 'Or will we be able to leave this morning after all?'

I smiled at him sunnily. 'I had a very nice bath last night, thank you, and you said you wanted to leave at about nine. It's now ten past which I think still counts as "about", don't you?'

Obviously not, judging from his expression, though I was saved from hearing his opinion on the matter by Janey, who roared up in her little black Twingo with Lily next to her in the front. Leaving then became complete chaos. Janey was practically running alongside the car, head stuck in the window while she gabbled last-minute messages. Lily had taken the opportunity to nip out of the car and was cavorting about, smiling maniacally while Oscar, Sally and Charlie tried in vain to catch her and say their own goodbyes at the same time. Maggie and Phil were noticeable by their absence.

Robert sighed in such a bad-tempered fashion when

we at last got away, amazingly enough without running anybody over, that I wished I had gone on the train after all. Fortunately his mood seemed to improve with every minute and every mile, until by the time we hit the motorway it was positively sunny. We spent the next couple of hours catching up on our mutual friends. I reckoned he needn't have looked quite so pleased when I said I'd lost touch with just about everyone as they'd all refused to talk to me, though it was nothing compared to how pleased *I* looked when he casually threw in that he'd heard Natasha was married and completely mired in domesticity and had become very boring. We stopped just before the outskirts of Paris to have the picnic Janey had insisted on providing (she said French motorway food was every bit as bad as its English counterpart) and sat down with a rather self-satisfied feeling at the good time we'd made so far. This despite the sedate pace I'd insisted on once I took over the driving – Robert called it something much, much ruder.

Janey's picnic fodder was as delicious as her normal cooking, so for the first few minutes there was silence apart from rather greedy chewing, until Robert offered me the last piece of *pan bagnat*. I shook my head regretfully. It was absolutely delicious – also very fattening – and I was regaining my lost weight at an alarming rate.

'Don't be stupid. One little bit isn't going to make any difference,' he scoffed, though I noticed he quickly helped himself lest I changed my mind. He, most unfairly, never has to worry about putting on weight. He took a large bite while subjecting me to an unnerving scrutiny which suggested that he was making up his mind whether I was well on the road to qualifying as a female sumo wrestler. He swallowed the last mouthful – he's always had excellent table manners – before saying, 'You look less skeletal than you did two weeks ago but, as I said, you're still on the thin side. You could do with putting on weight.'

'Come on, you only said that to get at George,' I said, trying hard to conceal my pleased smirk.

'Not true,' he protested. 'I've got enough problems in my life without adding to them by telling a woman she should put on weight when she shouldn't. My God, the first time she couldn't do up her jeans or some revolting urchin in the street yells, "Hey, Tessie! Done the ton yet?" she'd be round at my door holding me entirely responsible for the whole thing and swearing vengeance. Besides,' he said as I giggled, 'I didn't need to get back at George like that. I had other ways of doing it.' His eyes began to gleam. 'Talking of which,' he went on, 'why does George have it in for you now? Last time I saw him he was all over you like a cheap suit. So what provoked the change in attitude?'

I smothered a laugh. George would be flabbergasted to think someone had even mentioned cheap suits and him in the same breath. Robert looked at me expectantly. 'He fell in the swimming pool,' I said woodenly.

Robert began to grin. 'Did he now?' he murmured appreciatively. 'Big splash?'

'Very,' I confirmed.

His grin grew even wider. 'You alarm me, Nella. Is this the way you deal with all your over-ardent admirers, now?'

355

Actually ardent was another word that didn't come within George's orbit but I didn't see any reason why Robert should know that. 'Only some of them,' I said evasively. Then, 'If you must know, he was saying that everything pointed to the burglary being an inside job, and you had to be the prime suspect.'

'Did he say why?' he enquired with interest.

'Primarily because you cheat at cricket. He's still *very* upset you said he was LBW.' Robert began to smile. 'Also that you must be fundamentally dishonest because you sell reproductions.'

'Specially commissioned copies, if you don't mind,' he corrected me. 'So you ducked him! I wish I'd been there to see it.' He stretched out lazily on the grass. 'I'd give you a big kiss as a thank you only I'm too comfortable to move.' What a pity, I thought before I could stop myself. 'The police think an intruder broke in – presumably they are more qualified than George to make a judgement, though I daresay he might dispute that – but he's absolutely right about one thing. If it was an inside job I'm in pole position to be fingered as 'im what dunnit.' He smiled at my expression. 'I'm the only one out of all the guests who had enough time to work out how to disable the burglar alarm.'

'What difference would that have made, since it wasn't on?' I objected without thinking.

He pushed himself up on one elbow, staring at me. 'How the *hell* did you know that?' Then as I sat in dumb silence cursing my big mouth, his eyebrows rose. 'I suppose Janey told you.'

I nodded.

'I thought you two were being a bit OTT with such a pantomime of secrecy over a very mild joke! Now I understand.' He sighed in exasperation. 'Is there anything else you chose to keep back from the police?'

I shook my head and tried to look the picture of innocence. Not terribly successfully, if his expression was anything to go by.

'Good,' he said tersely. 'So I can be reasonably sure that we won't be stopped somewhere so you can be hauled back for more questioning! Just what did Janey think she was playing at? I suppose she must have been very well oiled indeed. How much had she drunk?' he demanded, glaring at me as if all this was my fault.

'Not very much,' I said quickly. 'You don't understand . . .' I explained how Janey had been drunk more on exultation that her fears that her marriage was over were groundless than a liberal quantity of her husband's premium cuvée.

'Of course Tom hasn't been mucking around with Solange,' he said impatiently. 'Janey must be mad to even think it. Any fool can see he adores her.'

'I would have thought that too, except where was Tom when Solange was playing hunt the asparagus?' I asked. Robert looked suspiciously blank and I said, 'Come on, I remember what you said to Venetia about it. You know where he was, don't you?'

He hesitated. 'All right then. He was at the bank, trying to stop them foreclosing on a mortgage on the vineyard. It dates from ages ago, when he bought a whole lot of extra land, and I don't know all the details but I think he's been hoping he could sort it out without letting Janey know what sort of mess he's got himself into.'

'From what she says about him, that's right up his street,' I said resignedly. 'Is it very serious?'

Robert pursed his lips. 'I believe so, but Tom doesn't normally talk about things like this. It slipped out by chance one evening when he'd had a jar or two under his belt, then he clammed up.'

'Poor Tom, he must be worried sick,' I said. 'I wish he'd tell Janey about it. She'd far rather they went bust than have him going off with another woman.' Robert raised his eyes to heaven with a 'typical woman' expression. 'But presumably this theft really is a blessing in disguise. Now he'll be able to pay the mortgage off with the insurance money, won't he?'

'He might be able to,' he said doubtfully, 'though the picture was under-insured so they won't get anything like the full value.'

'Janey's got a studio flat. Maybe if she sold that and they put the two together they could get enough to keep the bank happy,' I said, thinking out loud. 'Incidentally, why does Tom appear to blame you for the theft?'

Robert picked up a cherry tomato and examined it closely before saying, 'He doesn't really. He was worried about the canvas deteriorating, and the evening before it was stolen, he asked me to examine it. Not that I'm qualified to do restoration but he reckoned I could tell him if he needed to call in an expert. Problem was, Venetia wanted to go out, you lot came back for a drink, and I was knackered so I went to bed. By the time I went to have a look at it next morning it was gone. Of course he knows I'm not the thief, but he said if I'd kept my word and done as he asked *when* he asked, the picture would have been safely up in my room when the thief broke in.'

'It's not what you'd call a reasonable attitude, is it?' I said, helping myself to a plum.

'Losing two or three hundred thousand grand's worth of picture can make even the most reasonable of men turn illogical. He needs to blame someone, justly or not.'

'I had no idea you'd become this philosophical,' I said and got a dirty look. 'I suppose that means that you knew the alarm had been switched off too.'

'Yes, I did, Miss Marple-Bowden,' he said in an amused voice. 'And I'm very glad that your George didn't know about it. He'd certainly have done his all to have me thrown in clink without allowing me to pass Go. However, unlike certain other parties, I didn't tell anyone else about it.'

I made a face at him and he grinned and looked at his watch. 'We've been here for over an hour, we'd better get on.'

We gathered up the detritus from our picnic, and I saved myself a particularly juicy-looking plum for later, though Robert warned me what he'd do if I dripped juice all over the inside of his car. Mess he didn't mind – I'd gathered that from the stuff strewn over the floor of the car – but stick he objected to strongly. I hastily set about licking the last remnants of my previous plum off my fingers before I got back into the driving seat and grabbed hold of the wheel.

CHAPTER 22

As Robert and I got further into Paris, the traffic began to slow down, until by the time we joined the dreaded Périphérique, the massive ring road around the city, the signs warning us of *circulation difficile* were completely unnecessary – we could see it for ourselves. Robert was much better-tempered than most men would have been in a similar situation; he refrained from hitting the car, yelling at the people next to us as if they were personally responsible for blocking the road, or even blaming the driver, me, for the state of the traffic. Though he couldn't resist making one sarky comment about how much further ahead we'd be if I'd been able to resist canoodling with Charlie just as we were supposed to be leaving.

'We might have managed to get to that bridge up there, I suppose,' I said mildly, pointing to one about fifty yards ahead, 'but I doubt it. And I wasn't canoodling either. He offered to take the pictures back for me so I wouldn't have to lug them up to Kendal and down to London again. It was very nice of him.'

'So it was a little thank you note for his kind thought

that you were writing him, was it?' enquired Robert silkily.

'Don't be silly! We're having a drink next week and I was giving him my number.'

'Oh, I *see*,' he said in a voice heavy with innuendo.

'No, you don't,' I said stiffly, glaring at him and forgetting to move up the necessary three feet as the car ahead inched forward slowly. I got indignantly hooted by the car behind and, jumping back to attention, let the clutch out too quickly so the Saab jerked forward, engine spluttering, Robert smirking at my mortified expression. 'He's just a friend,' I said defensively. 'I like him, and for your information, I examined him closely at breakfast this morning—'

'Nice for you.'

I don't hit people when I'm driving. Sometimes I'm very tempted, though. 'And he can't be taking cocaine. He doesn't sniff.'

'Of course that settles it,' Robert said in such an infuriating voice that I might have foregone my vow of non-violence in cars if he hadn't snapped out suddenly, 'Come on! Pull into the right-hand lane, it's moving. Quickly, woman, move it! There's a gap . . .'

It was nearly six o'clock before we were on the other side of Paris and heading north; the delays with the roadworks meant we'd been caught in the rush hour and made us even later. 'I doubt we'll get to your parents' before midnight now,' Robert said, sounding fed up.

'Doesn't matter to me. I warned them not to expect me at any specific time and we aren't leaving until midday tomorrow so I'll be able to sleep in. But what about you?

You won't get to London until the small hours. Would you like to stay at my parents'? I'm sure there's room.'

He shifted position and tried to straighten out his leg a little. 'What I'd really like, Nella, if it isn't essential that you get to Chatham tonight, is to break our journey this side of the Channel. To be honest, my knee is beginning to give me real gyp and I'd rather not have to spend another five hours or so in a car this evening.'

I wouldn't have been human – or female – if I hadn't wondered for a fleeting moment if this was just some excuse to get me in what is popularly known as a compromising situation. It was highly unlikely. For the last hour or so I'd been aware that being stuck in a car without the opportunity to get out and move around hadn't been doing Robert's knee any favours at all, and really the only strange thing was that he hadn't cried 'Stop' before. 'That's fine,' I said. 'Where do you want to stay? One of those hotels that cater for travellers?'

He shuddered. 'Certainly not! If we've got an extra night in France we might as well enjoy ourselves, not turn it into a period of penal servitude. Let's go on a little further so we don't have to get up too early in the morning and then we can leave the motorway up here,' his finger jabbed at the map, 'and just see what we find.'

'Sounds OK to me,' I said absently, wondering exactly how Robert intended to 'enjoy' himself.

At one point it looked as if we might have to settle for one of the cut-rate boxes that cater for frequent travellers after all. We gave the first hotel we passed a miss on the grounds that we didn't need to go inside to see that we'd have to hock the car to pay the bill; the next we tried, in a delightful little village on the banks of a river, was fully booked with the overflow from a local musical festival and the patron proudly informed us that every hotel room for twenty kilometres around was occupied and suggested we head towards the coast. Despite this being a tourist area, none of the villages we went through had a hotel and we were beginning to wonder if we'd have to go back to the one where we'd got as far as opening the car door before hastily closing it again against the over-powering smell of drains. Then Robert sent us the wrong way at a vital junction and we nearly rejoined the motor-way back to Paris. Maybe I shouldn't have asked if he'd like me to take over the navigation as well as the driving. For about fifteen minutes I got the impression that Robert's plans for the evening involved a bath, a decent dinner and murder, possibly not in that order.

Fortunately, soon after that we chanced on Souteil, a one-time seaside town now firmly landlocked in the middle of a flat plain due to the sea retreating several kilometres. As well as narrow winding streets that climbed higgledy-piggledy up a low hill crowned by the crumbling remains of a castle, it had the Auberge du Nord, a venerable former coaching inn in the middle of town, that was so discreetly hidden away behind a high wall that we might have gone straight past it but for the elderly man in blue overalls and Breton beret at the garage where we filled up with petrol. He had enthused about it being an establishment *très sympa* with a truly welcoming *patronne*, and gladly gave us directions. As it was, we still nearly missed the small weathered sign with the Auberge's name to one side of a huge curved arch that must have been easily wide enough for two stagecoaches side by side and I had to reverse the car, much to the annoyance of the driver behind me, back to the entrance.

Robert got out, stretching stiff legs and flexing his knee, looking around with a sheer smile of pleasure at the cobbled courtyard, weathered brick and the way the roof dipped and swayed with age. 'I'm not going any further,' he announced. 'We stay here.'

'What if they don't have a room?' I asked. And what if they did, but didn't have *two* rooms? This, I have to admit, was a question that had been preying on my mind. I mean, if there was only one room left and if Robert declared that we might as well take it rather than keep on with our wearying search that might not get us two rooms anyway, how should I react?

'Let's go and see,' he said cheerfully, limping in through a half-open studded oak door, that looked as if it might date from the time when the sea was still lapping at the town walls, into a foyer decorated with a rose-patterned wallpaper that must have been the *dernier cri* in about 1950. A large lady with improbably orange hair sat behind a large desk, various important-looking pieces of paper spread out in front of her but in fact concentrating on knitting a cobweb-fine baby's shawl of incredible intricacy. Of course she had room for us, she said. She was so pleased we'd come to her, she loved having *les anglais* in her hotel, they were so civilised and never complained. At this we glanced at each other, wondering if this boded well for our stay. She would take us upstairs and show us where we were sleeping so we could be sure we liked it before we registered. She swept up something in her hand before I could see if it was one or two sets of room keys and still talking rapidly, most of it aimed at Robert who was obviously the sort of *anglais* she particularly liked (male and good-looking), judging by the weightily flirtatious looks she kept on sending him over one well-covered shoulder, led us up a flight of lethally well-polished oak stairs, made even more treacherous by a dip in the centre of each tread.

The inn went around all four sides of the courtyard and had been added to over the years with a fine disregard for logicalities such as having the rooms in a straight line, or even keeping to the same ceiling heights. One bit of passage had a sharp kink for no reason we could work out and we had to mysteriously go down one short flight of stairs then up another longer one before we reached the section where we were sleeping, above the arch to the courtyard. I'd been battling with the strangest sensation ever since we turned the last corner; it seemed that my sense of balance had gone for I felt as if I was listing to port, but Madame seemed quite upright when I looked. 'Voila!' she declared, throwing a door open to a room decorated with a particularly vivid pink wallpaper. I wasn't expecting the slight step and went in with a jolt, my steps gaining momentum as I crossed the room as if I was on skates. I was beginning to wonder if Janey had slipped some sort of delayed action Mickey Finn into the iced tea she'd included in our picnic when I noticed that this side of the bed was propped up on little wooden blocks under the legs, presumably to level it so you didn't fall out in the night. The building must be moving with age, I thought with a mixture of relief that I wasn't going crazy after all, and slight apprehension at the degree to which my room appeared to be tipping over to one side.

'Madame says this part of the building hasn't been altered since the fifteenth century, apart from things like the plumbing, so I suppose if it's lasted for six hundred years we can expect it to go on to tomorrow morning without falling out into the street,' Robert said from beside me.

'Hope so,' I said vaguely, though I still found it pretty unnerving to look out of the window and see that my hands, resting on the window ledge, were several inches further out over the street than my feet. Actually I found the pink counterpane-covered bed, a very large double bed, even more unnerving. Surely Robert wouldn't even think ... A room was one thing, *in extremis*, but a *bed* ...

'My room's even worse,' he went on. 'The bath's been placed down the slope so I'll be interested to see what happens when I run it. I doubt the water will even manage to reach the far end before it rises up to the overflow at the other.'

'Would you rather have this room?' I asked, eager to make amends for my silly fantasies, even if he didn't know about them. 'The bath's on the level, though it's not very big,' I added with a doubtful look at his lanky legs.

'No, it's fine, thanks. It'll be a new experience,' he said cheerfully.

Half an hour later, bathed, changed and freshly made up (on my part, not his) we were setting out to explore the town and find somewhere to eat. Actually it would have been rather more than half an hour later if I'd been left to my own devices. I had been having a sartorial crisis of some extent, that really familiar one that starts with 'I've got nothing to wear.' Well nothing that was clean, ironed, new and, most importantly, flattering. It was only an impatient knock on the door that made me seize up a top I'd already tried on once and taken off because I'd decided it made me look fat. It didn't really matter what I wore to go out to eat with Robert, I told myself, it wasn't *that* sort of dinner. Besides, he thought I was too thin. I put it on.

'Your time-keeping hasn't improved over the years,' he said disapprovingly as I appeared. It was all right for him. He belonged to the put-on-the-first-clean-thing-that-comes-to-hand school of dressing and it might look fine on him, it did actually I noted, looking at his navy shirt and jeans, but if I adopted it, I'd end up looking like your original ragbag. 'I suppose you've been dithering about what to wear,' he said, giving me a casual once-over.

'Yup.' There was no point in pretending. He'd been through this before and as he'd said so accurately, some things just don't change. 'But the results were worth it, weren't they?'

He looked at me again, with more attention this time. 'Not really,' he said in an offhand voice and grinned at my indignant expression, waiting just long enough for me to build up a smouldering head of miffed steam before he said, 'You've got good basics so you don't need to spend hours in front of a mirror to look nice.' I was just digesting this, a nice warm smug feeling at the compliment creeping through me when he added, 'Especially not when we're supposed to be going out for dinner. I'm starving! Shall we go before I pass out from hunger?'

I'd recovered enough of my sense of humour to be speaking to him again by the time we found the little restaurant in a tranquil little square so highly recommended to us by Madame, who had waxed lyrical about the quality of the service and the chef's magic touch with seafood. She had waxed so lyrical that Robert muttered the chef had to be either her son or her lover and the 'service' must be some other relative. Since the chef remained in his kitchen doing what chefs do we never got to see if Robert's theory was correct in that respect but we both detected a distinct resemblance to Madame around the nose and chin in the pretty waitress who took our order, though luckily for her she bore no resemblance to Madame in the waistline or hair areas.

Even if Madame was putting business her family's way she had done us proud. We sat outside at a table on a part of the pavement sectioned off by tubs of flowers from ordinary passers-by, sharing a bottle of very good wine and eating food which was amongst the best I'd had for a long time. Even better, unlike George, Robert wasn't neurotic about germs and was quite happy to let me sample what he'd chosen so I could see if he'd done better than me; indeed, he pinched more than one of my *moules*. Though actually I was enjoying myself so much I don't think I'd really have minded if the food had been cooked by my brother, which says a lot. I'd forgotten how much I liked just talking to Robert, especially now that I didn't feel he was simply waiting to go for my jugular each time I dropped my guard. I could relax and didn't have to watch every word I was saying. By the time he said, with a welcome degree of regret in his voice, that he supposed we really ought to let the staff close up, we were the last customers left and even the youths who had been hanging out in the square making eyes at the teenage girls mincing past had slouched off to find other haunts.

I leaned back with a happy sigh while the waitress unhurriedly went off to make up the bill. 'Thanks for all this.'

'What for?' he asked.

I shrugged. 'Everything. Allowing Janey to bully you into offering me a lift, suggesting that we stay here. After what happened yesterday, if I'd simply got on the train and gone home as I was originally supposed to, I'd have felt so flat and miserable about everything, but today's made it all different . . .' My voice trailed off and I looked down at the tablecloth, afraid that I might have said too much.

'You've got nothing to thank me for,' he said in an amused voice. 'I've been suiting myself entirely, I promise you.' Startled, I raised my eyes and he smiled at me in a way that did something very odd to my stomach. 'As I said, it made sense for you to come along, even if you've got the acceleration instincts of a snail. Since it's such a nice evening, shall we walk around the town a little before we go back to the auberge?'

Robert's smile had been making female stomachs, and ones made of much tougher stuff than mine, lurch pleasurably for years; it didn't mean anything. On either of our parts. I was just reacting to an attractive man. It happens. I was trying to think of the last time it had when the bill came and I was able to get rid of my last lingering feelings of self-consciousness over having a hormone system that apparently goes into overdrive over a display of white teeth (one front one slightly crooked) by having a vigorous discussion over whether we were going to split the bill or not. I won. We did. But even so, that relaxed feeling I'd had during dinner of being with a good friend had vanished to be replaced by something much more unsettling, something I didn't really want to think about.

We meandered slowly around, admiring the floodlit castle walls and deciding that as it was dark it probably wouldn't be a good idea to take advantage of the path that went around the top of them, wandering along the main square which was obviously the social centre for the whole of town and was still humming. Robert wanted us to have a drink in a particularly disreputable-looking bar so he could have a chance to play the table football at the back of the room. 'I was twelve the last time I saw one of those,' he said longingly. Luckily for me several youths got up and surrounded it in a noisy joshing group that looked as if it was going to be there for some time. Frankly, I hadn't fancied being the only woman in such a seedy dive, especially as an unshaven man in a grubby white singlet was already openly leering at my cleavage. At least he'd noticed I'd got one, unlike certain other parties, I though peevishly as we walked back down the hill towards the hotel.

Was it my imagination or did a pall of tension envelop us as we turned in under the arch that supported our rooms? Conversation died and we crossed the darkened courtyard only muttering occasionally, 'Watch out for that step,' or 'Can you remember the way to our rooms?' in hushed voices so we didn't wake anyone up. Robert even managed to swear in a whisper when he banged his knee on one of the many tables Madame liked to litter around the foyer to ambush unwary guests, though it has to be admitted that I'd never heard quite that range of expression used before at *any* volume. When I stumbled over a raised floorboard in the corridor upstairs, he shot out a hand to stop me measuring my length which certainly would have negated all our attempts to keep quiet, then withdrew it again quickly as if he'd been burned as soon as I recovered my balance.

'If we aim to leave at eight, we'll have plenty of time to get to your parents'. That OK with you?' he asked as we reached our rooms.

I nodded, for some strange reason finding it rather difficult to breathe. Actually it wasn't strange at all. I knew perfectly well what was going on, I'm not that self-deluded. But I do have a certain sense of self-preservation and I was well aware that the lines my thoughts, my wishes, were running along were not at all sensible. Anyway I didn't know what he felt. Not for certain anyway. 'Goodnight. Thanks again,' I said.

'It was my pleasure,' he said with another of those smiles. This time I was as sure as you ever can be of the message that I read in his eyes. I gulped, my stomach doing another loop the loop as several images flashed through my mind, none of them decent. All I had to do was tilt my head as he bent to kiss me goodnight so that instead of my cheek he met my mouth and we could take it from there... So it wouldn't be wise, there was no future in it – not even I could fool myself into believing that, but I was a big girl now, wasn't I? An adult even. I was entitled to do stupid things sometimes, and was it really so stupid to live for the moment for once? I'd done the sensible thing with George and look where that had got me. And when you walk into something with your eyes wide open so that you're fully armed against the consequences, that's not really stupid at all, is it? It's called seizing opportunities. Besides, I wanted to. I really wanted to.

He looked at me gravely. I thought for a horrid moment that he wasn't going to kiss me goodnight at all, then as I smiled rather tremulously his face cleared and he bent towards me. I tipped my face up.

CHAPTER 23

I didn't get much sleep that night. I spent most of it berating myself for being a bloody fool and wimping out at the last moment. God knows what Robert thought as I suddenly whipped my head away and bolted into my room muttering that I had loads of packing to do so I'd better start now. It turns out that I'm not very good at seizing opportunities, certainly not ones like that. There I was, about to do whatever we were going to do, when I'd been overwhelmed by a feeling that somehow I'd got on the high diving board when all I'd planned to climb was the little plank they allow the toddlers to jump off. It was all right for him; tomorrow he would go back to his real life without a backward glance, maybe even start patching up things with Venetia, and if he thought of me in the next few weeks it would be with a mild pleasure that we'd been able to cement our rapprochement in such a mutually enjoyable manner. That's how men think about one-night stands – that they're fun, that they're nothing serious, and, above all, that they're for one night.

There's walking into things with your eyes open knowing the risks, and there's walking into them knowing that you're just about to go in *waaay* too deep. So I fled.

In the end I got up off the bed and wandered restlessly around the room, thinking I might as well stick to the letter of the truth and get on with my packing. I folded every garment immaculately, taking care to do up all the necessary buttons, close the zips, even putting my shoes in facing each other and toe to heel rather than chucking them in any old how like I usually do. Anything in fact to keep my hands busy, even if I couldn't stop my mind buzzing. My mother would have been proud to see that her lessons on how to pack a suitcase so that you didn't crease the clothes had at last borne fruit, as I put the last beautifully cornered skirt on top of the pile in the case and straightened out a collar on a shirt just so. Of course she usually started with clothes that hadn't been lying in a crumpled heap on the floor, but you had to begin somewhere.

In the cold light of day I felt even worse, and acutely embarrassed to boot. How could I have reacted as if Robert was Dracula stopping by for a three-course meal when he'd only been about to give me a peck goodnight? I trailed downstairs, hardly able to bring myself to look at him, but he asked me in such a perfectly normal manner if I'd slept well and then went back to eating the liberal quantities of croissants Madame thought was necessary for a breakfast that I began to wonder if I'd imagined the whole thing.

My mother appeared so promptly on the doorstep as we turned into the drive at home that if I hadn't known she doesn't have any I'd have suspected she'd been on net curtain duty, ready to mount an ambush the moment the car drew up. I knew yesterday when I rang to say that I was travelling with an old friend and was staying overnight that I'd never get away with merely assuring her it wasn't George. Indeed, it was only the excuse of Robert's mobile's failing batteries that had saved me from the full maternal interrogation going into operation there and then.

What was Min doing here? I thought in alarm as a slim blonde figure appeared alongside her. She was supposed to be travelling up North with her beloved, wasn't she? But she was smiling as if she didn't have a care in the world, so it didn't look as if anything drastic had happened. She beat Mum in the race to reach the car and to give me a hug, saying in her usual breathless rush, 'Francis has gone to Glasgow of all places for the bank and says he'll meet me in Cumbria, so I thought I'd take the chance to go over the plans for the reception with Mum. Are you *sure* you don't want to be a bridesmaid? We can talk about it in the car because I'm going to drive you up. Dad's got something on this morning and doesn't want to leave until mid-afternoon. Besides, I'd like some company and it'll give us a chance to catch up. I haven't seen you for ages.'

'That'll be great,' I said, trying to cut across her flow. I know from bitter experience what Min is like when she gets going.

I was too late. 'And what have you been up to, little sister? Sudden change of plans, I hear?' she asked with a knowing smile, glancing over my shoulder. 'Not that I blame you. He's a lot more exciting than going on the train. Who is he?' she hissed in an all too audible whisper. 'The new Mr Right?'

'No, the old one,' Robert said in a highly amused voice as I went scarlet.

'You must remember Robert, Min? I'm sure you met when you came up to visit me one weekend,' I said woodenly as her eyes widened into an incredulous O. 'We were staying near each other in France and he kindly offered to give me a lift back.'

For once Min seemed to be lost for words, something I was very grateful for, although I could already see the what, where, when questions beginning to form. Mum's curiosity-meter, which always works at a pretty high pitch where her children are concerned, cranked into overdrive the moment she twigged who it was I'd been travelling with. She hadn't met Robert before, though she'd certainly heard enough about him, and he didn't stand a chance of getting away before she'd satisfied her nosiness to the fullest degree. She cut firmly across his protests that he ought to be pushing on, saying she was so delighted to meet an old friend of mine after all this time. He must be tired from the journey and the very least she could do to thank him for his kindness to me was to give him a cup of coffee and a slice of the excellent chocolate cake she'd brought from the WI Bring and Buy sale a couple of days ago. There was no need to worry about my luggage. Min and I could make ourselves useful and do that.

Recognising an immovable maternal object when he saw one, Robert met my eyes and meekly said that chocolate cake sounded wonderful. He was borne off inside while I jiggled his car keys in one hand and looked balefully at my elder sister.

'So you've made up with him at last. That's great. He's one of those men who improve with age, isn't he?' she said, though fortunately Robert was out of earshot this time. 'It's not fair. Nobody ever says that women look better with a few extra lines.' She stroked one of the imaginary crow's feet around her eyes that had recently begun to occupy her, then snapped her attention back to the matter in hand. 'So when did all this start? Not long ago, I imagine, if you went in for an unscheduled dirty stop out last night.'

'It wasn't like that,' I said, unlocking the boot of the car.

'Wasn't it?' Min sounded disbelieving.

'No!'

She looked at me hard, then said invitingly, 'So tell me all about it.'

'Look – I don't know where to start, and even if I did, Mum would have had Robert completely inside out before I was anywhere near finishing. I'll save it for the car.'

'OK,' she said, 'but you aren't wriggling out of telling me. I want to know everything.'

'Don't you always?' I grinned, for though Min drives me mad sometimes we actually get on very well. 'Tell you what, I really will tell you everything, providing you stop banging on about me being your bridesmaid. I'm sorry, I love you dearly, you know I do, but I am absolutely not, and I mean it, parading up the aisle behind you wearing a ballerina-length ice blue silk dress.'

She laughed. 'I suppose it does look better on Francis's sister than it would on you.'

'Yeah, well, it helps if you're fourteen,' I agreed.

'Right, it's a deal,' she said briskly. 'Though I'll make sure you're the one to get my bouquet. You look as if you might need it.' She skipped back out of reach of any retaliation, then peered in the boot. 'This suitcase I recognise, but these are nothing to do with you, are they?' she asked, looking at the stack of pictures in their cases.

'Those two with the pencilled N in one corner are mine, and *no*, you may not have a look inside.'

She made a show of being about to rattle one of them until I stopped her, then laid it flat in the boot of her car. 'If we put our suitcases on the back seat you needn't worry about anything toppling on these.'

'Good idea,' I said, fishing out a carrier bag containing some last-minutes presents I'd bought on a lightning dash around a supermarket between Souteil and Calais this morning. I didn't really expect the wine and cheeses to be the type to tickle the most discerning palates, but I reckoned being questioned by the police when you had been planning to do your shopping is pretty hard to beat as a plausible excuse for why you didn't spend hours poring over the goods in an upmarket emporium. I handed a Camembert and a Pont l'Eveque to Min. 'Here you are. Something to make your car smell nice.'

'Thanks.' She took an appreciative sniff and staggered. 'Mm, nice! I'll see if Mum's got a Tupperware box she can lend me.' Inside, we found Robert in the kitchen surreptitiously feeding bits of chocolate cake to a surprised but pleased ginger cat on his knee. My mother was bustling around asking him questions in her normal seemingly inconsequential way, but which as I knew to my cost, was in fact a highly efficient information-gathering technique.

'It's very good,' he said in an undertone as I slid in the seat next to him, 'but this is the third slice she's insisted on giving me, and they aren't getting any smaller!'

Mum broke off from finding out about Robert's credit card details, or something of the sort, and threatened me with a piece of cake too. I said I'd share Robert's and pulled his plate towards me, for which I got a grateful smile, the type which made me look away for a moment so I could sort myself out. Orlando didn't look so thrilled though.

'No thanks, no coffee for me, or I'll be stopping at every service station between here and Birmingham,' said Min as she rootled in the cupboard under the sink and came up with an old ice cream box, putting the cheese in it, then wrapping it in several plastic bags until she was satisfied it was sealed as tightly as an airlock on a space station. 'I'll go and put this in the car, lest I forget,' she said as she drifted out again, turning to say over her shoulder, 'you and I ought to leave soon, Nella. My car may be reliable but it doesn't like to go too fast.'

'That should suit you just fine,' Robert said with a sardonic grin as he got up, firmly refusing further offers of food and drink and saying he mustn't hold my mother up any longer. She looked as if there was nothing she'd like more, especially as I gathered from her frustrated air that he had deployed an expertise in dodging her questions that she wasn't used to encountering.

Even so, disappointment didn't stop her from looking after his departing car and saying in an approving voice, 'Oh Nella, I am glad I've met him at last. He is nice, isn't he?'

Mustering a smile, I said in as offhand a tone as I could manage, 'You know, Mum, there are many words I'd use to describe Robert,' – infuriating, opinionated, clever, impatient, forceful, generous, devastating, didn't want to think about that – 'but nice isn't one of them.'

'Why do you say that?' she asked, dropping her voice to a horrified whisper. 'Is it something to do with his *habits*?'

I laughed genuinely, jolted out of the forlorn mood I'd been in since I waved goodbye to him. 'As far as I know his habits are perfect, and no, I don't know precisely what they are these days, sorry to disappoint you!'

She smiled, well used to being teased by her children, and I took advantage of her temporary silence to say, 'And he's already got a girlfriend – a tall, beautiful redhead who used to share a flat with me. Venetia would have come back with us except she's helping out an old family friend with a domestic emergency.'

Wow! I deserved a pat on the back for that, I thought, feeling thoroughly pleased with myself. I know that you aren't supposed to lie to your parents, but surely you can mislead them a little. Besides, I didn't actually know what the situation was between Robert and Venetia; they could still be an item, couldn't they?

Needless to say I didn't get away with this sort of smokescreen with my sister, largely because she's had far more experience at pulling the wool over the parental eyes than I have and can recognise a half-truth from a thousand paces. However, there are other sorts of smoke-screen, and in a story as complicated as this one it was quite easy to 'lose' a few details, especially the ones concerning my ignominious flight into my bedroom last night. 'Fancy letting a chance like that slip through your hands!' she'd have said. The fact that I agreed with her wouldn't have made it any more palatable to hear.

'Oh, what a shame. I'd really hoped that you two might be getting back together again,' she sighed. So had I – well, not hoped, that was going too far – but I'd dreamed about it a little.

'Are you suggesting I should ignore your often given advice about not having anything to do with men on the rebound?'

'With someone like Robert it'd be a case of do as I do, not as I say,' Min replied seriously. 'Besides, when have you ever taken my advice? You certainly don't seem to be doing it with this Charlie bloke.'

'That's different,' I said defensively. 'He's not on the rebound. He and Sally are drifting apart – he told me so.' She raised her eyebrows eloquently. OK, so I knew perfectly well that men aren't always absolutely truthful about that sort of thing, but I believed Charlie. Decent men like him didn't mislead you like that. 'Anyway,' I went on, 'Sally's much better suited to George. They go very well together.'

'So by moving in on her boyfriend you're actually doing everyone a favour,' Min concluded sarkily and laughed as I stuck my tongue out at her.

The subject of her wedding kept us fully occupied for the rest of the journey. My grandparents had arranged for their large visiting family to be billeted for the weekend on various friends in the neighbourhood: Granny and her old friend Mrs Hudson were being distinctly competitive over who would be the first to have a great-grandchild and I was amused to see that my hosts had four unmarried sons, even if the youngest one was only nineteen. Min was taken in to have a drink while one of the sons, Robin, helped me with my luggage and took it up to my room. He stumped off upstairs with my two suitcases while I went to get the pictures out of the car.

I opened the boot and froze. Underneath the garment bags with Francis's suit and a dreamy little number from Ghost for Min there should have been two picture cases. I blinked and looked again. I wasn't wrong. There were *three* of them.

'Min!' I hissed from the drawing-room door and beckoned her out to the hall. 'We've got one of Robert's pictures in the car. How on earth did it get in there? I know I only put my two in.'

She cleared her throat, looking unusually self-conscious. 'Um, I was meaning to have a word with you about that.'

'Word about what?' Then light began to dawn. 'Are you telling me that you deliberately took one of Robert's pictures? Oh Min, how could you!' A huge lump of dismay settled like a stone in the pit of my stomach. 'Don't you think I've already been accused of picture theft quite enough times in one week?'

'Don't be silly! 'Course he isn't going to think you've

stolen it,' she said robustly. 'He probably hasn't even noticed it's gone yet. All you've got to do is ring him at that gallery of his and tell him I made a mistake and put it in my car. I'm quite prepared to take all the blame.'

'How very generous of you,' I said faintly. 'But I don't understand why you want a canvas you haven't even set eyes on.'

'I don't, stupid! I did it for you. Look, you might say that there's nothing going on between the two of you, but you were looking at him in the kitchen as if he was your last Rolo and you'd just been forced to offer it to that Maggie. I didn't hear any stuff about seeing each other in London, or even exchanging phone numbers, and well . . . I couldn't bear to think you were going to let him go again without a fight. When I was putting the cheese in the car I saw you'd left his keys sticking out of the boot and it occurred to me there was something I could do.' She shrugged. 'If I've got things wrong there won't be any harm done, will there? If I haven't . . . as you've got his picture you'll have to make contact at least once, won't you?' She grinned. 'No need to give you any advice on how to make the most of *that* particular opportunity.'

I stared at her, torn between outrage and admiration. She looked relieved, as well she might be, when I burst out laughing and hugged her. 'Minerva Bowden, you are completely outrageous. Did you use a trick like this to snare Francis?'

'Didn't need to,' she said smugly. 'Though I had to remind him that he wasn't the only pebble on the beach on one occasion. Cost me a fortune, what with the escort from the agency – an underwear model and *very* tasty – and dinner and champagne in the restaurant Francis and I usually go to, but it worked. The announcement went in *The Times* two days later.'

I waved her off and rang Robert at the gallery, the only place I knew to get hold of him, speaking, to my mingled relief and disappointment, to his partner who appeared to be completely unfazed by being one picture short. He said he'd get Robert to ring me. From then on I was kept so busy by my lively hosts who believed that if you were having a party weekend you should make the most of it that I didn't have time to wonder more than about twice every minute just what Robert was going to think of his picture mysteriously moving over to Min's car, especially after I'd assured him I'd checked I'd got the right ones. My mood see-sawed between fear that he must be smelling a super charged rodent about this and a bubbly feeling that even if he was, it didn't matter. I was still going to see him again. I refused to even contemplate he might send a messenger.

My grandparents' party went with a bang – literally, since two cousins set off sixty rockets at midnight. Everybody was in the best of moods, my grandfather made a speech about Granny still being as lovely as she was sixty years ago, and best of all from my point of view, Min had been unusually discreet. My parents were still labouring under the impression that I'd spent the last two weeks or so peacefully sunbathing by the edge of a pool so I hadn't had to spend most of the evening dodging behind my grandfather's prized potted palms to avoid being flapped over because of my horrible experiences.

And as I had hoped, prayed for given the current state of my bank balance, Nick thought it an excellent idea to be saved the trouble of looking for a suitable wedding present for Min by going halves with me over the pictures. He appeared to be quite happy to give me a cheque there and then and leave it at that. I promptly pocketed the cheque (slipped it in my bra, actually) but said didn't he think he ought to come over and take a look so he actually knew what he was giving his sister. Nick didn't agree that this was strictly necessary but said he'd drop by sometime in the morning. In fact, he and his girlfriend, an annoying silly girl called Lucinda, didn't turn up until just before lunch so I had to rush him up to my room for a quick viewing, Lucinda following in his wake.

I unwrapped the newspaper from around the first picture and drew out the *vendangers* returning home at the end of the day. 'Hey, this is nice!' he exclaimed, taking it from me and giving it a close look. 'Wouldn't mind it myself. What's the other one of?'

'Everyone getting very merry at a *fête du vin*.'

'Sounds right up my street,' he grinned and handed the picture back. 'Min'll really go for these. Well done, Nellie the Ellie.'

I screwed up a bit of newspaper and threw it at him; he dodged it, laughing. I hadn't noticed that Lucinda had also been busy unpacking until she said in a surprised voice, 'This one's really nice too, but I don't know why you think it's a pair to that other one. It's nothing like it.'

I was in the middle of doing the *vendangers* up again and I could see its companion, still wrapped, on the floor in front of me. 'You must have unwrapped Robert's picture. Can you put it back?' I said sharply. 'It got put in Min's car by accident and God knows what it's worth. I don't want to be held responsible for any damage to it.'

'OK,' she said amiably. I caught a glimpse of gold out of the corner of my eye as she began to slide it back and my head jerked up. Staying her hand, I stared incredulously at a glowing vivid picture, one I knew well; a sunlit beach under a jewel bright sky, a little boy playing in the sand, and Venetia's double, hair streaming in the wind, triumphantly holding a whorled shell up in the air.

CHAPTER 24

All I could think of was that I had to get Nick and Lucinda out of my room as quickly as possible. 'Um, on second thoughts, I don't think we should get the other picture out after all,' I said, amazed that my voice sounded even remotely normal. 'The frame is even more fragile than this one. I'd better take them both to a repair shop – you can have a proper look once it's been done.'

'Fine,' Nick said agreeably. 'But don't get them over-restored. You know how Min likes her things artfully distressed.'

'Genuinely distressed in this case,' I said, forcing a smile to my lips as Lucinda, who might have been a dab hand at giving the impression that she had cotton wool between the ears but knew a good picture when she glimpsed one, started saying that if that was the sort of picture Robert sold she'd certainly go along to his gallery. My heart missed a beat as Nick brightened with interest, saying he'd like to have a quick look too, then added that he and Lucinda had better get going; they were already late. Since they were supposed to have been somewhere for lunch twenty minutes ago he was dead right. I hung around on the drive for what seemed like hours, and was probably only five minutes, saying my goodbyes and see you soons. Nick left at last and, pretending I hadn't heard my hostess say we'd better go in to lunch ourselves, I shot back up to my room and drew Robert's picture out of its sleeve.

There's nothing like having your very worst fears confirmed. I'd been hoping that what I'd seen had been a figment of my imagination. It hadn't. I shoved it back with shaking hands, doing the flaps up so no one else could possibly get a glimpse, and wondered what the hell I was going to do next.

After lunch, I was being given a lift back to London by Robin and another of the brothers; mercifully, since I was incapable of making even the most basic sort of conversation, they appeared to think my shell-shocked state was the result of a mild hangover and let me sleep it off in the back. I stared unseeingly out of the window, thinking, thinking, thinking. *Why* had Robert stolen the picture? I'd heard him referring to the fortune his partnership in the gallery had cost him and how he was mortgaged up to the hilt, but surely he wouldn't have resorted to theft to pay off his debts? Or had it been Venetia's idea, and she'd persuaded him to take the picture to England to divert suspicion from her? Did it matter? I felt a tear trickle down my cheek. What did was that I'd let my dreams and hopes carry me away to a ridiculous extent, and minded them being dashed more than I did the realisation that, at the very least, Robert was an accessory to theft. Anxious not to alert the two men in the front to my tears, I did my best to sniff silently, which wasn't easy.

The picture had to go back to Janey and Tom, obviously, but how could I return it without letting them know how it had come into my possession in the first place? On second thoughts, I didn't want them to know it had anything to do with me. They might start thinking the local police had been on to something after all and I was acting from a belated fit of conscience. I certainly wasn't taking the rap for someone else. For a horrible moment I began to wonder if that was what Robert had intended all along, and felt my precarious composure start to wobble violently; that was one notion I really couldn't cope with. Except he wouldn't do that. A few hours ago I would have said confidently that he wasn't into theft either, but I was still certain on this one. Anyway, we all knew it was Maggie who'd shopped me to the police and I was absolutely sure she and Robert weren't in cahoots. So I could go back to thinking about what on earth I was going to do with my unwanted parcel.

The simplest answer would be to post it, label done in anonymous block capitals naturally. But mightn't it get damaged or pinched? Besides, it would probably need about fifty quid's worth of stamps and, call me mean, but I strongly begrudge spending my money on covering up somebody else's crime. If I sent it by carrier wouldn't I need to give a sender's address? Did they check these things? And that pretty well ruled out depositing it at a police station, saying that it was a stolen picture which needed returning to its owners. Even the most dozy copper was going to ask a few questions about that. What about taking it to one of the auction houses and leaving it there for a valuation? Then I could send an anonymous letter telling Tom and Janey where the picture was. Of course, I'd have to work out some form of disguise so that the person behind the desk at the auction house couldn't give a too accurate description of the mysterious woman who'd brought the painting in, but that shouldn't be too much of a problem. Didn't Felicity still have the red-haired wig she'd bought after a particularly brutal cut last summer?

It wasn't perfect but it might do. By the time we reached my flat I had pulled myself together enough to be able to converse quite lucidly with Robin and his brother, though I was relieved when they refused my offer of a drink. Just as well, too, since the only alcoholic substances in the flat were half a bottle of cooking sherry and one can of lager. Once they'd gone I began to roam around my stuffy, dusty flat, at a loss what to do next. I turned on the radio for company, and hid the picture behind the sofa, where it was out of sight but definitely not out of mind. The answerphone told me I had thirty-four messages. How on earth could I have *thirty-four*? Did I even know that number of people?

The first message was Oscar, saying he was back safely and to give him a ring when I had the time. The second from my mother said much the same, so did the third from Min. My telephone bill was going to be astronomical with all these call backs, I thought as I dialled up number four and froze as Robert's voice came out of the machine. I cancelled it as quickly as I could, then sat there cursing myself for not having at least listened to what he had to say. But he couldn't have an excuse for what he'd done;

there wasn't one, I reminded myself sternly, trying to ignore the warm friendliness I'd heard in his voice. How many of the remaining thirty messages were from him? I stared at the machine, horribly tempted to do a quick race through every one.

I was going to go mad if I stayed here on my own. I hesitated for a moment, then picked up the phone and dialled Oscar's number.

'Are you in bed?' I asked when he answered.

'My dear Nella, what do you think I am?' he asked, shocked. 'A geriatric who needs his cocoa and hot water bottle by ten o'clock? I'm getting over the journey, which wasn't nearly as nice without you to keep me company, by watching a video of *Bringing Up Baby*, if you must know. I just love Cary Grant.'

'So do I.' Thank God he wasn't watching *Greyfriars Bobby*. I was close enough to tears as it was. 'Can I come around and watch it with you?'

'Of course you can,' he said, probably alerted by my tone that something was up. 'Shall I come up and get you?'

I laughed. 'I know that the streets of London aren't supposed to be safe for a woman on her own after dark, but I think I can risk going from one end of the street to the other all alone, don't you?' Given the mood I was in, I'd quite appreciate meeting a mugger too; there's nothing like taking it out on someone else.

The telephone started to ring again as I rooted in my cupboard for a light jacket. I let the answerphone pick it up and as I let myself out of the door I heard Robert leaving yet another message.

Poor Oscar, he likes to gear himself up for the week ahead by spending his Sunday evenings slopping on the sofa in his tracksuit bottoms and no shoes watching a classic film and eating popcorn. Not many people know about this. So I expect the last thing he felt he needed was me clinging around his neck pouring out my problems. He didn't get to watch much of his video either, but then he knows the script virtually off by heart and can quote Cary Grant at length (he does a nifty Katharine Hepburn too) so my conscience wasn't as bothered as it might have been. I wouldn't necessarily agree that a problem shared is a problem halved, this problem was way too big for that, but at least telling Oscar was enough of a comfort for the time being.

'You look brown, Nella. Had a nice holiday?' asked Darcy, our junior copywriter, as I stopped and looked in dismay at my desk, which appeared in my absence to have been on an intensive breeding programme for Post-it notes. Each one bore an apparently urgent message – usually one that was going to involve me in several hours' work. Even the keyboard was sprouting yellow and pink paper, while the screen must have been covered a good week ago, judging by the dates on them. It was going to take me until midday merely to read them, I thought, fighting the urge to turn on my heel and walk straight out again to replenish my already depleted energy with a large Danish at the coffee shop over the road. Come on, Nella! I told myself. The last thing you need is to start comfort eating. Wasn't I miserable enough already without the scales giving a wail of protest every time I stepped on them?

Darcy was looking at me with a slightly offended air. I smiled at her. 'Sorry, I was miles away. My holiday was one ... that I won't ever forget,' I said absolutely truthfully as I sat down and began piling my messages in a large heap, noting with interest that three pieces of important copy needed to be ready by ten o'clock and a report finished by lunchtime. Three weeks ago I'd have leaped to it, began tearing my hair out and would have got at least some of it done in time. I really couldn't be bothered now. There were more important things to think about. To be honest, the world wasn't going to come to an end if I didn't do it all. I checked the top message, which was to come up with some immediate sparkling draft copy for a possible run of ads in the teenage press for a roll-on deodorant that might or might not be adding a new scent to its range.

'Nella, I've got to have this by this evening,' said one of the account executives, speeding past my desk and dropping a file on top of everything else without a single 'if you don't mind' or 'I'd be very grateful ...'

Hadn't I got enough on my plate right now? I thought in irritation, picking up the file and winging it back with remarkable accuracy, for me. Only a few pages fell out. 'I haven't got the time. Do it yourself if it's that urgent,' I called.

He stopped to turn around and look at me in surprise. I wasn't known for fighting back; perhaps that was why I seemed to get more of the dross work than any of the other copywriters. Then to my surprise he gathered up his scattered papers and said, 'Oh well, if you're too busy . . . Do you think you could do it by the end of the week?'

I hid a faint smile. It seemed that even if the bottom had dropped out of your world there were still some things you could refuse to put up with. Maybe I should tackle my miserable salary next, I thought as I said airily, 'Don't know, doubt it. I'll let you know tomorrow.'

In my new mood of refusing to take any more rubbish I handed over most of the messages for urgent copy-writing to Darcy, telling her to deal with them. When she began to protest I fixed her with an eagle eye and pointed out that she was supposed to be my assistant – so what had she been doing in the last two weeks, allowing my work to pile up like this? Probably buttering up others who she reckoned were more likely than me to help her onto the fast track to becoming a fully-fledged copy-writer. This ambitious little madam subsided and meekly asked me which one she should start on first. 'Oh, and there's another message from some early bird, rang before you got in this morning,' she said, handing it over.

I glanced at it, my heart doing a funny little hippityhop as I saw Robert's name. He must be desperate to get hold of me before I looked at the picture; shame it was too late. I handed it back to Darcy. 'If he rings again tell him I'm in a meeting,' I said curtly. Darcy looked as if she was about to start whining that she was a copywriter not a secretary-cum-receptionist, but something in my expression must have dissuaded her.

An hour later I was in the discussion corner having a brainstorming session about a new press campaign with one of the artists and a couple of account executives, and doodling an intricate series of circle mazes on my reporter's pad – it helps to get the ideas flowing freely, honest – when the phone went for me.

'Hi, Nella,' Robert said cheerfully. I was going to *kill* Darcy, I thought wrathfully. 'You're very difficult to get hold of. I must have tried you at your flat about ten times last night.'

So that was why there were an extra four messages when I returned to the flat this morning for a swift change after spending the night in Oscar's spare bed. 'I got back from Cumbria very late,' I said mechanically, conscious that there were three other people within hearing distance who were staring at me with varying degrees of irritation and disapproval for having the nerve to take a personal call during a meeting. I glanced at them and cupped my hand around the receiver in a fruitless attempt to muffle my voice. 'It's too late, Robert. I've already seen the picture, Nick's girlfriend took it out of the case by accident.' Why on earth was I trying to explain to him that I wasn't guilty of prying? As if it really mattered. He began to speak, and I cut across him, not caring if the others overheard me. All I knew was that I couldn't bear to listen to attempts at self-justification. I might find myself trying to believe them. 'How could you do it?' I demanded, furious to hear my voice wobbling slightly. 'Tom and Janey are your friends, too.'

'Have you told them about finding the picture?' he asked, taking advantage of a momentary pause while I took a shaky breath.

'Of course I haven't! Because then I'd have to tell them how I got it, wouldn't I?'

'Nella, you don't understand—' he began.

'No, and I don't want to!' I snapped. 'And do you know what makes me almost angrier than anything else? That George was bloody well right!' And I slammed the phone back down.

While everybody stared at me in surprise, Darcy stuck her head over the partition and said apologetically, 'Sorry, Nella. Sue was minding the phones while I popped to the loo and I forgot to tell her you didn't want to speak to him.'

Oh well. I would have had to speak to him some time. 'That's OK,' I said, 'no harm done,' though Mark, the account director in charge of the session, looked as if in his opinion having his meeting disrupted by this sort of dramatic personal call amounted to a lot of harm. He sighed audibly as the phone went again almost immediately with another call for me. I snatched it up and said fiercely, 'What's the matter with you? Are you quite incapable of getting the message that I don't *ever* want to speak to you or see you again?'

'But what have I done?' asked a plaintive voice. Not Robert's.

I was completely thrown, my mind blank, then I got that wanting to sink through the floor feeling. 'Charlie?' I said tentatively. 'I'm sorry. I thought it was someone else.'

'I was hoping that was the case – because I'd hate to get on your wrong side,' he said. 'We're still on for that drink this evening, aren't we?'

Soddit! I hit my forehead with the palm of my hand. The last thing I needed was to have to be social this evening, even with someone as relaxed as Charlie. But after the way I'd greeted him how could I possibly put him off? 'Yes, of course we are.' I tried to inject a bit of enthusiasm in my voice. I'd have to go home via the off-licence, and even if I hadn't been back long enough to turn the flat into a tip, it still needed a tidy-up and the application of a duster. 'Though I can't make it too early, I've got lots of work on.'

Mark nodded approvingly; this was showing the right attitude, even if being constantly on the phone wasn't.

'I don't mind, I'm just happy to see you at whatever time suits you,' Charlie said enthusiastically.

Oh no, this was another thing I didn't feel up to coping with right now. But, conscious of my increasingly impatient colleagues who, no doubt justifiably, didn't see why this meeting should overrun into their lunch hour just because I was fixing up my social life, I hastily told him to come round to the flat at half-past seven.

'Great,' he said, 'and I'm sure that like me you won't have had a chance to do any food shopping, so shall we go out for a bite to eat?'

'Yes, that'd be lovely,' I lied. 'See you later.' Oh well, unpacking would have to wait.

'Is anyone else likely to ring you in the next hour or so?' Mark asked with heavy sarcasm as I put the phone down.

'Don't think so,' I said breezily.

'Good, then we can get on.'

I staggered up the shallow flight of steps to my front door that evening, even later than I expected I'd be, my arms aching from carrying several carrier bags loaded with bottles and other essentials. I set the bags down with much ominous clinking and fished for my keys. Oh hell, Charlie was due in twenty minutes. Maybe if I was lucky he'd be late then I'd have a chance to do a lightning dust as well as change out of my work clothes and replace the makeup that had worn off during the day. Otherwise it was a case of one or the other. Which was the most important? Being male, Charlie would be more likely to notice a sparkling and dusted female rather than a sparkling and dusted flat, so there wasn't much of a contest, I decided as I dumped the bags on the kitchen table and shoved a bottle of white wine in the fridge.

I hadn't even got as far as flinging my jacket off when the phone went for the first time. I heard Oscar telling the machine that he needed to speak to me urgently and if I was there, to pick up the phone. Probably only wanted to catch up on the day's latest events, I thought, kicking my shoes off. I didn't have time for a long gossip now. It went again as I was doing a quick flick through my wardrobe, quick by necessity as most of my clothes were either in the laundry basket or still in my suitcase. This time it was Janey, sounding on top of the world and saying she must speak to me about something important and to ring her back as soon as I got in. I wondered if it was anything drastic and if maybe I should speak to her for just a minute or two. Charlie was bound to be late, men always were. I glanced out of the window as I havered over the phone and saw him getting out of a Golf parked about halfway down the road. He wasn't late, he was bloody well *early*! My indignation changed into panic as I remembered that so far I hadn't done anything, not even rubbed the mark off my knee where somebody had banged it with something filthy in the Tube.

She probably wanted to tell me about Tom's mortgages and how the insurance money would get them out of trouble. Except that they wouldn't be getting any once I'd returned the poisoned chalice hidden behind my sofa, would they? It would go back on the wall where it wouldn't be doing any good to anyone – and what would Tom do then? I wondered if I shouldn't burn the bloody thing, except that Mr Peters, the green fascist from next door, would be bound to report me for having an illegal bonfire. He'd threatened to do Felicity under the Clean Air Act once for lighting a barbecue. Admittedly the sausages had been on the carbonised side of well done, but all the same . . .

I came back to earth to see Charlie walk along the pavement looking for my number. The bell went almost immediately.

'I'm sorry, it's unforgivable of me to be early like this, but it didn't take nearly as long to get here as I thought it would,' he said as I opened the door. He looked different somehow, and I felt a bit awkward. Maybe it was seeing him in a navy suit and white shirt rather than the baggy shorts and polo shirts he'd worn most of the time at the cottage. It wasn't easy to imagine this sober businessman shimmying up and down the terrace doing a tango and making the women present have most unsuitable thoughts, but then Charlie was rather like an iceberg; ninety per cent of him was below the surface. I smoothed down my skirt in the vain hope that somehow I might be able to stretch the fabric to make it magically cover the smudge on my knee. Of course all it did was draw his attention to it, I realised crossly as I saw his eyes rest on my legs.

I assured him that it didn't matter at all, it was lovely to see him, then hesitated for a moment. 'Look, would you mind if I settled you down with a drink for a few minutes while I change out of my work clothes and clean myself up?'

'You look great as you are,' he replied, with more gallantry than truth, I feared. 'But go ahead. I know what it feels like when you haven't had a chance to freshen up. In fact, take a bath if you'd like.'

'Is it as bad as that?' I asked in faint alarm, wondering if I had smudges in places I hadn't noticed yet. I wouldn't have dreamed of suggesting to someone who had only just arrived for a drink that I might go off and have a bath, but now he'd mentioned it, there was nothing I'd like better.

He laughed. 'No, of course not! I hate to admit it but I haven't seen *Coronation Street* for a fortnight and I'm suffering from withdrawal symptoms. I was just thinking that if you were to relax in the bath for ten minutes or so before we go out . . .' he said, eyeing the telly in a longing manner.

'Shame on you, Charlie! Didn't I hear you telling Maggie one night that watching soaps was the visual equivalent of reading Enid Blyton when you're grown up?'

'She was being incredibly pompous about the social worth of *EastEnders*,' he replied, quite unabashed.

'I thought it was *Brookside* that gave us an unparalleled look into the lives of real people. But which ever one it was, does that excuse you hiding your own extensive knowledge of the soaps?' I said over my shoulder as I took the chilled bottle of wine he'd brought with him into the kitchen.

'You're excused anything when it comes to taking Maggie down a peg or two,' he said with a conspiratorial smile, leaning against the doorframe while I found the corkscrew and the glasses. I appreciate men who have the common sense to realise when they ought to keep out of the way of somebody who is having a busy couple of minutes, especially in a kitchen that's as small as mine. 'I mean it, honestly,' he went on. 'Why don't you take ten minutes out and relax, if that's what you'd like to do?'

I looked at him, wondering if he was really that keen to see *Coronation Street* or if he was just being nice. Good manners and desire fought a brief battle. Desire won. 'If you really don't mind, I won't be long.'

'Be as long as you want – until eight o'clock at least,' he said. 'But promise you won't tell Maggie.'

'I'm hardly likely to be speaking to her, am I?' I said.

'No, I don't suppose you will,' he said with a grin. 'Luckily for me!' He was looking around with blatant curiosity. 'This place is really nice. I like the way you've done it up. Do you live on your own?'

'At the moment. I've got a flatmate but she's in New York on a six-month secondment.' I found a little painted dish I'd picked up at a crafts fair and showed I wasn't entirely deficient in the hostess graces by emptying a packet of peanuts into it for him to have with his glass of wine.

He smiled his thanks and we wandered back into the sitting room. 'Have you heard from Janey since you got back?' he asked.

'Only a message to ring her,' I said, looking for the remote control and finding it eventually on top of the bookcase.

'I wonder if the Sydney's been recovered yet,' he said, settling himself down comfortably on the sofa. Not yet, I thought with an uncomfortable lurch of my stomach. Not officially anyway. 'Did your pictures travel up OK, by the way? Didn't get damaged or anything, did they?'

'No, they're fine.' I was unpleasantly aware of the painting stacked a couple of feet behind his head. 'Or at least I presume they are. I haven't had a chance to look at them both yet.'

He nodded, his attention on the television screen. I took the hint, hearing the volume go up as I went down the corridor to the bathroom.

Five minutes later I was just getting into a bath with enough bubbles in it to have preserved the modesty of an elephant, when I realised to my irritation that I'd left my glass of wine on the kitchen table. I was tempted to forget it, but this bubble extravaganza was going to be a bit of a waste if I couldn't complete the fantasy by having a chilled glass of wine, wasn't it? I shook the worst of the bubbles off, wrapped myself in a towel and opened the door very quietly, checking that the coast was clear. I didn't particularly fancy showing myself off to Charlie in a striped towel and a silver butterfly hairclip. Reassured by the noises drifting down the passage, I tiptoed to the kitchen.

The door to the sitting room was slightly ajar, the back of Charlie's foot just visible through the gap. I stopped on the way back to the bathroom, wondering what on earth he was doing on the floor. Had he dropped something – a contact lens, maybe? Ought I offer to help him find it? I'd take a peek to check if he was in the blindly-patting-the-carpet position that I knew well from Oscar. No need to burst in in this attire if all he'd done was drop his keys.

What I saw through the crack in the door nearly made me drop my glass. *Coronation Street* was blaring away, the Rover's Return didn't appear to have changed much in the five years since I'd last caught a glimpse of it, but far from being glued to the screen Charlie was kneeling with his back to the television, opening one of my picture cases. He laid the wrapped picture carefully on the floor and taking a Stanley knife out of his pocket began to rapidly, but carefully, slit through the parcel tape that held all the protective layers of newspaper together. I watched, too surprised at this extraordinary behaviour to even think of moving, as he peeled away the layers like the skins of an onion. Something had been put face down over the glass of my picture so that it fitted snugly into the ornate frame. He scrabbled at it, murmuring with satisfaction as his fingers finally got a grip and lifted another, smaller picture out, placing it face down on the carpet. Quickly, as if he had practised this, he wrapped my picture up again, fastening the layers from a fresh roll of parcel tape he had in his pocket until it resembled the original wrappings closely enough for me never to have noticed there was anything different, and shoved it back in the case, leaning it up against the wall as if it had never been moved.

Then at last he picked up the second picture and turned it over to look at it. I was sure I already knew what it was. But it didn't make it any less of a shock to see him holding up something I knew so well; a framed oil painting of a sunlit beach under a jewel bright sky, a little boy playing in the sand, and Venetia's double, hair streaming in the wind, triumphantly holding a whorled shell up in the air.

CHAPTER 25

I don't think I made a sound but something, some instinct, caused Charlie to spin around. I suppose if I'd had any brains at all I could have easily scarpered back down the corridor into the safety of my bedroom long before Charlie, hampered in speed terms by keeping a tight grip on the Willard Sydney, had flung the door open, but I was so confounded by seeing him with something I knew was still safely stowed away behind the sofa that it didn't even occur to me to make a dash for concealment. He stared at me in silence, apparently almost as shocked as I was. 'Oh bugger!' he said eventually. 'Bugger, *bugger*!'

'So it was you who stole the picture,' I said stupidly, still rooted to the spot, my brain clamouring, *It wasn't Robert! It wasn't Robert!*

He raised his eyebrows, looking for a moment like the person I thought I knew. 'I don't expect you'd believe me if I said I was a private detective charged with getting it back? No? I suppose I'd better admit it. Yes, it was me.' He sighed deeply. 'It was going so well, too. Why the bloody hell couldn't you have stayed in the bath like you were supposed to?'

'I wanted my glass of wine,' I said, and then added dumbly, 'was it all a put-on then, about wanting to watch *Coronation Street*?' Discovering that someone who only a few days ago was appearing in some of your naughtier fantasies has apparently used you to transport stolen property does tend to scramble your brains a little. Otherwise I'm sure I would have got on the case earlier.

'What do you think?' he asked contemptuously. 'You're very nice, Nella, but you're incredibly gullible. How many men do you know who would turn up here for a drink and suggest that you go off and have a bath without having some sort of ulterior motive?'

'None,' I said honestly and added, hoping to tweak his conscience, 'but I thought you were different – a really, decent, considerate person.'

He smiled briefly. 'And now you know better. Sorry to disillusion you.' So conscience-tweaking didn't work; it had been worth trying though. 'God, you're a pain,' he said crossly. 'Another two minutes and I'd have had this locked in the boot of my car and you'd never have known a thing about it. You've got a real talent for being where you're not wanted, you know. The only lucky thing is that you aren't very observant. I watched you chase into that hut after that bloody dog of Janey's and I was sure you were going to find the picture then. If you'd only looked up you'd have seen it resting across a couple of beams a few feet above your head! I couldn't believe my luck when you walked out without it and carried on yakking, nor when you said you hadn't had time to look at your pictures yet. It was all going my way.' He looked at me with acute dislike. 'Now you've gone and wrecked everything.'

'I didn't mean to,' I said inanely, as it occurred to me it might be a good idea to humour him. After all, as he'd said, I'd just gone and wrecked a near-perfect crime. He was both taller and a lot fitter than me. I could still visualise him in his swimming trunks about to dive into the pool, and I remembered his muscles clearly. He had, I couldn't repress a shiver, a Stanley knife in his pocket and last, but definitely not least, he was in a suit and I was in a bath towel. I wondered if I would be able to run back down the passageway and into the garden before he caught up with me. There wasn't actually any way of getting out of it but I was pretty sure that if I screamed loudly enough, Mr Peters from next door would ring the police. Not to come and rescue me, but to complain about the amount of noise I was making. Still, the result would be the same.

Charlie must have caught the flicker of my eyes for he frowned. 'You'd better come in here and sit down where I can see you, while I decide what I'm going to do with you.'

You might say that my blood ran cold at his tone. In the circs I was hardly going to argue, was I? Especially as I remembered that the key to the kitchen door had been put in a drawer safely hidden away from burglars and damsels in need of a quick exit. And after what I'd said to Robert this morning, he was hardly likely to be coming around hammering on my door, was he? So I could forget about any ideas of a white knight coming to my rescue. I was on my own here. I obediently edged past him, keeping as wide a berth as possible, and sat down on the edge of the sofa, anchoring the towel with my knees, noticing with a sort of hysterical incredulity that I'd kept a tight grip on my wine glass. No point in letting it go to waste. I took a large swig, I needed something to keep my spirits up. He moved over to the fireplace and, keeping a possessive grip on the painting, leaned over to flick off the television. The silence was almost deafening. I could hear the blood pumping in my ears. I looked up at him and he looked at me. I don't think either of us was absolutely certain of what to do next. I licked my lips nervously. Didn't popular wisdom say that in these situations the best thing is to keep them talking? 'Why did you do it?' I asked.

'I need the money of course,' he said, as if this should have been self-evident to anybody. 'Have you got any idea how expensive it is trying to lead any sort of decent lifestyle in London these days?' Well, yes, I had. I was trying to do exactly that myself. 'The salary I earn is absolutely pathetic, doesn't even *begin* to meet my most basic outgoings – you know, things such as rent, taking girls like Sal out, decent suits and proper bottles of wine. And now I've got a couple of people who I owe money to on my back. They're getting really insistent that I pay them – soon.'

'These people – are they dealers?' I asked, too appalled to think of holding my tongue.

'Of course not,' he said indignantly. 'What do you think I am? I'm not completely insane. I do quite enough damage to my body with the amount I drink without adding the contents of a pharmaceutical laboratory to it as well. I couldn't afford it either,' he added in an aggrieved voice. 'I like an occasional flutter, it's the only chance I've got of making any real money, apart from things like this,' he gestured to the Sydney with his free hand. Did he mean he'd done something like this *before*? 'Only I haven't had much of a run of luck recently. I thought Mack understood it was a temporary difficulty but he says he's got money problems himself. I got a message before we left for France that if I don't settle my account by the end of the month I'll soon be walking on crutches.'

Charlie looked at me without seeming to see me, then went on: 'I could have sold my car and told everyone I was becoming an out-and-out green – that might have kept Mack satisfied for a while – but I'd still have had to find another twenty grand somehow.'

'So you decided to supplement your bank balance with a rather nice painting.'

'Except it isn't nice, I don't even like it.' Did this make the theft more acceptable? 'Though I know you do,' he added witheringly, as if this implied I favoured highly coloured pictures of dinky windmills with fat white horses drinking out of the mill-stream and chocolate-box kittens playing with neon balls of wool. 'I heard you telling Janey how nice it would look up there,' he said, gesturing with his chin at the empty space above the fireplace, which now that he reminded me, was absolutely the perfect space for a Willard Sydney.

'So there was someone in the hall! What were you doing, going to the loo?'

He nodded. 'You two were nattering so hard you

wouldn't have noticed a herd of rhinoceroses charging down the passage. I didn't think much about what Janey was saying until I'd put Sal in the car and came back for her handbag. And there was the picture, unalarmed, unguarded, unwanted. You lot were behind a shut door, no one was going to know I'd come back to the house and Sal was so sound asleep she wasn't going to notice if we went back to the cottage with some extra luggage. And it'd solve so many problems. I'd get enough from flogging it to cover all that I owed, even have a bit over for a seed fund to make some serious money, Janey wouldn't have to look at it any more and Tom's obviously in need of some dosh too. I wasn't ever going to have an opportunity like this again.' He looked at me seriously, as if I couldn't possibly disagree with his point of view. 'You could almost say it would have been a crime *not* to have stolen it.'

'An almost philanthropic gesture, you might say,' I commented before I could stop myself. The filthy look he gave me reminded me that I was supposed to be humouring him, not putting his back up.

'I couldn't believe how easy it was – as if someone *wanted* me to have it,' he said. 'I stopped on the way back and hid it in that old hut, reckoning if it was found by someone it was hardly going to be a disaster, but the only person who even went in there was you. Then the police settled on *you* as chief suspect.'

'Was it you who set them on me?' I asked, my fingers tightening around my glass. I emptied it before I broke it and set it down on the floor beside me.

For the first time since he'd begun to start talking he

looked slightly less certain of himself. 'Not really.' He didn't meet my eyes. 'They already knew about you sharing a flat with Venetia and saying you were going to steal the picture. They asked if I thought you were joking, and I, well,' he cleared his throat, 'I said you were a pretty serious sort of person, that's all. It was just a red herring, Nella. I knew they wouldn't be able to pin anything on you,' he added, looking at me with wide eyes as if I couldn't help but sympathise with what he'd done.

I bloody well could, as it happens. 'So that makes it all right, does it?' I said furiously. 'Do you have any idea of what you did to me, Charlie? I have never been so frightened in my life!'

'You try having some East End gorilla threatening to break your leg and then you'll know what fear is,' he said dismissively, as if this settled the matter. 'And they let you go soon enough. Your *shining honesty*,' he put a distinctly nasty twist on the words, 'won through, didn't it?'

I counted to ten lest I say something that was going to get him really angry. And then to twenty. 'But weren't you taking a terrible gamble by hiding the Sydney with my pictures? I nearly unwrapped them to show them to my brother, but . . . something came up and I didn't have the chance.'

'But I *like* gambling, Nella. That's why I owe so much money,' Charlie said, no doubt stating the obvious. 'And Sal's not stupid, you know.' Unlike a certain Nella Bowden. 'She was bound to wonder what was going on if I suddenly produced a large picture-shaped parcel of my own for us to take back, wasn't she? But she'd have seen nothing untoward in us taking something of yours back. And if we'd got stopped by Customs . . .' he smiled slightly, 'they were *your* pictures. I'd made certain I hadn't left any fingerprints on the wrappings. Have you got any idea how difficult it is using parcel tape when you're wearing washing-up gloves? And you'd already been under suspicion once, hadn't you?'

I stared at him dumbly, wondering how it was you couldn't tell what a cold, manipulative bastard lay concealed under Charlie's friendly unassuming surface. And a remarkably clever one who seemed to be able to rescue almost any situation too. Look at the way he'd immediately come on to me the moment he realised that the pictures weren't going back with him after all, or how he'd arrived early this evening so that I would be stressed, tired and even more susceptible to his ingenious suggestion to get me out of the way.

'With talents like that I'm amazed that you aren't making a fortune in organised crime,' I said spitefully.

He shuddered. 'I'm not a criminal.' Really? 'And I can't stand violence.'

I was glad to hear that.

'I don't make a habit of doing this, you know,' he said, with a touch of indignation. 'But this was irresistible. I stood to lose nothing, only win,' he went on reminiscently. 'And it was going so well, until you came along.' He glanced at me with such savagery that I shrank back slightly, clinging onto my towel as if it was a suit of armour.

'Well, I'm sorry to have upset your plans,' I said nervously and quite untruthfully.

'Perhaps you haven't.' He eyed me thoughtfully, stroking his chin. I felt my heart speed up painfully. What was he intending now? To tie me up with the parcel tape? Take me hostage while he sold the picture? Would he allow me to get dressed first? It might take some time to fence a painting like that and I couldn't spend weeks in a towel.

'I'm sure you're intending to call the police the moment I leave the flat,' he said pleasantly, 'but I really wouldn't, if I were you. You see, if you do, I'll be forced to tell them how I planned the theft with my accomplice, a supposedly *very* respectable art dealer called Robert Winwood, and that it was *he* who took a stolen picture worth a quarter of a million quid into the country, in one of his carrying cases too. That part has the undeniable benefit of being true. Robert will be taken into custody for questioning, of course. They'll have to let him go eventually, but there's bound to be lots of publicity.' He cocked his head on one side, looking meaningfully at me. 'Of course he knows all about how your whole career can be wrecked by a wrongful arrest, doesn't he? Wouldn't it be a pity if it happened for the second time? For the second time . . . *because of you.*' I felt as if the wind had been knocked out of me. Charlie's eyes twinkled merrily. 'If you want to have cosy little chats with Oscar you really ought to have them out of earshot of someone reading their book.'

He leaned down and picked up the picture and smiled at me in a terrible parody of the smile I used to find so attractive, or perhaps it wasn't a parody. I could see beyond it now. 'So shall we say, Nella, that you're going to forget that I ever came to your flat this evening, that you ever saw this,' he shifted his grip around it slightly, 'or that you know anything about a missing Willard Sydney? It would be best for everyone.' He waited, and I stared back stonily. 'What point is there in you stirring up a whole lot of trouble?' he asked in a reasonable voice. 'It won't do any good to anyone, but if you keep quiet, Janey and Tom get their money, Robert gets to keep his reputation and the job he loves so much – and I get to keep two whole legs,' he added with grim humour.

I'm ashamed to say I was tempted to cave in and do as he wanted. I had a nasty feeling the threat to Robert was a very real one – maybe to me, too. Charlie hadn't actually got around to saying he'd finger me too – he'd probably taken that as read. And I was still in a towel. Except . . .

'There's only one problem, Charlie.'

'What?' he demanded. 'Do you want to be cut in on what I get for the picture?'

I hadn't actually thought of that. 'Considering that you used me to smuggle it into the country, I would have thought it was reasonable, wouldn't you?' I took a deep breath, hoping that my voice wasn't going to betray me. 'Except there's no point – it's worthless.'

'Don't be stupid!' he said. 'I'll get at least fifty thou.'

'Bit of a generous estimate, isn't it? I thought you usually only got about ten per cent of the market value for a stolen picture.' Charlie looked rather startled at this information (gleaned off an episode of *The Bill*, but I kept my source to myself). 'Sorry, Charlie, but you won't even get two hundred quid for this one. It's one of

Robert's reproductions. As you said yourself, Tom needs the money. He's already sold the original.'

He started, then recovered himself. 'Nice try, but not true,' he drawled, nonetheless turning the picture over and examining the back. 'As I thought, you're talking rubbish,' he said with a certain degree of relief. 'It doesn't have a marker on it to show it's a copy.'

'Come on, Charlie, this is the era of the microchip. You can't possibly *see* it!' I said as scornfully as I could. 'But I can assure you, it'll take an expert only five minutes to tell you what's in your hands was painted this year.' He shook his head, though he seemed to be just the teeniest bit uncertain. I looked at him earnestly, trying to be as convincing as possible. 'It'll put that Mack bloke in a *really* bad mood when he discovers you're trying to palm him off with a fake.'

Charlie rubbed his chin thoughtfully. 'If it's a fake, why did Tom call the police?'

Why did he? 'Er, well he had to once the alarm had been raised, didn't he? Otherwise everybody would have smelt a rat,' I said, speaking more rapidly as I warmed to my theme, desperate to convince him and get him out of here, without the picture, as quickly as possible.

'Maybe,' he said doubtfully, then his expression sharpened. 'Come off it, Nella! Janey wouldn't have told you to steal a fake.'

'But she didn't know it was one – Tom hadn't told her. Robert was telling me about it in the car. That's how he met Venetia, you know, when he came to take photographs so his artist could start doing the copy.'

'I thought Venetia said she'd met him at some party in

London,' he said, frowning as if searching his memory for her exact words. Damn! That's the trouble with over-embroidery. Your stitches go all awry.

He hesitated, looking as if he wasn't sure whether to believe me or not. I held my breath, hoping, hoping, then he smiled at me coolly. 'Never mind, it doesn't matter either way. A mate of mine will be able to tell me what this really is. If you're telling the truth,' he shrugged, 'I'll have to find some other way of raising money. And if you aren't,' his voice changed, 'you'd best remember what I said to you. If I go down, your Robert goes down with me.'

'He's not my Robert,' I said sadly and with absolute truth. Nor would he ever be, not now.

'Isn't he?' Charlie said sceptically. 'More fool him then. *I* certainly wouldn't have let an opportunity to drive through France with you go to waste like that. At the very least I'd have staged a breakdown that meant spending the night at some out-of-the-way hotel.'

I looked fixedly at my hands, fiercely willing myself not to blush. For once the gods listened to me, or at least I think they did; at any rate Charlie didn't snigger knowingly.

'Shame about all this. We could have had quite a thing going,' he said with just enough regret. 'Remember what I said. I meant it.' Then, grasping the picture securely under one arm, he was out of the door and away.

For a couple of seconds I was too relieved that he'd actually gone to do anything, even move, then I was filled with such a marvellously energising burst of rage at being taken for an almighty ride like this that I leaped up and, grabbing my towel, ran out on the doorstep shrieking at the top of my voice, 'Stop thief! Stop him, someone, he's just burgled my flat! That man there! Yes, him, the one with my picture under his arm!'

Charlie was about thirty feet away, strolling speedily but without panic down the street. He looked incredulously over his shoulder and broke into a run. 'Catch him!' I yelled to a businessman carrying a briefcase on the other side of the road. He stared at the demented female in a towel yelling accusations at an apparently respectable bloke in a suit and pretended he hadn't heard. 'Wimp!' I snarled. There was nothing for it, I was going to have to do it myself.

I was never going to catch him, I realised in dismay as I belted down the street. He had far too much of a head start. I was beginning to get a stitch and he was already unlocking the rear door on his Golf. I hardly had the breath to shout any more. He flung the picture on the back seat, and got in, starting the engine while I was still a good twenty yards away. Then I nearly tripped over a paving stone with astonishment as a man got out of a car parked further down the street and ran back towards us. Charlie must have seen him too for he revved up frantically and began jerking back and forth with loud protesting noises from his engine and at least one crunch which indicated that the person who had parked behind him was going to need a new bumper. He got the car aligned and started to move, but had to slam on his brakes to allow another car to pass. Before he could get moving again Robert had flung open the rear door and seized the picture.

Charlie half spilled out of the car, leaving the engine running and lunged at him. 'Give that to me!'

'No. It's not yours,' Robert said calmly.

'Watch out, Robert!' I panted, arriving at last, as Charlie put a hand in one of his pockets. 'He's got a knife in there!'

With a dexterity that amazed me, I managed to keep a grip on the towel and catch a quarter of a million pounds' worth of Post Impressionist just before it hit the pavement as Robert wheeled around to grab Charlie's shirtfront. 'A knife? What have you been doing to Nella?' he demanded, twisting his hand in Charlie's tie so it tightened in a stranglehold around his neck.

'Nothing, I promise you,' I said quickly. 'I only know because I saw him putting it back after he'd undone the wrappings on the picture. Let go!' I added frantically. Charlie's face was going a strange shade of puce and he was making funny gurgling noises. 'You're going to garrotte him!'

'Good,' Robert said tersely, though I was relieved to see that he loosened his grip a little. So was Charlie, judging by the deep breaths he was taking. Needless to say, now that someone had come to my aid, the street was slowly filling up with males who were gamely giving the impression that of course they would have been prepared to leap into the breach, but it just so happened someone had got there first. 'You'd better go and ring the police, Nella,' Robert told me.

'Is there really any need for that?' I squeaked. 'We've got the Sydney back and I'm sure Janey and Tom won't want this sort of publicity. You can just see the tabloids going to town with "Château tenant steals valuable picture," or something. Wouldn't it be better just to let him go?'

'How sensible of you, Nella,' Charlie said in an approving voice.

Robert hesitated. 'Please,' I added.

With obvious reluctance Robert released him. Charlie staggered backwards quickly out of his reach and said in heartfelt tones, 'Thank you, Nella.' He looked at the picture in my arms and sighed. 'Oh well, as I said, it was worth the risk. I almost won and I didn't lose anything. You might say it was the ultimate perfect bet. The only thing I do regret . . .' He cocked his head and smiled at me. 'I don't suppose you'd have dinner with me one evening?'

'No, she would *not*!' Robert said fiercely.

Charlie grinned and got into his car, blowing me a kiss out of the window. Robert took a step towards him and he gunned the car into gear and took off as if the hounds of hell were after him.

CHAPTER 26

So my white knight had turned up after all. I gave Robert a shaky smile, my heart still racing. 'Thank God you were here. How did you happen to be on the spot?'

He waited, eyes fixed on the end of the road, as if to make sure Charlie really was turning the corner and not coming back again. Then: 'I had to speak to you somehow, Nella. I was going to bang on your door until you let me in, only Charlie was walking up your steps as I arrived, so I decided I'd wait in my car until you were alone. I'm obviously not very good at this surveillance lark, though. I was reading the paper and not concentrating on the job in hand, hence being so slow off the mark when you started shrieking like a banshee.'

'At least you got here, and you got the painting back,' I said, lapsing into tongue-tied silence as I recalled what I'd said to him this morning and looked down at my now very filthy bare feet. I definitely needed that bath now, except it had probably gone cold. Also an interested group was gathering around us, one or two of the men goggling openly at my unusual street wear. I did a speedy check to ensure everything was still decently in place and mumbled, 'I left the door of the flat open. I'd better get back before half the criminal element of South London take it as an open invitation to go in and do the place over.'

Robert took the picture off me, taking care, so it seemed, to keep his distance and not actually brush up against me. 'May I come to get the case for this?' he asked with a painful politeness that made my heart sink. 'I really appreciate the brave efforts you made to get it back, but you needn't have gone to so much bother. It isn't genuine.'

'Er . . . actually,' I began.

He sighed. 'It's true, I promise you. Tom couldn't face the fuss if anyone knew he was settling his debts by flogging an heirloom so he commissioned a copy off me. I was supposed to have done a swap the night before I left, only . . .'

'So *that's* why he blamed you for the theft of the Sydney,' I said as we reached my front door and I closed it behind us.

'Quite,' Robert said. 'And Tom was already having enough problems with the insurance without them discovering he'd had the forethought to have a perfect copy made of his missing picture, so I took it back to London while he made up his mind what to do with it – which is why it was in my car.' He rested the picture against the wall and turned to face me. 'And that's the whole story. The truth. If you don't believe me you're welcome to ring Tom.'

'I don't need to,' I said in a low voice, trying

desperately to formulate the words to tell him I already knew how wrong I'd been.

'So you've been speaking to Janey. Tom said he'd told her.'

I shook my head and said miserably, my insides shrivelling up, 'I worked out what had happened earlier this evening.' Round about the time I saw Charlie with the picture and realised it had a twin hidden only a few feet away. Bit late really. If only Robert would look even a little bit understanding ... but no, I suppose that was too much to ask. 'Robert, I'm so sorry,' I said finally, looking away so he couldn't see my face beginning to screw up. 'I should have known that you weren't a thief.'

'It was a perfectly reasonable assumption to have made,' he said coolly. 'I think I'd have done the same if I'd discovered an apparently valuable picture hidden away in your luggage, except I like to think that I might have allowed you to tell me what it was doing there before I condemned you out of hand.'

He was being so bloody reasonable that each measured, fair word was like a knife twisting in my stomach. I knew Robert, I thought with a sniff. He didn't *do* reasonable, not with people he cared about. He did flaming rages, enthusiasms, indignation, passion ... no, don't think about that. I even longed for him to look at me with that familiar murderous expression; at least it would mean he was feeling *something*. I had really blown it this time, beyond all possible redemption, and it was hardly surprising, was it? All I could do was nod in agreement, too dispirited to say anything more in my defence. 'About the picture—' I began.

'Forget it,' he said briskly. 'The only thing that does mystify me is how it got mixed up with your things.'

'That was Min.' I looked away in embarrassment. 'She ... she was trying to make sure that we met up again.'

'She certainly achieved that!' he said with a tinge of amusement in his voice. Then it turned to ice. 'But presumably your sister didn't know about Charlie or she'd have realised she was on a hiding to nothing.'

'What do you mean?'

He smiled at me, not a very nice smile as it happens. It was about as warm as a November afternoon. 'Come on, Nella. There's only one reason why a woman has all her clothes off within twenty minutes of a man arriving in her flat.'

I stared at him, my heart beginning to race. Was I imagining things or did he really object more to me being half undressed around Charlie than about Charlie legging it down the street with someone else's picture? 'Two reasons actually,' I corrected. 'The second is because she's having a bath.'

'A *bath*?' he said incredulously. 'Is that how you entertain your gentleman callers these days?'

'I was alone,' I said repressively. 'And Charlie wasn't in the least bit interested in getting my clothes off; all he wanted to do was get the wrappings off that picture.'

'Shows a lamentable sense of priorities if you ask me,' Robert murmured, his expression as he looked at me making me think that perhaps the sun might rise again tomorrow after all.

'But I'm not worth a quarter of a million pounds. At

426

least I daresay my mother would say that I am, but she's biased,' I burbled, trying to force myself to concentrate on the job in hand and not do something dramatic to persuade him to go on looking at me like that – such as dropping the towel. Lest I be tempted to do just that I took an extra hard grip on it while Robert stared at me, as if he was wondering whether I'd finally flipped. It just seemed too complicated to explain so I reached behind the sofa and hauled out the picture case. 'You see, *this* is what came out of your car.'

I stepped back a pace and watched his face change as he opened it up. He drew out the picture inside and looked at it, then looked at the one against the wall, then very carefully as if he couldn't believe what he was seeing, placed the one he was holding next to its twin. I hoped he knew which one was which because I certainly didn't. After a long silence he chuckled. 'I wonder what Tom would have done to me if I'd rescued his precious picture only to drop it and smash it on the pavement! Good thing you caught it,' he said, eyes still on the two pictures. 'So George was right about it being an inside job. He'd be very upset to know he fingered the wrong person though. Who'd have thought it of *Charlie*? Though I suppose he does have that reckless edge.' He swung around to give me a hard look. 'Why did you insist on letting him go?'

'Not because I can't bear the idea of him behind bars, I promise you,' I said quickly. Robert still looked suspicious. 'He said if he was arrested he'd name you as his accomplice, said the publicity would ruin your reputation. Maybe he was exaggerating, but I thought it was too much of a risk. I've already done for one career of yours, haven't I?' I looked down, scuffing the carpet around with a grubby foot. 'I was going to let him get away – when it comes down to it, it's only a picture, but,' I shrugged, 'I thought that perhaps he wasn't as clever as he thought – after all, *I'd* caught him in the act. He was bound to get caught eventually. And he'd probably finger you then anyway, so I reckoned I'd better try and get it back from him right away.'

'You chased after Charlie when you knew he had a knife on him? Are you out of your mind, Nella?' Robert demanded, a welcomingly murderous look in his eyes. 'Didn't you think for a single moment of what he might do to you?'

'Er ... no,' I admitted, then added, 'but he said he didn't like violence.'

Robert stared at me as if he wanted to grab my shoulders and shake sense into me then he began to laugh. 'So you charged into battle on my behalf dressed in a *towel*. My darling, you are quite, quite mad!' At last I found myself in his arms, being hugged so tightly I could hardly breathe. 'I admit this outfit is a great deal more enticing than your average suit of armour, but perhaps you ought to save it for indoors in future,' he said, slackening his grip slightly and looking downwards appreciatively. 'When Wonder Woman goes out defending justice and apprehending a criminal or two she usually wears something a bit more ... secure,' he added as the towel slipped slightly. 'But you shouldn't have taken the risk, my brave, brave darling!'

I protested a bit indistinctly that I hadn't been brave, I

hadn't really thought what I was doing, but he ignored that, telling me to shut up, then making sure I shut up by kissing me. Usually I object to men trying to make me be ~t. Not this time. At some point the towel gave up the and fell off completely and after that things _gressed like they tend to when your towel has fallen off. I didn't object to that either.

It was some time later, quite a lot later in fact, and we'd got to the stage where other appetites had to be satisfied and were waiting for a pizza to be delivered. Neither of us felt comfortable about going out just in case that arch chancer and opportunist Charlie was waiting to see if he could turn his hand to a bit of breaking and entering to add to the rap sheet he had already. Robert had offered to get us a takeaway but I was still so overwhelmed by this only dreamt-of turn of events that I was reluctant to let him out of my sight, even if only for a few minutes. I could see this might present a bit of a problem tomorrow morning when we both had to go to work, but I'd deal with that later.

Robert had taken delivery of an extra large Pizzaman special with extra just about everything and I was closing the door behind him when Oscar, white as a sheet, belted up the steps. 'Nella! Are you all right?' he panted as he saw me.

I grinned at him. 'I can assure you I've never been better.'

'I've been worried *sick* about you! I've been trying to get hold of you all evening – I've been speaking to Janey and I've *got* to tell you about that picture. Anyway, I dropped in at Mrs Patel's for milk first, and she said she'd heard you'd been attacked by a naked man in the street and taken off in an ambulance – head injuries, she thought.'

Wow! This neighbourhood had a pretty good rumour machine operating, even if it did get some of the details wrong. I lifted my arms and gave him a twirl. 'As you can see I'm completely fine.'

The colour began to come back to his face. 'What have you been doing?' he demanded reproachfully. 'Janey says she can't get hold of you either. First all I got was the answerphone, then it seemed as if it was off the hook.'

'Er, yes, I can't have replaced it properly,' I said, blushing and trying not to laugh at Robert's guilty expression. He must have knocked the receiver off when he put three cushions on top of the telephone so we wouldn't get distracted from more important things by the continuous sound of Oscar and Janey leaving messages.

'Oh,' Oscar said, coming inside and sitting down. His gaze rested briefly on Robert and on his bare feet before coming back to me. He must have been really worried about me not to have copped on to this interesting development straight away, I thought, feeling deeply touched. 'But what's been going *on*, Nella? Presumably there was some truth in this story; even old Mrs P doesn't make up naked men chasing you down the street out of thin air, so who was he?'

'It was Nella doing the chasing, in a towel,' Robert said with relish in his voice. 'That's a memory I shall cherish for a long, long time.' His eyes met mine and he smiled at me in that way that did serious damage to my blood pressure and heartbeat. As a result my explanations to Oscar as he stayed on to share our pizza were somewhat disjointed and he had to get me to repeat several of the salient points.

'So what happens now?' he asked, looking at the two pictures propped up side by side against the wall as if he wasn't absolutely certain he wasn't suffering from double vision.

'I imagine that Tom will hand the original, as he planned, over to the American millionaire who desperately wants a Sydney to complete his collection and is prepared to pay a handsome sum for it. The copy will go back to Château du Pré to hang on the hall wall, where no one will be any the wiser,' Robert said. 'Though since rather a lot of people are in on the secret by now maybe Tom will come clean about it.'

'Surely not if he ever wants to speak to Venetia again,' Oscar said. 'She'll go into orbit, won't she?'

'I doubt she'll mind that much,' Robert said offhandedly. 'She'll still have the copy one day, and the money's going towards protecting her inheritance. She stands to benefit more than anyone by the sale of the Sydney too. She gets all of her mother's share of the château and vineyard on Tom's death, and under the French inheritance laws she'll get part of Tom's half as well so she'll end up with the largest part of the business.'

'Really? I wonder if that's why she's decided to shack up with a winemaker – keep the business in the family so to speak,' Oscar said with a sly smile, and looked at the two of us with wide eyes. 'You mean you haven't heard?' He knew damn well we hadn't. 'She's gone off with

Carlton! Janey told me this evening. He was round at Napier's all last week laying siege, and apparently Venetia discovered after a couple of days of unadulterated Napier that he wasn't really as attractive as her adolescent fantasies,' there was a sort of unsurprised snort from Robert, 'and she moved into Carlton's pad at the weekend. According to Janey, Venetia's not saying how long this is going to last, but Carlton says he knows a good thing when he sees one. He was over this afternoon asking Tom for his daughter's hand in marriage.'

'Very tactful of him,' murmured Robert. I shot him a quick look but his face showed nothing but a mild amusement which told me nothing of what he felt about this news. 'And I expect Tom immediately said yes and the sooner the better, thus ensuring Carlton plays in *his* cricket team again next year!'

'Something like that,' chuckled Oscar. 'Janey's already trying to decide if the twins should wear blue or red velvet as page boys.' His eyes strayed back to the pictures and he sighed. 'I still can't believe it was Charlie who did it. I liked him.' So had I, I thought sadly. 'Still, I said Robert couldn't have stolen the picture,' he said to me with a certain amount of 'I told you so' satisfaction.

'Don't mention it, please,' I begged.

'At least you only thought I was a thief this time,' Robert said lazily, putting an arm around me. 'I can live with that. Heaven knows I've been called a shark and worse enough times by some of our artists over our commission rates, but I'm not keen on being called a pervert.'

'Who did that?' I asked indignantly.

'You did,' he said casually. 'When you told the police I was the Bakersfield prowler.'

'I never did!' I exclaimed vehemently.

Robert turned his head around very slowly, and stared at me. 'Didn't you? Then what *did* you tell them?'

'Nothing,' I said miserably. He didn't seem to understand what I meant. 'Literally nothing. They rang me for an alibi for you and I said I didn't know you.'

'Bloody hell! Is that *all* you did?' he exclaimed. 'I can still see the smug look on the Sergeant's face as he came back and told me I'd picked the wrong one to bail me out. Actually, once I'd calmed down I couldn't really blame you for refusing me an alibi, not after the way I'd been mucking around with Natasha. Didn't like to admit it, though.' He grinned. 'And I'd have done much the same to you in similar circumstances, still would if it meant preventing you spending a night with Charlie. Or George,' he added reflectively. I got the impression he'd happily consign George to a night in the cells even if it wasn't going to be in the good cause of keeping him away from me. 'You know, I didn't believe at first that it could have been you who shopped me as the Bakersfield prowler. Someone who could do something like that wasn't acting from spur-of-the-moment temper, but real malice. Not your sort of thing. But that bastard Sergeant had been going on and on about the fury of a woman scorned and revenge beating strong in the female breast, then you said it had been all your fault . . .'

'I meant you missing your meeting at Chambers.'

'Oh God!' he groaned. 'I just assumed . . . And of course the Sergeant did nothing to correct me. He probably reckoned I was less likely to bring a suit for wrongful arrest if I believed my girlfriend was behind it.'

It had never occurred to me that all our friends would have been blaming me for Robert's actual arrest. Since none of them would speak to me, I hadn't had the chance to find out either. No wonder I'd been so comprehensively cold-shouldered.

He looked at me contritely. 'It's my turn to apologise. I should have realised.'

'Shush!' I commanded, putting my hand across his mouth to add weight to my words. 'I got a few things wrong about you, didn't I? So shall we call a moratorium on the apologies? It's over and done with – *stop that*!' I hissed as he began to nibble my fingers. 'You're embarrassing Oscar.' He beamed at me unrepentantly and kissed them again.

Oscar was studiously chewing a piece of cold pizza and gazing pointedly at the two paintings as if he was trying to compare the brushstrokes. He turned back to us with a distinct expression of relief as I separated myself from Robert so that I could bring in the bottle of wine that Charlie had brought. I hadn't seen any need to tell Robert where it came from; he might have got on his high horse and refused to drink it which would have been a pity since it was very good, much better than anything I ever bought, and probably one of the many reasons why Charlie was so deeply in debt. 'So what was Tom's reaction when you told him you'd got the picture back?' Oscar asked as I refilled his glass.

'Er, we haven't got around to it yet,' I said, trying hard to stop myself from looking self-conscious. 'One or two things came up.' I heard an imperfectly suppressed snort of laughter from beside me.

'As far as he knows, Nella still has me marked down as one of the great art thieves of the new century, but I suppose we shouldn't keep the news from him any longer than strictly necessary,' Robert said. 'Maybe you could ring him for us, Oscar – from your flat.'

Oscar grinned. 'Yes, it's time I was going, isn't it? I'll tell Tom you're guarding the pictures in a secret location and can't be reached, and you'll ring him tomorrow.'

As I opened the door for him he turned to me with a smile that I knew very well. 'At last. Taken you two long enough, hasn't it? I was beginning to think all that effort might have gone to waste.'

I stared at him in disbelief. 'Oh come on. Don't pretend you've been trying to throw us together!' I exclaimed. 'You've never stopped chucking me at George.'

'But I told you I'd decided you and George weren't suited. Is it my fault that you didn't believe me?' he said solemnly, though his eyes were twinkling. 'Hasn't it occurred to you just how many times you've just accidentally "found" yourself in Robert's company during the last few days?'

I put my hands on my hips and glared at him. 'You promised to stop interfering,' I began, then as his face fell in the most comical manner, I laughed and hugged him. 'But just this once I'll forgive you.'

'Good.' He returned my hug. 'Because otherwise

435

you'd have to have a go at Janey too. It was her idea as well!' On this parting shot he went off down the steps, casually whistling, turning around to give me a jaunty wave from the bottom.

It was beginning to seem as if the only person who hadn't been actively interfering in my love-life was Maggie, I thought with some amusement as I closed the door. 'I might find myself getting quite jealous of Oscar if you go on cuddling him like that,' Robert said.

I put my arms around his waist and gave him a cuddle of his own which he seemed to think was very satisfactory. 'Oscar reckons you're only getting this because of his incomparable matchmaking skills.'

Robert grinned and kissed the top of my head. 'I hate to disappoint him, but long before he saw the light I'd already decided that, come what may, I was going to get you back somehow.'

'Had you?' Keeping my eyes on his chest because I wasn't sure if I wanted to see his expression while he replied, I asked quietly, 'When was that? Before or after Venetia?'

'Before, of course,' he said, then added gently, 'hey come on, you haven't been imagining this is some sort of rebound thing, have you?' He pushed my chin up so I had to look at him. Well, of course I'd had a nasty niggle or three along those lines. I'd been trying not to attend to them, but it was difficult. 'I'm fond of Venetia, but that's as far as it ever went. And once I'd seen George being all proprietorial with you and I realised that it wasn't just a perfectly reasonable dislike that made me want to bop him on the nose, I knew Venetia and I were finished. Just in case you're thinking I'm some kind of real bastard,' he said with a faint smile, 'her interest in me was wavering and I knew it wouldn't be long before she was off like a rocket with a man who interested her more, which is exactly what happened.' There was a pause. 'Though to be honest, I'm just a little offended at being dumped for *Napier*.'

'But she was talking about getting married to you,' I said, hardly able to think for relief. 'Said that love in a garret would be all right if it was with the right person.'

'*She* might have been talking about marriage, I certainly wasn't,' he said firmly. 'Venetia's always thinking about getting hitched – one reason why she has such a high turnover of men. Most blokes get scared if their date starts thinking about the wedding stationery before the end of their first meal. But if it's Carlton who is calling the shots this time, it might work out. I hope it does,' he added with a distant friendliness in his voice that was immensely reassuring. 'And whatever Venetia may think,' he added, 'my flat is *not* a garret, it's very nice and you'll like it.'

'Will I?' I asked.

'Well, you'd better, since I intend you to spend a lot of time there.'

I liked the sound of that, but just had to check something. 'This time I'll be spending at your place wouldn't include putting in a bit of time with the washing machine, would it?' I asked with mock suspicion.

'It's very nice of you to offer,' he grinned at my squeak of protest, 'but I've already got Janice who comes in to do it for me. It wouldn't be fair to deprive her of a job – besides, I'm sure she's better at it than you are. Anyway,' he traced a finger around my mouth, 'you'll be far too busy exercising your other talents.'

I smiled at him. I liked the sound of that even better.

Now you can buy any of these other bestselling
Headline books from your bookshop or
direct from the publisher.

FREE P&P AND UK DELIVERY
(Overseas and Ireland £3.50 per book)

Olivia's Luck	Catherine Alliott	£5.99
Backpack	Emily Barr	£5.99
Girlfriend 44	Mark Barrowcliffe	£5.99
Seven-Week Itch	Victoria Corby	£5.99
Two Kinds of Wonderful	Isla Dewar	£6.99
Fly-Fishing	Sarah Harvey	£5.99
Bad Heir Day	Wendy Holden	£5.99
Good at Games	Jill Mansell	£5.99
Sisteria	Sue Margolis	£5.99
For Better, For Worse	Carole Matthews	£5.99
Something For the Weekend		
	Pauline McLynn	£5.99
Far From Over	Sheila O'Flanagan	£5.99

TO ORDER SIMPLY CALL THIS NUMBER

01235 400 414

or e-mail <u>orders@bookpoint.co.uk</u>

Prices and availability subject to change without notice.